Twisted Values

Art Wiederhold

Order this book online at www.trafford.com
or email orders@trafford.com

Most Trafford titles are also available at major online book retailers.

Print information available on the last page.

ISBN: 978-1-4907-9480-8 (sc)
ISBN: 978-1-4907-9483-9 (e)

Trafford rev. 04/15/2019

 www.trafford.com

North America & international
toll-free: 1 888 232 4444 (USA & Canada)
fax: 812 355 4082

Chapter One

Eva's husband jokingly referred to her as a "mutt". It was in reference to her blend of Asian, Arabic and Latin ancestry. It gave her a cute, exotic look that used to make most men turn to watch her pass by. With her dark brown hair, deep hazel eyes, sensuous lips and perfect figure, one could say that she could even stop traffic. Men always hit on her in college and even after she was married.

But that was 20 years ago.

Most men didn't stop to look at her anymore. Even her own husband barely bothered with her lately. The only man she knew who still paid attention to her was her husband's best friend, Al. They used to chat often. She liked being around him. He was easy to talk to. He listened and he had a good sense of humor.

They were instantly attracted to each other when they met several years ago. In fact, it was obvious to anyone who saw them together that they were drawn to each other. Even her husband Vince noticed it and he often joked about it.

Eva took it good-naturedly and shot back at him. One day, she even asked what he'd do if she did fuck Al. Caught off guard, Vince simply said if she did fuck him, there wasn't much he could do about it.

"I would just have to let nature take its course," he said.

Eva looked at him and smiled. Her smile made Vince a bit uncomfortable. He knew her well enough to know that she would go out of her way to make that happen if and when she had a chance—and that Al wouldn't be able to resist her. He even teased Al about it and Al told him that when it came to Eva, anything was possible.

As time passed, she came up with excuses to be with Al when Vince wasn't around. Of course, Al didn't mind.

Eva was super-hot and sexy and he liked her. They even joked about having sex with each other. In fact, their jokes became more and more erotic with Al telling her on several occasions: "I'd love to bury my face in your pussy and eat you until you scream."

One day, she looked him straight in the eyes and smiled.

"And then what?" she asked

She usually responded with if he played his cards right, maybe that would happen one day. This time, the attraction was way off the scale. In fact, she noticed that Al had a very large bulge in the front of his jeans which he didn't bother to conceal.

"And then I'll bury something else in your pussy," he said. "Something nice and hard."

"That is so tempting," she said as she ran her fingers over his bulge.

That's when Al suddenly took things up a notch. He just grabbed Eva by the shoulders and stuck his tongue in her mouth. Eva was caught by surprise. Instead of pushing him away, she actually responded by kissing him back.

With passion.

It felt like lightning struck her, too. That's when Al ran his hands down her back to her ass and squeezed it. She pressed her body against his erection. As they kissed, she gyrated against him, like she was fucking him. He responded by thrusting back and forth so that his bulge rubbed against her crotch each time. She was on fire now and she just about sucked his tongue out of his mouth. She humped him harder and harder until she actually came. So did Al. They stopped after a few minutes. Both were breathing heavier and she was flushed. She smiled at him.

"That was really nice," she said. "Real nice."

"Now what?" he asked. "Do we take this further?"

"We'll see," she said as she rubbed the wet spot in his jeans.

Ever since then, she always felt horny whenever she was close to Al. So did Al. And nature *was* taking its course. When no one else was around, they French kissed and dry humped until they both came. God how she wanted to have an affair with him!

And Al's touches grew bolder and bolder. Eva got into the practice of unzipping her shorts or jeans whenever they were alone. This enabled him to slide his hand into her panties and play with her pussy and clit until she came. Sometimes, he just flicked her swollen clit to get her off.

Sometimes, he slid hid middle finger into her cunt and "fucked" her. Sometimes he did both. While he played with her cunt, she unzipped his jeans, pulled out his prick, and jerked him off until he came. As she did, she watched his foreskin roll up and down and became even hornier. Soon, Al started raising her shirts and sucking her nipples while she kept tweaking his knob until they both came. She kept jerking him off and watching as he shot several spurts of cum all over himself. Then she stopped and licked the cum from her fingers.

"Next time, I'm gonna fuck your brains out!" she said.

One lazy Sunday afternoon, Eva decided to turn up the heat. Vince was off playing baseball and she knew he'd be gone most of the day. So she drove to Al's house wearing nothing but her tiny jogging shorts and a T-shirt.

When he let her inside, she immediately threw her arms around his neck and French kissed him. He responded by running his hands all over her. She led him to the sofa where they kissed again while he played with her nipples. She laid there sighing as he rolled up her T-shirt and swirled his tongue over each nipple.

"Wait!" she said.

She sat up and peeled off her shirt. Her breasts were firms and perfect. He leaned over and sucked each nipple while he massaged her crotch. She unzipped his pants and pulled out his prick. He almost came when she jerked him off. She let him go and lay down. He kissed his way down her body, lingered at her navel, and slowly pulled her shorts down.

She was naked now.

And he obviously loved what he saw. She closed her eyes as he slid his tongue up and down her slit.

"Yes!" she thought. "He's eating me! This is the day!"

He buried his face in her cunt and licked away. She gasped, moaned and convulsed. Then she came. It was a long, wonderful, deep orgasm that caused her to rock from side-to-side. He made her come twice more. As she lay panting, he stood and removed his clothes.

This was the first time she ever saw him naked.

And she liked what she saw, too.

She sat up, grabbed his prick, and slid it into her mouth. He gasped as she sucked it and bobbed her head back and forth. After a minute or two, she let him go and laid back with her legs wide apart.

"Fuck me!" she said.

There was no stopping him now. He moved between her thighs and eased his prick into her cunt. She pulled him to her and wrapped her legs around his hips. It was the moment she'd been hoping for. She felt him move in and out and quivered with each thrust.

"Yes! Fuck me!" she moaned.

She soon moved with him. It felt better than she hoped it would. In fact, she loved it. They fucked faster and faster. She matched him thrust for thrust. He loved the way she fucked and how tight her cunt was.

It didn't matter that they were cheating. Nothing mattered but the intensity of their lovemaking and the pleasure they were giving each other.

He came first. When she felt his cum spurting into her, she also came. They kept fucking as hard as they could until both were totally spent. She smiled up at him and they kissed again. They had done it. They had crossed the line and committed adultery.

Eva didn't care. She'd finally had full out sex with Al and his half hard prick and pool of cum inside her pussy felt wonderful. She sucked his prick until he was fully erect again and lay back down. He slid his prick into her cunt and they moved together slowly.

"I finally have you all to myself!" she whispered. "I'm all yours now."

They moved together perfectly. It was as if their bodies were made for each other. His thrusts were deep and strong and she quivered with every one of them. The second one lasted longer than their first and felt even more exciting.

"I'm gonna come," he whispered.

"Come in my pussy. Make me yours!" she gasped as she fucked him faster.

The timing was perfect, too.

They both came at the same time and kept fucking until he slipped out of her. She looked down at the stream of white that oozed from her throbbing cunt and smiled.

"I am yours," she said as they kissed.

They fucked twice more that day. Each time, he came inside her cunt. She decided that she would always let him cum inside of her and the consequences be damned. As she beamed up at him after their last fuck, she said: "I love you."

She went to his house the next day. This time, they went up to the bedroom and spent the entire morning and afternoon exploring every part of each other's bodies and they fucked in at least four different positions. Each time was better than the last and each time, she screamed "I love you!"

And each time they fucked, she let him come inside of her.

Two nights later, she showed up at Al's house again and they repeated what they'd done before and again Eva cried out that she loved him each time she came.

When she finally got home around midnight, she admitted to Vince that she and Al were lovers and that she planned to fuck his brains out every chance they got. She also told him that he was welcome to "fuck any other woman you have a mind to" as long as she could keep fucking Al.

Vince laughed and told her that he'd already fucked two other women at work, so it was fine with him if she fucked Al. They both stared at each other then busted out laughing. Vince also told her that since Al planned to marry a very sexy Filipina soon, he might go after her.

That Friday, she arrived at Al's place with a small overnight bag and announced she was his for the entire weekend.

"Since Monday is a holiday, that means we will be together for almost four whole days. Do you think you can keep up with me, Al? I feel very horny and you know I like to fuck a lot!" she said as she put her arms around his neck.

"I'm gonna give it my best shot," he said as they kissed...

That same weekend, Vince took one of the women he'd bee fucking to a small inn in the next town. When Monday evening rolled around, it was more than obvious that everyone was really happy.

That was the last time that Al and Eva fucked for the next couple of years. Three weeks after that, Al married a cute, sexy Filipina named Rinna—who was quickly became Eva's best friend.

Rinna was the same height as Eva and had short, jet black hair and dark brown eyes. Her natural tan gave her an exotic appearance and her perfect figure and long sexy legs always attracted attention. Even now men always stopped to watch her go by and many stopped to talk to her where she worked or was out by herself.

She also attracted the attention of Vince who got an erection whenever Rinna was around. Everyone knew this but Rinna herself, who seemed to be oblivious. Besides, she had become best friends with Eva.

The two women became nearly inseparable. They went everywhere together. They especially liked to hang out in the casinos on weekends. Rinna's husband wasn't too crazy about her casino nights but he let her go anyway, especially if they had nothing special planned. Eva's husband didn't seem to care, unless she lost money. Then the fights started.

But she kept going anyway.

When she felt upset or depressed, she usually sought the comfort of Rinna. They'd have lunch together and talk. Often, they ended up back at the casino. Over time, Eva realized that she had become attracted to Rinna.

Physically attracted.

She'd never felt that way about any other woman. At first, she tried to hide her feelings. But as time went on, she started displaying them.

It first manifested while the two were just walking through the park. They were walking very close to each other when Rinna tripped over a root. Eva reached out and grabbed her hand to keep her from falling and, to Rinna's surprise, she didn't let go. They just continued walking and talking while they held hands like it was the most natural thing in the world.

"Did I ever tell you how beautiful you are?" Eva asked.

"No. I think you're beautiful, too," Rinna replied as they smiled at each other.

"You're really sexy, too. If I was a man, I'd ask you out on a date," Eva said.

Rinna laughed.

"Well, we always go out together and now we're holding hands. Maybe we've been dating all along," she joked as she squeezed Eva's hand.

"Maybe," Eva smiled.

"I kind of like this," Rinna said.

"Me, too," Eva agreed. "I have a confession."

"What?" Rinna asked.

"I am sexually attracted to you. I think I have always been. When I am with you, my pussy gets warm."

Rinna giggled.

"No. It's true. In fact, I feel very warm right now," Eva said.

"My pussy gets warm when I'm with you, too," Rinna admitted. "I love you, Eva."

Eva beamed and squeezed her hand harder. They stopped and looked into each other's eyes for a long time.

"I love you, too. I love you so much that if I had a dick, I'd make love to you right now," Eva said softly.

Eva slid her tongue into Rinna's mouth. Surprised, Rinna did the same. The kiss was soft, sweet and amazingly erotic. They stopped, smiled at each other, and kissed again. This time, it became more passionate, like a kiss between lovers. They stopped and caught their breath.

"Wow! That was really nice. I've wanted to kiss you like that for a long time," Eva said.

"I'm really surprised you did that, Eva. But I liked it, too. Maybe too much," Rinna said.

They kissed again.

That's when Rinna realized that she wanted Eva. She'd never had such feelings for a woman before and it excited and it scared the Hell out of her. Their kiss grew deeper and hotter. Rinna began to feel moist between her thighs and she sucked Eva tongue with more and more passion to let her know she was willing. Eva responded in kind but was also frightened of where this was going. She wanted Rinna more than ever and she slid her hands down her back and fondled her behind.

"Yes," Rinna whispered.

They hurried back to Rinna's house. Once inside, they kissed again. Rinna's head began to spin. They went to the sofa and sat down. They kissed again. This time, Eva gently ran her hand up and down Rinna's thigh. Rinna parted her knees and kept sucking Eva's tongue. Eva's touches were sexually arousing. So much so, that Rinna started doing the same to Eva to let her know she was interested.

That's when they heard Al's car drive up to the house.

They stopped what they were doing, giggled at each other and greeted him when he came in.

"Next time," Rinna whispered.

But Eva didn't press the issue.

She was new at this and wasn't sure where to go next or even if Rinna wanted to go any further. Besides, she valued her friendship and needed her to have someone to confide in. She was a little worried that if she pressed things, Rinna might become aloof.

Or she might piss off Al whom she still wanted to fuck.

She didn't hide it from Rinna, either. She had told her about their brief fling just before Al married her. Rinna said that since they weren't married at the time, it didn't bother her.

"But I am surprised that you actually cheated on Vince like that. Does he know?" Rinna asked.

"I'm sure he's figured it out. He knows I'm attracted to Al. But he hasn't said anything about it yet," Eva said. "Besides, Vince has his eyes on another woman and would do just about anything to get into her panties."

"Oh? Who is she?" Rinna asked.

"You," Eva said. "Vince told me that he'd love to have sex with you because he thinks you're the hottest woman he's ever met. I just laughed but don't be surprised if he tries something."

"He keeps saying nice things to me," Rinna said.

It started the first time he saw her in shorts. Rinna, he thought, had the most beautiful legs he'd ever seen and the sight of her smooth, tanned limbs gave him an instant hard on. He began to fantasize about having sex with her a lot and oh-so wanted to turn those fantasies into a reality.

So he told Rinna how sexy she was and how she had the sexiest legs on Earth. Rinna knew that Vince was attracted to her. She had seen his prick bulge in his jeans several times. The idea that the sight of her legs gave him an erection excited her. She wondered if Vince would try to do more than just look. If he did, she wondered how she'd react.

A couple of days later, Al had a barbecue. Everyone was a little drunk and Vince started coming onto Rinna.

"I want you," he whispered as he leaned close.

"You can't have me. I'm married," she said with a sly smile.

"How about I just borrow you then?" he teased as he put his hand on her knee.

She giggled but let him slide his hand up her thigh and under her shorts. She almost jumped out of them when he touched her cunt. It ended there.

The next time, they were at a museum. Al and Eva wandered off to check on an exhibit in a side gallery while Rinna wandered around the section dealing with the history of women's fashions. Vince followed her and stood very close.

When no one was around, he leaned close and kissed her on the neck. She pushed him away.

"Stop that! Someone might see us!" she said.

They kept walking around. When they came to a darker area of the gallery, Vince kissed her again. He was directly behind her and as he nuzzled her neck, he reached around and squeezed her breasts. He heard her moan softly and realized he'd aroused her. So he kept nuzzling her and playing with her nipples.

Rinna began breathing heavily. She felt his erection pressing against her behind and smiled. This went on for a several minutes. That's when Vince slid his hand down her belly and into her shorts. She quivered as he stroked her cunt.

"You like this?' he asked as he teased her swollen clit.

"Yes!" she whispered.

They stopped because they heard other people approaching. That was the first time that any man but Al had ever touched her cunt.

The next time was at another barbecue. This time, they were at a park. Rinna went off to locate a bathroom. Vince waited a few seconds and followed. He knew that Eva was keeping Al busy, so he wouldn't be missed.

When Rinna exited the bathroom, Vince was waiting outside. She saw that he already had an erection and smiled. They ended up in a shaded area between several trees. That's when they exchanged their first French kiss. As they kissed, Vince ran his hands all over her body. By then, his erection was pressing against her crotch and the contact was making her crazy.

Vince reached under her T-shirt and played with her nipples. She was really horny now. So horny that she raked her fingers along his bulge. Before long, he had his hand in her panties again and his middle finger was moving in and out of her wet, hot cunt. She unzipped his jeans, reached inside and pulled out his prick. This was only the second one she had ever touched or seen and she kept her eyes on the shiny knob as precum oozed from the slit and covered it with each pump of her hand.

They kept at this until they both came. And that wasn't the only time this happened. They did this every time they were alone together. Rinna realized that she was very attracted to Vince and they'd end up fucking sooner or later.

The last time, they almost did just that.

It was about ten a.m. when Vince paid her an unexpected visit. He had taken the day off from work and decided to surprise her. As soon as she opened the door, he grabbed her and stuck his tongue in her mouth. She relaxed and sucked it while she rubbed his crotch. They kept at this for few more minutes. She felt him unzip her shorts and slide them down her body along with her panties. She quivered with excitement as he felt her. She undid his jeans and pulled out his erection and jerked him off nice and easy.

When precum emerged from the slit, she massaged it into his knob and shaft and kept jerking him off. By now, his middle finger was working her slit and she was shaking all over. She began to moan loudly as she jerked him faster.

He suddenly stopped fingering and dropped to his knees. To her surprise—and delight—he gripped her ass and pulled her forward so he could bury his tongue in her cunt. Rinna almost screamed as she came. She came hard, too, and fucked Vince's tongue.

"Wonderful! I love it! I love it!" she moaned as she came again and again.

Vince stopped and stood up. Rinna looked at his long, hard dick and smiled. She knelt down in front of him and ran her tongue all over his shaft, balls and knob several times before sliding half of it into her mouth. As she sucked, she played with his balls. Vince spurted seconds later. Rinna almost gagged on the first shot but managed to swallow all of it and the others that followed. She kept sucking his dick until Vince's balls ached and he told her to stop.

They hugged for a long time, and then Vince zipped up his jeans.

"Do you fuck as good as you suck?" he asked.

"Do you fuck as good as you eat pussy?" she countered.

They laughed. On the way out, he felt her cunt again. She smiled.

"Next time?" he asked.

"Definitely!" she replied.

"Has Vince tried anything with you yet?" Eva asked.

"Yes. I let him touch my pussy a few times and I squeezed his dick. The last time, we had oral sex," Rinna said.

"Would you fuck him if you had the chance?' Eva asked.

Rinna laughed.

"Maybe. Is he any good?" she teased.

"Oh, he's real good," Eva said.

"Is he as good as Al?" Rinna joked.

"Almost. They're real different from each other. If you really want to find out, give Vince a try. But if you do, I'm going after Al again," Eva said half in jest.

Rinna laughed it off but the seeds had been planted. She began to wonder what it would be like to fuck Vince. She already knew from the bulges she saw in his jeans that he had a really big dick and she began to wonder what it would feel like inside her cunt. In fact, she even mentioned it to Al.

He laughed it off and told her to go for it if she really wanted to, but not to be surprised if he went after Eva. He knew she had a slutty side that came out when she drank.

Big time.

A couple of years earlier, Rinna met a man at the casino bar named Will. He was tall, broad shouldered and very handsome. He bought her a drink and they sat down at a table and chatted. Will made her laugh. He bought her a second drink and that's when he slid his hand along her inner thigh.

"And what are you after?" she smiled as he moved his hand under her skirt

"Guess!" he said.

She giggled and parted her legs. She had allowed Vince to feel her pussy a few times when no one was looking, so she saw no harm in letting Will do the same. By the third drink, he had his middle finger moving inside her very wet cunt and she wondered what it would be like to fuck him. She parted her legs more as he fingered her faster. She began to quiver all over now.

"I have a room in the hotel upstairs," he said.

"Let's go," she said.

She held his arm as they went to the elevator. She realized that she had just agreed to have sex with a man she'd met less than two hours ago. She was about to cheat on her husband but it didn't matter. She was anxious to feel Will's prick inside her cunt.

They entered his suite and hurried to the bed where they quickly undressed each other. As she lay on the bed, Will spent several wonderful minutes sucking her nipples while he "fucked" her with his middle finger. She moaned and squirmed as he played with her. At the same time, she wrapped her fingers around his prick and slowly jerked him off.

Will kissed his way down her body and buried his tongue in her cunt. Rinna moaned loudly as he ate her and soon began fucking his tongue. She erupted seconds later. She gripped his hair and humped his face as she came again and again.

He stopped and knelt over her. She smiled up at him and opened her legs wide.

"Fuck me!" she said.

He teased her a few times by moving his cockhead up and down from her ass crack to her clit. She was on fire now.

"Fuck me!" she demanded.

As soon as his huge prick parted her quivering labia and plunged deep into her cunt, she knew she was his. She gripped his hips and moaned as he fucked her with long, deep, easy strokes. Will's dick deliciously massaged every bit of her cunt with each and every stroke. After a few thrusts, she moved with him.

Yes she was cheating.

Yes she was fucking a total stranger.

But it felt wonderful! Too wonderful to stop.

They fucked faster and faster. Rinna suddenly screamed and came. As she did, she fucked Will as hard as she could until she felt his cum spurt into her.

"Don't stop, Will! Keep fucking me! Fill my pussy with your cum!" she ranted.

They rested for a little while, and then she straddled his dick and impaled herself on it. That's when she showed him why Filipina's are called "little brown fucking machines". Will was amazed. Rinna was terrific and she used her inner cunt muscles to do things to his dick that he'd never felt before.

This time, they climaxed together and Will pumped another good load of cum up into her cunt.

Rinna wasn't finished. She grabbed his dick and slid it into her mouth for what Will later described as the best blowjob he'd ever had. She sucked and licked his shaft and knob and played with his balls until he grew rock hard again.

Rinna got onto her hands and knees.

"Fuck me!" she said.

Will laughed and slid his dick into her cunt again for what proved to be a very long, very intense fuck which concluded with a simultaneous orgasm and him pumping yet another load into her cunt.

They caught their breath.

"How long will you be in town, Will?" she asked.

"Two more nights," he said.

"Want to do this again tomorrow?' she asked.

"Hell yeah! When can you get here?" he replied.

"I'll meet you in the bar at seven," she said. "I love the way you fuck and I want to do this every night until you leave."

"I don't have a problem with that. But won't your husband have one?" Will asked.

"I'll worry about that later," she said as she stroked his dick.

She got home well after midnight with a satisfied grin on her face and a pussy full of cum. She told Al what happened and told him that she couldn't help herself. She also told him that agreed to meet Will the next two nights.

"It's exciting fucking someone else for a change. It's different and I let myself run wild. So I'm going to fuck him the next two nights even if you tell me not to," she said.

"Did you let him cum inside of you?" Al asked.

She smiled and hiked up her skirt to show she wasn't wearing panties, and then she used two fingers to pry apart her labia so he could see the pool of cum inside her. By then, he was rock hard. She smiled and took his hand and led him upstairs...

The next night, she and Will fucked four different ways and he flooded her cunt with cum. The next night, Rinna didn't get home until ten the next morning and she could barely walk straight. She showered and fell asleep on the sofa. That's where Al found her when he got home from work at four that afternoon.

He wasn't really surprised she did that. She admitted that she had allowed Vince to play with her pussy several times and had even made her come a couple of times. She also admitted that she had jerked him off and was planning to fuck him sooner or later.

It wasn't her only "slip", either. After that, she fucked several other men she met at the casinos and each time, she got home with the same results. There was no stopping her when she was drunk and horny and, if she liked the guy, she'd end up fucking him. It was a side of her that Al didn't know about until it started happening and he realized there was nothing he could do about it On a couple of nights, she even left her panties at home on her pillow so he'd know not to wait up for her.

He usually laughed about it.

Rinna had become a slut.

Most other men would divorce their wives over this, but Al and Rinna adored each other and he was willing to indulge her "hobbies". At least she did it openly, so she wasn't really cheating and she even told Al that he could fuck other women if he wanted to as that would only be fair.

"Since I've had a lot of different dicks in my pussy, you can stick yours into as many different pussies as you want," she said. "You can start with Eva because she's nuts about you and go from there. I know there's a certain woman at work you're dying to try, too."

Al said that he'd probably take her up on that.

.Vince had said on more than one occasion that he'd really love to fuck Rinna. And Al told him that if he managed to do that, he was going to fuck Eva half to death. Vince laughed and told him to go for it since he knew that Eva was crazy about him. The two men shook hands and said it was a deal.

Vince also told him that he'd been fucking this young woman at work every chance he got and that Eva already knew about that.

"She'll be after you again—big time. So let her 'catch' you. Then I'll go after Rinna. I'm betting that she can fuck like crazy, too," he said.

"She certainly can," Al smiled.

So everyone knew exactly where they stood and the table was set. But nothing happened for several weeks and the two women kept hanging out together. They laughed and held hands and deep kissed and caressed each other's thighs as their mutual attraction grew and grew. But they still were too chicken to take it further.

Eva noticed that Rinna always wore her shortest shorts when she knew Vince was around and that she always kept her eyes glued to his crotch to see his reaction. Eva didn't mind because she was openly flirting with Al.

"You already know what I have between my legs. It's yours whenever you want it," she whispered when no one was around. "I'm yours, Al. I will always be yours. Remember that."

When things went bad between Eva and Vince, she always confided in Rinna, who was a good, sympathetic listener. Rinna knew that Eva needed someone to vent to and was more than happy to be that person. When Rinna wasn't available, Eva talked with Al. He always listened to her and his way of putting a lighthearted spin on her problems always made her feel good. They liked each other a lot. Rinna knew this and didn't mind, even though she knew about their fling.

About a week later, Eva and Vince had another bitter argument over her casino habits. They each said some nasty things to each other. Vince stormed out and went to work and Eva headed to Art's house to talk to Rinna.

But Rinna was out shopping and Al happened to be on his patio, drinking beer. When she arrived, he handed her one. It was a very warm day and Eva had on her dark green running shorts and a T-shirt. Al admired her long, tanned legs a she sat down with him. He always liked her legs. They looked so smooth and silky and were perfectly shaped. She still had a nice behind, but there was a bit more of it now.

"Do you still think I am attractive?" she asked after a while.

Al responded by putting his hand on her thigh. She smiled. He used to do that quite often when no one else was around and, as before, she didn't try to discourage him.

"Of course I do," he said as he moved his hand upward. "Why'd you ask?"

"Vince said I was getting fat," she said. "Am I?"

"To be honest, you have put on a few pounds, but it actually becomes you. I can't believe he even said that," Al said as he moved his hand higher and higher. Eva knew what he wanted and she parted her legs.

"So you'd fuck me?" she asked.

He laughed. Eva always had a blunt way of talking. He decided to answer her by sliding his hand beneath her shorts to her panties. She smiled and let him feel her cunt again. It was just like old times. She loved the attention and the fact that he found her alluring. It had been ages since he did this and she found herself missing his caresses.

That day, he went so far as to slide his hand down into her shorts. It was the first time he'd touched her cunt in a while and his gentle touches made her quiver all over. She raised her t-shirt to reveal her breasts. He swirled his tongue over each nipple and made her breathe heavier.

"That's so nice. I've really missed this," she whispered as she squeezed the bulge in his jeans.

He kept sucking her nipples and fingering her clit until she orgasmed. It was a strong, almost bone-jarring type of come, too.

They'd always stopped short of actually having sex. Today was different. Eva was upset and horny and looking for reassurance that she was not ugly or too fat.

"I take it that means you would," she said.

"Definitely," he assured her.

"Maybe one day, we will both get our wish," she said as he rubbed her clit. "Oh, God! I'm so wet!"

That's when they heard Rinna drive up. Al stopped and turned as she came to the patio. She hugged them both. She noticed the obvious erection in Al's pants and looked at Eva, who just sat there with a sly grin on her lips.

"Did I interrupt something?" she joked.

"Maybe," Eva smiled.

"Can we go to the casino tonight?" Rinna asked.

"We? You have a mouse in your pocket?" Al teased.

"No. Me and Eva," Rinna said as she playfully pushed him.

"I guess so. Just don't lose the house," he said.

And off to the casino they went. Al's attentions had made Eva feel good about herself, at least for a little while. But even he had said that she'd put on a few pounds.

That night, as they played slots, Eva asked Rinna if she thought she was getting fat.

"I really haven't noticed," Rinna said.

Eva stood and spun around slowly while Rinna watched. She sat down and looked at her.

"Be honest. Am I getting fat?" she asked.

"Well, your ass is a little rounder," Rinna said. "But it makes you look even sexier."

"That's what Al told me," Eva said. "Vince said I'm too fat and that I need to lose weight."

"I think he's nuts," Rinna said as she put her hand on Eva's thigh.

Eva smiled at her and parted her knees. She was still feeling horny from her brief encounter with Al. Eva's hand crept upward to the edge of her shorts then moved down again. She kept stroking her like this for several minutes and Eva's cunt was soon very wet.

"I love you, Rinna," Eva whispered. "If you want me, I'm yours."

"I'm not sure how to do this. You excite me, Eva. You make me nervous, too," Rinna said as she caressed her.

They stopped before anyone could see them and went back to playing the slots. Eva was so horny that her head reeled. She wanted to tear Rinna's shorts off and bury her face between her legs.

They played for another hour and decided to drive to the restaurant in the park for a snack. It was about six. They never made it to the park. Instead, they went back to Rinna's house and had a glass of wine while they sat on the sofa.

"Have you fucked Vince yet?" Eva asked.

"No," Rinna lied.

"Are you going to?" Eva asked as she stroked Rinna's thigh.

"Probably. I like to play with his dick and I've sucked it so I wonder what something like that would feel like in my pussy," Rinna admitted.

"Do you tell Al about it?" Eva asked.

"Yes," she said with a smile. "What about you?"

"I think about Al all of the time lately," Eva said. "And I want to fuck him more than anything on Earth. In fact, I'm dying to have sex with your husband again."

Rinna laughed.

"Do you plan to do anything about it?" she teased as she continued to stroke her thigh.

"Maybe. If I did, would you be mad at me or Al?" Eva teased back.

"Neither," Rinna said after a few seconds. "Right now, I'm thinking about something else."

Eva laughed.

They made eye contact. Eva felt almost mesmerized now. She studied Rinna's face as of seeing her for the first time. She was cute and oh-so sexy.

Rinna kept stroking her inner thigh slowly and gently. Eva parted her legs and smiled. Rinna moved closer. The attraction was now powerful. Too powerful to resist. Their lips touched. Eva opened her mouth and shivered as their tongue's met. She had never kissed another woman and the waves of excitement that now surged through her made her actually shiver.

Rinna felt it, too.

She moved her hand upward to Eva's panties. Eva sighed as Rinna gently felt her. She felt herself grow warmer and wetter and sucked Rinna's tongue harder. She ran her hand up under Rinna's shorts and massaged her cunt. Rinna's legs parted.

Eva shook all over as Rinna's eased her fingers into her cunt. Her legs were wide open now. Rinna moved her fingers in and out of Eva's cunt. Eva caught her signal and did the same to her. They sat there and kept doing this until they made each other come.

Eva came first. When she did, she shook all over and emitted a loud, "YES!"

Rinna came moments later. They clung to each other for a while and exchanged several more kisses. When they recovered, they looked at each other and smiled. They had always been attracted to each other. Now, they had taken their first steps toward doing something about it.

"I love you, Eva," Rinna whispered. "I think I loved you from the moment I met you."

"I think I felt the same way about you. I was just too chicken to tell you. I was afraid of how you'd react. Wow. I'm glad we finally did something about it. I'm glad you feel the same way about me as I feel about you."

"Now what?" Rinna asked.

"I'm not sure. This is new for me. I've never felt attracted to a woman before," Eva said.

"Me neither. I guess we can take this one step at a time and see where it leads," Rinna said as they kissed again.

But Eva and Al's relationship was about to heat up big time. Both wanted to take it beyond what they'd already done.

A couple of days later, that's exactly what happened.

Rinna came home unexpectedly. She heard a sound coming from the living room and went to check it out. That's when she saw Al and Eva on the sofa. He had his tongue in her mouth and one hand in her shorts and she was jerking him off. She stood and watched them for a little while. The sight of Eva's hand moving up and down Al's prick made her feel wet between her legs. She was also excited by the way his hand was moving inside Eva's shorts. She then cleared her throat to let them know she was there

They stopped and looked at her. She noticed that Eva still had Al's dick in her hand and she became as red as a tomato at being caught. Instead of blowing her top, she surprised them by remaining calm and smiling.

"As long as you've started, you might as well finish," she said as she walked into the kitchen.

She stood on the doorway and peaked at them. Eva's shoulder and arm were still moving up and down and since she was moaning, she knew that Al's fingers were inside her cunt. She watched until Al came and she saw his cum spurt several times as Eva kept pumping him.

The idea that Eva and Al were having sex made her feel hornier than she'd ever felt before. No longer able to control herself, she stepped in front of them.

"Don't stop," she said. "Keep doing it."

Rinna undid her belt and allowed her shorts to slide down her legs to her ankles. Al and Eva watched as she kicked them to the side and peeled off her panties. Eva was still pumping Al's prick. Rinna stepped close, got on the couch and straddled Al's legs. Eva smiled and guided his prick up into Rinna's cunt then sat back and watched as she bounced up and down on it. Al groaned and grabbed her hips.

As they fucked, Eva peeled off all of her clothes and stepped in front of them. Rinna smiled and caressed her cunt. Eva breathed heavier and heavier. Rinna eased her middle finger up into Eva's cunt and moved it in and out. Eva shivered all over, her excitement heightened by the fact that the beautiful Rinna was doing it.

Rinna kept riding Al's prick faster and faster. She felt her entire body tremble and leaned against him to let him play with her nipples.

"Yes!" she cried as she erupted.

The orgasm was powerful. One of the best she'd ever felt. She moaned and shook as waves of intense pleasure surged through her. As she came, she felt Al's cum jet into her. The sensation made her come even more. As she came, she frigged Eva's cunt as fast as she could. Eva screamed and came. She gripped Rinna's shoulders to keep from falling. Rinna leaned toward her and gently swirled her tongue over each of Eva's nipples.

After a few seconds, Rinna stood and sat down on the loveseat. She smiled at Eva.

"Go for it," she said. "I want to watch you fuck."

Eva gave Al's half hard prick a few pumps then slid it into her mouth. Al moaned as she sucked it and played with his balls. When Eva felt he was iron hard again, she lay on the floor and opened her legs wide. Al got between them and slid his prick into her gorgeous, tight cunt. Eva shivered and wrapped her arms around his hips.

"Fuck me! Make me yours!" she shouted.

Rinna watched as the settled into a good, deep, slow fuck. It was obvious this is what they'd both wanted to do for a long, long time. They weren't just fucking. It looked like they were making love.

She loved watching his prick move in and out of Eva's gorgeous cunt. She watched as they fucked faster and faster. Eva came first and shook all over as she fucked him back with everything she had. He matched her thrust for thrust then finally came. He shot what was a surprising amount of cum deep into Eva's convulsing pussy as she held on and begged him for more.

Al pulled out when his prick went flaccid. Eva was still in sexual Nirvana and didn't mind at all when Rinna moved close and French kissed her. Before long, they were locked into a very passionate embrace. Al watched in awe as the fingered each other through a series of good, hard comes that left them both exhausted.

"That was awesome," Eva said after she caught her breath.

Rinna helped her back onto the sofa. They looked at each other and laughed. It had been a spontaneous threesome and Rinna had let out her inner slut in a way that neither Al nor Eva imagined.

Rinna sat up and smiled at Al.

"Why did you do that?" he asked. "I'm not complaining but this was so unexpected and not like anything you'd ever do."

"I'm not sure why. I just got so excited watching you and Eva that I had to join in. Wow, Eva. You have a very sexy body," Rinna said as she stroked her breast. "I've wanted to do this with you for a long, long time."

She ran her hand along Eva's thigh. Eva smiled as she stroked her cunt, amazed that Rinna thought of her as a lover. She'd had similar feelings for Rinna. Now everything was in the open. She'd gotten to finally have full sex with Al and Rinna had encouraged them to do it.

"You're so sexy. So irresistible," Rinna said as she played with Eva's cunt.

Watching them made Al hard again. Eva watched his prick grow. She got onto her hands and knees. Rinna did the same.

"Fuck us, Al!" she said.

Al got behind Eva and slid his prick into her cunt. He fucked her as hard as he could. Eva fell to her elbows and shook all over as she came. Al quickly pulled out and plunged his prick into Rinna's cunt. Eva watched as they fucked hard then simultaneously came.

After that, they all got dressed and went out to dinner.

The next day, the women got together again to further explore their attraction for each other. They had a few glasses of red wine. In between glasses, they French Kissed and felt each other up.

"You want to have an affair with my husband?" Rinna asked as she stroked Eva's slit.

"Yes. A long, steamy affair, too," Eva said as she opened her legs wider. "I want to feel his dick inside my pussy. I want him to fill me with his cum over and over again."

"Okay," Rinna smiled as she moved her fingers beneath Eva's panties and into her slit.

Eva shook all over. This is the furthest Rinna had ever gone with her and she was on cloud none over it. She smiled at her and ran her tongue over her lips to let her know she was all hers now. Rinna moved her finger in and out her cunt slowly. Eva gasped and convulsed as she came. She gripped her chair and bit her lower lip to keep from screaming. Rinna smiled and pulled her fingers out of Eva's sopping cunt.

"Wow. That was nice," Eva said.

Your pussy smells good," Rinna said as she sniffed her fingers. "So, now what should we do?"

"Well, you said that think about having sex with Vince. If you had a chance, would you really do it?" Eva asked.

"I already have," Rinna said after a pause.

Eva giggled.

"I knew it!" she said. "Vince is more interested in your pussy than he is mine anyway," Eva said. "He said that he loves your legs and your cute, tight ass and even said he'd love to get at what you have between those legs. He's always been attracted to you. I thought you knew that," Eva said.

Rinna told her about it.

She had just returned from her morning jog. She was wearing only a loose t-shirt and her silk running shorts. Vince pulled up outside the house and asked if he could borrow one of Al's tools. Rinna let him in and led him upstairs to where Al kept his tool kit. Vince was behind her and he ogled her ass and legs the entire time and he became very hard. She watched as he looked through the tool kit and found the wrench he needed.

She turned to lead him back downstairs and was surprised when Vince squeezed her behind. She just stood still, not sure of how to react for a few seconds as he continued to feel her. When he ran his fingers along the crack of her ass, she quivered.

"I want you, Rinna," he said softly. "I want you more than anything else on Earth."

She turned to face him. He smiled at her and gently massaged her crotch. She was wet now. Very wet and horny. She kind of like the attention, too.

She opened her stance. Vince ran his fingertips along her slit through her shorts while she watched the front of his jeans bulge more and more.

"You have the sexiest legs and ass I've ever seen. I'm dying to get at what's between those legs, too," he said.

"Maybe I'll let you," she said.

That's when Vince's cell phone beeped.

He ignored it and kept fondling her. She was breathing heavier now as she felt her cunt get warmer and wetter. His bulge seemed huge now as his prick strained against his jeans. She leaned against the wall and closed her eyes. Vince could hardly believe he was getting this far with her. His touches were making her tremble now. He slipped his fingers into her shorts and gently caressed her soft pussy. Rinna moaned.

His phone beeped again and again.

"You'd better answer that," she said softly. "It might be important."

He stopped and answered it.

"I was expecting this call. I have to go now. I'll see you again later," he said.

She escorted him to the front door and watched as he drove away.

Vince tried again the next morning.

He came to the house to return the wrench. When the doorbell rang, Rinna was doing her usual housework. When she did, she always wore light clothes, like a T-shirt with no bra and her jogging shorts. When she opened the door, Vince ogled her legs and smiled.

"I brought the wrench back," he said as he held it up. "I'll put it back in the tool box."

He saw that her nipples were erect and winked at her. By then, he was starting to get an erection. Rinna led him inside and watched as he put the wrench away. When she turned around, she felt his hand on her ass.

"God, you look so sexy in those shorts," he said as he fondled her.

She didn't try to discourage him. She turned to face him and smiled as she watched his prick grow. She enjoyed his reaction. He reached over and caressed her crotch. She opened her stance and let him continue as she watched his bulge get bigger and bigger. She leaned back against the wall and closed her eyes like she did last time. Vince slipped his middle finger under her shorts and past her panties and into her cunt. Rinna trembled as he moved it in and out nice and easy.

She was on fire now.

She groped his erection and marveled at its hardness. He fingered her a little faster and sent shivers through her body. She tweaked his knob through his jeans a little while. He slid his finger into as deep as he could and wiggled it around.

Rinna gasped and came.

It was a sudden and hard orgasm. She moaned loudly and shook all over. All the while, she kept playing with his knob. Then she felt him stiffen as the front of his jeans filled with warm, sticky liquid.

She had made him come. She kept playing with him until she felt his prick go soft. Meanwhile, he made her come a second time as he massaged her clit nice and fast. She gripped his shoulders and screamed.

"Yes! Yes! I love it!"

By then, Vince's hand was inside her panties and his mouth and tongue were on her right nipple. Without her realizing it, he had raised her shirt so he could suck it and she didn't mind it one bit.

Vince had her where he wanted her now. She was ready to let him fuck her in every hole of her body as many times as he wanted. He took her hand and led her to the dining room table and turned her around. She leaned forward and sighed as he caressed her ass. She heard him unzip his jeans. He pushed aside her shorts and moved close. She felt the head of his prick move slowly up and down her slit and opened her stance. Then he eased his prick into her cunt slowly.

Deliciously.

"Yes!" she sighed as he fucked her.

He grabbed her hips and pistoned in and out of her moist, tight cunt. She just leaned on the table and sighed with each deep thrust.

His prick felt so damned good, too.

So wonderfully hard and wicked. She shivered as he moved faster and faster. He reached around and played with her nipples to heighten the intensity. Rinna moaned and thrust her ass back up at him.

"Oooh! I'm yours, Vince! Anytime you want me, I'm all yours! Fuck me!" she sighed.

Rinna's cunt was as tight and exciting as he imagined it would be. He was beside himself now as he finally got to fuck the woman he was most attracted to.

Rinna came first and screamed as it rippled through her quivering body. It was intense and incredibly deep. He kept fucking her as hard as he could and finally came. She sighed as she felt his cum jet into her. He grabbed her hips and fucked her harder. This caused her to keep coming and coming.

When he was spent, he fell on top of her, panting.

That's when they heard Al drive up to the house.

Vince pulled out his shirt and adjusted it so it covered the wet spot in front of his jeans while Rinna ran upstairs to put a bra on. They both smiled and acted like nothing happened but Al knew differently because of the slight aroma of sex in the air.

Since he had been fooling around with Eva, he didn't say anything to them. He just decided to let things work themselves out.

"So you did it!" she giggled.

"Yes," Rinna confessed. "And I plan to do it again."

"In that case, I'm going to fuck Al into the mattress," Eva said with a giggle as Rinna slid her hand under her shorts again.

She leaned back and sighed as Rinna played with her clit. She was so horny that she came within seconds. Rinna kissed her as she continued to finger her faster and faster. She loved the way Eva's cunt convulsed around her fingers and grew wetter and wetter. Eva put her arms around Rinna's shoulders and sucked her tongue passionately as she came again and again and again.

"I love you, Rinna!" she cried as she shook all over.

She pulled up her T-short to expose her breasts. Rinna leaned over and gently tongued and sucked each nipple while Eva moaned in ecstasy. Before long, Eva was happily sucking Rinna's nipple and her hand was deep inside Rinna's shorts.

After she made Rinna come several times, they sat back to catch their breath. This was the closest to having all-out sex they'd ever come and their hearts were now pounding out of control.

Rinna looked at the clock.

"Al will be home any second," she said as she readjusted her clothes.

Eva did the same and they kissed. It was a long, very deep kiss, too. One that spoke volumes about their feelings for each other.

"Now what?" Eva asked. "Where do we go next?"

"I'm not sure. This is new for me, too. I guess we can just follow our feelings," Rinna replied as she stroked her cheek. "I've never felt this way about a woman before and I'm not sure what we should do."

"Me neither," Eva admitted.

"By the way, Al's planning another barbecue this Sunday. Can you guys come?" Rinna asked.

"No problem. We'll be here. We'll bring the drinks as usual. I have to warn you that I plan to dress very sexy so I can attract Al," Eva said with a grin.

"I'll do the same," Rinna said. "Maybe we can start something crazy."

"I'm game if you are," Eva said.

Chapter Two

That same night, the girls decided to go to the casino. When they arrived, the place was packed. The separated to find empty slot machines to play and ended up on opposite sides of the casino.

Around 10 o'clock, a handsome younger man moved onto the unoccupied seat as the machine next to the one Rinna was playing. He smiled and said 'hello'. She returned the greeting and the two struck up a light, fun conversation as they played.

"Are you married?" he asked.

She showed him her wedding ring. He sighed.

"Just my usual luck. All the real pretty ones are always taken. Where are you from?" he asked.

"The Philippines," she said.

"No wonder you're so pretty. I've heard a lot of interesting things about the women from your country," he said.

"Like what?" she asked.

"Well, I'd rather not say. I might offend you," he said.

"That's okay. I'm sure I've already heard them," she said with laugh.

"Are any of them true?" he asked.

"Most of them are," she said.

At that time, a waitress walked by with two drinks. He tipped her and she handed one to Rinna and one to him. She sniffed it.

"What is it?" she asked.

"A rum and coke," he said. "It's on me."

She thanked him and sipped it. It tasted sweet but strong. They chatted a while longer.

"I'd sure like to find out if what I heard is true one day," he said.

"Maybe you will one day," she said.

The drink made her feel very relaxed and a bit giddy. She was tipsy now. When she got tipsy, she got horny. He ordered them each another drink. They continued to talk. As they talked, he put his hand on her knee. She looked at him and scowled. He withdrew it and they kept talking. She noticed that the talk had been steered to more sexual things.

"You have the sexiest legs," he said as he again placed his hand on her knee.

"Thanks," she said as the booze really kicked in.

He gently stroked her inner thigh and told her how sexy she was and how smooth her legs felt and how he'd love to see what she had between them. She giggled at his comments but didn't bat his hand away. He moved it further up her inner thigh to the edge of her shorts.

"I bet you have the prettiest and tightest pussy on Earth," he whispered.

"My husband thinks so," she said with a grin as he parted her knees.

"That lucky bastard. I wish I could get as lucky as he is," he said as he eased his hand up into her shorts.

Her cunt felt like it was on fire now. She felt horny, too, real horny. She looked at his pants and saw what appeared to be a very large bulge. She wondered how big his prick really was and how it would feel to get fucked with it.

"You might," she teased.

He was now gently running his fingers up and down the front of her panties. Her legs were wide apart now and she was squirming a bit.

"Come home with me tonight," he urged.

"I can't do that. My husband would go crazy if I stayed out all night," she said. "Ooohh!"

He slid his finger into her cunt and moved it in and out. She quivered all over and knew that she really wanted to fuck him—a lot.

"Okay. I know a real quiet and very private place we can go to here in the casino. We can go there. Then you can show me if what I've heard is true," he pressed as he continued to finger her.

"Are you sure no one will see us?" she asked.

"I'm positive. It'll just be you and me," he assured her. "There's an office that's hardly ever used right behind the poker table area. It even has a big leather sofa."

"How do you know about this?" she asked as her head began to spin.

"It's my uncle's office. He only uses it during the day and I have a key to it," he said. "Want to go with me?"

She was on the verge of coming now and her body screamed for sex. She smiled at him and nodded. He led her across the casino to an ornate looking wooden door. She watched as he took a key from his pocket and opened the door. They went inside and he turned on one of the lamps. There was a big desk, two leather chairs and a large leather sofa with a coffee table in front of it along with other furnishings.

She smiled and walked to the sofa. She turned and nodded as he undid her shorts and slid them down her legs along with her now-soaked panties. She sat down and opened her legs. He knelt between them and buried his tongue in her cunt. She gaped and moaned as he ate her. At the same time, he fingered her cunt. She groaned and moaned and came. It was a good, long orgasm, too.

By the time her fog cleared, he was standing over her naked. She stared at his prick. It was the longest one she had ever seen, too. She reached up and stroked it a few times. When it became even harder, she leaned back and put her feet up on the sofa. He grinned as he moved between her legs. She felt his knob tease her labia a few times and closed her eyes as he entered her. He went in very deep, too. So deep, she felt his head touch the back of her cunt. She reached up and gripped his arms and they began fucking. It was a nice, deep, slow fuck, too. His huge prick felt delicious as it moved in and out her cunt and he loved how tight she felt.

She had done it again.

She was fucking a man she had met only an hour ago. And God! It felt so good! She moved with him now. She threw her hips upward to meet his thrusts and tightened her cunt muscles around his prick. He moaned and fucked her slower, to savor the way her cunt felt as it massaged his prick.

"Harder! Do it harder!" she whispered as she felt herself about to explode.

He fucked her faster and faster. She shook all over and came. As she did, she fucked him faster, too. She came twice while they fucked. Both were good, body shaking comes that took her breath away. She fucked him back as hard as she could.

"I'm gonna come!" he gasped.

"In me! I want to feel you come inside me!" she screamed.

They fucked harder and faster. She came again. Just as she did, she heard him grunt. He rammed his cock into her as deep as he could and flooded her with cum. She fucked him as fast as she could and stopped when he grew flaccid and slid out.

She smiled up at him.

"Wow! That was great!" she said.

"Yes you are. Do you cheat on your husband often?" he asked as he stroked her thigh.

"No. This was my first time," she lied. "I'm not really sure why. I guess it was the alcohol and I like the company."

"My name's Jake," he said.

"Rinna," she said with a smile.

"Do you have time for one more?" he asked as he stroked her pussy.

She smiled and lay back with her legs wide open and sighed as he slid his prick into her again. She was more sober now, but since they'd already fucked, she felt she might as well enjoy another one. He was good at it, too.

Before long, they moved together and she moaned and sighed with each good, hard thrust of his prick. At the same time, she threw her hips up at him to take every bit of him inside her. They fucked nice and slow now, to take their time to really enjoy it.

"My God! That's good. So good! Fuck me, Jake!" she moaned

They kept moving together faster and faster. This time, they both came together. She shook all over and screamed as he again filled her cunt with his cum. They kept at it until they couldn't move anymore.

He stuck his tongue into her mouth for a good, deep kiss afterward.

They rested a few minutes and talked. Then they dressed and exchanged phone numbers. Jake promised to call her when he got back to town. She told him she'd like to meet earlier next time and spend most of the night with him.

"Great! I'll get us a suite upstairs. That way, we can fuck as much as we like," he agreed.

To her surprise, he grabbed his wallet, took out two one hundred dollar bills, and put them in her hand. She stared at the money then at him.

"For services well rendered," he said. "Consider it a gift."

"I'm not a—"she began.

"Nobody said you were. I just thought that someone like you deserved a thank you gift. Money is all I have, so I gave it to you. I hope you're not offended," he said.

She smiled and put the money into her purse.

"I'm not. Thanks," she said.

That's when she realized that she not only cheated on Al, but that she would most likely do it again. She'd spent her life having sex with only one man. Now, she had the itch. And it needed to be scratched often. It also occurred to her that since she had taken Jake's money that made her a prostitute in every sense of the word.

"So, I'm a prostitute," she smiled as she headed back to the slots.

When she walked back to the slots, she felt his cum deposits squishing around inside her cunt. The sensations made her smile. It felt strange to have another man's cum inside her pussy—but it also felt exciting. Just like it did when she fucked Vince.

A few minutes later, Eva found her and tapped her on the shoulder. Rinna smiled and Eva noticed that she looked kind of flushed but happy.

"Have you been drinking?" she asked.

"A little," Rinna said. "What time is it?"

"Almost one," Eva said. "We'd better go home."

As they walked out, Eva noticed that Rinna's legs seemed kind of wobbly. She was walking like she felt a little sore, too.

"Are you okay?" she asked.

"Oh, yes. I'm very okay," Rinna said. "Very, very okay."

Eva stared at her and laughed.

"You've been fucked!" she said.

"No I haven't," Rinna denied.

"Yes you have. That's why you're walking like that and you look so happy. You've been fucked in it was obviously a really good one," Eva said.

"No. Really," Rinna protested.

Eva spotted what appeared to be line of shiny liquid running down Rinna's thigh. She reached over and rand her fingers through it and sniffed them.

"That's cum—and you have a pussy filled with it, don't you?" she said.

"I, er—" Rinna began.

"Don't you?" Eva pressed.

Rinna smiled.

"You really did it! You fucked someone here tonight. And it was a good hard one, wasn't it?" Eva asked.

Rinna blushed.

"How was he?" Eva asked.

"He was great. He had a long, really hard dick and he knew how to use it. We fucked twice, too. I didn't mean for it to happen, but he's young and handsome and he got me drunk. So I agreed to fuck him," Rinna admitted.

"Al is gonna kill you! Are you gonna fuck this guy again?" Eva asked as they got into the car.

"We exchanged phone numbers and he said he'd call me when he got back to town. If he does, we'll meet here and we'll have sex again. Lots of sex," Rinna said.

"You're a cheater!" Eva teased.

"So are you. You've been fooling around with my husband for a long time. Besides, this isn't the first time I've slipped," Rinna said.

"You mean you've fucked other men?" Eva asked as they left the casino lot.

"I've fucked lots of other men—including Vince," Rinna said with a grin. "I like feeling strange dicks in my pussy once in a while. Dicks are like potato chips for me. I can't have only one."

"Wow! I never knew that. How many other men have you fucked?" Eva asked.

"I don't know. I've never counted them. A lot. When I drink, I get real horny and when I do, I end up fucking somebody," she said. "Sometimes, I don't get home until the next afternoon—especially if I really like the guy."

"Does Al know about that?" Eva asked.

"Oh yes. He can tell by the way I look when I get home and because I have a pussy full of cum. And he knows that I'm not going to stop. So you can fuck him whenever you like," Rinna said. "I know you want to and so does he."

Eva laughed and nodded.

"Now I'm really gonna fuck Al into a mattress! I didn't know you were such a slut!," Eva said.

"You should try being a slut, too. It's a lot of fun. Today, I got paid $200 to be a slut. So we can make good money doing this," Rinna suggested.

"You're a prostitute?" Eva asked.

"I guess so. This isn't the first time I got paid to fuck and I know it won't be the last. Men love Asian pussy and they're willing to pay for it. As pretty as you are, I know you'll make lots of money," Rinna said.

"Maybe I'll try it," Eva said. "Are we still on for this weekend?"

"Definitely!" Rinna said.

"I can hardly wait!" Eva said as they laughed.

Al was still up watching TV when Rinna got home. He watched her walk in and smiled. She looked at him and blushed.

"I guess you had a great time tonight," he said.

"Um. Yes. I did," she replied as she sat down next to him.

He leaned over and smiled when he caught the unmistakable aroma of heavy sex on her.

"I know that scent," he said. "I've smelled it hundreds of times. "How was he?"

"Who?" she asked nervously.

"They guy you had sex with tonight. From the way you smell and walk, he must have fucked the Hell out of you," he observed.

She almost died. There was no sense in denying it now. She'd been caught.

"We've been married a long time, Rinna. You can't lie or hide things from me. You know that I've fooled around a little with Eva. Hell, you even caught us at it. So if you want to have sex with other men, I won't stop you. After all, it's your pussy and you can share it with whoever you want. Just remember who you're married to and tell me when you decide to stray," he said calmly.

"You're not mad?" she asked.

"A little bit. But now I know that I have the green light to go as far as I like with Eva. I also know that Vince has been coming onto you a lot lately. Have you two fucked yet?" he replied.

She nodded.

"I thought so," he said. "Just don't go wild and turn into some sort of slut on me.

"I won't," she promised. "Don't you do it, either."

"Deal!" he agreed.

The next day, Art hired a carpenter to do some complicated work around the house. The man arrived at nine after Art left for work. Rinna let him in. She was dressed in her green jogging shorts and a T-shirt and nothing else. The carpenter smiled when he saw her. She smiled back and led him into the kitchen where the work was to be done.

They chatted while he set up his tools and got the lumber out of his van. He quickly realized she wasn't wearing a bra and that her nipples seemed to be getting hard. So was he. Rinna was obviously flirting with him now.

The carpenter's name was Frank. He was over six feet tall and very handsome. Frank flirted back playfully but he really wanted to fuck her. Rinna realized that, so she amped up her flirting. She stood near him with her feet slightly apart and chatted while he kept working. She could tell by the obvious bulge in his jeans that he was horny, too.

She decided she wanted to fuck him—a lot.

"When you're finished here, there's something upstairs in the bedroom I need you to take care of," she said softly.

"Oh? And what would that be, exactly?" Frank asked.

"This," she said as she pulled aside the crotch of her shorts to expose her freshly shaven cunt. "It takes a very special tool to take care of me and I think you have exactly what I need."

"Are you serious?" he asked as he nearly came in hi jeans.

"Yes. I am very serious. Have you ever fucked a Filipina before?" she teased as she revealed more of her cunt.

"No," he said as he eyed her prize.

"Then I am going to show why we're called little brown fucking machines," she said.

Frank left his tools on the kitchen floor and followed her upstairs. Within seconds they were both naked and Rinna was sucking his prick while he ate her pussy. His prick was hard and thick. Just the way she liked them, and she loved the way he tasted.

He loved the way she tasted, too. He sucked her clit and licked her cunt until she'd come twice. She fell onto her back with her legs apart and smiled when he slid his prick home. She gripped his arms and opened her legs wider as they fucked. He fucked her nice and slow with deep, easy strokes that massaged her entire cunt. All the while, he kept telling her how sexy and tight she was. Frank lasted longer than she had hoped. In fact, he made her come again and again. She arched her back and fucked him as hard as she could until she felt his cum streaming into her cunt.

He emptied a good sized load into her, too.

They stopped and he dressed. She watched as he finished the job. By the time he was done, he was fully erect again.

Frank left the house an hour later with wobbly knees and a limp dick. Rinna had worn him out and he had done the same to her. When she told him that she normally charges for her favors, Frank laughed and adjusted the final bill by $250.

They also exchanged phone numbers because he said that he certainly wanted to do this again soon as she was the finest woman he had ever had sex with.

"Tell your husband that the job didn't take as long as I expected so I lowered the bill. That should explain the difference," he smiled. "You have the best cunt in the world, Rinna. The very best!"

She hurried up to shower to hide her activities from Art. As the water cascaded over her body, she smiled at warm, tingly sensation inside her cunt...

Al smiled when she showed him the bill. He knew exactly how she got it lowered.

"Was he good?" he asked.

She blushed then giggled then nodded.

"Do we need him to do any more work around here?" she asked.

"Wow. He really must have been good! I'll let you know," he joked. "Maybe you can get us a discount again. Hell, if you make him real happy, he might do the job for free!"

"I can try!" she said with a giggle. "American men love Filipina pussy!"

"Yes we do," Al smiled as they hugged.

That night, she thought about how many different ways she could use her pussy to save lots of money. There were auto repairs, appliances to be bought or fixed, more carpentry work, etc. She was sure that most of the men she dealt with would gladly knock a couple of hundred dollars off their prices for the chance to fuck her. But most of those guys were older and unattractive. She had her standards. She had to be very attracted to a man before she'd fuck him.

As she always put it, she didn't fuck trolls.

"My pussy is like an ATM," she told Eva. "A lot of men want it and they're willing to pay me. If I like the guy, I'll have sex with him. If I don't, all of the money in the world won't get me to fuck him. I don't like men who give me the creeps or come on too strong or stink of alcohol and cigarettes. They have to be clean and good looking and nice."

Eva just sat and stared at her.

"I never knew you were a prostitute," she said. "And now you have me thinking about trying it. A lot of men come on to me. Maybe they'll pay me for sex."

"I'm sure they would. You're really sexy and exotic. Men go crazy for women like us. Use your pussy to make money," Rinna urged.

Rinna returned to the casino a couple of nights later. As she played her favorite slots, a young, handsome man walked over with two drinks. He sat down beside her and handed her one of them.

"Are you Rinna?" he asked.

She stared at him.

"How did you know my name?" she asked.

"Jake told me all about you and even emailed your photo. I have to say that the photo didn't do you justice. You're far more beautiful in person," he said.

She smiled and sipped the drink.

It was rum and coke, heavy on the rum.

"Thanks," she said.

"My name's Tom," he said as they shook hands.

"What did Jake tell you about me?" she asked.

"He said you were fun and sexy and great in bed. So I decided to look you up and find out how great you are for myself," he replied.

"Oh," she said hesitantly.

"I want to have sex with you, Rinna. Lots of sex. I have a room upstairs in the hotel. We can go there. I'll pay you the same amount that Jake did," he offered.

She thought about it and grinned.

"Have you ever had sex with a Filipina before?" she asked.

"Never," he said.

"In that case, you're in for a real treat," she said.

When they got to his suite, they started out by kissing and undressing each other. By then, Tom was rock hard and his prick looked massive. She ran her fingers up and down the shaft a few times, and then gave it several pulls. To her delight, it became even harder. While she did this, Tom sucked her nipples and moved his finger in and out her wet cunt.

She smiled and got onto the bed with her knees bent and legs spread open. He got between and slid his prick into her tight, hot cunt. She groaned and dug her nails into his hips as they fucked. He fucked with long, deep and hard thrusts that sent shivers throughout her entire body. It felt awesome, too.

"Ooohh yes! I love it!" she moaned as she fucked him back.

Tom was thrilled with her tightness and enthusiasm. She didn't just go through the motions like a typical hooker. She was really fucking him and enjoying it as much as he did. In fact, she was giving him the best fucking he'd ever experienced.

"Fuck me, Tom! Fill my pussy! Fuck me good!" she moaned as his prick plunged into her time and again.

When they came, it was at the exact same instant and she clung to him and thrust back as hard as she could until he was finished. He lay on top with his prick still buried in her cunt. She used her inner muscles to play with it until he grew hard again...

Three hours later, she was back in the casino with her pussy filled with cum and another $200 in her purse. It was fun and easy money. She was surprised that men were willing to pay someone her age for sex. But Filipinas earned reputations for being great sex partners. American sailors dubbed them Little Brown Fucking Machines. Rinna was no exception. Al often called her that, too.

All of a sudden, her pussy was a hot commodity.

She played the slots for a few minutes. A second man wandered over and sat next to her. He also handed her a drink. She smiled at him

"Hi, Rinna. I'm a friend of Jake's," he said. "My name's Trey."

"Glad to meet you, Trey. I charge $200," she said.

"Great. Let's go to my hotel room and fuck ourselves silly," he said.

"That sounds good to me," she agreed as they headed for the lobby.

Rinna left the casino around midnight. Her pussy ached from the pounding Trey had given her and a stream of cum was running down her inner thigh. She had fucked two total strangers in one night and was going home a winner. She felt sexually sated and she had an extra $400 in her wallet just for opening her legs for them.

"Yes," she said as she climbed into her car. "I am a prostitute now."

When she got home, Al smiled as she staggered to the sofa and plopped down next to him. She grinned back at him. He knew that grin well, too. He had seen it hundreds of times before.

"Again?" he asked.

She nodded.

"How many?" he asked.

"Two. I made $400," she said happily.

"So you're a whore now?" he asked.

"Yes. At least for a while. Is that okay?" she asked.

"No, but it's your pussy to do with as you like. Since I'm fucking Eva, I can't bitch about what you're doing. Just be real careful. There are a lot of creeps out there and I don't want anything bad to happen to you. After all, I do love you," he said as they hugged.

She smiled.

"I know," she said. "I promise not to fuck too many men."

He laughed.

"How many is too many for you?" he asked.

"I'm not sure yet," she replied.

The next morning, she met Eva for breakfast at a local IHop. Eva prodded her to tell her about what she did the night before. Rinna told her everything. Eva looked at her and shook her head.

"You're really a prostitute now?" she asked.

"Uh-huh. I've had sex with three different men and I made $600. It's a lot of fun and they pay me to do what I really love to do. All of the men were very good looking, well dressed and they had money to burn. So when they offered it to me, I took it. Maybe you should give it a try," Rinna said.

"You really think that anyone would pay me for sex?" Eva asked.

"Of course they would. You're very sexy and exotic looking. Men go for women like us," Rinna assured her. "And you don't have to do it all the time. You can fuck as many men as you want whenever you feel like it."

"How many do you plan to fuck? Eva asked.

"Maybe three or four each week," Rinna said. "And it's all cash, too. So no taxes."

"You do know it's illegal, right?" Eva pointed out. "You could get arrested if anyone complains."

"None of my men will complain. I think as long as I'm not obvious about it, or I arrange to meet men ahead of time, I'll be fine. I won't get caught."

"So you charge $200 each time?" Eva asked.

"That seems to be the going rate. I'm sure if I played hard to get, I'd be able to drive the price up. You could charge whatever you want as long as they're willing to pay you. How much you make is up to you."

"Maybe I'll try it later. Right now, I'd want to swap husbands with you," Eva said.

"That should be easy enough. Al's having a barbecue this Saturday. Let's put on our sexiest clothes and make them as horny as possible. Then we can swap and fuck the daylights out of them as much as we like," Rinna suggested.

"I know. It's not like they haven't fucked us before," Eva said.

That Saturday, the girls put their plan into motion.

They were at Al's house barbecuing as they usually did on warm, sunny Saturdays. Since it was very warm, Rinna wore a short, frilly red skirt that highlighted her shapely legs and behind.

Eva also wore a short skirt that barely covered half her thighs. Even Rinna admitted that Eva looked especially hot that day.

As the afternoon passed and the drinks flowed freely, Rinna noticed that both Vince and Eva seemed to be paying a lot of attention to her legs. Vince often ogled her legs anyway as he found Rinna very sexy and attractive. A few times, she noticed that he'd gotten erections while watching her.

That made her smile. The fact that he got hard when he looked at her both pleased and excited her. In fact, she began to get damp between her legs.

Eva made sure that wherever she went, Al got a real good look at her. Rinna noticed that Al had kept a close eye on Eva the entire afternoon.

She smiled.

Their little plan was working. Both men were obviously erect. But would they try to do anything?

They cooked, ate and drank and laughed. Rinna glanced at Vince who made his prick "dance" inside his jeans. She smiled at him and nodded. It was time to get things going.

She went back into the house to get more ice for the drinks. Vince said he was heading for the bathroom and followed her inside. Instead of going to the bathroom, he stopped next to Rinna.

"You're the sexiest woman I know, Rinna and your legs are fantastic," he said as he leaned close.

She felt his warm breath on her face as she leaned against the fridge. She could see the huge bulge in his jeans as it bobbed up and down. He leaned closer.

"I love your ass, too. It's so perfect. I want you, Rinna. I want to have sex with you more than anything on Earth," he said as he slid his hand along her thigh and up under her skirt.

She trembled as he ran his fingers over her panties. Rinna was drunk now and more than a little horny. She opened her stance and let him touch her and quivered as he ran his fingertips along her slit.

"I want you," he whispered.

She closed her eyes and sighed as he massaged her clit. As her libido ignited, she reached down and ran her fingers over the bulge in his jeans. Vince's prick felt massive.

Long and thick.

She squeezed it a few times and was surprised that it grew even harder and longer. She wondered what it would feel like to get fucked by him. Vince moved her panties aside and slid a finger up into her cunt. Rinna moaned as he moved it in and out several times. At the same time, she kept fondling his prick.

"Let's do it, Rinna," he whispered as he fingered her faster.

She smiled at him and nodded. Then she slowly slid his zipper downward.

Eva also made her move. She walked over to Al and stuck her tongue in his mouth. Al reached up and slid his hand under her skirt and eased his middle finger into her sopping cunt. She reached down and groped his prick. When it was good and hard, she freed it from his jeans and proceeded to jerk him off.

Al was already worked up and he spurted seconds later. She kept pumping him and sending white streams of cum onto the grass while he fingered her to a good, hard orgasm.

At that moment, Rinna was also jerking Vince off as fast as she could. She was amazed at how thick and hard it was and wondered how it would feel moving inside her cunt. Vince was also busy fingering her cunt. She squirmed and quivered each time he touched her clit.

"Let's do it, Rinna," Vince urged.

She nodded.

He moved her panties aside. She opened her stance and shook with excitement as she felt his knob move along her slit. It teased her labia for a second or two then slowly pushed past them and into her cunt.

"Yes!" she sighed as he moved it all the way in.

She gripped his shoulders as quivered as he moved it in and out slowly. God, it felt so good, too. Vince grabbed her hips and fucked her faster and faster. She moaned and moved with him, savoring the way his dick felt inside of her.

They were fucking! They were actually fucking!

Out in the yard, Eva was busily sucking Al's prick. Al shook all over as this was the most intense sex they'd ever tried. She was good, too.

So good, that he stayed rock hard.

Eva stopped and stood up. She removed her panties and straddled Al. He sighed as she lowered herself onto his prick. It was the very first time they'd done this. Eva's cunt was oh-so tight and hot.

"I've got you now!" she said as she moved up and down nice and slow. "Fuck me, Al. Fuck me good!"

She bounced faster and faster. He held onto her hips and moved with her, driving his prick as far up into her cunt with each thrust as he could. Eva moaned and gasped each time as he hammered it home.

"Fuck me! Fuck me!" she moaned as they moved together faster and faster.

Rinna lay on the kitchen table with her legs wrapped around Vince's hips as they fucked like there was no tomorrow. She'd already come several times, too. Vince knew this but kept going. She dug her fingers into his shoulders and moaned as her surroundings spiraled out of control.

She was so far over the edge that she barely heard it when Vince groaned. She felt his warm cum jet into her with each subsequent pump of his prick and fucked him back as hard as she could. They kept going until Vince sighed and slipped out of her. He stood and watched as a river of white goo ran out of her still quivering cunt.

She grinned up at him as she massaged it into her cunt and along her ass crack. She reached over and squeezed his flaccid prick. A prick that was now slick and wet with their combined juices.

She rolled his foreskin back and forth a few times until he got harder. When she thought he was hard enough, she laid back and placed his prick at the opening to her cunt. Vince smiled and slid it all the way in for another good, easy fuck.

Al rammed his prick in and out of Eva's hot, wet cunt as hard and as fast as he could. She clung to his shoulders and stuck her tongue into his mouth. As they kissed, she began to quake all over. He sensed she was on the verge of orgasm and fucked her even faster. Eva screamed and shook all over as she came.

It was a good, deep orgasm that made her see white. Al didn't hear her as he was too busy filling her cunt with his cum until it ran out and coated his balls. They held each other tight and kissed as they returned to Earth.

Eva stood and they watched as more of Al's cum dripped to the ground.

"You like my pussy?" she asked with a wicked grin.

"I love your pussy," he said as he ran his fingers along her slit.

At the same time, Vince and Rinna were writhing in the throes of their combined orgasms. Rinna dug her fingers into his shoulders and moaned loudly as they kept fucking until they were both spent.

"Wow!" she sighed as she came slowly back to Earth.

"Incredible!" Vince whispered. "Just incredible."

The men didn't know it but Eva and Rinna had planned the entire thing. They had made up their minds to swap husbands for one good, hard fuck just to get everything out into the open.

As Rinna and Vince emerged from the house with the ice, Eva gave her a wink to indicate she had fucked Al. Rinna winked back and nodded. That's when she spotted Eva's panties on the patio. She picked them up and handed them to her and they both giggled for a long time.

Al laughed, too.

"You planned this, didn't you?" he asked.

"That's right. How'd you like it?" Eva asked.

"This was your best idea ever," Vince said. "You plan on doing this again?"

"We sure do," Rinna assured them. "We can swap whenever you want."

Al smiled.

"Are you really sure about that?" he asked.

"We are," they both said.

"So I can fuck Eva whenever I want?" Al asked.

"As long as I know about it, it's okay with me," Rinna replied

"And I can fuck you whenever I want to?" Vince asked.

"As long as it's okay with Al. Is it?" Rinna smiled.

"I guess so," Al agreed.

"Good!" Eva said.

They had a few more drinks and finished eating. By then, everyone was horny again. Eva slid her skirt up and smiled at Al. He reached over and caressed her cunt.

"Let's go up to the spare bedroom," she said.

Rinna and Vince watched as they raced into the house. Rinna smiled at Vince.

"There's more than one bedroom inside," she said.

She led him to the smaller bedroom and shut the door behind them. He smiled as she slowly removed her clothes. She watched as his prick grew longer and thicker as he, too, stripped. She walked over and wrapped her hand around it. He quivered as she slowly beat him off until he was at full salute. At the same time, he sucked her right nipple and fingered her cunt, which was still sticky with his earlier deposit.

She walked to the bed and laid down with her legs wide apart. He moved onto the bed and got between them. She bent her knees and sighed as he slid his prick deep into her cunt. She moaned louder as he fucked her. She gripped his shoulders and fucked him back; savoring each and every thrust of his prick as it deliciously massaged her cunt.

Vince was big.

And oh-so hard and thick.

She fucked him faster and faster as she felt herself coming. He matched her with good, hard and deep strokes that made her teeth chatter. This was one of the very best fucks of her life.

"Yes! Oh God! Yes! Use me!" she cried as she shook all over.

Her orgasm caused her cunt to literally convulse and suck at his prick. The sensations made him come, too. He kept fucking and fucking until he'd fired every last bit of cum he had left into her and she fucked him back harder and begged him for more.

Just down the hall, Al was on his back, driving his prick up into Eva's cunt while she rode him. Her cunt was exquisitely tight and warm and she knew how to use her inner muscles to make each thrust feel incredibly exciting. She moaned loudly as she bounced up and down on his prick. And she really loved the way it felt inside her body.

Al watched as Eva's head fell back and she sighed and moaned. He reached up and played with her nipples. She quivered and rode him faster.

"I love it! Yes! I love it!" she moaned as she came

He grabbed her ass and rammed his prick as far up into her as he could. Then he came and filled her with every bit of cum he had left. She fell on top of him and stuck her tongue into his mouth as she fucked him slower and slower until her orgasm subsided.

"I am yours now," she said. "Forever and ever. Yours."

Rinna looked down at the stream of white oozing from her slit and smiled. This wasn't the first time in her life that her cunt was filled with cum from someone other than Al. She felt deliciously wicked and sexy.

Vince smiled at her.

"This was the greatest sex of my life. You're great, Rinna. I mean that," he said.

"So are you. Anytime you want my pussy, you know where to find me," she said as she stroked his prick.

They decided to make their swap an all-night thing of nearly non-stop sex. Both women seemed to be insatiable and they found all sorts of ways to keep Al and Vince hard. Rinna and Vince fucked three more times before they collapsed into a deep slumber. Al and Eva finally gave out around three a.m. and he fell asleep with this prick still buried in her cunt.

When they woke the next day, it was nearly noon. Rinna woke to the delicious sensations of Vince's prick moving in and out of her cunt. She soon caught his rhythm and moved with him until they both came.

Eva woke Al with a blowjob. When he was good and hard, she mounted him and fucked him nice and slow. When they both came several minutes later, she stuck her tongue in his mouth and milked him of every drop of cum he had left.

The couples staggered down to the living room about an hour later. All of them moved slowly. They looked at each other and laughed.

"Now this was one Hell of a night!" Vince said. "I never dreamed we'd do anything like this. It was terrific! Rinna sure knows how to fuck."

She blushed and slapped him playfully on the arm.

"You call Filipinas little brown fucking machines. I just wanted to show you that we are," she joked. "That's the most sex I've ever had in one day. I can hardly walk!"

"Me neither," Eva said happily. "Wow. We really did it, Rinna. We swapped husbands just like we planned. I guess no one has any complaints about it. Right?"

"Hell no!" Al smiled.

"Ditto!" said Vince. "Are we gonna do this again?"

"If you like," Rinna said.

"I like. If it's okay with you, Al," Vince said.

"Since we've started this, I don't see why we can't do it again. I love having sex with Eva and I'd love to do it again real soon," Al said as he felt Eva's behind.

Vince checked his watch.

"It's almost two. I gotta get home and shower. We have to be at the mall for a presentation at four. I'll call you when we get home. Maybe we can all go out for dinner," he said.

"Talk to you later," Al said as he saw them out.

He watched them drive away and looked at his wife.

"This was some crazy day," he said.

"Did you enjoy fucking Eva?" she asked as they sat down on the patio.

"Yes I did," he replied.

"That's why we set this up. Vince has been trying to get into my panties for a long time, too. So I decided to let him again," she said.

"How was it?" he asked.

"I'd say it was as good as the sex you had with Eva," she teased.

"Now what? Did you get this out of your system? Or do you want to keep doing it?" he asked.

"I'm not sure," she said. "Maybe. What about you?"

"Let me think about that," he said. "Right now, we need to shower and get some rest."

The next morning, Al woke to the wonderful sensation of Rinna riding his prick, like she did almost every morning. He gripped her behind and thrust back. This fuck was hard and intense, too.

And it was short.

As always, they erupted together. Rinna kept fucking him until she was wiped out. She collapsed on top of him and stuck her tongue into his mouth while he gently fingered her slit from behind.

They stopped and went out to breakfast. Al watched her intently as she ate. She looked positively elated and he knew it was from a day and night of nearly non-stop sex.

"I know what you're thinking," she said. "Yes. I loved every minute of it."

"I can see that. So tell me, how many other men have you had sex with besides Vince?" he asked.

"Three so far," she admitted. "They all paid me, too."

"Oh. So you're a hooker now?" he asked.

"Uh-huh. Do you mind?" she asked.

"Would it make a difference if I said it did?" he asked.

She giggled.

"No," she replied.

"I figured that. So how long do you plan to keep doing this?" he asked.

"For as long as men want to pay me," she answered. "I love to fuck and I love the money. I'm going to become a total slut. I'm going to fuck every good-looking man who is willing to pay for my pussy."

"Wow! Are you sure about that?" he asked.

"I'm very sure," she said.

"Does Eva do it?" he asked.

"Not yet, but she's thinking about it," Rinna said. "Do you think men would pay her for sex?"

"Hell yeah! She's gorgeous and exotic. That's a combination men can't resist. She's like you in that respect," Al said. "And you both know how to make men happy."

"I knew you'd say that. So do you plan to fuck other women besides Eva?" she asked.

"I'm not sure," he said. "It's hard to top the two of you and I don't know if I can handle any more women right now."

"I think you should," she said. "Really. You need to find yourself another pretty Asian playmate. Just don't become too emotionally involved with her. That would complicate things for us."

"The last thing I need to make this even more complicated than it already is," he said. "I think I'll just stick to you and Eva right now."

She grinned at him.

"We're that good?" she teased.

"Oh yeah. Maybe too damned good," he said.

She laughed.

"Even so, I think you should look around more," she said. "You might find someone special right under your nose. Just don't make her too special."

"Do you have anyone in mind?" he joked.

"As a matter of fact, I do. She's right under your nose, too. You see her almost every day and she's kind of cute," she said.

"You mean I already know her?" he asked.

"Uh-huh. You've introduced us and we've even had her over here a few times," she replied.

"Oh! Her!" he said with a laugh. "Yeah, she is cute."

"You should try to get into her panties. I bet she can really fuck, too. She has the body for it," she said. "She has nice legs and very cute ass and I bet her pussy is nice and tight."

The woman was a short, thin Vietnamese woman named Li. She was around 35 years old with short black hair and virtually no breasts. But she had a nice, sexy body that aroused him. They worked together and had become friends over the years. She was nice, down-to-Earth, and pretty shy around every man but him. She was also old-fashioned and traditional.

Most American ignored her because of her lack of breasts and shyness. Al was the one who welcomed her into the department and trained her and they hit it off immediately. He found her warm and cute and funny. She liked his honesty.

Rinna also knew that Li liked Al a lot and that he was also attracted to her. If she could get the two of them involved with each other that would leave her with more time to fuck other men and make lots of money doing it. They had also become friends.

"She's a real possibility. But she's never even had a boyfriend, so I'd have to take things slowly with her. She's also very shy and very tradition minded. You know, old fashioned when it comes to things like dating and sex," he said. "She probably wouldn't think of sleeping with anyone she's not married to."

"She sounds like a real challenge for you," Rinna teased.

"She would be and I don't want to offend her or scare her. She and I are good friends and I don't want to ruin that, either," he said.

"I'll leave that up to you," she said. "I have to shower and get dressed. I'm almost late for work."

Chapter Three

Rinna worked part-time as a desk clerk for one of the hotels downtown. Whenever she was there, men liked to come up and chat with her. She was cute and gregarious and they liked her Gracie Allen way of looking at things.

A few men had attempted to date her over the years, but backed off when she said she was married. One guy, Charlie, didn't seem bothered by that. He kept talking to her and coming on to her each week.

She kind of liked Charlie, too.

So she never rebuffed him and kind of hinted that she'd be interested in going a lot further with him. He wasn't aware of her extramarital activities yet or the fact that she'd be willing to fuck him for the right price. So she played her little game with to see how far he was willing to go to get into her panties.

He wasn't pushy about it and he didn't seem full of himself like a lot of men she met. So they kept talking and making each other laugh. A couple of weeks later, Charlie offered to take her to dinner. It was late and she'd missed lunch, so she agreed to go with him.

They headed over to a small bistro near the hotel. They ordered dinner and Charlie ordered a bottle of Rose' wine. They ate, talked and drank. Rinna was feeling tipsy and her guards were down. And she was getting horny.

"This is kind of like a date," she said.

"Almost. We're just a couple of friends having dinner. If this was a date, we'd be doing other things," he said.

"Oh? What other things?" she asked.

"This," Charlie said as he whispered in her ear.

Rinna blushed and giggled.

"That's more than just a date," she said. "Way more!"

"Are you open to any of that?" he asked as he placed his hand on her knee.

She smiled at him.

"Maybe," she said.

He inched his chair closer and slid his hand up under her skirt. He was amazed when she parted her legs and allowed him to feel her panties. He ran his hand all over her crotch. She looked at him and nodded as he slowly slid his fingers past her panties and into her cunt.

"If you want that, it'll cost you," she said.

"How much?" he asked.

"How much can you afford?" she asked.

"I'll pay for dinner and give you this." he said as he handed her all the cash he had in his wallet.

She took it without counting and smiled.

"We can get a room at the hotel. I get them for free," she said.

"Let's go!" Charlie said happily.

Charlie took his time with her that night. He slowly undressed her then kissed and licked his way down her body to her cunt. She sighed as he ate her. He licked her gently and slowly to make sure she also enjoyed it. After he made her come twice, he slid his surprisingly long prick into her cunt for what proved to be a slow, masterful fuck. Once she caught his rhythm, she fucked him back.

And he lasted a very long time.

So long that she came again and again before he fired his load deep inside her cunt. As he came, he kept fucking her and fucking her and fucking her. Rinna moaned and held him tight as she moved with him.

Then he came again.

After he emptied his second load into her cunt, he pulled out. She smiled up at him as she lay panting for breath. It had been one of the best fucks of her entire life, too. It was so good, she almost paid him!

"I can't believe we did this. I can't believe you finally let me into your panties. You're terrific, Rinna. I'd love to do this with you every week," he said as he ran his hand all over her breasts and belly.

"I'm game if you are," she said.

"Fantastic!" he said. "How about next Wednesday?"

"Sure thing. I'll be at the hotel that night and I'll make sure we have a room," she said.

"I'll take you to dinner first," he said. "What time do you have to be home?"

"Whenever we're finished," she smiled as she jerked him off. "Whenever I can't make you hard again."

They fucked twice more that night. She got home around eleven. When she sat down at the kitchen table to count what Charlie had paid her, she was stunned to see it was almost $400. Al watched her count it.

"I guess that you'll be fucking him again soon, huh?" he asked.

"Next Wednesday," she said. "I might be home a lot later."

"I won't wait up," Al said.

"Good. But I'm all yours until then," she smiled as she grabbed his dick...

So here she was on a Wednesday night. She had clocked out at five and had dinner with Charlie. Now she was in the room on her hands and knees getting slow-fucked from behind by his exquisitely long prick.

There was no pretense this time. Charlie knew what she was and he was more than happy to pay and she was more than happy to let him use her cunt for his playground.

They fucked four times. Each time, he also made her come and shot what seemed to be a huge load of cum into her cunt. Then she gave him something to think about by sucking his prick until he came in her mouth. She smiled as she swallowed it.

When she got home early the next morning, she had another $400 in her purse and a "date" for the following week.

She called Eva to tell about it.

"He really paid you that much??" she asked.

"Oh yes. I didn't ask him for that, but he said I'm worth it. He bought me dinner, too," Rinna said.

"Maybe I should try it," Eva said.

"Yes you should. Al said that as sexy as you are, you could make a lot of money, too," Rinna said. "I just tell men to pay me what they think I'm worth. So far, I'm surprised at how much they pay."

"Al really said I was sexy?" Eva asked.

"Yes. I think you're very sexy, too. Once a man sees your pussy, he'll pay a lot to get into it," Rinna assured her.

Two mornings later, Rinna was lying on her back in bed with her legs wide open sighing and moaning with pleasure with each good, deep thrust of Vince's prick. He had arrived unexpectedly a few minutes earlier and Rinna led him straight up to the bedroom.

Vince had spent the first few minutes eating her pussy while she stroked his prick. As soon as she came, he slid around and rammed his prick into her trembling cunt. The sudden thrust made her come even harder and she screamed with delight as it rippled through her. She grabbed his arms and opened her legs wide. After a few good thrusts, she moved with him.

"Oh yes! Fuck me, Vince! Fuck me good. I'm yours now. I'm yours whenever you want me!" she moaned.

To Vince, Rinna had the best and tightest cunt on Earth. It wrapped around his prick so perfectly and she really knew how to fuck. He moved faster and faster. Rinna matched him stroke for stroke. Soon, she began to tremble.

"I'm coming, Vince! Make me yours! Fuck me!" she cried as she dug her fingers into his arms and threw her body up at him.

It was too much.

Vince shot line after line of cum into her cunt. Rinna kept fucking and fucking as she came. He felt her cunt suck at his prick. He felt her quiver as they kept going and going. Vince fired one last load into her and collapsed on top of her chest. She screamed as her orgasm triggered and undulated beneath him.

They locked into a deep, long kiss. Vince sat up and smiled at her.

"You're the best," he said as he stroked her thigh. "The best."

"You're damned good, too," she smiled as she pumped his prick.

When she couldn't make him hard again, she laughed. He did, too.

"I'm sorry, Rinna. But you wore me out," he apologized. "Maybe tomorrow?"

"Maybe," she said. "I really like having sex with you."

"Does this bother you at all?" he asked.

"Not really. As long as Al is having sex with Eva, I don't feel guilty about having sex with other men—especially not with you," she replied. "Does it bother you when Eva fucks Al?"

"Not in the least," Vince said. "We have open marriages now. We can all fuck whoever we want. Eva said that you and she planned all of this a while back but it took a little while to get the nerve to actually go through with it."

"Yes it did. We've been good little wives for a long time and now we both want to let our inner sluts out and have some fun," Rinna said.

She had often fantasized about fucking some of the men she'd met at the casino. Now that she'd already done it, she knew she'd do it again. She had also fantasized about having sex with Eva, who she always considered to be very sexy. She loved her long, shapely legs and kept thinking about what was between them. They had already started down what promised to be a very different and exciting road. Neither was sure exactly how to proceed. They wanted each other, too.

A lot.

The very next day, things heated up between them.

Eva had come over around eleven. Rinna prepared a light meal and they chatted and joked while they ate. Eva had worn a short skirt and Rinna was wearing her usual jogging shorts and T-shirt.

They ate and chatted and felt each other's thighs as they grew hornier and hornier. Before she knew it, they were kissing. As their passions soared, Eva slid her hand into Rinna's shorts and gently teased her already moist slit. Rinna sucked Eva's tongue harder and slid her hand under her skirt. Eva parted her legs.

"You are so very beautiful," Eva said. "So very sexy."

"So are you," Rinna replied.

Their kiss had ignited a fire, too. One that they both felt as the heat wave surged through their bodies. Eva raised Rinna's t-shirt and sucked her left nipple. Then she eased her hand back into her panties. Rinna writhed and moaned as Eva did her. When she came, she screamed and shook all over.

She fell back onto the sofa with her legs apart. Eva pulled off her shorts and stopped to admire her rich, dark triangle. She ran her fingers over Rinna's cunt a few times then slid her middle finger inside of her. Rinna gasped as Eva "fucked" her.

Then she came again, only harder. Eva moved downward and ran her tongue over Rinna's slit. Rinna moaned loud and shook again. She could hardly believe her friend was eating her and she loved the way her warm, soft tongue caressed her labia. Eva had never eaten a woman before and she went about it gingerly at first, savoring Rinna's aromas and the sweet salty taste of her cunt. Rinna seized Eva's hair and pulled her face into her cunt.

"Eat me, darling! Make love to me!" she said.

Rinna did.

She licked and sucked Rinna's cunt and even fingered her through one orgasm after another. Rinna shook and moaned and cried out as she begged her to keep going. When she'd had enough, she lay still and panted for air.

Eva stood and pulled up her skirt. Rinna reached over and peeled off her soaked panties. Eva sat down with her legs apart and feet up on the sofa. Rinna felt her for a little while, then got on her knees and slid her tongue along Eva's slit.

"Yes! I love it! I love you!" Eva moaned as Rinna ate her as if it was the most natural thing for her to do.

Eva erupted.

Rinna kept going and going. Eva kept coming and moaning and stroking her hair as she bounced up and down on the sofa. Then Rinna became adventurous. She slid her finger up into Eva's ass and "fucked" her. The sensations drove Eva wild and she came harder than she had ever come before in her entire life.

"I love you, Rinna! I really love you!" she screamed.

"That was the best sex I ever had. It was really special because I made love with you. I've always felt attracted to you, Eva. I've always wanted to eat your pussy. This was better than I hoped it would be, too," Rinna said as she caressed Eva's breasts.

"It was incredible. To be honest with you, I think I fell in love with you the day we first met. I've never had feelings for any other woman. I love you, Rinna. I truly love you," Eva said as they kissed again.

Eva giggled.

"You have something crazy in mind again, don't you?" Rinna asked.

"I sure do. Wouldn't it be wild if we could get our husbands to have sex with each other? I'd really love to watch Vince suck Al's dick. Wouldn't you?" Eva said.

Rinna laughed at the absurdity of the idea.

"I don't think that will ever happen," she said.

"Me neither. But wouldn't it be fun if they did?" Eva asked. "After all, they really like each other."

"Yes. But not like that! That's the most insane idea you ever had, Eva. It'll never happen. But I admit, it might be interesting to watch," Rinna said.

"Then lets' see if we can make it happen," Eva said.

"Okay. I'm game," Rinna smiled.

That night, they went to the casino. This time, they stayed close together the entire night. They played the slots, but their minds were not on what they were doing. They kept glancing at each other and giggling the entire time.

Around ten, they decided to leave. As they got into Eva's car, they leaned close and made eye contact. They spent several seconds looking at each other, and then kissed. This time, it was as if lightning struck them.

They stopped and smiled at each other.

"Wow. Did you feel it, too?" Eva asked.

"Oh yes. That was amazing," Rinna said.

They kissed again with the same sensations. That's when they both knew they were sexually attracted to each other and both were thinking about taking this further. That's why Rinna didn't object at all as Eva slid her hand along her thigh to her panties and gently raked her fingers over her cunt. She sucked Eva's tongue harder and placed her hand on Eva's thigh again and slid her hand under her shorts. Eva smiled and parted her knees as Rinna played with her cunt and hungrily sucked her tongue. Her cunt was on fire now.

So was Rinna's.

"So you'd like to try some pussy, eh?" she joked.

"Sure. Why not? It might be a lot of fun," Eva said as she maintained eye contact with Rinna.

"Well, I have a pussy," Rinna said.

"I know," Eva whispered as she put her hand on Rinna's thigh.

Rinna opened her legs and stroked Eva's inner thigh. They leaned toward each other. They were just about to kiss when the casino security van rolled by. For some reason, they stopped.

Eva sighed.

"Damn guard!" she heard Rinna say.

"The guard is gone," Eva whispered as she put her hand on Rinna's thigh again.

Rinna smiled and leaned closer. Their lips touched. The sudden, almost electric sensation caused them to giggle. They decided to try it again. This time, they maintained contact for a few seconds. Soon, their tongues merged. Their kiss lingered and grew more and more passionate. As they kissed, they massaged each other's crotch. Rinna was on fire now. She was breathing heavy and Eva's touches were driving her half crazy.

Eva unzipped Rinna's jeans and slid her hand into her panties. Rinna opened her thighs and trembled as Eva's finger danced gently over her labia and clit. She undid Eva's shorts and slipped her hand down into her panties. She felt something warm and soft and exciting. Eva sighed as Rinna played with her clit. For a long time, they sat there French kissing and playing with each other. Rinna came first and squirmed around in the seat. She diddled Eva's clit faster and faster until she came, too.

"That was nice," Eva sighed.

"Very nice," Rinna agreed.

They kissed again.

Before they could take this even higher, they were interrupted by another set of headlights. They stopped, smiled at each other. Eva started the car and they headed home. Whenever they stopped at a traffic light, they kissed and felt each other. At one point, they drove into a small park and kissed for a long, long time as they made each other come again and again.

When Rinna got home, she found Al seated in front of the TV. She sat down next to him.

"I'm having sex with Eva." She announced.

"I figured that. I always knew you were attracted to each other. You go everywhere together and you even hold hands when you walk side-by-side. Have you actually started anything?"

"Yes," Rinna admitted.

He laughed.

At that moment, Eva was telling Vince about the affair that had ignited between her and Rinna. He smiled at her and then laughed.

"It had to happen sooner or later. It was obvious that you two had the hots for each other, so it was only a matter of time until you followed through with it," he said.

"I didn't know we were so obvious," she said.

"You wear your emotions on your sleeve and I could tell you wanted Rinna as much as I did. Now we're both having sex with her," he said. "Nice, isn't it?"

She nodded and smiled.

The following night, Rinna and Eva returned to the casino. This time, they separated. Eva went to her favorite slot machine and sat down to play. After a few minutes, she noticed a handsome man standing behind her watching her play. She turned and smiled at him.

"I'm Phil," he said as he offered her a drink.

"Eva," she said as she took it.

She was wearing tight shorts that left little to the imagination. He ogled her legs as she watched his dick get hard. He clearly liked what he saw.

"You amazingly sexy," he said.

"Thanks," she replied as she pretended not to notice his hand moving up her thigh.

"You have incredible legs," he said as he stroked her thigh.

"What's between them is incredible, too," she teased.

"Are you offering it to me?" he asked. "If you are, I'm interested."

"Maybe," she said as she parted her legs.

He moved his hand to her crotch and gently stroked her. She smiled as her pussy grew warmer and warmer.

"How much will you cost me?" he asked.

"Whatever you're willing to pay," she replied to her own surprise.

"My room is upstairs," he said. "You're not really in the business, are you?"

"Maybe tonight I am," she said as she followed him to the elevators.

Rinna was already upstairs, moaning and sighing as Jake fucked her from behind. She loved the way he fucked, too. His stroked were slow and deep and strong and his prick massaged every part of her cunt as it moved in and out.

He had texted her earlier and told her he'd be at the casino that evening. Of course, she agreed to meet him again.

"Oh that's good! That feels so good! Fuck me, Jake!" she sighed as he gripped her hips and thrust harder.

They moved faster and faster. He fucked her harder and harder and she moaned with each, long, deep thrust of his prick. He began breathing harder now. Rinna felt herself erupt and she shook all over as the powerful orgasm swept through her sweaty body. Her quaking caused him to come, too, and he started pumping line after line of cum deep into her cunt. They kept fucking and fucking.

Rinna came again and again.

She was no quivering all over and begged him to fuck her harder. He did his best to comply as he kept going. He fucked her slower now as he savored the way her cunt hugged his prick. After another minute or two, he exploded again.

Jake emitted a long, deep moan as he emptied his final load into her. When he couldn't move anymore, he stopped and eased his now limp prick out her cunt. She rolled over and pulled him on top for a good, deep kiss.

"That was magical!" he said after a while. "Each time with you is better than the last. Lately, you're all I think about, Rinna. And I want you more and more."

"My pussy is all yours whenever you want it. Call me and I'll meet you anytime and anywhere. God that was great!" she said.

They kissed again and got dressed. He handed her $300 this time. She smiled and slid the cash into her purse.

"You are one fantastic fuck!" he said.

"So are you," she assured him.

Eva and her new lover started out with a nice, easy 69. When he was super hard, they stopped. She laid back and opened her thighs. He smiled and slid his prick into her for a nice, long, easy fuck.

His prick was long and thick.

Longer and thicker than any she'd felt before and he knew how to use it to make her feel every deep and delicious thrust. She was surprised that she had let him pick her up so easily and even more so that she had agreed to have sex with him for money.

She was now a prostitute.

Just like Rinna. A pussy for hire and she didn't feel guilty about it at all. All she cared about was the hard, strong prick that was moving in and out her oh-so-willing cunt and the wonderful sensations it was sending throughout her body.

They fucked and fucked and fucked. Eva came once.

Then again.

Each orgasm was deep and powerful. Her body shook uncontrollably as she gripped his shoulders and fucked him back as hard as she could. She soon heard him groan and his thrust grew erratic as she felt his cum jet into her again and again. They kept going for a few more thrusts, then he slipped out of her and buried his tongue in her mouth for a long, mind-numbing kiss.

"How was I?" she asked as they dressed.

He reached into his wallet and handed her all the bills he had. She counted it and was astonished to see $275. She smiled at him.

"I guess you really like me," she said.

"You are not only drop-dead gorgeous, you're the best fuck I ever had in my entire life. I'd like to make this a regular thing—if it's okay with you," he said.

"Sure. Here's my cell phone number. Call me whenever you want and we'll do this again. Anytime at all," Eva said.

She met Rinna at the bar a few minutes later. They looked at each other, smiled and laughed.

"Welcome to the club," Rinna said as they hugged.

Vince and Al were shooting pool down in Al's basement. Al told him what Rinna had suggested and he laughed.

"You might as well do it," Vince said. "I told Eva that I'm fucking this young blonde at work and that I plan to keep fucking Rinna. So if Rinna said you should look for another woman to fuck, I say go for it. There must be someone you'd like to have sex with."

"You have to admit, this is one fucking weird situation," Al said as he took his shot.

"Weird but fun. I just get the feeling that we're all gonna get burned somehow. I'm enjoying it, but things like this never turn out good," Vince said. "All I know is this shit wasn't in our wedding vows."

"Mine neither," Al said.

"Well, do you have someone in mind?" Vince asked. "Besides Eva."

"Maybe," Al hedged. "But I don't want to start anything that I can't finish. I'm not sure how to approach her or how she'll react."

"You're talking about that little Vietnamese woman you work with, aren't you?" Vince asked.

"Uh-huh," Al admitted. "She's very nice and kind of shy. We talk a lot and she brings me lunch once in a while. She likes to cook and she's real good at it and she's very happy when I eat it and compliment her."

"I know what you mean. I'd be careful with her, too. She might want something permanent. I don't think she's the type to become part of a fling. You said she was kind of old fashioned and very tradition bound."

"That she is," Al said.

"Are you going after her?" Vince asked.

"I'm kind of afraid to," Al replied.

"How do you feel about Rinna being a hooker?" Vince asked.

"I'm not all that crazy about it, but there's no way to stop her from peddling herself to any man who's willing to pay," Al said.

"As good as she is, she'll probably make lots of money. Do you think she'll be able to talk Eva into trying it?" Vince said.

"Probably. They both love sex and money and lots of men would gladly pay to get into their panties," Al said. "Would that bother you?"

"Maybe a little. I don't care as long as I get to fuck whoever I want," Vince replied. "Like you said, if Eva decided to do it, there isn't shit I can do about it."

Eva smiled as she showered the next morning.

She had finally crossed the line and sold her pussy to a man she'd met at the casino. What's more, she really enjoyed it.

Phil had fucked the daylights out of her. He was so good, that her pussy still tingled when she thought about it. She knew that if he called, she'd fuck him again. She'd also fuck other men if they were willing to pay her.

She had started out with the intention of only having regular sex with Al. Then Rinna ignited an affair with her and the two of them admitted that they loved each other. Now Rinna had convinced her to become a pussy for hire.

Her life had taken a few unexpected turns. So had everyone else's. Vince admitted he was having an affair with a much younger woman at work and that he preferred to fuck Rinna instead of her. That was fine because she'd rather have sex with Al anyway and Al seemed more than willing to fuck her.

"What a strange web I've woven!" she said.

Rinna was very open about her sexual activities. When she got home that morning, she told Al she had sex with Jake and he'd paid her $300. She also told him that Eva had finally joined the "club" and that they both planned to keep selling their pussies for a while.

The idea that his wife was selling herself to other men made Al so excited that he just about tore her clothes off. They didn't stop fucking until after sunrise and both agreed it was the wildest, most intense sex they'd had in a long time.

Eva decided to turn up the heat on Al. She decided that she wanted Al and would to everything she could to make him hers. She knew he was sexually attracted to her and usually got an erection whenever they were close to each other.

Two days later, she stopped by the house to see if Rinna was home. She beamed when Al answered the door and let her in.

"I thought you were at work," she said.

She wore the same green jogging shorts that hugged her ass and showed off her shapely legs. He ogled her as she sat down on the sofa. Al told her that Rinna had to go to work to cover for another woman who had called in.

Eva smiled.

"So it's just you and me today, huh?" she asked.

"Yes," he said as he sat next to her.

She put her arms around his shoulders and stuck her tongue into his mouth. He eagerly kissed her back and slid his hand up her thigh. When he reached her panties, she opened her legs and shivered as he fondled her cunt. She sucked his tongue harder as she silently begged him to take here there and then.

She broke off the kiss and pulled up her T-shirt to reveal her already erect nipples. He leaned over and sucked one nipple then the other while he massaged her swollen clit. She gripped his head and held him against her as she moaned.

"Yes! Yes! I love it!" she cried as she suddenly came.

She fell against the arm of the sofa and smiled at him as he pulled her shorts and panties off. He whistled when he got his first real look at her gorgeous brown muff.

"I'm all yours now," she said.

Al unzipped his jeans and pulled out his erect prick. Eva wrapped her fingers around it and gave it several easy pulls to make it longer and harder. Then she let him go and laid back with her legs wide apart.

Al buried his face in her cunt. She writhed and sighed as his tongue danced over her labia and clit. She came seconds later and fucked his tongue crazily as she begged him to keep going. She came again and let out a long, happy sigh.

He moved between her open thighs and slid his prick into her cunt. She gasped and wrapped her arms and legs around him. Before she knew it, they were engaged into a nice, deep easy fuck. Eva sighed with each deep thrust and threw her hips up at him. At long last, she was fucking Al—and it felt wonderful.

Eva's cunt felt incredibly tight. Al loved the way her walls caressed his prick as he moved in and out. She made it feel even more incredible when she tightened her cunt muscles around his prick. This made it feel more intense. More erotic.

They fucked for what seemed like a wonderfully long time. Then Eva came again. As she did, she fucked him harder. This caused Al to come, too. He groaned loudly and fired stream after stream of cum deep into her hungry pussy as he fucked her faster and harder.

"Yes! I love it! Fuck me!" she screamed as she arched her back and came again. "My God! That feels so good! So very good!"

They stopped when each was completely spent. Eva grinned up at him as she rubbed her cunt.

"I love the way your cum feels inside my pussy," she said

"That was terrific, Eva. Amazing!" he said after a while. "From now on, it's going to be nearly impossible to keep my hands off you when we're alone."

"You can touch me, eat me and even fuck me whenever you like and as much as you want," she said.

"You have the sexiest ass I ever saw," he said as he caressed her crack.

She put her legs up and used her hands to spread her cheeks apart. The sight made him rock hard again. He moved between her legs and slowly eased his prick up into her ass until he was balls deep. She sighed. She sighed louder as he proceeded to fuck her. Vince had used her like this many times and she always enjoyed it. Al's prick felt perfect to her and she began to move with him.

"My ass is yours now! All yours! Fuck me, Al! Make love to me!" she gasped as she came.

He grunted and came, too. He kept fucking her as fast as he could until he emptied every drop of cum he had left into her ass. They spent several minutes kissing each other passionately after that.

"Anytime you want me, I'm all yours," she vowed.

When Rinna got home that evening, true to his word, Al told her what happened. Rinna listened quietly then smiled.

"Now that you've fucked Eva, I guess it's okay if I keep fucking Vince and other men?" she asked.

"If you really want to. Do you?" he asked.

She smiled.

"Yes. Is that okay?" she replied.

"Well, it's your pussy. If you want to share it with someone else, there's nothing I can do to prevent it," he said.

"You really can't, can you? To be honest, I really enjoy having sex with different men—and women. Lately, it's all I think about," she said.

"How much?" he asked.

"A lot!" she giggled as she squeezed his prick.

Things were kind of normal for the next couple of days as neither woman felt like going to a casino. In fact, Rinna was grateful for the break.

But it was short at best.

Vince dropped by right after Al went to work. He'd called ahead of time so Rinna was expecting him. She wore a white T-shirt and her dark jogging shorts and greeted him at the door by groping his prick.

"I've been thinking about you," she said as she led him to the sofa.

Before long, they were locked into a torrid kiss. Vince slid his hand down into her shorts and she pulled out his prick and jerked him off nice and easy. As she watched his pre-cum ooze from the slit in his knob and make it shiny, Vice fingered her clit.

"Let's do it, Rinna. Let's fuck," he urged.

It was right then she knew that she wanted to fuck him. She wanted to feel his massive prick moving in and out of her cunt. By now, he was massaging her clit harder and she quivered and moaned as his fingers sent electrifying sensation surging through her body. She pumped his prick faster and faster. Vince moaned. She felt his prick stiffen suddenly and squeezed it harder as she beat him off.

"Oh God!" he gasped as his cum spurted from his prick.

She kept beating him nice and slow. Each pump of her fist elicited another spurt of cum. Rinna watched each spurt, too, as it shot out of his prick and decorated the front of her T-shirt. At the same time, Vince played with her clit, causing her to squirm and tremble as she neared her own climax. Her legs were wide open now and Vince's middle finger was moving in and out of her slit.

She came seconds later. As she did, she fell back against the armrest of the sofa and quivered. She looked at Vince and smiled at his half-hard prick as it bobbed up and down. Still lost in an orgasmic fog, she barely noticed as Vince slid her shorts slowly down her thighs. By then, she was virtually screaming "fuck me!" as she watched his prick grow hard again. As for Vince, he nearly came again as he slowly revealed her cunt with its perfect triangular patch of black hair, swollen clit and moist, partially open slit.

She nodded as he pulled off her shorts tossed them onto the loveseat. She opened her legs wide and sighed as he moved between them and slid his prick into her cunt.

"Ooh yes!" she said as she felt it fill her entire cunt.

She bent her knees and gripped his arms as he moved in and out slowly so they could both savor the moment. After a few east thrusts, she moved with him. It felt wonderful. Wicked.

Vince was in Heaven now. Rinna's cunt was warm and moist and oh-so tight and he loved the way she was moving with him. Fucking him.

"This is perfect," he said. "So perfect."

They moved faster and faster. She moaned and quivered with each hard thrust as every part of her body screamed, "Fuck me!" She felt herself coming and fucked him faster. She wanted them to finish together. Wanted to feel him come inside her pussy as he filled her.

Vince groaned and began fucking her harder still. Rinna came and screamed as she shook all over. Vince came seconds later. Much to his delight, she wrapped her arms around him and kept fucking him as he fired wads of cum deep into her cunt until he was completely drained.

Just as they finished, they heard Al coming up the walk. They stopped immediately. Rinna grabbed her clothes and retreated into the bathroom to clean up. She came out just as Al entered the house. She greeted him and sat down on the sofa and acted like nothing happened.

He just looked at her and smiled.

Vince excused himself and left. As soon as he drove away, Al pulled Rinna's shorts off. She parted her legs and nodded as he undressed and eased his prick into the pool of cum that was still inside her cunt so he could feel it squish around his prick. The sensation was so erotic that he came after just a few hard thrusts. Rinna felt him cum and fucked him back as hard as she could, enjoying the weird feeling of his prick moving inside her in the double pool of liquid. She moaned and came soon after.

Al pulled his still erect prick out of her cunt and slid up into her ass. Rinna gasped as he bent her almost double and fucked her until he went soft and slid out of her.

She smiled up at him.

"That was awesome," she said. "What made you try that?"

"I just wanted to find out what it felt like to fuck you right after you had sex with another man," he said. "When I saw his cum oozing out of your pussy, I just couldn't stop myself."

"And?" she asked.

"It was weird and crazy sexy," he said.

She laughed.

"It was, wasn't it?" she asked. "So my fucking other men turns you on?"

"Kind of," he admitted. "But you've always turned me on anyway."

"I know," she smiled.

The following night, the women headed out to the casino and the men got together for a few drinks at Al's house.

"We sure as Hell are in a weird situation," Al said. "Not only are we fucking each other's wives, but they've decided to become prostitutes. Right now, they're at the casino fucking other men for money. I have to say that I never saw this shit coming."

"Me neither. But as long as I get to fuck Rinna, I don't care what Eva does. I know you sure as Hell don't mind fucking Eva! And she's wild about you. I see this as win-win for everybody," Vince said.

"I just never expected our wives to go down this path at their ages. Since they're both red-hot and really know how to fuck, I think they'll make a lot of money for a while. Let's enjoy the wild ride until they get this out of their systems and hope that nothing bad happens to them," Al said.

"I agree," Vince nodded. "Anything happening with you and that woman at work?"

"Not yet. We're friends and we talk a lot. We have lunch and breaks together. But she's very shy and unassuming. If she feels anything more toward me, she hasn't said," Al replied.

"You going after her?" Vince asked.

"I am thinking about it—a lot," Al said. "Rinna told me to do it, but that might lead to something we don't want."

"Fuck! Risk it anyway. If it all goes wrong, you can always blame it on Rinna. After all, she started all of this shit," Vince said.

At that very moment, Rinna was in one of the Casino's hotel rooms bouncing up and down on the long, hard prick of her latest client. She had met him less than 10 minutes after entering the casino and liked what she saw so much, she agreed to fuck him.

They had started out by slowly undressing each other. This quickly became a good, heated "69" which then became a good, hard fuck. His prick was at least 9 inches long and very hard and she sighed and moaned with pleasure as she rode him nice and easy. He also moaned as he fondled her ass.

"Oh God! You're so tight! So wonderfully tight!" he sighed.

Rinna smiled and squeezed his prick with her cunt muscles and fucked him even slower. He moaned louder.

"I'm gonna come!" he cried as he gripped her hips and fucked her as hard as he could.

The sudden change caused Rinna to come and she began quivering and moaning as she kept fucking him. Seconds later, she felt his cum spurting into her and rode him even faster.

"Yes! I love it! Yes!" she cried.

To her surprise, he was still hard.

He flipped her over and kept thrusting. She gripped his shoulders and trembled with each thrust as he made her come more and more. He kept at it for another few minutes then fired another load into her cunt.

He sighed and pulled out. She looked down at the stream of cum running out of her slit and smiled. They dressed and chatted a while. He handed her $200 and escorted her back to the casino. That's where they exchanged phone numbers and she found his name was Ryan.

She watched him leave and smiled. Ryan had really pounded her. She felt warm and tingly between her thighs and was still a bit wobbly when she walked to her favorite slot machine. As she sat down to play, she wondered how Eva was doing.

A few minutes later, Eva walked slowly over to her and tapped her on the shoulder.

"How'd it go?" Rinna asked.

"Good and bad," Eva said. "I just got fucked in my ass by a guy who had the biggest dick I ever saw."

"How'd that happen?" Rinna asked.

"He said he'd pay me another hundred if I let him fuck me in my ass. Naturally, I agreed and went up to his room. That's when I found out how big his dick was! I've been fucked in my ass before, Rinna, but that guy almost split me in two. His dick went in deeper than anything else did before and I almost screamed when I felt it moving inside me. He went all the way in, too. When he fucked me, it hurt at first. After a few thrusts, I got used to it and relaxed. He fucked me a long time, too. He even made me orgasm! I mean a real, good one, too. I almost passed out from it. That was really good. Now if anyone else wants to do me that way, I'm ready. My ass has been broken in good tonight," she said.

"Did he pay you?" Rinna asked.

"He sure did. He said my ass felt so good that he paid me an extra $150. So I did good tonight," Eva smiled.

"I think we're through for the night. Let's go home," Rinna said.

Along the way, they talked about swapping husbands again. They decided to convince Al and Vince to go out on the town that weekend. Knowing what their wives were up to, the men quickly agreed.

When Saturday rolled around, they all got together for dinner and drinks. It was a real informal night out and they bar hopped. As the night wore on, Vince made several passes at Rinna which she happily accepted. He managed to fondle her behind a few times and even got his hand between her legs. She reciprocated by groping his prick. Al was also busy with Eva. Since both women wore loose, skimpy shorts, it was easy for the men to get at their cunts. The men wore shorts, too.

They had all tacitly agreed to swap mates when they started out that evening. What they didn't know at the time was their little sexual adventures would trigger unforeseen events. In fact, it would be the night when all barriers came down and lead them to entanglements and relationships they never imagined.

When they left their third bar, Eva and Al sat in the backset of the car while Vince drove. Almost immediately, Eva unzipped Al's shorts and pulled out his prick. She'd been playing with it all night. Rinna watched as Eva moved her head downward and slid Al's prick into her mouth and proceeded to suck away. Rinna unzipped Vince's shorts and slowly jerked him off as he drove. He was glad it was only a short distance to Al's house as Rinna's hand was driving him crazy.

By the time they got there, everyone was more than a little horny. Vince and Rinna sat on the sofa while Al and Eva shared the smaller love seat. Both men still had their pricks out, too. Vince watched as his wife stuck her tongue into Al's mouth for a long, passionate kiss. At the same time, she rubbed his prick and caused the bulge in his shorts to rapidly expand.

Rinna was also busy. She grabbed Vince and kissed him. She laid back and pulled him on top of herself. At the same time, she pumped his prick. She stroked it until it was good and hard, and then smiled up at him.

"Fuck me," she said.

Vince didn't hesitate. He undid her shorts and panties and pulled them off. Rinna bent her knees and threw open her thighs. Vince got between them and eased his prick into her cunt. She moaned as he went in deep and wrapped her arms around him.

While they were doing this, Eva peeled off her shorts and mounted Al's prick. She stuck her tongue into his mouth again and bounced up and down while he held her close. She fucked him nice and slow, too, so she could really enjoy the feel of his prick massaging her cunt.

On the sofa, Rinna was happily fucking Vince back with all she had. His prick felt wonderful, too. It fit her cunt perfectly and she let him know it by using her inner muscles to grip him with each thrust.

Vince moaned several times as they moved together.

"Nobody on Earth can fuck as good as Rinna!" he thought.

Al and Eva fucked faster and faster. Then Eva came. It was sudden and powerful. As she came, she fucked him slower. Seconds later, he spurted his load up into her cunt.

"Oh yeah! Fill me, Al. Fill my pussy with your cum!" she moaned as they fucked faster and faster. "Make love to me!"

Vince was watching Al fuck Eva from the corner of his eye. He watched her ass move up and down and saw Al's prick move in and out of her each time. Watching his wife fuck his best friend like some wanton slut fascinated him. Eva had a shapely ass and good tight cunt and watching Al's prick move up and down as she rode him made him even hornier and he fucked Rinna with a lot of energy as his own prick grew harder and harder.

And the harder he grew, the more Rinna moaned "fuck me!" as his prick pistoned in and out of her tight, wet cunt.

Rinna emitted a loud moan as she came. She clung to Vince's arms and fucked him back like a wildcat as he emptied his load into her cunt. He came a lot, too. So much that it squirted out of her cunt with each hard thrust. They kept going for several; more hard strokes, then Rinna melted into the cushions and sighed happily.

"Wow! That was the hardest fuck I've ever had!" she said after she caught her breath.

When it was over, they sat back to rest. No one bothered to dress. That's when Al noticed that Vince seemed to be looking at his prick, which was still slick and shiny with his and Eva's combined cum.

Seeing Al fuck his wife had turned him on more than anything else he'd ever seen. Watching Al's prick moving in and out her cunt while she fucked him back made him hornier than ever and made his dick harder as he fucked Rinna. It was like witnessing a live porno movie.

But now, he was seated across from Al and looking at his prick and for some reason, he couldn't turn away. He seemed mesmerized by the way it glistened with his and Eva's combined liquids. It was one of the most erotic things he'd ever seen along with his friend's cum oozing from Eva's open cuntlips. He gaze was fixed on Al's knob which was very shiny at the moment and as he looked at it, he felt his own prick stir.

Eva was seated on the sofa with one leg up on the cushion and her legs apart as she watched Vince's prick get harder and harder. She looked where he was looking and was somewhat surprised that he was getting excited by looking at Al's prick.

"Is it Al's dick that's turning him on? Or is he turned on because it's still shiny from fucking me?" she wondered.

Al was eyeing Rinna who was still lying on the floor with her thighs wide apart. He was fascinated with the stream of thick, white cum oozing from her cunt. And it aroused him. In fact, he became hard again in a few seconds.

This didn't get past Rinna, either. She reached over and jerked Vince off. When he was fully erect again, Rinna pushed him onto his back and impaled herself on his prick for what proved to be a good, long and hard fuck. She moaned and gasped as she bounced up and down on Vince's prick, well aware of the fact that he was steadily getting harder and longer with each bounce. His prick was long, thick and strong and it hit all of the right places as they fucked. Vince reached up and played with her nipples. Rinna's head fell back and she quivered with lust as she rode him harder and harder.

"Gimme your dick! I want it! Fuck me!" she screamed as she felt herself come.

By then, Eva was sucking Al's prick. When he was hard enough, she lay down on the floor and opened her legs. Al smiled and mounted her for a second fuck that proved to be even better than the first. Eva met each and every thrust of his prick with a hard thrust of her own as she gripped his shoulders. She wasn't just fucking him anymore. She was making love to him. Giving him everything she had and then some to let him know how she felt.

"I love you, Al! I love you!" she cried as she wrapped herself around him.

Vince and Rinna came first. After draining each other with a last burst of hard fucking which culminated with Vince adding a second and bigger load of cum to what she already had in her cunt, they stopped to watch Eva and Al go at it.

Again, Vince's attention went to the sight of Al's prick moving in and out his wife's cunt as she begged him to fuck her faster.

Eva glanced at Vice and noticed that his prick was getting harder and harder as he watched her fuck Al.

"Let's really give him something to look at," she said as she started fucking Al harder.

The sight of Al's prick moving in and out his wife's cunt fascinated Vince. It was the most erotic thing he'd ever seen and the longer he watched, the harder he grew until he had a massive boner.

Rinna pushed Vince onto his back and slid her cunt onto his prick. As long as his prick was hard, she was going to make good use of it. She moved up and down slowly at first and used her muscles to massage every bit of his prick each time. Vince moaned and played with her nipples which caused her to moan as well. They fucked faster and faster. Each hard thrust caused Rinna to quiver with pleasure.

"Fuck me, Vince! Gimme your dick! Gimme all of it!" she moaned.

Al had never seen his wife fuck anyone before or act so slutty. This made him even more excited and he fucked Eva with everything he had. She screamed and came, then fucked him faster until she felt his load jet into her again.

Vince watched her come and fucked Rinna harder and harder. Then they both came at the same time and spent the next few moments writing with each other. Vince pulled out and sat against the couch and watched as Al gave Eva several more slow, easy thrusts while she said "I love you" over and over again.

Al pulled out and sat back. That's when he realized that Vince was looking at his prick. And he was. The way Al's and Eva's juices now glistened on Al's shaft fascinated him. Even half erect, he could see that

Al's prick was fairly large and the fact that it had now been inside Eva's cunt several times began to turn him on.

A lot!

Al looked at him and made his prick "dance" to watch his reaction. Vince stared at Al's glistening knob. The more he looked at it, the harder his own prick became. The others sat and watched as Vince's prick rose slowly upward until he was fully erect and his knob gleamed with cum. Rinna reached over and jerked him off to make sure he was good and hard and laid back with her legs wide open.

"Fuck me!" she said.

When it was over several minutes later, they were all covered with sweat and the entire room smelled of sex. They rested for a few minutes. This time, everyone was too spent to do anything else so they dressed and parted company.

"This was one strange night," Al said as he got into bed with Rinna.

"Why did Vince get hard when he saw your dick? What with that?" she asked. "I know he really likes to watch you fuck Eva. That probably has a lot to do with it."

"Probably. I like watching him fuck you, too," Al said. "You really put everything into it. You're like a porn star."

She laughed.

"I've never watched anyone fuck outside of a porno movie. That was really wild," she said.

"Yes it was," he replied. "We'll have to do this again soon."

The next night, Rinna headed for the casino. After a few minutes on the slots, a tall, very good-looking man approached her. She smiled.

"You're one hot looking woman," he said.

"Thanks," she smiled.

"My name's Harry," he said as he held out his hand.

"I'm Rinna," she said as she shook it.

"You're a Filipina. Is it true what they say about women from your country?" he asked.

"There's one way to find out," she said. "But it'll cost you $200."

He reached into his wallet and took out four $50 bills and handed them to her. She smiled.

"I'm all yours," she said as she followed him to the elevators.

Rinna's new client proved to be very energetic. They started out slowly with a nice, easy fuck. His prick was long and fairly thick, so it massaged every part of her inner walls deliciously. He used slow, deep thrusts and went in all the way to his balls each time while he played with her nipples. She moved with him, too.

As they fucked, he commented on how tight she was and how gorgeous her body was. They moved faster and faster and faster. She heard him grunt. He leaned forward and fucked her faster as he fired line after line of cum into her cunt.

To her surprise, he was still rock hard when he pulled out.

He flipped her onto her belly, shoved a pillow beneath her to elevate her behind, and proceeded to fuck her again. This position made it feel even more exciting and she soon came. As her body shook, he fucked her harder and harder.

Rinna cried out with passion as he triggered a second orgasm.

And a third.

"Ooh yeah! Fuck me good! Use me, Harry! Use me like you want!" she cried.

He fucked her harder and harder, then leaned forward and emptied another good load of cum deep inside her flooded cunt. He pulled out, spread her cheeks and eased his prick up into her asshole.

Rinna bit her lower as he pushed into her. She wasn't expecting this and it caught her by surprise. She relaxed her muscles and sighed as he fucked her slowly. After a while, she began to enjoy it.

Harry fired one last load off into her ass and eased his now limp prick out of her.

She rolled over and smiled at him.

"Did you get your money's worth?" she asked.

"Oh Hell yeah," he said. "You're the best I've ever had. I'd like to do this again soon."

They got up and dressed and he escorted her down to the casino. He stopped to kiss her as he handed her squeezed her behind. She responded by squeezing his dick.

"How about next week?" he asked. "I'm single so I can't think of anything better to spend the Money on."

"Okay. I'll see you here the same time next week," she agreed.

When she returned to her favorite slot, another man walked over and handed her a drink. She took it and smiled. Fifteen minutes later she was in his room moaning and crying out as he fucked the daylights out of her.

She got home around two a.m. Al was still up watching TV. He smiled at her as she sat next to him.

"How many tonight?" he asked.

"Two," she said as she leaned against his shoulder. "My pussy is filled with cum."

He took her hand and led her up to the bedroom…

Eva said she was staying home with Vince. When Vince called her to tell he he'd be home very late, she put on her workout clothes and headed over to the YMCA. She spent over an hour using the Stairmaster and another 45 minutes weight training with light weights.

When she got ready to leave, one of the men walked over to her.

"I've been watching you all night," he said. "I can't help it. You're the sexiest woman I've ever seen."

"Thanks," she said.

"My name is Lance," he said as they shook hands.

"Eva," she replied.

"Are you married?" he asked.

"Yes I am," she said.

"Damn. Just my luck. All the really sexy women are taken," he said as they laughed.

"Sorry," she said.

"Do you fool around?" he joked.

She smiled. Her smile almost made his knees buckle.

"Maybe," she replied.

"Oh? What would it take for me to have a date with you?" he asked.

"Money and a great big dick," she said.

"I don't have money. But I do have a good sized dick," he said. "How much money?"

"That depends on what you think I'm worth," she said.

"Let me think about that," he said as he headed for the locker room to shower.

Eva did the same.

When she left the YMCA an hour later, she saw Lance seated on the steps outside. He smiled at her.

"I went over the ATM," he said, as he showed her the cash.

She grinned.

"This is your lucky night!" she said.

Lance actually too her to his apartment which was a few blocks away. They spent the next five hours fucking in as many different ways as they could think of. To her delight, the handsome Lance lived up to his name.

His dick was a good 11 inches long and really hard and each time he thrust into her, he did it nice and slow and deep. She'd never had anything this big in her cunt before, nor had anything ever massaged every nook and cranny of it like Lance's dick. He made her come after only a few thrusts and she kept coming and coming all during their tryst.

They fucked in three different positions and by the time he'd exploded deep inside of her, she was totally exhausted and feeling great all over. In fact, he came inside of her three different times and she finished off the evening by sucking his dick until he was totally limp.

When she got home a little past midnight, Vince was still out.

She didn't care.

She'd had some really good sex with Lance and she was $200 richer.

"Yes. I am a prostitute now," she said as she looked at herself in the dresser mirror. "My pussy is a valuable commodity."

Chapter Four

When Rinna and Eva arrived at the casino two nights later, they decided to head for the bar. They sat down and ordered drinks as they looked over their potential customers. A few minutes later, a tall, broad shouldered Nordic-looking man walked over and sat next to Rinna.

"I'm Lars," he said.

"I'm Rinna and this is Eva," Rinna said as they shook hands.

"I've seen you ladies around here several times. Each time, I've watched you leave the casino with men. Are you in the business?" he asked as he placed his hand on Rinna's knee.

She smiled and parted her legs.

"Yes we are," she said.

He smiled.

"Me and a few friends are having a party up in my suite tonight. I'm lining up the entertainment. If you ladies are interested, we'll make it worth your while," he said.

"What kind of entertainment are you looking for?" Rinna asked.

"Sexual," he replied as he ran his hand along her thigh. "Are you interested?"

"Maybe. How many men would we have to entertain?" Eva asked.

"Ten," he said. "Plus you can have as much to eat and drink as you like. We'll have plenty of food, booze and weed. All we need are a couple of hot looking ladies to make it complete," her said.

"How much?" Rinna asked.

"What do you normally make?" he inquired.

"We get $200 per client," Rinna said.

"That's sounds fair enough. We all have plenty of cash and we'll even set up a brandy snifter for tips. Each of us will pay you as we go along, so you could make a lot of money tonight—if you can handle that much sex."

"That's a lot of fucking and sucking," Eva said.

Rinna smiled as he played with her cunt.

"Okay. We'll give it a try. When do we start?" she asked.

"Right now," he said.

The celebrants had rented the Presidential Suite. When Rinna and Eva arrived, all of the men applauded. There were 10 men. All were under 30 years and good-looking, too.

Rinna smiled at Eva.

"Now that I see how handsome all these men are, this is going to be a real pleasure!" she whispered.

Lars handed them each a mixed drink while the men gathered around to look them over. One man whistled and commented that Lars had exceeded their expectations by finding "the two most beautiful women on Earth."

"It's show time," Rinna said as she finished her drink.

They walked to the middle of the room, introduced themselves and did a striptease to a slow tune that was being played. The men whistled, clapped and hooted as one article of clothing after another hit the floor until both women were naked.

They spun around and posed in various positions, and then each retreated into a separate bedroom. Within minutes, all of the men were naked. After that, the party became a blurring succession of big pricks as each man took his turn fucking them and getting sucked off. The party grew wilder and wilder. At any given point, Rinna had two men fucking her at one time while she sucked another one off and jerked on two other pricks. She felt them come in her cunt and ass countless times and swallowed quarts of cum. She was fucked in every imaginable position and in every hole for more times than she could count.

The combination of the alcohol and second hand weed smoke made her feel hornier than ever and she threw herself into the party with incredible gusto as she begged them to keep fucking her.

And they did. In several different positions and on various pieces of furniture. They used her cunt and her ass with equal gusto and they all came inside of her. She also sucked several dicks and swallowed what felt like a gallon of cum. Their dicks came in all sizes and widths, so each fuck felt different. The men oohed and ahhed and commented on how great she was, how tight she was and how hot she was. Each of them stuffed $100 bills into her jar or purse.

Eva fared the same and several of them fucked her in her ass, too. In fact, at one point she was riding one man's prick and sucking another while a third happily fucked her in the ass. That's when Eva realized that she actually liked getting fucked in her ass and that her rear channel easily adjusted to accommodate every sized dick.

"My ass is made for fucking!" she thought as the party continued.

Rinna also got fucked in her ass a few times. Although she wasn't wild about it, she eventually learned to like it after the sixth prick found its way into her ass and made her entire body quiver with each good, deep thrust while she sucked another guy's dick.

The men seemed tireless, too. Whenever one man came in her pussy and pulled out, another man took his place so the fucking seemed to be nonstop. They didn't care that her cunt was filled with loads of cum, either. In fact, they seemed to enjoy it more that way.

In short, they were gang banged for the entire night in what became a sexual marathon.

They staggered out of the suite and down to Rinna's car around 10 the next morning. Both felt very tired and sore and they had purses stuffed with cash. When they got inside the car, they took the money they'd made, counted it and divided it equally. Rinna whistled.

"We each made $2,800! That's a lot of money for one night," she exclaimed.

"And a whole lot of fucking in one night. My pussy and ass are sore and I'm having trouble sitting comfortably. It was great, but I don't ever want to do anything like that again," Eva said.

"I came so many times that I almost passed out," Rinna said.

"We've become real sluts, Rinna. We'll fuck anybody anywhere as long as they pay us," Eva said. "We are now walking pussies for hire."

"You say that as if it is a bad thing," Rinna joked.

Eva laughed.

"We've become whores at an age when most women give up the trade. Men go after us because we're exotic and they're willing to pay us good money for our services," Rinna said. "I'm kind of proud of that."

"Me, too. To be honest, I'd rather have sex with Al," Eva said. "It feels very special when I'm with him. Is that way for you and Vince?"

"I love to fuck him, but that's as far as it goes," Rinna said. "He'd been chasing after me for a long time, so I decided to let him catch me."

"Look at the time! Our husbands are gonna kills us! We didn't even come home last night!" Eva said as she looked at her watch.

"We'd better get going," Rinna said as she started the car.

When Rinna got home, Al was watching TV` in the living room. She plopped down next to him and smiled.

"How many?" he asked.

"At least 10," she said. "I think I got fucked about 25 times. We each made $2,800."

"I'm glad you don't charge me. I don't think I could afford you," he joked.

"I'm going to stop for a few days. So is Eva. Those guys almost fucked us to death," she said.

"That's good," he smiled.

"So I'll be all yours for the rest of this week. I hope you can keep up with me," she teased.

"I've always been able to before," he smiled.

"I know. I'm counting on you," she said.

Four nights later, Rinna was again at the casino playing her favorite slots. She was having a good day, too.

Within 10 minutes of entering the casino, a well-dressed man approached her. After a drink and a short chat, she went up to his room for what proved to be a nice, long and easy fuck. He was slow and gentle and she fucked him back the same way. She decided that he was one of the best she'd had in a while, too. It was more like they were making love. It was so pleasant; they both came at the same instant. She clung to him and moaned as he pumped his entire load into her while they French kissed.

She cleaned up in the bathroom and collected her fee. When she returned to the casino, she met another man with broad shoulders and a pleasant smile. She spent the next two hours in his room screaming with pleasure as he fucked her in four different positions. In between fucks, she played with his prick and sucked it to make him hard again. When all was said and done, he paid her double her usual price because she was "that good".

Her pussy felt pleasantly tired when she returned to the casino. She decided that she wouldn't fuck anyone else that night. Her mind was lost on her machine and she didn't notice the tall, well-built, dark haired man behind her until he said something.

"You're really cute," he said.

She turned, looked him over and smiled.

"Thanks," she said.

"You mind if I sit next to you and talk?" he asked.

"No. I don't mind," she replied.

They talked for a long time. The man made Rinna laugh and she felt at ease with him. She made him laugh, too. He bought her one drink. Then another and another. She agreed to have dinner with him so they went to the casino restaurant. The place was dimly lit and the food was good.

His name was Troy.

They talked more and more. She felt his hand slide up her inner leg. Since she was wearing jeans, she let him do it. Besides, she liked him now. Maybe she liked him too much because she parted her legs. Troy stroked her inner thigh. His touches were warm and exciting and she was surprised that she was letting him touch her like this.

"You're so beautiful," he whispered. "So very sexy. Come with me."

"Where?" she asked as his fingers danced over her crotch.

"To my suite," he said as he gently rubbed her.

"Why?" she asked as she subconsciously teased him.

"To have sex. Lots and lots of sex," he said. "I want what you have between your legs."

"You're already touching that," she joked as he traced her labia with his fingers.

"I want to do more than just touch it," he said.

Rinna was very drunk now and horny. Troy leaned closer and closer. Before she could think, their lips made contact. Then their tongues merged. She felt her heart racing faster and faster as her inner fire ignited.

Troy realized she was on the fence now and decided to gamble. He slowly undid the buttons on her jeans while they continued to kiss. When Rinna didn't object, he undid her belt and the top button and slid his hand down into her panties. She quivered as she felt his fingers dance over her cunt, stoking her fire even further. She moaned softly as he slid them along her swollen and moist labia. When he eased a finger into her cunt, she nearly bit his tongue off.

She gripped his arms as he moved the finger in and out of her slit. He stopped kissing her and moved it upward. She smiled at him and parted her legs as Troy played with her clit. She was too drunk and too horny to make him stop, too. So she looked at him and smiled dreamily. He kept doing this until Rinna shook all over and came. It was a nice, long and pleasant orgasm, too.

He kept his hand on her cunt and gently moved his finger in and out of her as her labia twitched. She caught her breath and smiled at him as her cunt throbbed and screamed for more. She forced herself to think clearer now.

"That was nice," she said as she looked at the obviously huge bulge in his slacks.

"I have a suite on the sixth floor," he said.

"That's nice," she said.

"We could go there if you like," he said as he slid his middle digit into her cunt again.

"And what would we do when we got there?" she teased as she parted her legs again.

"We could take our clothes off and have sex," he said. "Lots of sex."

"Oh?" she teased.

"I have a big, hard dick and I'm dying to see how it fits into your tight little pussy," he said.

"I bet you do," she said. "But I'm afraid I'll have to say no."

"Why? I thought you liked me," he said.

"I do like you. If I didn't, I wouldn't let you touch my pussy like this. I'm tempted to go with you, but I'm a married woman and my husband is expecting me home in a few minutes," she said as she decided to tease him. "I don't want him to get mad at me."

"What if I offered to pay you?" he suggested.

"How much would you pay me?" she joked as she fingered her faster and faster.

"How about two or three hundred dollars?" he offered. "Cash."

By then, her legs were wide apart and her entire body was trembling from the delicious sensations Troy was sending through her. She was very, very wet now and super horny.

"That's a lot of money," she whispered as his finger moved in and out of her cunt nice and easy.

"Not for someone like you. How about I make it $400?" Troy asked.

Rinna looked at the huge bulge in Troy's pants. She reached over and ran her fingers along it. Her touches made it dance. She'd already fucked other men for money and Troy was offering her much more than any of them did.

She decided to play "hard to get" to see how much more he'd offer. She had already decided to fuck him, but as long as he was willing, she was going to keep negotiating with him. To keep him interested, she let him play with her pussy while she fondled his prick. He leaned closer and kissed her. Rinna responded by sucking his tongue as it entered her mouth. Her cunt was on fire now.

"Let's do it, Rinna," he urged as he fingered her clit again.

She fidgeted and squirmed now as she felt another orgasm coming on. Her legs were wider apart now and she was breathing harder. She located his cockhead through his pants and tweaked it few times. Troy unzipped his pants to see what she'd do. Rinna reached inside and wrapped her fingers around his surprising thick and long shaft. She felt it grow even harder and freed it from his pants. She now looked down at the large, dark head as she continued to stroke it, surprised at herself for doing this.

Troy smiled and frigged her faster. She responded by jerking him off faster and faster and faster.

"I'm gonna come," he whispered.

Rinna aimed his prick at the underside of their table and stroked him faster. She felt it stiffen and spasm. Troy grunted softly as he ejaculated, thrilled beyond words that Rinna was actually doing this. Rinna was horny and somewhat embarrassed. Her fingers were now sticky with Troy's cum. When she thought he was finished, she let him go and used a napkin to wipe her hand. As she eyed his still half-erect prick as he used his muscles to make it "dance".

"That was great," he said as he continued to finger her. "Great."

At that time, Rinna was glad the café was dimly lit and that everyone else there was too busy doing other things to notice her or Troy. She grabbed his prick and played with it again and felt it get bigger and harder with each pump of her hand.

Every cell in her body was screaming "fuck me!"

"Let's do it, Rinna. Let's go upstairs and fuck," he pressed. "You know you want to."

That's when she came again. Harder. She suppressed a moan and gripped her seat to keep from sliding off. God, how she wanted to fuck him! She bucked her hips up and down a few times as the orgasm raced through her. She squeezed his prick harder and beat him faster. Troy sighed as she made him come again.

"I'll make it $500," he offered. "I've got to have you!"

"Wow! I appreciate your offer, Troy. If I was in the business, I'd take you up on it, too. But like I said, I'm married and I need to get back home now. Okay?"

"Oh. I understand," he said. "Maybe next time?"

She smiled as he took his hand out of panties.

"Maybe. We'll see," she said as she playfully squeezed his prick again and gave it few strokes.

She kept at it for a little while, intrigued that he had gotten hard again so fast. Troy eased his hand back into her panties. They kept at this until Troy shot yet another load onto the underside of the table and he had made her come again. By then, they were both spent and pretty satisfied.

"Now, I really want you," he said. "When can I see you again?"

"I usually come here every week. Maybe we'll see each other again soon," she said.

"I will definitely be looking for you, Rinna," he assured her as he zipped up his pants.

"Good," she said.

She buttoned up her jeans. Troy ogled her ass as she got up and walked out of the restaurant, so sorry that she got away.

Rinna wobbled out to her car and sat behind the wheel. She realized that she wanted to fuck Troy and wondered if she had played too hard to get. He did seem super interested. Hell, he had offered to pay her $500which was more than double what she usually made.

"We'll meet again," she said as she started the car.

While Rinna was enjoying her trade at the casino, Eva was at her house fucking Al. In fact, at that very moment, she was lying on her back naked with her legs spread apart, cooing and moaning as Al's tongue worked her slit.

She knew that Rinna would be gone the entire evening and decided to take the opportunity to spend time with Al. When she showed up wearing nothing but her jogging shorts and a tank top, Al practically dragged her up to the bedroom.

They started out with as long, exciting "69". This led to her begging Al to fuck her in her ass, which led to another long "69". Then Eva impaled herself on Al's prick and rode him until their bodies gleamed with sweat and he'd spurted every last drop of cum he had left into her cunt.

Now, he was eating her again while she sucked his prick. Neither one of them cared what Rinna nor was Vince up to.

Rinna got home after one a.m. and smiled and waved at Eva as she got into her car and drove off. Al greeted Rinna at the door and they simply looked at each other and laughed. This time, Al didn't ask her how many men she served that night and Rinna didn't volunteer the information.

The next morning, they chatted over breakfast as usual. This time, Rinna told Al all about her encounters and her intriguing almost-fuck with Troy.

"Really if he had shown up earlier, I would have fucked his brains out. I was already exhausted when we met but we did tease each other for a long time. How was your night with Eva?" she said.

"Fun as usual. She's very sexy and energetic. Hell, we'd just finished another good, hard fuck a few minutes before you arrived. Eva is something else in bed!" he replied.

"I still think you should branch out and have sex with at least one other woman," Rinna urged.

"I doubt if that's possible. I can hardly keep up with you two now. Another woman might kill me," he said.

"At least you'll die smiling," she joked. "Look Al. I'm fucking just about every man who's willing to pay for my pussy. So feel free to fuck as many other women as you want. Just don't get romantically entangled with any of them."

"Promise me that you won't, either," he said.

"Okay," she said.

Vince was still out when Eva got home. She laughed. She knew he was off fucking that blonde from his job. She really didn't care who he fucked as long as she got to fuck whoever she wanted.

"We sure have a strange marriage now. I never imagined anything like this when we got married 20 years ago. Now anything goes and it's all in the open," she said as she went in to shower.

Chapter Five

Al and Vince were seated on the sofa in Al's den watching a baseball game. As they drank beer, they talked about the game and a few other things.

"You know, I really love fucking your wife," Vince said. "Once she gets going, she never seems to get tired. If she's like this with her clients, I know they're getting their money's worth."

Al laughed.

"Eva's the same way," he said. "She doesn't hold back. We'll have to arrange a weekend swap soon. We can switch on Friday night and meet up again Monday. We can spend the entire time having sex in as many ways as we can imagine."

"I'm up for that!" Vince said.

That same night, Rinna and Eva headed for the casino again to do a little "fishing". They each wore very short skirts and sleeveless blouses and they immediately turned heads when they walked into the place.

Eva wished Rinna good luck and slowly walked to her favorite slot machine. Rinna headed for the bar to get a drink.

Eva scored first.

While she was playing the slots, a tall, rather good looking man walked over and started a conversation. She kind of liked his demeanor, so she chatted freely with him. As they talked, they had several drinks and Eva felt loose and horny.

She was wearing a short skirt that night, and her new acquaintance spent much of the time admiring the view as it slowly crept up her thighs. She also noticed that he now had a big bulge in the front of his slacks.

A very big bulge.

After a while, she felt his hand on her thigh. Rather than push him away, she smiled and parted her knees. The man smiled and eased his hand upward. The higher it went, the more she parted her thighs while maintain a smile and eye contact.

He soon reached her panties. Eva opened her legs wider and sighed as he felt her. Her pussy was already warm and moist and she welcomed the sexual contact. She reached over and squeezed his bulge.

"I know a very secluded area. No one will see us there," he whispered.

She nodded and followed him across the casino floor and through a set of curtains. They went down a dimly lit hall and through a side door to a small, empty banquet room. She smiled and slid up onto a table. He knelt before her, reached under her skirt and slid her panties off. She laid back and opened her legs wide. He buried his tongue in her cunt and proceeded to eat her. She was so horny, so far gone, that she came in seconds and began humping his tongue. He kept eating her until she'd come again.

Then he stood and unzipped his pants. Eva stared as he pulled out his huge, rigid prick. Without a word, he slid it into her cunt and gave her one of the slowest, deepest fucks she'd ever experienced and she happily moved with him.

To her delight, he brought her to another orgasm. Then he came, too. She held him tightly as he emptied his cum into her cunt. It felt so warm and pleasant. And he came a lot! They kept fucking and fucking until he was completely drained.

He pulled out and straightened up. Then he helped her off the table. He bent down and picked up her panties. She smiled when he put them into his jacket pocket.

"Souvenir—if you don't mind," he said with a smile.

"They're all yours," she said.

He took $200 out of his wallet and handed it to her. She shoved the bills into her pocket and kissed him and headed back to her machine. Along the way, she went to the ladies room to clean the cum from her cunt in case she got another nibble.

At the same time, Rinna was upstairs in a suite with a man she'd met a few minutes earlier, happily sucking his prick while he tongued her pussy. His tongue felt unusually long, too, and he made her come twice within 10 minutes.

As she lay on her back with her legs wide apart, she felt him slide his unusually long prick into her cunt. She wrapped her arms around his hips and they began fucking. It was a hard, deep and very intense fuck. Since she was still caught up in her orgasm, the sensations of his prick plunging in and out her cunt kept her coming and coming. She was soon almost blind from the orgasms but still managed to hang on and fuck him back with everything she could. She soon felt him spurt into her and fell back with her arms apart.

He came a lot, too.

So much that it ran out of her cunt and slid between her cheeks. She moaned and sighed as he kept at it. He kept going and going. She began to see white now. It was, by far, the longest single fuck of her life. She could hardly believe that he could keep fucking like that and coming and coming.

She finally heard him emit a long, satisfied groan as he fell on top of her. When he pulled out, she smiled at the river of cum that ran out of her cunt like a white waterfall. He grinned at her and grabbed his wallet. She got up and dressed and kissed him again as he handed her $250 and told that she was the very best he'd ever had. She handed him a business card with her cell phone number.

"Call me when you want to this again, Steve," she said.

"How much for an entire weekend?" he asked.

"I don't think I can handle you for an entire weekend. You wore me out tonight. But we'll see," she smiled.

It proved to be a busy night for both Rinna and Eva. By the time they left the casino, it was nearly five a.m. Both women had fucked three different men and both had trouble walking back to the car.

"My ass and pussy are filled with cum now," Eva said as she started the car. "That's the most sex I've had in one night in a long time."

"Me too. My pussy is still throbbing," Rinna added. "We made a lot of money tonight, too. How many different men do you think you could handle in one night?"

Eva shrugged.

"That depends on how they fuck. Each man does it different. Maybe four or five would be my limit. What about you?" she asked.

"Maybe the same," Rinna said.

"You know, I really like being a prostitute. I love to have all sorts of strange dicks in my pussy and I love getting paid for it. We could get rich doing this," Eva said.

"If it doesn't kill us first," Rinna smiled. "I'm really exhausted now. "My first guy almost wore me out."

"He must have been real good," Eva remarked.

"And real hard, too," Rinna giggled.

"Slut!" Eva teased.

"Tramp!" Rinna teased back.

They laughed.

When Rinna got home, she saw that Al was still up watching TV. She sat next to him and leaned against his shoulder. He put his arm around her.

"I did three tonight," she said tiredly. "So did Eva. We each made over $600."

"That's a lot in one night. I suppose you're too tired for another one?" he asked.

"Maybe. We'll see after I shower."

"Yeah," he replied.

Rinna and Eva met for lunch the next day and ended up at Eva's house afterward. As they stood facing each other in the living room, they embraced. Rinna stuck her tongue into Eva's mouth for a deep, warm kiss while Eva stroked her behind.

"This is great and all, but I really want to fuck Al!" Eva said.

"You mean again?" Rinna asked.

"Let's swap again. The guys will really go for that!" Eva said as she ran her fingers along the inside of Rinna's thigh.

"Let's do it next weekend," Rinna said as she smiled at her

"Deal!" Eva grinned as she fondled her crotch.

Rinna smiled and opened her stance. Eva undid her shorts and slid her hand down into her panties.

"Yes!" Rinna whispered as Eva's finger entered her cunt.

She reached down and undid Eva's jeans and returned the favor. Both women began to breathe harder and harder. Their cunts were sopping wet now and their bodies trembled as they stood their "fucking" each other with their fingers. Rinna stuck her tongue into Eva's mouth as she came. It was a good, long orgasm that made her squirm. Eva came soon after.

"Oh my God! I love it!" she sighed as Rinna kept fingering her.

Eva came again and again. So did Rinna as Eva's fingers never left her pussy, either. When they stopped, they looked at each other. Without a word, Eva knelt and tugged Rinna's jeans and panties all the way down.

"Your pussy smells so good," she said as she moved close.

Rinna quivered as Eva ran her tongue along her slit. She let her head tilt back and shook harder as Eva proceeded to lick deeper. This was, by far, the most erotic moment of her entire life. Her gorgeous best friend was making love to her with her tongue and it felt so wonderful.

So right.

Rinna soon came again. As she did, she humped Eva's tongue.

"More! More! I love it! I love you!" she cried.

She stumbled to the sofa and sat down. Eva stood before her. Rinna smiled and pulled her jeans and pantries down. Then she stopped to admire Eva's near perfect cunt. She leaned over and slid her tongue into Eva's slit.

Eva moaned.

Rinna licked her slit harder and sucked her swollen clit. Eva rocked back and forth and came. She came hard, too.

"I love you, Rinna!" she screamed.

They sat and smiled at each other. They had finally fulfilled their fantasy. They had sex with each other. It was their first taste of pussy but they knew it wouldn't be their last.

"My pussy is yours whenever you want it," Rinna said. "I'm all yours, Eva. Every inch of me is yours."

"I'm yours, too," Eva said as they kissed again.

Before they knew it, they were totally naked and locked into a good, long "69". They kept at it until both had come multiple times and were finally too worn out to continue. Rinna was elated with her first lesbian experience, especially since it was with Eva, a woman she found incredibly sexy and she loved dearly.

"Wow. Sex with you is better than sex with Vince," Eva said. "I truly love you, Rinna. I think I always have."

Rinna beamed.

"And I truly love you, Eva," she said.

They went into the living room and drank some wine. After a few minutes of chatting, they ended up in bed naked again. This time, they spent a long time in a nice, easy 69 until they'd both come a couple of times.

"I never thought I'd fall in love with a woman, but I'm glad it's you," Rinna said.

"I love you, too," Eva said as she stroked Rinna's cunt. "I love the way you feel and smell and taste. I love the way you kiss and the way you eat me."

They had lunch and decided to go to a casino. Once they got there, they went to their favorite machines and played the slots while they trolled for customers.

While Eva really didn't care who she had sex with as long as they had money, Rinna was kind of choosy about who she slept with. She refused to sleep with anyone who was drunk or reeked of booze or anyone she felt looked too sleazy. She liked handsome, well-dressed men who were sure of themselves and had enough cash to pay her for her services.

This night, she was really picky.

One guy attempted to kiss her but she turned her head and shoved him and he got the message. She didn't like his looks at all and he really turned her off big time.

The next guy bought her a drink. It was a fairly strong one, too, and it made her a little light headed and horny. She was so horny that she let him put his hand on her thigh while they talked. After a while, he slid it up her leg to the edge of her shorts and she pushed it away. He reeked of cigarettes and alcohol anyway and she decided she wanted nothing to do with him. He left after he apologized.

The next struck gold. Mostly because she'd had two drinks and she kind of liked him. Before she knew it, he had his hand under the leg of her shorts and he was gently running his finger up and down her cunt through her panties. She was so tipsy that night that, instead of shoving him away, she opened her thighs. She smiled at him as he teased her swollen clit, but when he tried to slip a finger past her panties and into her cunt, she pulled his hand away and clamped her knees tight.

He smiled and stayed to talk. She had another drink and smiled as he slid his hand up her thigh to her panties again. This time, she opened her legs wider and allowed him to touch her and touch her. She was hot and wet between her legs now and he even managed to slide two fingers into her cunt.

Almost automatically, her legs parted. She just sat there and maintained eye contact with him as he explored her. She was surprised at herself. And the more this guy moved his fingers in and out her cunt, the wetter and hornier she became. She sat there and breathed hard as he played with her. She watched the bulge in his pants grow and briefly wondered what it would feel like to fuck him.

Soon her legs were wide apart and she was shaking all over. As waves of pleasure rippled through her body, she hoped like Hell that no one else could see what was happening. His fingers were going a little deeper with each move and she began to imagine that it was his prick instead.

A minute later, she came. As she did, she clamped her knees shut and pushed his hand away. She could hardly believe he'd gotten so far and she knew he wanted to get even further. When he offered to take her up to his room, she hesitated playfully to see what he'd try next.

"Let's go up to my room and finish this the right way," he whispered as he slid his hand up her thigh. "I've got to have you. You're so beautiful. So sexy."

Again her legs parted. Again his fingers entered her still throbbing cunt and wriggled around inside of her deliciously.

"Come with me," he urged as he made her come again.

This time, she had trouble staying seated and had to grip the sides of the chair. His fingers felt so good moving inside her pussy and the size of his bulge made her curious about how big his prick was and how it would feel inside her cunt.

"Let's do it," he urged as he massaged her g-spot and made her come even harder.

She almost screamed "fuck me!" but managed to stifle it as she shook and shook. Damn, it felt so good. When he withdrew his fingers, she smiled at him and nodded.

Ten minutes later, they were both on his bed naked and fucking like crazy. He was good, too. Much better than she had expected and he made her come several times. He was really delighted that she let him come in her pussy, and boy, did he ever do that!

She finished him off with a blowjob.

He was so thrilled with her that he tipped her an extra $100. She gave him one of her cards and told him to call her if he wanted to meet her again.

Eva had her own encounters at the casino. Only she was far more receptive than Rinna. The first guy took her to a dark area of the casino. Once there, she let him pull down her shorts and panties and eat her pussy until she came. When he was finished eating her, she turned around and leaned against the wall with her feet spread apart. He got behind her and slid his prick into her cunt for a nice easy fuck. Just before he came, she turned, grabbed his prick and sucked it until he blew his load into her mouth. She kept sucking until she swallowed all of his cum. When they were finished, he surprised her by taking out his wallet and handing her $200.

Before she could say anything, he thanked her and left. Stunned, she put the money in her purse and went out to the casino, smiling like the Cheshire Cat.

An hour later, she allowed a man to play with her cunt while she jerked him off. They kept at this until they both came. He tried to fuck her but couldn't get it back up. So she finished him off with a blowjob. The man said she was terrific as he handed her $150 and walked away.

The next guy took her up to his room for a good, hard and intense fuck that left her panting for air. He had placed a cushion beneath her ass to raise her hips. This made the fuck deeper and harder. This was a first for Eva, too. And she really enjoyed the intense sensations that his prick sent through her body with each thrust.

She left his room on wobbly legs and made her way back to the slots.

Rinna walked up an hour later looking tired and happy. Eva laughed.

"I did two tonight," she said.

"Just one. I didn't care for the looks of the other men who hit on me, so I brushed them off," Rinna said. "Ready to go home?"

"Sure. I'm kind of tired anyway," Eva agreed.

Al just got home from work when Rinna arrived at the house. She told him about her adventure and they went upstairs to shower. She also told him they were trying their luck again the next night.

Al smiled and carried her over to the bed...

The next night, the casino was kind of dead and neither of them got any hits. They left early and stopped in a secluded park and started French kissing. Before Rinna realized it, Eva had pulled her shorts and panties off. She then buried her tongue in Rinna's cunt and ate her until she came.

Rinna pulled Eva's shorts and panties off and quickly returned the favor. When Eva came, she seized Rinna's hair and held her in place while she fucked her tongue until she came again. They quickly scrambled into the back seat and locked into another good, long "69" until they each couldn't come anymore.

Eva felt exhilarated now. They exchanged several more kissed as they dressed and professed their love for each other.

"You know, this might sound crazy, but I think I fell in love with you the day we met. I tried not to let it show because I wasn't sure if you were interested. Now that I know that you feel the same way about me, I'm sorry I waited so long. Vince is right. You're the sexiest woman alive," Eva said.

"You're very sexy, too, Eva. I've wanted to make love with you ever since I saw you. I've never had such feelings for another woman before and I wasn't sure how to approach you. So I'm real happy you approached me," Rinna said. "Sex with you is exciting and a lot of fun. I'd like us to be lovers forever."

"So do I. Can I still fuck Al?" Eva asked.

"Sure. Can I still fuck Vince?" Rinna asked.

"Whenever and wherever you like," Eva assured her.

Eva watched as Al greeted Rinna at the door with a hug and a kiss and wished he was hugging her. She knew that Rinna was in for a good night of lovemaking. She wasn't. In fact, Vince wasn't at home when she got there. He was coming home later and later these days. When he did, he barely noticed her.

Still feeling neglected by Vince and bored, Eva began cruising the sex sites on the internet while masturbating. She did this every day, too. Each time, she managed to make herself come. It was good, but she really needed to feel a good, hard prick in her cunt.

On Wednesday, she decided to return to the casino. She wore her skimpiest shorts and a T-shirt. She made it a point to walk around the casino to show herself off, then sat down at her favorite slot machine and started playing. A few minutes later, a rather good-looking man walked over and sat beside her. He was ogling her legs as her shorts left almost nothing to the imagination.

"You like what you see?" she asked.

"I definitely do," he said. "You have terrific looking legs."

"Thanks," she smiled. "Would you like to see what's between my legs?"

"I sure as Hell would," he replied. "Is that an offer?"

"Maybe. I can be had for a price," she said.

"How much?" he asked.

"We can discuss that after. You can pay what you think I'm worth," she offered.

"Deal!" he said.

She followed him to the elevators then into his room on the 9th floor. She smiled because he was already hard and it looked huge. They went to the bed and slowly undressed each other while he nibbled on her ears, shoulders and nipples and she stroked his prick. He pushed her onto her back and buried his tongue in her cunt. She gasped and moaned as he ate her while he moved a finger in and out of her cunt.

"More! More! Make me come! Make me yours!" she cried as she shook all over.

As she lay with her legs parted, he slid his prick into her cunt. She moaned louder and gripped his hips as they fucked. His stroked were deep, strong and powerful. They sent shivers all though her body and she fucked him back as hard as she could.

"Fuck me! Fuck me! I love it!" she moaned as she arched her back and came.

He fucked her even faster.

She came again and again and again.

The she felt his cum spurt into her again and again and again. They kept fucking as long as they could. Eva lost track of her orgasms. She felt warm all over. This had become the longest and most intense fuck of her entire life.

When he finally pulled out, her cunt was flooded with cum. It ran out of her open labia and made its way between her ass cheeks to the mattress. She looked up at him and smiled. She saw that his prick was still half erect. She reached out and gave it several strokes then slid it into her mouth. Now it was his turn to gasp as she sucked him dry.

After they dressed, he reached into his wallet, took out a bunch of bills and handed them to her. She counted it and smiled. He'd paid her $250.00!

For something she enjoyed as much as he did.

"I'd give you more but that's all I have on me," he explained. "Jesus! You're fantastic!"

"So are you. What's your name?" she asked.

"Tony. Yours?" he asked.

"Eva," she said as they shook hands. "If you're ever in the area again, give me a call."

She wrote down her cell phone number and gave it to him. He stuffed it into his wallet and grinned.

"You can count on that!" he said.

Eva returned to the casino floor and started playing the slots with her extra cash. After an hour passed, a tall, well-dressed man walked up and handed her a mixed drink. She took and smiled and they spent the next few minutes chatting while he stroked her inner thighs.

"Are you in the business?" he asked.

"Maybe. What do you have in mind?" she asked coyly.

"I have a room at the hotel. We can go there and fuck the shit out of each other," he said.

"Do you have money?" she teased.

"Yes," he assured her,

"Then I have the pussy," she said.

They spent two hours in his room fucking in various positions. He was especially attracted to her firm, round ass so she let him use her back door as much as he liked. His prick was the perfect size for her ass, too. He was thrilled at how tight she was and even more thrilled that she let him fuck her without using rubbers and letting him come inside her.

When they fucked missionary style, she wrapped her arms and legs around his body and fucked him back with everything she had until they were both too exhausted to do anything else. Before she left, he buried his tongue in her cunt and made her come several more times. Eva finished him off with a good blow job.

After she dressed, he handed her three $100 bills. She wrote her cell phone number on a piece of hotel stationery and handed it to him. He smiled and put it into his wallet.

"I've fucked lots of women but I have to say that you're the best. I mean that, too," he said as he escorted her to her car. "I'll call you when I come back to town."

"Do that," Eva said as she kissed him.

"Have you ever considered making this your profession?" he asked.

"Not until now. Why?" she said.

He reached into his wallet and took out a business card. She looked it over. It had a photo of nude woman and website address.

"What's this?" she asked.

"It's an online dating club. Women register for free and the site advertises your services to its registered male clients. The men are pre-screened so you don't get any creeps and they pay well. You could make a lot of money with that pussy of yours and you can fuck as many men as you want any time you want," he explained.

"Will they pay what you paid me?" she asked.

"I think so. They might pay more. Give it a try," he urged.

She thought about the money she just made and how much more she could make. She smiled and put the card into her purse.

They kissed again and said good-bye. She left the suite and wobbled down to her car. Tony had fucked her very well indeed and she even got paid for it.

She laughed as she drove home.

"I'm a prostitute!" she shouted.

While she was doing that, Rinna was in a hotel room at another casino. She was on her hands and knees getting fucked from behind by a man she'd met less than 15 minutes after she entered the place. He was tall, dark haired and had a very long dick which he moved in and out her cunt with a sensual, easy motion that caused his prick to massage her g-spot with every stroke.

He fucked her for a long, long time. When she came, she saw stars and began to quiver all over. She fell onto her elbows to take his prick even deeper. He thrust harder and faster which gave one good orgasm after another.

He was so good, she could barely talk.

"Can I come in your pussy?" he asked.

She nodded and emitted a long, deep moan as she came yet again. Seconds later, she felt him spurt into her. It was good, hard spurt, too. He fucked her faster as he came and came and came. She felt his cum running down her inner thigh and wondered how one man could come so much at one time.

He finally went limp a few good thrusts later and slipped out of her. She rolled over and stroked his cum-coated prick, then slid it into her mouth...

A half hour later, she made her way back to the casino floor. He "lover" had fucked her again. This time, in the missionary position. It was a harder, faster fuck that left her moaning and gasping when she came.

When he was finished, he handed her $300 and said he'd like to see her again. She gave him her card and told him to call her when he was in the area.

She got herself a drink and sat down at the slots. A few minutes later, another man approached her and made her an offer. When she said it wasn't enough, he increased it. She smiled and followed him up to his hotel room...

Chapter Six

The next day, Eva got together with Rinna at her house for another morning of good, hot sex. This time, they ate each other until neither could orgasm anymore.

When Al got home, Rinna said she had fallen in love with Eva.

"It's real, too. I can't keep my hands off her and we seem to be so perfect in bed. Does it bother you that I love a woman?" she asked.

"Not at all. If you're going to fall in love with a woman, Eva's the perfect choice. It's funny. After all this time, we discovered that we both like pussy, especially Eva's pussy," he said.

She laughed.

"I never expected this to happen, but I'm happy it did," she admitted. "I've secretly wanted to get into her panties since we first met but I was too chicken to try anything. I didn't know she felt the same way about me!"

"So me, you, and Vince are all having sex with Eva. You and Eva are fucking Vince and me. It's kind of weird but also kind of fun," he said.

"As long as no one gets hurt," Rinna said.

He nodded.

"And you're both prostitutes because you love the money and the sex. Which do you love more?" he asked.

"I'm not sure. Maybe the sex," she admitted. "It's exciting being fucked by so many different men because each guy does it differently."

"So you plan to keep doing it?" he asked.

"For a while. As long as men want to pay for my pussy, I'll sell it to them," she said.

"If you do, be careful," he cautioned. "There are a lot of creeps out there. And it is illegal."

"Are you planning to fuck other women?" she asked.

"Not right now. Two is more than enough to keep me happy," he said.

"What about later?" she asked.

"We'll see," he hedged.

He actually did have someone in mind, but was unsure how to approach her. She was kind of shy and probably inexperienced but they had become friends. Rinna had met her several times, too. In fact, she had even urged him to have sex with her.

About a week later, Eva was seated at the PC with her pants off rubbing her clit when the doorbell rang. She stopped and called out.

"Who is it?"

"It's me, Al," the man said. "I'm working on my house and I need to borrow Vince's jigsaw. Mine just died."

She decided to have a little fun and to see if her husband's friend was still attracted to her. Without bothering to dress, she went to the door and opened it. He took one look at her cunt and got an immediate erection.

"You like?" she asked.

"Oh Hell yeah," he replied as his bulge expanded.

"I was playing with my pussy when you rang the bell and I didn't feel like dressing," she smiled as he followed her inside.

She wiggled her behind as she walked; knowing that he'd always liked the way she looked in tight jeans. She stopped at the sofa and turned. As she did, she fondled his bulge.

"Since you always liked my pussy, I thought I'd show it to you."

His eyes never left her muff.

She sat down on the sofa and spread her legs wide. Then she reached down and spread open her cunt lips to show him her dark pink walls and swollen clit.

"I've always loved your pussy," he said.

"I hope you are going to do more than just look at it," she said.

Without saying a word, he knelt down in front of her, pulled her toward him and buried his tongue in her cunt.

"No more joking! Take me!" she sighed as his tongue moved up and down her labia.

She shut her eyes and moaned as he ate her. It had been such a long, long time since she'd experienced such excitement. She began to hump his tongue. He moved to her swollen clit and gently sucked it.

"Yes! Oh god, yes!" she cried as she came.

She gripped his head and pulled him into her as she fucked his tongue until she came again and again. While she was still gasping from her orgasms, he took off his jeans. She grabbed his erection and pumped it several times as she watched his foreskin move back and forth over his knob. She smiled up at him and slipped it into her mouth while she massaged his balls. When he was longer and harder, she stopped and lay back with her legs wide apart.

"Oooh yeah!" she moaned as he entered her.

They moved together smoothly, as if they'd been lovers forever. She wrapped her legs around him and stuck her tongue in his mouth. They continued to fuck for a long, long time as she gave herself to him.

Totally and eagerly.

The difference between the way he fucked and the way her husband fucked her fired her libido. Each thrust felt deeper and stronger. She used her inner muscles to squeeze his prick as she fucked him back to show him how much she loved it.

He understood and responded. He thrust harder and harder. Each thrust made her quiver and moan.

"Fuck me! Fuck me! Fuck me!" she moaned as she matched him with equal vigor. "Oh, God! I love it! I am all yours now."

By some miracle, they erupted together. It was one deep and perfect orgasm that rippled through them both at the exact same instant. She felt his sperm jetting into her and milked him as hard as she could. He stayed inside of her for quite some time while she held him tight.

"I've wanted to do this for days," he whispered.

"Me, too. You can have me anytime you want from now on. I am yours. All yours," she said softly. "My pussy belongs to you."

They got up. She led him to the basement workroom so he could find the jigsaw. Neither bothered to dress and he kept his hand on her ass the entire time. By the time they returned to the living room, he was rock hard again. She grabbed his prick, gave it a few strokes and led him to the sofa.

She leaned back and opened her legs then closed her eyes. He moved between her legs and slid his prick into her cunt. She wrapped her arms and legs around him and they fucked. As they did, she savored every thrust of his prick as it pistoned in and out of her hungry cunt.

They fucked twice more that day. Each time, he came inside her cunt. Each time, they came together in one big orgasm. Each time, it was perfect.

She smiled at him and touched his cheek. The look in her eyes was obvious.

"I love you," she whispered. "You don't have to say anything. I just thought I'd tell you how I feel about you."

He pulled her to him for a long, deep kiss.

"I'll see you soon," he said.

He dressed.

She walked him to the door and kissed him while he gently stroked her cunt.

"That's all yours," she repeated. "I am all yours—forever."

As she watched him drive away, she smiled.

"At least he still finds me attractive," she said as she vowed to give herself to him any time he wanted her.

Before she stepped into the shower, she studied her body in the mirror, especially the part between her legs. She smiled at the cum that dripped to the floor.

That Friday the couples were out on the town together. Rinna had had several glasses of wine and was fairly drunk. Somehow or other, the conversation turned risqué. Rinna went to the restroom to clean up a little. Vince said he was going to the men's room. Instead, he followed Rinna to the back of the club.

She smiled when she came out of the restroom. She noticed that he had an obvious bulge in his pants and giggled.

"Is that for me?" she joked.

"It can be if you want it to be," Vince joked back. "All that sex talk made me horny."

"Me too," she said as she playfully squeezed his prick.

To her delight, it grew bigger. She ran her fingers up and down the shaft as it grew and grew.

"I've missed your big, hard dick," she said as she played with him.

"Want to see if it'll fit in your pussy?" he asked as he reached between her legs and stroked her crotch.

"Yes," she said as she opened her stance.

He stroked her harder. She shivered a little as she enjoyed the contact. Vince was amazed she was letting him do this and letting him know she was willing to go further. That's when they saw someone else coming. Rinna stopped and winked at Vince. He just grinned because he now knew that he had a real good shot at her.

They left the club a couple of hours later. Both Rinna and Eva had a case of the giggles by then and just about everything made them think of something dirty or sexual and caused them to laugh.

Al invited Eva and Vince in for some coffee. Rinna went to the kitchen to make it. A couple of seconds later, Vince left to go to the bathroom. He spotted Rinna in the kitchen. He walked up behind her and fondled her behind. She smiled and wiggled it against him. This gave Vince an immediate erection.

Rinna turned.

Their faces were only inches apart. She smiled and grabbed his prick.

"Yes," she whispered.

"Yes what?" he asked as he fondled her crotch.

"Yes I want to see if your dick will fit inside my pussy," she replied.

In the living room, Al and Eva were locked in a very torrid kiss. There was no doubt what Eva wanted or how horny she was. As soon as Vince followed Rinna into the kitchen, she sat next to Al, unzipped his jeans and started stroking his prick. When he was nice and hard, she leaned over and slid it into her mouth. Al came seconds later. As he flooded Eva's mouth with cum, she hungrily swallowed every bit of it.

Rinna unzipped Vince's jeans and pulled out his prick. She stroked it until it became good and hard while he moved his finger in and out of her already wet cunt. Vince moved closer and they kissed. It was a deep, hot kiss that made Rinna stroke his prick faster. He pushed aside her panties and eased it up into her cunt. Rinna gasped and put her arms around his neck as he began to fuck her.

She sucked his tongue harder as she moved with him. They were both so horny that they came less than three minutes later. Rinna held on and kept fucking back until she felt his cum running down her inner thigh.

She smiled at him and sighed as she slowly came down to Earth. His prick was still inside her cunt and she used her inner muscles to squeeze it while he fondled her ass. It had been another perfect fuck.

Both Rinna and Vince heard the sound Al made as he came. They stopped what they were doing, laughed and carried the coffee into the living room just in time to see Eva cleaning her lips with a napkin.

She blushed when she saw them.

Nothing else happened that night. They finished their coffee then Vince and Eva left for home. Along the way, Eva asked Vince when he planned to fuck Rinna again.

He laughed.

"Soon I hope," he said. "That's really up to her. Doesn't that bother you?"

"Not at all," she said. "Want to know why?"

"Not really. As long as it doesn't bother you, I guess I can go for her, huh?" he said.

"Knock yourself out, lover!" Eva said with an almost cat-like grin.

Vince did a few days later.

He went to the house to see if Al wanted to go to the ballgame with him. Rinna answered the door. She was in the middle of housecleaning and had on her jogging shorts and a T-shirt and nothing else. Vince took one look at her and got an immediate erection.

And it was noticeable.

Rinna stood and stared at his crotch as the bulge grew and grew. Vince kind of blushed and half apologized. Rinna laughed and invited him in.

"I'm sorry, Vince. But Al had to work overtime. He's not here now," she said.

"But you are and that's even better," Vince said.

"Would you like something to drink?" she asked as they went into the kitchen.

"Okay," he said.

She opened the fridge and frowned.

"All I have is a bottle of white wine," she said.

"That's fine," he said.

She poured them each a glass and leaned against the sink while they talked. She realized that Vince kept staring at her legs and crotch. She began to feel a little bit edgy, but in a nice kind of way. They kept talking and had another glass of wine. Vice could see she was getting a bit tipsy. He also knew from past experiences that she became a little horny when she got drunk. He decided to gamble. He put down the glass and walked up to her. They stood just inches apart now, their eyes locked on each other. Rinna felt her heart beat faster and faster and wondered what Vince would do.

"I think you're the most beautiful woman on Earth, Rinna," he said softly as he touched her cheek. "And there's something that I've always wanted to do to you."

"And what do you have in mind?" she asked with a nervous smile

He reached up, put his hands on her shoulders, and kissed her. Caught by surprise, Rinna let him continue. Before she knew it, their tongues had merged and he was holding her even closer. So close that she felt his erection press against her crotch.

That's when her libido took over.

Before realizing it, she began rubbing her cunt against his prick. Surprised, Vince grabbed her behind and squeezed it as he moved with her. There was nothing covering Rinna's cunt but a thin layer of cloth, so each movement sent delicious tingles all through her body. She humped him faster and faster. Vince slid both hands down into her shorts and fondled her crack. Rinna moaned and sucked his tongue harder as she humped away.

"I've got to have you, Rinna," Vince said as he slid his hand down into her shorts and raked his fingers over her quivering, wet cunt.

She let out a low moan as he teased her clit. She moaned louder when he slid a finger into her cunt and wriggled it around. God, she was so incredibly horny. That's when she felt Vince move her shorts downward.

He backed off and unzipped his jeans. Rinna smiled as he pulled out his prick. She reached down and wrapped her fingers around it. It was long and hard and warm. She gave it a few easy pumps while he managed to pull her shorts down to her knees. She let them fall to her ankles and kicked them off.

He ran his fingers over her cunt hairs as she played with his prick. He was finally going to fuck his fantasy woman. She stepped close and guided his prick to her cunt. He gasped as the head pushed past her labia and entered her. They moved toward each other and Rinna sighed as his prick filled her. It was spontaneous and far more erotic and exciting than she hoped it would be.

He gripped her ass and started moving in and out of her nice and easy. She held onto his shoulders and savored the way his prick massaged her inner walls. It felt wonderful.

Full and thick and hard.

"Yes!" she sighed as he thrust harder.

"You feel so tight! So perfect," he whispered as they fucked faster.

She moved with him and emitted gasps and moans as they thrust harder and harder. His prick massaged her g-spot with every inward move and caused her to quiver with pleasure. Before she realized it, she was fucking back like mad as her orgasm suddenly erupted and raced through her entire body.

"Yes! Yes! Yes! Yes! Yes!" she cried as she came and came.

She felt his warm cum spurting into her as he came, too. It flooded her cunt and ran down her inner leg as they kept fucking and fucking until each was totally spent. She let him go and sighed as she looked at his half-hard prick that now glistened with their combined juices. Her cunt still throbbed deliciously as it slow oozed a stream of white down her leg.

"That was wonderful," she said after a few seconds.

That's when they heard the front doorbell ring. They tried to ignore it but it rang again and again. Rinna slid her shorts back on and went to the front door. She opened and smiled as Al walked in.

"I forgot my keys," he said as he studied the obviously flushed look on her cheeks.

"I thought you had to work late," she said.

"They realized they had enough people so I came home," Al said as Vince walked in.

"You're just in time to go to the game with me. I have two free tickets," Vince said. "The game starts in an hour."

"Let's go," Al said. "I'll see you later, Rinna. Wait up for me."

She laughed.

Then she looked at the shiny streak on her inner thigh and wondered if Al had noticed it. She figured that he knew she was fucking Vince. He had to know, just as she knew he'd fucked Eva. He had said it was okay with him.

When Al returned, Rinna was waiting for him on the sofa. He sat next to her and gave her a hug. She smiled.

They both laughed.

"I saw the streak on your thigh this afternoon and the flushed look on your faces. It was easy to see that you'd been fucking the Hell out of each other just before I got home," he said.

"We did," she replied honestly.

"How is he?" he asked.

"Good. Real good. How's Eva?" she replied.

"Real good," he said.

Rinna giggled as they raced up to the bedroom.

Vince had already made up his mind. He was going after Rinna. It was impossible to hide his attraction for Rinna. After all, he got an erection whenever he saw her in shorts. He'd always loved her legs and she had a very cute ass to go with them. And he really loved what was between those legs, too.

Now that he's seen and put his prick into it, it was all he could think about. Rinna was the hottest, sexiest woman he knew and he was thrilled that she was willing to have sex with him.

He looked at Eva.

Since she had started working out, she was looking sexier and sexier, too, but he was more interested in having sex with Rinna. He knew that Al was certainly attracted to her. That was more than obvious. She was also attracted to him. And they'd had sex a few times.

That didn't matter to him. He wanted Rinna.

His next move was when they were standing in line waiting to get into a show at the nearby arena a few days later. It was packed and Rinna was right in front of him. He took a chance and fondled her behind. She glanced back at him and giggled. So he tried it again. This time, he ran his fingers along her crack. He moved up first then slowly back down to where he could gently massage her crotch. Rinna responded by reaching behind her and grabbing his crotch to show him she liked what he was doing and was willing to fuck him.

"When?" he whispered.

"I don't know. We'll have to see," she replied as she played with the tip.

She also noticed that Eva had her hand on Al's crotch. She was obviously squeezing his prick and he was fondling her ass. She smiled.

Eva turned and winked at her. The wink told Rinna all she needed to know.

When they got inside, they sat so that Rinna ended up next to Vince and Eva was next to Al. As soon as the lights went down, Rinna felt a hand on her thigh. She parted her legs and let Vince fondle her cunt through her panties while she played with his prick. How she wanted to fuck him! She wanted to feel that prick of his inside her pussy again.

Eva was seated next to her and breathing heavy as Al's fingers danced over her cunt while she jerked him off. It was almost obvious what they were doing but Eva was at the point where she had virtually no shame.

Rinna smiled.

They had managed to swap mates in the arena. It was done deliberately, as if everyone had agreed to it without having to say anything. They kept at this for nearly the entire performance. Vince had even managed to make Rinna come a couple of times and she had unzipped his jeans, pulled out his prick, and quietly jerked him off until he spurted a line of cum all over the back of the seat in front of him.

When Eva sensed that Al was about to come, she leaned over and slid his prick into her mouth. Rinna didn't notice as she was too busy enjoying what Vince was doing and jerking him off. By the time they left the arena, they were all sexually satisfied.

Rinna wondered if they had anything else planned for the evening as she was still horny. But nothing else happened that night and their lives returned to normal for a few days. Rinna knew that Vince wouldn't give up and she didn't want him to. The idea of fucking him excited her to no end. Just thinking about their almost fuck always made her horny. And when she was horny, she just about fucked Al half to death.

And that night, she was hornier than usual...

Chapter Seven

That Saturday, Eva and Rinna went to the casino. While Rinna played the slots and sipped her rum and coke, a handsome young man sat down at the machine next to hers. He smiled at her. She smiled back and they started talking.

"Do you remember me? We met a few weeks ago," he said.

She studied his features and smiled. She'd let him feel her cunt. He'd even made her come a few times and she had come very close to fucking him.

"Oh, I remember you," she said. "You almost made me forget I'm married."

"When I saw you tonight, I thought I'd come by to say hello. You look even sexier than you did that night," he said as he put a hand on her knee.

"Thanks," she said as she continued playing.

They chatted as she played. The chat was pleasant and sort of funny. In fact, they made each other laugh quite a bit. As time passed, he got her another drink. Then he invited her to have dinner with him. She decided she liked him enough to do that and they went to a small bistro inside the casino. The place was romantically lit.

They ordered six small plates and shared as they talked more and drank. Rinna was feeling relaxed and dreamy. And he was certainly very interested in her. Before much time passed, she felt him put his hand on her thigh. She looked at him and smiled.

His hand moved upward and under the leg of her shorts to her panties. Almost automatically, Rinna parted her thighs to invite him to play with her pussy. She really liked this guy. Maybe too much. She shivered slightly as he ran his fingertips up and down her slit through her panties. She parted her legs even more now to show him that she liked it. He smiled at her and slid his fingers past her panties and into her now very moist cunt.

"You like this?" he whispered.

"Oh yes," she said as she trembled.

He eased two fingers deep into her cunt and massaged her g-spot. Rinna almost bit through her lip to keep from screaming as delicious sensations rippled through her body. That's when she looked down and saw that he'd freed his erect prick from his pants. Caught up in the throes of passion, she reached down and started beating him off. The more she played with him, the more she realized that she wanted to fuck him.

"Yes I like what you're doing," she said.

"Want to do more?" he asked as he rubbed her spot harder.

That's when she came. It was a good, powerful orgasm that nearly blinded her. As she suppressed her screams, she kept jerking him off faster and faster until he spurted lines of cum all over the underside of the table.

He zipped up his pants and stood up with his hand extended. She took it and followed him out of the bistro and over to the elevator. Before the fog cleared from her brain, she was on her back in a king sized bed and he was pulling off her shorts and panties. She watched as he undressed and climbed in with her. She briefly shut her eyes to make the room stop spinning. That's when she felt his tongue moving all over her cunt.

"Yes! Yes!" she moaned.

Her libido was now in overdrive. She rocked from side to side as she begged him to keep eating her. Minutes later, he made her come again. She screamed as she erupted and humped his tongue.

"Fuck me!" she yelled. "I need to feel your dick inside me! Fuck me!"

He moved between her legs and rammed his prick home. She wrapped her arms and legs around him and screamed as he fucked her with a nice, hard rhythm. She soon moved with him. As they fucked, she realized that she had finally crossed the line. She was having an extramarital fuck with a man she'd met only a few hours ago.

And she loved it.

His prick was straight and hard and thick. It deliciously massaged every part of her cunt as he fucked her. She dug her fingers into his back and thrust her hips up to take all of it inside her with each stroke. And it felt so damned good!

"Fuck me harder! I want to feel it!" she moaned.

He moved faster and faster. She matched his strokes and used her inner muscles to squeeze his prick. The sudden change caused him to quiver, ram his dick into her harder and come. When Rinna felt his cum splash against the walls of her cunt, she came, too.

"Oooh yeas! Gimme your dick! I love it! Fuck me!" she cried as her orgasm tore through her body.

They kept going until he finally went flaccid and popped out of her. Rinna looked down at her cunt and watched as a line of snow white cum ran out of her pulsing cunt.

She reached over and gave his prick several easy pumps. To her delight, it quickly became hard again. She smiled at him.

"Ready?" she asked.

"Oh Hell yeah!" he said.

They finished undressing each other and fucked a second time. This one lasted longer and he did it softer and gentler. Rinna decided that she liked the feel of a strange dick moving inside her cunt much more than she thought she would. She liked the way he fucked, too. It was nice and pleasant. Almost like Al. They both came again about 20 minutes later. This was so strong, it left both of them drained and bathed with sweat.

He smiled at her.

"What's your name?" he asked.

"Rinna," she replied. "What's yours?"

"Mitch," he said as they shook hands and laughed. "Are you married?"

"Not tonight," she joked.

He laughed.

"I like the way you think!" he said as he slid his prick into her.

They started in the missionary position as Mitch slow fucked her for a long time. They switched around so that Rinna was on top and she slowly bounced up and down on his prick while he played with her nipples. They kept at this until Rinna came and fell to the side. While she was still moaning and writhing, he flipped her onto her belly and fucked her from behind until he emptied his cum deep into her cunt again.

She smiled at him.

"I'm sorry I didn't do this with you the first time," she said.

"Better late than never," he said as they deep kissed.

As they dressed, Mitch admired her flawless body.

"Would you like to make this a regular thing?" he asked as he handed her $200.

"How regular?" she asked as she put the money into her purse.

"I get into town every couple of months on business. I could call you when I return and we can get together. If you like," he said.

"I like," she said as she gave him her cell phone number. "Try to call me the day before so we can set things up."

"You have got yourself a date!" he said as they kissed again.

When Eva saw them in the lobby ten minutes later, she was surprised to see them kiss. It was a deep, French kiss, too. She waited until the guy left then walked up to Rinna. She looked obviously flushed. Like she always did after having sex.

Eva smirked.

"Did you two have sex tonight?" she asked.

"Oh yes! Mitch fucked the Hell out of me—three times!" Rinna admitted. "Damn, he was good, too. I didn't think he'd get it up so many times, either. I'm really tired now and my pussy's filled with cum—a lot of it. How did you do?"

"I didn't have any luck at all tonight," Eva said. "I wish I'd had met that guy you were with. I could use a real good fuck!"

"Maybe you'll have better luck next time," Rinna said.

The next night, the couples went out on the town. They had dinner at a local restaurant and they'd all had several drinks. As usual, Eva was hanging onto Al and openly flirting with him. Rinna didn't seem to notice or mind and Al sure as Hell didn't.

Everyone knew where this was going when they returned to Al's house. Rinna went to the kitchen to get a bottle of wine from the fridge. Vince followed. He saw her bent over at the fridge as she looked for the wine and walked over and fondled her behind. She remained still and just let him fondle her. When he slid his hand between her legs, she stood up. She opened her stance and allowed him to keep doing it for a while.

She liked Vince and if he wanted to touch her ass or pussy, that was okay with her. Especially since she was feeling the effects of the alcohol at the time. She also knew that Eva was probably groping Al's prick and he most likely was playing with her pussy. So why not let Vince have some fun?

She turned and smiled at Vince. Then she put her arms around his shoulders and stuck her tongue into his mouth. The kiss caught him by surprise. It was totally unexpected and incredibly erotic. As he kissed her back, he reached down and unbuttoned her jeans. When she didn't object, he slid his hand down into her panties and gently played with her clit.

She kept sucking his tongue passionately. He stroked her clit faster and faster. She got very moist and very warm. Vince was only the fourth man to touch her like this and she was showing him that she really liked what he was doing.

A lot!

A sound coming from the living room caused them to stop. Rinna buttoned up her jeans and smiled at Vince. Then she squeezed his prick.

When they entered the living room, Eva was busy adjusting her jeans and blouse. She looked at Rinna and smiled. Rinna giggled.

They sat and chatted for another hour and the wine flowed freely. The entire time, Rinna noticed that Vince was ogling her legs so she made sure he got a good look up her shorts. She picked up the empty wine bottle and winked at Vince then went to the kitchen. Vince followed.

As soon as they were out of sight, Eva stuck her tongue in Al's mouth and grabbed his crotch.

She unzipped his jeans and pulled out his erection. Al undid her shorts and pulled them off. She smiled and leaned back with her legs wide apart. Al moved between them and slid his prick into her hot, moist cunt and they proceeded to fuck like crazy.

Once they reached the kitchen, Rinna and Vince became locked in an increasing torrid embrace. Rinna was so horny at this point that she just leaned against the table and smiled as Vice pulled her shorts down and off. While he was kneeling between her legs, he reached up, gripped her ass and pulled her toward him. Rinna sighed as she felt his tongue dance over her labia. She sighed louder as he sucked her clit. She came in less than a minute.

Vince stood and freed his erection from his jeans. Rinna grabbed it, gave it several pulls and eased her ass onto the table. She opened her thighs wide and gripped his shoulders as he slid his prick into her cunt.

It felt nice.

Exciting.

She closed her eyes and moaned as he moved in and out. His was just the third prick to enter her and the idea that she was fucking him made her heart race. She moaned as it slid all the way in, then out, then in again.

Vince was thrilled. He was again fucking Rinna, the hottest and sexiest woman he knew and her pussy felt just as warm and tight as always. They fucked and fucked for several minutes. Rinna came first and moaned loudly. Vince fucked her faster and faster. She moved with him and kept coming harder and harder. Then she felt his cum jetting into her cunt.

"Oooh yes! Yes!" she cried.

Neither Al nor Eva heard her.

Both were caught up in their waves of orgasmic bliss and still fucking like crazy on the sofa. They finished a few moments later and were straightening up just as Rinna and Vince returned to the living room.

Rinna and Eva smiled at each other.

"Now it's official," Eva said. "We are all cheating."

The men looked at each other and laughed.

When Eva and Vince left, Rinna sat next to Al on the sofa and touched his hand. He held it tightly and smiled.

"This is fun," she said.

"Yes it is," he agreed as he hugged her.

"What do we call it?" she asked.

"Wife swapping?" he suggested."

She laughed.

"That kind of sounds funny. Should we keep doing it?" she asked.

He shrugged.

"Do you want to?" he asked.

"Maybe. It's kind of fun and exciting to have sex with another man. The only man I'd ever had sex with in my life was you and I really love it. But this is different so I think I'd like to do it again," she said. "And I want to keep fucking other men."

"Don't get too carried away with this. We need to remember that you and I are married to each other and shouldn't do anything to ruin that," he said.

"I think we can do that," she smiled.

That weekend, the women decided to book a single suite at a nearby hotel for Friday night. When they told the men about it, Al wanted to know why they only booked one suite.

"It only has one king-sized bed, too," Eva smiled.

"Why only one?" asked Vince.

"You'll see," they both said.

When they arrived at the hotel, Rinna told Al and Vince to wait ten minutes before coming up to the suite, so they could prepare their surprise for them. The men agreed as they realized that their wives had something very special in mind that night.

When they entered the suite, Rinna called out for them to come into the bedroom. They did and stopped in their tracks when they saw both women lying on the bed stark naked with their legs apart.

"You can fuck both of us as many times as you like," Rinna said.

"And in any hole you want," Eva added.

Al and Vince quickly disrobed while their wives stroked their pussies. To Al's surprise, Vince got onto the bed first and slid his prick into Rinna's cunt. She wrapped her arms around him and bent her knees. As he watched his friend's prick move in and out of Rinna's willing pussy, Al's own prick got longer and harder than he ever though it could. He got into bed and rammed it deep into Eva's cunt.

"Yes!" she screamed as she clung to him.

The four of them fucked and fucked like crazy. Rinna moaned and obviously came. As she did, she fucked Vince harder. He grunted and filled her cunt with his cum. Rinna moaned and begged him to keep fucking.

Al only half noticed.

At that moment, he and Eva erupted simultaneously. They gripped each other and kept fucking and fucking. Vince was surprised to hear his wife scream.

"I love you, Al! I love you!"

Almost immediately, both men pulled out. Eva grinned at her husband as he moved between her legs and sunk his prick into her cum-filled cunt. He never once imagined that he'd get sloppy seconds from his own wife, but for some reason, he just couldn't resist fucking her while she was filled with another man's cum.

"Ooh yeah!" he sighed as he felt the sticky pool engulf his shaft as it moved in and out.

The warm liquid heightened the sensations and made his prick grow harder than ever. He leaned into her and fucked her with long, deep strokes to make sure cum coated every inch of his prick. The squishing sensations Eva now felt as Vince's prick pounded her made her quiver all over. She realized that he actually liked fucking her this way. He liked the feel of Al's cum around his prick.

Meanwhile, Al had sunk his prick into Rinna's cunt and was experiencing a similar sensation. He had to admit that it felt strangely erotic and, to his delight, his prick grew fully erect again after a couple of thrusts.

Rinna also enjoyed it. She clung to Al and matched him thrust for thrust as they fucked. It was weird. It was exciting. It was sensuous.

Vince fucked Eva as fast as he could now. He was on the verge of coming and she was already in the beginning throes of her orgasm. She shivered beneath him with each hard thrust and threw her hips up at him each time to take him even deeper.

He'd never seen his wife like this. She was a total slut now. A living, breathing sex machine that kept begging him to fuck her harder.

Eva gasped and moaned now.

"Fuck me, Vince! Fuck me good. Fuck me!" she said as she came.

It was a good, bone shaking come, too. She gripped his arms and screamed as she arched her back. Vince hammered away at her until he finally added his own cum to the load that was inside her.

"Oh my God!" Eva sighed as she felt him spurt inside of her.

He laid on top her; his prick buried in her cunt, and enjoyed the feeling of his cum mingling with Al's and coating his prick.

Rinna and Al were now writhing in an orgasm. Eva watched as cum squirted from Rinna's cunt with each hard thrust of Al's prick. The sight of her moving in unison with Al made her feel even hornier. Vince, too. As he watched them fuck, his prick began to rise.

That's when Eva reached over and grabbed Vince's prick and slid it into her mouth. Vince gasped as Eva sucked him off and she obviously reveled in the combined taste of his and Al's cum that now coated his prick.

"No one," he thought, "can suck a dick like Eva!"

She swirled her tongue up and down his shaft and around his knob several times, then proceeded to suck away as she slowly jerked him off. Vince moaned as she fondled his balls and let his load fly. He grunted and shook as he came. This time, he fired his load into Eva's hungry mouth and she gladly swallowed every drop.

While she did this, he looked at the pool of white goo inside her cunt. Caught up in the moment, he turned around and buried his tongue in her. The cum tasted sort of sweet and a tad salty. As Eva continued to suck his prick, Vince went down on her. He was now turned on beyond belief and tried to lap up every bit of cum his tongue could reach while he fingered her asshole. Eva came and came and came but kept sucking his prick until it finally grew limp and slipped from her mouth. Vince stopped and lay next to her. Both were breathing very hard.

That's when Al and Rinna came. Rinna cried out as she erupted and Al just about double over as he filled her cunt to overflowing with his cum. There was so much of it that ran out of her cunt and oozed between her ass cheeks to the mattress. They kept fucking and fucking until they were exhausted.

They rested for a while and joked about their experiences. Eva teased Vince about the way he seemed to love the taste of cum.

"If you like it that much, maybe you should suck Al's dick," she joked.

"You try it and you'll be sorry!" Al joked.

"Don't worry! I don't swing that way and you know it!" Vince assured him.

That's when Rinna decided to take advantage of Vince's half-erection. She reached over and grabbed Vince's prick. After she gave it several pulls, he was nice and hard again. Rinna got onto her hands and knees and smiled.

"You know where to put that!" she said.

He did, too.

He was more than happy to fuck her good, tight pussy again. He went in balls deep, savored the feel of her cunt for a few moments, and then fucked her. Rinna moaned happily and dropped to her elbows so she could take him in even deeper. They settled into a good, long and intense fuck.

Meanwhile, Eva sucked Al's dick until he was fully erect again. Then she got into the same position as Rinna.

"Ass or pussy?" Al asked.

"You choose!" she said.

She gritted her teeth as he eased his prick into her asshole for what proved to be another, very long and exhilarating fuck. He ass was perfect and oh-so tight. He gripped her cheeks and fucked her nice and steady.

"Use me, Al! I'm yours! Fuck me! I love you!" Eva cried as she enjoyed the feel of his hard prick moving in and out of her ass.

They continued along these lines for the entire night. By check-out time, none of them could move. Rinna said her pussy was sore—but in a nice way. Eva said both her pussy and ass felt happy.

The men just looked at each other and laughed.

"Did we just have an orgy?" Eva asked as they dressed.

"Oh yeah," Al said. "And it was terrific!"

"Yes it was," Rinna agreed. "You both know how to use your dicks and tongues. We have to do this again soon."

"But not too soon," Al said. "I'm wiped out."

After they got home, Al and Rinna plopped down on the sofa to rest. She smiled at him.

"That was a lot of fun," she said. "I kind of like swapping."

"So do I. What made you and Eva decides on this?" he asked.

"I'm not sure. It just seemed like a great idea," she said.

"It sure as Hell was. You know, it felt really weird and sort of erotic to fuck you right after Vince did," he said. "And he sure seemed to enjoy fucking Eva after I came in her pussy, too. How did it feel to you?" he asked.

"Strange," she said. "Nice but strange. What was really strange was watching Vince eat Eva after you both had come in her pussy. He really seemed to enjoy that!"

Al nodded as he wondered what was up with that.

Vince wondered the same thing. For some reason, he felt compelled to eat Eva after he saw the pool of cum in her cunt. Maybe it was the way she had sucked his prick or the way it felt to fuck her immediately after Al had come inside of her. He wasn't sure what it was, but he did enjoy it.

Maybe too much.

Eva was surprised at him, too. He had done things that were very much out of character for him. She didn't care because she got to fuck Al most of the night. She also realized that several times during her orgasms, she had shouted out that she loved Al. She knew Vince heard it, but so far, he hadn't mentioned it.

Two days later, Eva and Rinna went to the casino together. As usual, they went their separate ways once they walked onto the casino floor. As Eva played her favorite slot, she became aware of a young, handsome man watching her. She turned and smiled at him. He returned it and walked over to chat.

After a few more minutes, Eva found herself in a small, dark room off the casino floor. She was leaning forward on a table with her jeans off, sighing and moaning as his massive, hard prick plowed her cunt from behind.

It proved to be a good, hard and long fuck. Eva came after a few minutes and shook all over. Her lover proved to have great stamina. He gripped her hips and kept fucking and fucking. Eva came again and again as she begged him to fuck her harder. When he finally came, he emptied so much cum into her cunt that gobs of it dripped onto the carpet.

They stayed still until they recovered. As Eva pulled her jeans back on, he handed her $150 and said she was the best piece of ass he'd ever had. Eva thanked him for the cash, stuffed it into her pocket and returned to the casino.

Rinna also had good luck that day.

She met a good-looking older man who bought her lunch. Afterward, she agreed to go up to his suite with him. Once there, they stripped and proceeded to have sex.

A lot of it.

He proved to be nearly tireless. In fact, he fucked her in three different positions after eating her pussy. He was good, too. So good, that Rinna lost count of how many times he made her come. And each time, he pumped what felt like a quart of cum into her cunt. When it was over, they dressed and he insisted on paying her. After some hesitation, she agreed to accept his money, even though she realized that would make her an actual prostitute. The man gave her $300 and said he'd love to see her again.

When she met up with Eva an hour later, both women looked so tired that they each knew what they'd been up to.

"How much?" Eva asked.

Rinna showed her the three $100 bills.

"He fucked me three times. Hard, too. So he must have figured I was worth it. How much did you get?" she asked.

"Half that, but it was all he had in his wallet," Eva said.

"You want to keep trying tonight?" Rinna asked.

"Oh yes," Eva smiled.

They returned to their spot and pretended to play. After another 20 minutes, a handsome younger man struck up a conversation with Eva. As they talked, she let him stroke her inner thighs while she watched the bulge rise in his pants. Ten minutes later, she was lying on his bed in his hotel room and he was slowly undressing her.

Rinna also scored again.

This guy just about bent her double and fucked her in her ass. She was glad his prick was normal sized and she didn't mind doing it this way. He used her rear channel twice and each time, she let him come inside of her. By the time she left his room, she could hardly walk straight but he did pay her $400. It was the most she'd made from a single client. A half hour later, she had her third client.

This was a nice, slow and easy fuck and he even made her come. She felt so good afterward that she handed him her cell phone number.

"The next one is free, Harry," she said with a smile. "I like the way you fuck. It's like you were making love to me."

"I was," Harry said as he paid her. "I really was."

At this time, Eva was also servicing her third client. They started out with a nice, long "69" and ended with an equally nice, deep fuck that left Eva moaning for more. She chatted with him, exchanged numbers and dressed. He handed her $250.

"I'll call you next week," he said.

"Do that, Vic," she smiled.

They got home after four a.m.

Rinna woke Al when she walked into the bedroom. She sat on the bed and smiled tiredly.

"I've reached my limit for a while," she said.

"Saturday is New Year's Eve. We'll be going out on the town with Vince and Eva. You ladies have anything special in mind?" he asked.

"Maybe," she smiled.

When New Year's Eve rolled around things suddenly grew wilder.

They were at a party at a local hotel. The package included two suites, food and drinks and the usual crazy stuff that went along with a party. The four of them had been drinking heavily. Al was dancing with Eva and he was dancing with Rinna. The floor was dark and they were dancing close.

Real close.

Rinna noticed something hard pressing against her crotch.

"Is that what I think it is?" she asked playfully.

"It is. I can't help it. I got hard dancing with you," he apologized.

"That's okay. I don't mind," she smiled as she moved even closer.

He pulled her against his body so that his erection rested against her cunt. She smiled and began to move to the beat of the music by thrusting her hips back and forth. He realized that she was purposely rubbing against his prick, so he pulled her closer and moved with her. He felt Rinna's heart beat faster and faster with each thrust and realized she was horny.

Very horny.

"That feels nice," she whispered.

"Want me to keep going?" he asked.

She nodded and humped him faster. God, she was horny that night. He gripped her behind and pulled her tight against his body. She responded by grinding her cunt against his prick while he humped her.

"I'd love to fuck you," he whispered.

"I know. I want to fuck you, too," she said as they humped harder. "God, this feels so good."

Vince was driving her crazy. She always knew that he wanted to get into her panties and at that moment, she was willing to give herself to him again.

They humped faster and faster.

"Let's fuck," she whispered as she neared her climax.

Vince led her to a very dark corner of the ballroom. Rinna undid her shorts and tugged them down. Vince pulled out his very erect prick and pulled her toward him. She grabbed his prick and guided it into her open cunt then sighed when he plunged it in. They fucked for about a minute before Rinna felt Vince's cum spurt into her cunt. It was just long enough for her to have an orgasm, too.

The music ended and the lights came back on and everyone returned to their table. That's also when he noticed a flushed look on Eva's face and wondered if she and Al had been doing something similar.

Eva winked at her.

Rinna blushed.

"I have an idea on how to make this the perfect celebration," Eva said.

"We're way ahead of you," Al said as he stroked her thigh under the table. "After midnight, we'll swap and spend the rest of the night fucking like crazy."

Rinna beamed.

"That means you get to do whatever you like with me, Vince. I'm very horny tonight. I hope you can keep it up," she said.

It was then that he realized that Rinna had a somewhat slutty side which emerged after she'd had a few drinks. He decided to try and exploit it, too.

Later, as Al and Eva danced very close, she watched Rinna hump Vince.

"Take a look at our spouses over there," she said.

Al did and laughed.

"You don't seem surprised," Eva said.

"I'm not. Rinna gets horny when she drinks too much. From the way Vice is smiling, I'm sure he doesn't mind what she's doing one bit," he said.

"Do you think they'll end up fucking each other again?" Eva asked.

"Probably, he said as he squeezed her ass.

"I'm glad that I wore a loose, short skirt tonight," Eva said. "That way, we can fuck right now and no one would notice."

The dance floor was pitch dark, save for the annoying strobes. Al raised the front of Eva's skirt and ran his hand over her bare muff like he did earlier. It was still sticky with his earlier deposit of cum. This made it easier on him as he pulled out his prick and eased it into her. She moved her hips back and forth to the rhythm of the music as they fucked. His prick felt wonderful, too.

"This is just the beginning," she whispered. "I'm going to fuck you silly tonight."

Vince and Rinna had gone back to their dark corner. This time, Rinna leaned with her hands on the wall while Vince fucked her from behind. His prick felt even bigger as he used her this way and she moaned softly with each good, deep thrust.

"I'm your slut tonight, Vince! Use me however you like," she moaned.

When the music ended, they wobbled back to their table. To Al and Vince's surprise, Eva leaned over and locked Rinna into what appeared to be a long and passionate kiss. Caught by surprise, Rinna let herself respond. They kissed for a long time, too.

When they stopped, the men laughed at Rinna's expression.

"You two have something going?" Al asked.

"Not yet—but maybe soon," Eva smiled.

Rinna blushed.

At midnight, they had the traditional champagne toast. When it was over, they couples decided to head up to their suites.

Within seconds, Rinna and Vince were totally nude and locked into a torrid embrace on the king sized bed. After several minutes of good foreplay, Rinna opened her legs wide. Vince got between her thighs and plunged his prick into her. She moaned loudly and wrapped her arms and legs around him for what proved to be a very good and very long fuck.

There were no worries or restrictions now. It was just the two of them in a beautiful hotel suite, naked and fucking.

Vince could hardly believe his luck.

Rinna was now his for the entire night. Her flawless, smooth sexy body and hot tight cunt were all his to enjoy. He loved the way she moved with him and how she threw her hips up at him each and thrust. Rinna didn't hold back. When she fucked, she really got into it. She was his perfect sex machine.

Rinna loved the way Vince's prick filled her cunt and the way he used it. His thrusts were deep and strong and his prick massaged every part of her cunt.

They fucked and fucked and fucked. At long last, Rinna came. It was good, deep orgasm that shook her entire body. As soon as she came, Vince did, too. He grunted and fucked harder as he added yet another load to the pool of cum that was already in Rinna's cunt.

Al and Eva spent several wonderful minutes giving each other oral sex. After he made her come at least twice, Al stuck a pillow under Eva's hips. He draped her legs over his arms and proceeded to fuck her nice and easy. Eva was delighted with the intensity of his strokes in this position. She sighed and moaned with each thrust and begged him to keep going. This was, by far, the best sex they'd ever had with each other and the fact that they could do this all night and for as many times as they wanted, made it all the more special.

For the rest of the night, she was Al's wife. She liked the sound of that, too. Maybe too much. She was surprised that everyone went along with this idea. Each of them was living out their fantasies for one whole night.

After a long, good fuck, she and Al came at the same instant. She gripped his arms and fucked him back as hard as she could while he flooded her cunt with cum—again.

As she came, she felt herself sailing above the clouds.

"I love you, Al!" she cried. "Oh, God how I love you!"

The next morning, they met in the restaurant for a late breakfast. Rinna noticed that Eva seemed to be glowing all over. She had obviously loved spending the night with Al. Rinna wondered if Eva loved it a little too much. The way she kept looking at him and smiled spoke volumes as to how she felt, too.

"Should I worry?" she teased.

"Maybe," Eva teased back. "How many times did you do it?"

"At least five. We never did sleep," Rinna beamed. How about you?"

"I lost count," Eva bragged. "Wow. What a night! We have to do this again soon."

Al laughed.

"That's fine with me," he said.

"Me, too," Vince said. "That was the best night I ever had. Thanks to Rinna."

Eva scowled.

"The best?" she asked.

"Well, next to our wedding night and honeymoon," Vince replied.

They laughed and ate and laughed some more. When they got back home, Al pulled Rinna to him and gave her a long, deep kiss. She held him tight and smiled.

"Is she as good as me?" she asked.

"No one is that good," he assured her.

"I'm glad you said that. I was starting to worry. I think Eva's in love with you," she said.

"You don't need to worry. I'm not in love with her. I just like having sex with her once in a while," he said.

"Good. What shall we do today?" she asked.

"How about we rest for a few hours then go out to eat?" he suggested.

She nodded.

For the rest of the winter, things quieted down. It was one of those winters where the area was hit by one snow storm or ice storm after another, making roads and streets too dangerous for travel. Because of this, the four friends rarely saw each other.

Al and Rinna spent most of their time together and Vince ignored Eva more and more, which made her more miserable and frustrated. She wanted to have more sex with Al, but Rinna kept running interference. Rinna also kept Al so busy that she didn't even think about Vince.

In short, things had gone back to normal.

The girls didn't even make it to a casino for an entire month. Eva felt trapped and snowed in. Bored and horny, she surfed the sex sites and masturbated just about every night, jealous of the fact that Rinna was getting laid daily. She made several futile attempts to reignite the flames in Vince and finally gave up.

The next month, they caught a slight break in the weather, so Eva and Rinna headed for their favorite casino. Even though it was a Saturday evening, the place looked nearly deserted. What made it even worse for Eva was that male prospects seemed to be kind of scarce, so no one was trying to pick her up. Since Al was keeping Rinna more than satisfied, so she didn't even think about fucking anyone else.

That night, the girls made out in the back seat of Eva's car before heading home. Eva was so horny that she just about exploded the second Rinna's tongue touched her clit. Rinna made her come three times that night and Eva's cunt was still throbbing nicely when she got home. She and Rinna followed this up with another great lovemaking session the very next morning and afternoon.

The next day, another snowstorm hit and virtually shut the city down. The next few days brought much of the same. As the weeks passed, Eva grew more frustrated. She wanted to feel a good, real and hard prick in her cunt. She wanted a man.

"Even when we go on double dates, you never leave Al's side. I have no chance to fuck him again when you cling to him. Vince has also complained because he's been wanting to get into your panties again in the worst way," she said.

"Maybe we can do something about that," Rinna said. "This Sunday is supposed to be very warm. Why don't we talk our men into going to the park for a cookout? I'll find some way to arrange it so that we can swap husbands for an hour or two."

Eva smiled.

"That sounds great! Let's do it," she said. "If that fails, we can go back to the casino."

"Okay," Rinna said.

"That way, maybe we'll both get laid," Eva said.

"You mean that you'd fuck a total stranger?" Rinna asked.

"Sure. Right now, I'm so damned horny I'd be willing to do it," Eva said. "It's not like we both haven't done it before. So let's get this picnic going before I do something stupid."

Rinna bounced her idea off Al.

"That way, you can take Eva off someplace and fuck her again and I'll fuck Vince," she explained. "We haven't done this for a few weeks so it should be a lot of fun. It was the last time. Remember?"

Al grinned.

"Are you sure about this?" he asked.

"I'm sure," she replied. "And if the afternoon goes well, maybe we can swap for the entire night."

"Okay. Let's do it," he agreed.

Vince was more than eager to get back into Rinna's panties, so he readily agreed to the idea.

The weather was perfect for their picnic, too.

They were sitting in a gazebo drinking beer after their cookout when Al stood up and took Eva's hand. She smiled at Rinna and walked into a group of trees a few yards away. It was time to do what they had come there for. Eva had worn only a T-shirt and some running shorts that day. There was no sense putting on panties as she knew she wouldn't really need them. She had also been flashing her pussy at Al all afternoon.

Rinna had on her loose silk shorts that left little to the imagination and the sight of her perfect, sexy legs had given Vince a very obvious erection. Rinna saw him ogling her legs and began to move around to give him better views. She even flashed her pussy at him a few times. He got her another beer and sat next to her.

While she lifted the bottle, he put his hand on her thigh. When she didn't object, he slid it up her leg. Rinna was kind of horny again and not thinking straight. As he neared her crotch, she parted her knees and smiled.

"You like to touch my legs?" she asked.

"Yes I do," he said.

"How about my pussy? You want to touch that? You can if you like," she said as she opened her legs wide. "Go ahead. I don't mind."

Stunned, he eased his hand under her shorts and raked his fingertips across her cunt. She looked at him and smiled. He traced her cuntlips several times and realized she was getting moist. So he massaged her clit.

"I like it," she said.

"Can I see it?" he asked.

"Okay," she said.

She pulled aside her shorts to give him a good view of her soft, black triangle. He ran his fingers through her cunt hair, and then felt her labia. She smiled at him as her heart beat faster and faster.

"Yes. I really like it," she said softly as he rubbed her clit.

She trembled slightly as she obviously enjoyed the sensations. Her labia were moist and swollen now and she was breathing heavier. Vince took a chance and slid a finger into her cunt. Rinna moaned and opened her legs wider. He went in deeper and wriggled his finger. She quivered and came.

Suddenly.

"Oooh yes! That's nice," she sighed as he kept playing with her.

He leaned closer.

Her cunt smelled wonderful. So wonderful that he pressed his face against her crotch and slid his tongue over her labia. Rinna quivered harder and came again. Encouraged, he slid his tongue into her cunt and licked away. She moaned louder and came yet again.

"My God!" she gasped as he kept licking. "Oh God! Yes!"

She was lying on her back now and humping his tongue. He stopped for a few seconds as she sat back up. She was breathing very hard now and her heart literally raced in her chest. She was amazed that she had allowed him to do that.

"That was very nice," she said at last. "Really nice."

Vince slid two fingers back into her cunt and wiggled them around. She opened her legs wide and arched her back as she came again. She moaned and gasped as waves of pleasure tore through her quivering body.

He unzipped his shorts and pulled out his erect prick. Her legs were draped over the edge of the table and wide open. Vince moved between them and teased her labia with his knob by moving it up and down nice and easy.

She looked at him. She wanted to scream "Fuck me!" She wanted to feel that prick moving inside her cunt. She parted her legs a bit further. Vince stopped. She felt his knob press against her partially open labia and smiled when he slid it into her.

It felt nice, too.

Real nice and exciting.

Then he started to move in and out slowly. She closed her eyes and enjoyed the sensations for a few thrusts. She then wrapped her arms around him and started to fuck him back. And she did it with incredible zeal, too. Vince leaned into her now and hammered away at her cunt. He thrust harder and faster. Rinna dug her fingers into his arms and matched him. She wanted to fuck him until they both went blind.

"Yes!" she moaned. "Yes! Fuck me, Vince!"

He fucked her faster and faster. Rinna held him tight and matched him. He felt her body quiver and heard her cry out as she came. As she did, her cunt walls convulsed around his prick several times.

"Oooh God!" he groaned as he came.

She felt his cum spurt into her and fucked him faster and faster. After a while, he slowed his thrusts and began to pant. That's when she realized he was spent. She lay still and let him finish.

"That was wonderful," she whispered.

Al and Eva had secluded themselves under an old stone bridge where they'd be out of view from anyone else. Eva had been flashing her pussy at him all afternoon to show him she was more than willing. So they found a nice, secluded spot.

Al spread a blanket on the grass and sat down. Eva stood over him and thrust her hips at him. He smiled and peeled off her shorts and panties then buried his tongue in her muff. She stood with her legs wide apart and fucked his tongue. She came minutes later. She dropped to the blanket, rolled onto her back and spread her legs. Al pulled out his erect prick and buried it in her cunt for a nice, long and easy fuck.

"I love you! I really love you!" Eva moaned as she came. "Fuck me harder now! Give it to me!"

Al leaned into her and hammered away. After several good thrusts, he emptied his cum in Eva's cunt and kept fucking her until he had nothing left. They kissed for a long, long time before dressing and heading back to the gazebo.

Eva saw the expression on Rinna's face and smiled.

"I have a pussy full of cum, too," she whispered.

Rinna blushed and elbowed her. Eva laughed.

On the way home, the wives decided to swap husbands again. Eva went home with Al and Rinna went to Vince's place.

Once in the bedroom, they quickly undressed each other, locked lips and tumbled onto the bed. Within seconds, Vince's hard prick was moving in and out of Rinna's cunt and she was begging him to fuck her harder. She loved the way his prick moved inside her cunt and she fucked him back with equal enthusiasm. And he loved the way they seemed so perfectly matched and the way her cunt hugged and massaged his prick with each good thrust.

"I'm gonna come!" he moaned.

She dug her nails into his sides and fucked him harder. She had to feel him come inside of her. When he did, she came, too.

"I love it! I love your dick! Fuck me!" she cried.

She was his private slut now. Her body was his to do with as he pleased. As long as she could feel that hard prick working her cunt, she would be his.

Al and Eva were on the bed naked. She was on her hands and knees and moaning happily as he fucked her from behind. He also played with her nipples as he fucked and this added to her intense pleasure.

"I'm yours, Al. I'm yours. Fuck me, darling! I love you!" she moaned.

That was the third time she had said this to him. While he loved to fuck Eva, he wasn't in love with her. Her body was smooth and tanned and her cunt was exceptionally pretty and tight. She also gave great head and he loved the way she always swallowed his cum each time. Eva held nothing back when they had sex.

Neither did he.

Eva screamed as she came hard. Her body trembled and she broke out in a sweat. He fucked her faster and faster then rammed his prick into her as far as he could. She sighed as she felt his cum jet into her.

"Yes," she thought. "I will always let you cum inside me."

After a long night of fucking, the men dressed and went to work. Vince smiled at the naked beauty on his bed with her cunt filled with his cum. They'd fucked five times that night. In five different positions. The last one had been a strain for him, too.

Al pretty much staggered to his car.

Eva had totally outdone what they did on New Years' Eve. Hell, she fucked the daylights out of him. When it came to sex, she was as good as Rinna. Maybe better.

That morning, Eva and. Rinna went to a local café for breakfast. They both looked at each other and laughed.

"So how many times did you fuck Vince?" Eva asked.

"I'm not sure. How many times did you fuck Al?" Rinna replied.

"We did it about three or four times," Eva said. "Do you plan on fucking Vince again?"

"I think so. What about you?" she asked.

"I'm gonna keep fucking Al every chance I get. So I guess this means that we're husband swappers," Eva said.

"Something like that. This is nuts," Rinna said. "I didn't mean for it to happen. It just sort of happened. When it did, I just enjoyed the moment. You too?"

"I think mine was more intentional. I've been teasing and flirting with Al ever since we met years ago. We fooled around with each other a few times but until a couple of months ago, that's as far as we went. Now that it's happened, I don't want to stop—ever!" Eva said.

"Ever?" Rinna asked.

"That's right," Eva said. "You know, Vince has had the hots for you ever since he met you. Now that he's had you, he'll keep after you," Eva said.

"I can handle him," Rinna said. "Just don't steal Al from me."

"I won't," Eva promised. "Are you still gonna fuck other men?"

"Sure. As long as they're willing to pay me, I'll fuck them. How about you?" Rinna asked.

"Yes if the guy looks good and has cash," Eva admitted. "Want to go to the casino today?"

"Sure. It's been a while. Let's go," Rinna agreed.

When they got there, they separated as usual. About ten minutes into playing, a man walked up and sat down beside Rinna. They smiled at each other and started talking. Before she knew it, he had his hand on her thigh.

"You are the sexiest woman I've ever met and I'd love to really get to know you—intimately," he said.

She smiled.

"Maybe we can make that happen," she said. "Do you have a room at the hotel?"

"Yes I do," he smiled. "What would it take to get you up there?"

"Money," she said.

"I have money," he smiled.

"And I have a hot, tight pussy. Let's go," she said.

Eva was also busy.

The man she had previously fucked showed up and, after some small talk, she again followed him to that small, secluded room off the casino. This time, she started him off with a nice, long blowjob. When she felt he was hard enough, she stood and allowed him to pull of her jeans and panties. She sat on the desk with her legs apart and sighed deeply as he ate her pussy. She came twice before he turned her around and slid his prick up into her cunt.

"I love your pussy," he said as he hammered away. "You're so tight. So wonderfully tight!"

He fucked her harder and harder. Eva came again and shook all over. He gripped her hips and fucked her even harder. While she was still coming, he fired his wad deep into her cunt and kept going until he was totally limp.

He eased out and smiled as she dressed.

"You have a terrific tight body," he said as he handed her $200. "I'll see you again. Soon."

"You can count on it!" she said with a smile.

Rinna's man fucked her twice and came in her cunt each time. She was exhausted now. He had made her come a few times, too. They dressed and joked about it all. Then he handed her two $100 bills and thanked her for the privilege.

His prick was huge, too. In fact, she'd never seen or touched anything like it and had wondered how much of it he'd get inside her cunt. He moved in slowly at first then fucked easy. His massive prick deliciously massaged every bit of her cunt and each good, long and deep stroke sent her sailing more and more toward what proved to be a powerful orgasm. Rinna could hardly believe this was happening or that she was actually getting paid to do what she loved so much. She wrapped her arms around him and moved with him.

"Give it to me! Give me all of your dick! Fuck me!" she moaned as they moved together.

When she came, she dug her nails into his shoulders and fucked him as fast as she could. He emptied all of wad into her cunt. Instead of pulling out, he rested on top of her until he grew good and hard again.

Their second fuck was even better than the first. In fact, she almost offered to pay him!

She smiled and returned to the casino. She got a drink from the bar and sat down to play. Soon, a second man found her. There was some idle chit-chat for few minutes, and then he suggested they go to his room and fuck.

"That sounds good to me, but it will cost you," she said.

"How does $200 sound?" he asked.

"Like music to my ears," she replied as they headed up to his room.

He proved to be young and energetic and quick to recover. They managed to fuck three times within the next hour. Each time, they tried a different position. By the time they were through, Rinna had so much cum inside her cunt that it made a strange squishing sound when she walked. She hurried to the bathroom to clean up and dress. When she came out, he handed her the money and asked for her phone number. She wrote it down on the hotel stationary and told him to call her when he wanted to fuck again.

She staggered back to the slot machines and sat down. Her cunt still throbbed and she ached all over. She had been fucked like mad by two different men in less than three hours. She was tired and happy and $400 richer.

She smiled.

It was easy to be a prostitute. Too easy. Men were more than willing to pay for what she had between her legs. The idea pleased her, too.

About an hour later, Eva wobbled up to her and sat down. Rinna saw the tired look on her face and laughed.

"How many?" she asked.

"Two. How about you?" Eva asked.

"The same," Rinna said with a grin. "Let's get out of here before more men see us. I think I've had enough dicks for one day."

When she dragged her tired body home, Al greeted her at the door. She walked in a plopped down on the sofa. Then she smiled at him.

"Busy night?" he asked.

"Yes," she replied. "I did it with two different men. I had a great time and they paid me. You're right, Al. I can make lots of money renting my pussy out."

"So you're going to keep doing this?" he asked.

"For a little while," she smiled. "I'm sorry, too. This isn't what you expected when we got married."

"It sure wasn't. I suppose Eva's doing it, too?" he said.

"Yes. We both got into this by accident. We just wanted to fuck different men. We never expected to get paid for it," she said. "Especially at our ages."

He laughed.

Chapter Eight

Things settled down for a few weeks as the winter worsened.

Rinna and Al went about their normal life and Eva went back to being ignored by Vince and getting sexually frustrated. About the third week, she was climbing the walls and started pushing Rinna to swap husbands again.

Rinna agreed and the pair put the wheels into motion once again. This time, the setting would be incredibly romantic because Rinna won a four night stay at a resort for two couples. They agreed to spend the first night with their own husbands then swap for the rest of their stay.

Vince got another chance at Rinna the second day at the resort. Eva was off doing the shops and Al was touring a nearby landmark. He and Rinna were seated on a balcony that connected their two suites and the booze was flowing freely. Rinna had been to the pool so she had on a robe and a small red bikini, The entire time Vince had been touching her legs and she didn't mind it one bit.

Rinna was again drunk and horny and her legs were wide apart. She smiled and giggled as he felt her through her bikini panties. She smiled even more as he slid his finger intro her very wet pussy.

"I like that," she said dreamily.

"Can I see your pussy again?" he asked.

"Out here? No way! Somebody might see us," she said.

"We can go inside," he suggested as he rubbed her clit.

She smiled and stood up. He followed her into the suite and into the bedroom. As he watched, she dropped her robe to the floor. Then she untied her panties and dropped them. He stared at her cunt. She spun around slowly and wiggled her behind. He walked over and fondled her cheeks.

Rinna laughed and squeezed his bulge.

She walked to the bed and lay back with her legs wide apart.

"Are you gonna do more than just look?" she teased as she rubbed her muff.

He knelt down and started licking her cunt. She moaned and bent her knees. She gripped his hair and pulled him into her as she fucked his tongue. She erupted a minute later and screamed out in ecstasy.

"More! I love it! Eat me!"

He gripped her thighs and buried his tongue in her cunt. She moaned and writhed and begged him to keep doing it. She was so drunk and so horny that she couldn't think straight. She wanted to come and come and come and she didn't care who was doing it.

By then, he had freed his erection from his shorts. When he stood, Rinna saw it and wrapped her fingers around it. He gasped as she jerked him off and literally begged her to let him fuck her. She was coming out of her fog then and she slowed her strokes as she eyed his knob. She was stunned that she actually had his prick in her hand and that she was jerking him off. She decided to finish what she'd started and jerked him off faster and faster. Vice grunted and fired lines of cum across her body. One line landed on her chest between her breasts. She pumped him until he was small again, and then let him go.

"Wow!" he said after a while.

She undid her bra, tossed it onto a nearby chair. Then, while Vince watched, she massaged his cum into her breasts and nipples in a slow sensuous manner that made him hard again. She smiled at his erection.

"You come back very fast," she said as she ran her fingers over the knob.

"You make me that way," he said as she stroked her cunt. "You're the sexiest woman alive, Rinna. I'd give anything to fuck you."

"Anything?" she teased.

"Yes. Anything," he assured her as he pushed her down on the bed and sucked her left nipple.

She quivered and closed her eyes. He licked the other nipple then moved back down to her cunt. She threw her legs open and pulled his face into her cunt. This time, she literally screamed when she came.

It was that good.

While she lay panting, he moved between her thighs. She felt his prick move slowly along her open labia and wondered if he'd try to put it in. That's when she felt his hardness move past her labia and into her cunt.

Vince began moving in and out nice and easy. She lay with her legs wide open and her knees bent and let him do it a couple of times. It felt so good, she moved with him. His strokes were hard and deep and she matched them eagerly now.

He was delighted. Rinna's cunt was tight and soft and he loved the way her walls hugged his prick as they fucked. She wrapped her arms and legs around him and fucked him back like she did the first time.

"Yes! I love it! Fuck me!" she said as they moved together faster and faster.

After several more good, hard strokes, they both came at the same instance. Rinna moaned and groaned as her orgasm tore through her body and Vince pumped every last bit of cum he had deep inside of her.

When they couldn't move anymore, they stopped. Vince pulled out and watched as his cum oozed from her open slit. He was amazed that they had fucked again. She grinned at him.

"We'd better get cleaned up before Al and Eva come back," she said. "I don't want them to catch us like this."

He laughed.

He figured that most likely, Al was busy pumping cum into Eva's cunt at that moment.

She got up and raced to the bathroom to shower. He returned to his suite to do the same. Neither of them wanted to have to explain anything to their spouse. But he had to admit that Rinna was a terrific sex partner. In fact, he thought she was much better at it than Eva and decided that he'd fuck her every chance he got.

Rinna was thinking along the same lines.

She also realized that she enjoyed swapping. She enjoyed the thrill of having a strange prick in her pussy and having men hit on her. She also wondered if she should have an affair with Vince and how such a thing would affect her life. Did she want to go down that rocky road? She wasn't sure.

But she was sure that she'd fuck Vince again and again.

"I admit that I love to fuck you," she told him. "Although I'd love to keep doing it, I'm married so I don't want to ruin what I have with Al. At least for now. But whenever you want, I'll be glad to open my legs for you," she said.

"When can we do this again?" he asked.

"I don't know," she replied. "We'll see."

They had dinner at one of the resort's restaurants. As they talked, they put everything on the table. And they laughed about it.

"Since it's obvious that we've been "wife swapping", why don't we do it officially for the rest of our time here?" Eva suggested. "We have three whole nights left here. I'll spend them with Al and Rinna can be with Vince and we can all fuck as much as we like."

"I'm all for it!" Vince said. "How about you guys?"

"Sure. Let's do it," Rinna agreed.

Al nodded and smiled.

For the rest of their stay, Al spent every minute with Eva and Vince spent his time with Rinna. It was as if they were married to each other. Neither Eva nor Rinna bothered to wear panties. They wanted to be able to fuck wherever and whenever the mood struck them.

By the time their stay was up, all four of them were physically exhausted. Rinna had spent most of the time with her legs wide apart and having her cunt stuffed by Vince's prick. They had fucked more times than she could count and her body—and cunt—ached.

Vince was nearly tireless in bed. He got back up quicker than she expected and each fuck seemed to last longer. He'd even straddled her body and fucked her breasts. That had been a first for her and she grew fascinated watching the knob of his prick moved back and forth between her breasts as he pushed them together and played with her nipples. She watched as his large, dark pink knob moved back and forth faster and faster and took on a shine as it became coated with precum. The sight virtually mesmerized her and she grew hornier and hornier.

"Yes! Fuck my breasts, Vince! Fuck them," she breathed as she began to orgasm.

When Vince suddenly came, his first shot hit her right on the lips. His next shot landed on her chin and the next few struck her lips and cheeks.

She was so startled by this that she instinctively licked her lips. It was sweet and salty and sticky, kind of like some exotic dessert. Vince kept fucking away and coming more and more. Soon, her neck was coated with lines of cum and the valley between her breasts was slippery.

That's when Rinna came, too.

It was a good, hard orgasm that made her moan and writhe around. Vince took a chance and moved upward so that the head of his prick touched her lips. Since Rinna was still in the throes of her orgasm, he mouth was partially open. Vince eased his prick into her mouth so that the head rested on her tongue.

She swirled her tongue over the knob a few times to get an idea of what it tasted like. She decided that it wasn't bad. Vince eased it further into her mouth. She felt the knob touch the back of her tongue and really enjoyed it. So did Vince. He moaned loudly. She felt his prick spasm in her mouth as he came. She felt his cum spurt into her mouth and sucked harder.

"Yes!" she thought.

Vince moaned louder as she sucked and sucked and sucked. Eventually, he pulled his prick out of her mouth. It was totally flaccid and he had the biggest smile on his face she'd ever seen. She smiled up at him. There was a streak of cum between her breasts, too. She reached down and massaged it into her nipples while Vince watched and grew hard again. She grabbed his prick and gave it several pumps to make it harder then smiled.

"Fuck me again, Vince," she whispered. "Make me all yours."

Vince immediately slid it into her cunt for yet another, good long fuck. Rinna fucked him back with equal vigor as if to prove she was his fuck slut.

Al and Eva were also inseparable.

As they explored the resort, they managed to find several beautiful spots to fuck. They fucked in empty cabins, next to a lake, on a hillside and at the boat house. No matter where they happened to be, they found a good spot to have sex. Each time Eva came, she told Al she loved him and said she was his and his alone.

And the more he fucked her or ate her pussy, the more he wanted to have sex with her. Her body was tan and lean and tight. Her cunt was perfection itself and she really knew how to suck a dick.

And unlike Rinna, Eva liked to be fucked up her ass, which he found to be exquisitely tight and silky smooth. By the time they were finished, Eva had a cunt, ass and belly full of his cum and kept telling him to give her more!

They met for breakfast the next morning. Rinna and Eva smiled at each other, and then giggled.

"Our flight home leaves in eight hours," Al reminded them. "That gives us plenty of time for more great sex—if you want."

"We want!" the others said at once.

By the time they boarded the flight, they were worn out. Al noticed that Rinna was having some trouble walking to her seat. So was Vince.

"You wore each other out," he commented.

"Yes we did," Rinna smiled. "So did you and Eva. This was terrific. We need to do this again soon."

"True. But not too soon," Eva said.

When they got home, they were so tired that they slept through half the next day. Rinna and Al went to dinner that night.

"That was fun," she said. "It was like Vince and I were married and on a honeymoon. How was it with Eva?"

"The same. A few months ago, I never would have thought of doing anything like this. What made you and Eva want to try it?" he asked.

"It was mostly Eva's idea. She told me that the two of you had had sex before you and I got married and she was dying to have you again. Mostly it's because Vince stopped having sex with her. He says she's too fat. Do you think she's fat?" Rinna asked.

"Not in the least. Vince seems to be a lot more interested in you. I think he has been ever since he saw you. Now that we've done this a few times, I'm sure he'll want to keep doing it," Al said.

"I know Eva does! She's crazy about you, Al. She told me that she loves you," Rinna said.

"She's told me that several times," he admitted.

"Do you love her?" she asked.

"I'm not sure," he said. "I admit that each time we do this, I feel more and more drawn to her. There's definitely some sort of connection between us. How about you and Vince?" he asked.

"He hasn't said and I don't feel that way about him. I love to have sex with him but that's it. I think it's because I've known him for such a long time and I feel comfortable with him," she said.

She smiled.

"You know how much I love sex. When we swap, I become a total slut with Vince. I know what he wants and I'm really happy to give it to him. Eva said that she becomes your slut, too. Anything goes with her," she said.

He laughed.

"You've become more and more open to this, haven't you?" he asked.

"Why not? I think we're all having lots of fun and no one is getting hurt because we're not cheating. And in the end, I still belong to you and only you. Nothing will ever change that," she said.

Later that week, Al and Vince got together at a bar for few beers. Vince brought up the subject of their extramarital activities and they laughed at how things were going.

"Tell me, Vince—just how do you feel about Rinna?" Al asked.

"Your wife is super-hot!" Vince replied. "I never imagined I'd ever get to have sex with her. Now, she's all I think about."

Al laughed.

"I'm starting to feel the same way about Eva," he admitted.

"That's fine with me. I know that she's nuts about you and always has been. If she had her way, she'd marry you," Vince said.

"We have strange lives," Al said.

"And stranger wives! But what the Hell. We're all having fun so there's no harm done," Vince said. "We're all doing things that we've only fantasized about and our wives are the ones who got all of this going."

"Yeah," Al said. "It's been weird. Exciting as all Hell but weird."

They knew that Rinna and Eva were at the casino that night. Most likely, they were in some suite fucking and loving every second of it.

They were right.

The girls hit the casino around six and separated as usual. This time, Eva scored first when one of her previous clients spotted and walked over. Minutes later, she was up in his room getting fucked up her ass.

This guy always liked to use her this way. He liked her pussy but he said her ass was tighter and he loved the way it gripped him when he fucked her. And Eva loved to feel his prick moving in and out of her ass.

Around seven, Rinna spotted Jake and walked over to him. It had been months since she last met him and they hurried up to his room. She stayed with Jake for the rest of the night, too. When she left around midnight, she had fucked him four times and sucked his dick. Each time they fucked, Jake managed to make her come.

He kissed her deeply and pressed a wad of bills into her hand. She almost gave it back to him but he insisted she take it. She thanked him with another long kiss and went down to the casino. When she stopped to count it, she saw that it was nearly $400.

"He's so damned good that I should have paid him!" she said with a smile.

She found Eva seated at her favorite machine.

"You look very well fucked," Eva observed.

"I met Jake tonight. I've been with him the entire time. He's fantastic!" Rinna said dreamily. "You look well-fucked, too."

"I am. I had three different men tonight. My wallet is filled with large bills and my ass and pussy are filled with cum. Want to go home now?" Eva said.

"Oh yes. Jake wore me out. I need a good night's sleep before I go to work tomorrow," Rinna said.

Rinna went to work at 11. Around three, she saw a familiar figure approach the desk. She smiled happily.

"Charlie! How nice to see you again. It's been months!" she said.

"I've been in San Diego on business. I'm back now so I thought I'd stop by and ask you out to dinner tonight," he said.

"I'd love to. Should I get us a room?" she asked.

"Definitely. I'll see you at six," he said.

She called Al and told him not to wait up for her. He laughed. As soon as he hung up, he dialed Eva's phone.

"Rinna's going to be gone all night," he said.

"I'll be there in 20 minutes," she almost shrieked.

She arrived in nothing but her T-shirt and lime green running shorts.

"We are going to make love all night," she said as she kissed him.

Rinna lay on her back with her wide apart and her arms around Charlie's neck as she savored each and every deep, slow thrust of his prick. They moved together perfectly as each tried to give the other as much pleasure as they could. She realized that Charlie wasn't just fucking her. He was making love to her. He was making sure that she enjoyed it as much as he did.

She did.

"I love it, Charlie. I love it. Make love to me!" she moaned.

Each thrust was slow in and slow out. It massaged every bit of her cunt and sent tingles through her g-spot. She came after about 20 thrusts and shook all over. Charlie kept fucking her and fucking her. She came and came and came.

"I love it! I'm yours! Fuck me!" she cried as she shook even harder.

When Charlie finally came, he filled her cunt to overflowing. He fell on top of her and they kissed for a very long time.

"You don't have to pay me anymore, Charlie. Ever!" she said.

"Can you stay the entire night?" he asked.

She began thrusting her hips up at him again until his dick became hard.

"Of course I can," she said. "I'll stay with you as long as you want."

Neither one slept that night. Rinna lost track of the number of times they fucked and the number of good orgasms she'd had. She never knew that any man could get up so often or come so many times in just a few hours.

Charlie was tireless.

Hell, he was superhuman.

And she could hardly get enough of him.

Eva and Al didn't sleep either. Just as Eva had declared, they made love all night. Al used her cunt and ass several times and she just about fucked him to death. When they were through, they staggered downstairs. They were just about to go out to lunch when Rinna came in.

The women looked at each other and broke into laughter.

As they ate, Al looked at each of them. They both almost glowed.

"Of all the men you really like to have sex with, who's your favorite?" he asked.

"You are!" they both said at once.

"After you comes Vince, then Charlie, then Jake," Rinna said.

"I don't have a particular favorite. They're all different and yet they're all the same. They make me come and they pay me. You are my favorite lover, Al. You always will be, too," Eva said.

"Okay. Who is your favorite woman to have sex with?" asked Rinna.

"You both are in a dead tie. It's impossible to choose between you. Since you're my wife and I love you, I'd say you have the edge, Rinna," he replied.

"In that case, I'm going to do everything I can to win the top spot," Eva said.

"And I'm going to do whatever I must to make sure that never happens," Rinna said.

"You're on!" Eva said with a smile as they shook hands.

It was then that Al realized how much trouble he was in for.

About a week later, the couples decided to attend a wine tasting party at a nearby winery. The party also included a one night stay at a nearby B&B so no one would have to drive home under the influence.

The wine "tasting" consisted of several full goblets of various wines and snacks. Rinna and Eva managed to get themselves wasted. The party dragged on for several hours. When he thought Rinna was drunk and horny enough, Vince made his move. They were seated at a table under a tree when he put his hand on her thigh.

She winked at him and smiled as he moved it higher and higher. Rinna parted her thighs. She wore a short skirt that night, so he had a clear shot to her cunt. She trembled a little as he felt her through her panties.

And she was horny enough to let him go even further. She looked around for Al and Eva. They were across the balcony chatting with a group of other people and laughing. She knew they wouldn't miss either her or Vince for a little while.

Vince stood. She took his hand and went with him. He took her down a flight of wooden steps to a more secluded part of the terrace. It was fairly dark there and no one else was around. He pulled her to him and they kissed.

It was a long, deep kiss. Vince pulled up her skirt. She giggled as he pulled down her panties then stepped free of them. When Vince kissed her cunt, she quivered all over. She stood with her skirt up around her hips and feet wide apart and sighed as he ate her. She was so horny that she came moments later. When she did, she gripped his head and fucked his tongue until she came again.

Vince pulled out his already stiff prick. Rinna smiled, turned around and leaned on a table with her legs apart. Vince got behind her, teased her most slit with his prick a few times then slid it in. He went in very deep, too. All the way to his balls.

"Oooh, yes!" Rinna moaned as he fucked her.

He fucked her nice and easy for several thrust then went faster and faster. Rinna came again. Then she felt him ram his prick into her as far as he could. He moaned and trembled as he came. As he did, he filled her cunt with his cum.

Lots of cum!

They fucked for a little longer. When Vince was completely limp, he withdrew. Rinna turned to face him and they watched as several globs of cum leaked from her open cunt and landed on the wooden deck between her legs.

"I like the way you do that, Vince," she whispered.

"You're damned good, too," he said. "Do you like it enough to do it again soon?"

She answered by stroking his prick and sticking her tongue into his mouth.

Al and Eva had also managed to locate a private area. In fact, they were less than 100 feet from Vince and Rinna. Eva had also worn a very shorty dress for the party and she made a point of telling Al that she didn't bother with underwear that night.

While Vince and Rinna were fucking, Eva was lying on her back on a table with her dress up around her hips enjoyed a good, hard fuck from Al. He had already eaten her through two good orgasms and she had sucked his prick. Now, here they were, enjoying a good, hard and almost public fuck at the winery.

Al was real good at hitting all of Eva's erotic triggers, too. In fact, he was far better at this than Vince ever was. She had come to the party with the intentions of fucking him. She wasn't worried about getting caught by Rinna, either. She figured that Rinna was probably fucking Vince at that very moment anyway.

As always, she and Al climaxed at the exact same time. As she did, she fucked him with everything she had and whispered that she loved him as he emptied every last drop of cum deep inside her cunt.

When they all returned to the party, Eva winked at Rinna and licked her lips slowly. Rinna giggled and blushed.

That night, everyone got what they wanted. Eva spent the rest of the night with Al and Rinna spent the night fucking Vince into the mattress. When they met for breakfast the next morning, they all looked worn out but happy.

Vince watched as Rinna sat next to Al, took his hand and leaned on his shoulder. He realized that the bond between them was unbreakable. Although Rinna loved having sex with him, that was as far as it would ever go.

He didn't mind that at all.

Eva sort of frowned at Rinna. Although she loved Al very much, he obviously loved Rinna beyond words. She knew that he was fond of her and realized that would have to be enough.

She spent the next two weeks trying to ignite some passion in Vince. But Vince kept telling Eva she was too fat and he really had no interest in her. Even though Al didn't seem to mind the extra pounds she'd put on, she wanted to look her very best for him. After all, she had Rinna to compete with and she was very sexy and beautiful.

It was silly to think of Rinna that way. There was no actual competition. But she wanted to make herself irresistible to Al—and any other man who might want her. She kept going to the YWCA during the day. And she kept surfing porn sites while masturbating after she got home because her trysts with Al were rare at best.

"You and Vince seem to be getting closer," Eva said at breakfast the next day.

"It's kind of hard not to grow closer when you fuck someone," Rinna said. "I guess you and Al pretty close now, too."

"But not as close I'd like," Eva said. "As you probably know, I'm crazy about him. I'll give myself to him anytime and anyplace he wants me to. But I'll never become as close to him as you are. To Al, we're just great fuck buddies."

"That's the way I feel about Vince," Rinna said. "Al is the only man I'll ever love and I still can't believe he lets me do this. But I also want to try other men. For 20 years, I've been very faithful to Al. It was like I was living in a convent. Now that I'm out, I want to try everything."

"Me too. I'd like us to swap husbands again soon. Any ideas?" Eva asked.

"Not really. Vince fucked the daylights out of me last time, so I'm good for a while. I'll have to think about it for a few days and get back to you," Rinna said as she ran her hand along Eva's thigh. "Right now, I'm thinking of other things."

"I have the same things in mind. Let's got to your place and make love. It's been a while since we did that and I really miss your pussy," Eva said.

They did.

They made love in as many different ways they could think of and fell fast asleep in each other's arms. They got up around two, dressed and went out to lunch. As they ate, they talked about everything else but another swap. This told Eva that Rinna wasn't interested right now.

Chapter Nine

Eva and Rinna headed for a local casino as they normally did on Saturday night. When they got there, they had a drink together then went their separate ways to play different slots. Rinna preferred the penny slots. Eva liked the dollar ones which were on the opposite side of the floor.

About an hour after she started playing, a young, dark-haired man walked over and started talking to her. He told her that she "really filled out those jeans nicely" and added that he'd like to see what's under all that denim.

"My pussy," she said with a smile.

"Is it a pretty one?" he teased.

"Oh yes. It's real pretty," she assured him

"Can I see it?" he joked.

"Maybe," she joked back. "If we had a place where no one could see us, maybe I'd show it to you."

"Well, I have a room on the third floor. We could go there," he suggested. "Then maybe you'll let me do more than just look."

She laughed at his boldness.

"How old are you?" she asked.

"Thirty-one," he said.

"I'm much older than you are," she said.

"So what? I have a nice, hard dick and I'm anxious to see how it fits inside your pussy," he said.

She looked at him.

"You're serious?" she asked.

"Very serious. What do you say?" he asked.

That's when they heard a woman's voice calling. He turned and scowled as a rather short, blond woman walked up and hooker her arm in his.

"I've been looking all over for you. It's time to go to dinner," she said.

Without saying a word, they left. She smiled and watched them walk off. She figured the blonde was his wife or girlfriend. Since he'd tried to hit on her, Eva thought that relationship was probably on the rocks.

And her timing really sucked, because she was about to let him take her upstairs and fuck the daylights out of her.

"Damn it," she thought as she kept playing.

Rinna was busy on the other side of the room playing the penny slots. She was engrossed in her game that she failed to notice a middle aged man who slid into the seat next to her. When she finally saw him, they both smiled.

"Having much luck?" he asked.

"A little bit. How long were you sitting there?" she asked.

"About 10 minutes. Sorry if I startled you. Are you a Filipina?" he said.

"Yes I am," she said.

"I like Filipinas. They're cute and sexy," he said.

She said nothing and kept playing.

"You're very cute and very sexy," he continued. "Are you married?"

She showed him her wedding ring. He smiled.

"Do you have a boyfriend on the side?" he teased.

She giggled.

"Of course not," she said.

"If you'd like to have one, I'm available," he joked.

"I don't think so. My husband would kill me," she said.

"You don't have to tell him," he said. "I know I sure as Hell won't."

She laughed.

"And just how would we do this without getting caught?" she joked.

"Well, we could meet here like we just did. Then I could get a suite upstairs in the hotel. We can go to dinner, have a few drinks then go to my suite and have sex," he said with a grin. "Do you have to be home by a certain time?"

"Before midnight," she said.

"That would give us plenty of time," he said. "You can show me if it's true what I've heard about Filipinas."

"Oh? And just what have you heard?" she teased. She was enjoying this little game now.

"That Filipinas are really great at sex," he replied. "Are you?"

"My husband thinks so," she said.

"I'd love to find out if it's true," he said.

"I guess you'll have to find yourself a single Filipina and find out from her," Rinna said.

"Is that a 'no'?" he smiled.

"Definitely," she said. "Better luck next time."

"I'm glad I didn't upset you. You have a good sense of humor," he said.

"Thanks. I don't mind joking sometimes," she said.

"I'll see you around. Bye," he said as he got up and left.

Rinna smiled.

At least he wasn't an asshole like a lot of the men who try to hit on her. In fact, he seemed really nice. She kept playing for a little while. The man came over again with two drinks. He handed her one.

"I'm back," he declared.

"So I see. What's the drink for?" she asked.

"You can consider it a peace offering or an apology," he said. "Whichever you prefer. I got out of line with you a little while ago and I want to make it up to you."

"I already told you I didn't mind joking with you. But thanks for the drink," she said.

"My name is Ron. What's yours?" he asked.

"Rinna," she replied.

They continued to chat for a little while. Ron kept telling her how pretty she was and how much he wished she wasn't married. She blushed at the compliments and kept playing while they talked. She was starting to like him.

A lot.

He made her laugh and she made him laugh. In fact, they hit it off great. They had two more drinks and Rinna felt a little tipsy. She was glad that Eva was driving that night because she was in no condition. The more she drank, the more she let her guard down and the more she became attracted to this handsome, younger man. He had deep blue eyes, too. The kind of eyes that held her gaze and made her get lost in them.

Then, out of the blue, he asked what she'd do if he tried to kiss her.

"I'm not sure," she said.

"Then let's find out," he teased as he leaned close.

Before she could react, he kissed her on the lips. She blushed and moved back. Then they laughed.

"I guess I'd let you," she joked. "I wasn't expecting that."

"That was really nice," he said. "Can I have another one? A real one this time?"

"Here? In public?" she asked.

He looked around.

"We could do it on the other side of that door," he pointed. "I don't think anyone will see us there."

She smiled at him.

"Just a kiss?" she asked.

"Are you saying that you'd be willing to go further?" he asked.

"Maybe—for the right price," she teased.

"What do you usually charge?" he asked as he slid his hand along her inner thigh.

"How does $200 sound?" she asked.

"That's not a problem and I have a feeling that you're worth every cent of that," he agreed.

"Okay," she said.

They made their way to the door. It opened into a dark room. Ron took her hand and pulled her to him. His arms were strong and she practically melted into him. He pressed his lips to hers. She met them warmly. After a few seconds, his tongue entered her mouth and merged with hers. The kiss made her feel tingly all over so she kissed him back with passion as her cunt grew moist. His hands moved down her back and fondled her behind. She responded by kissing him harder. She felt something hard grow in the front of his pants. It pressed against her. Their kiss had given him an erection. She felt him hump her and moved with him as her libido kicked in.

He moved his hand to her left breast and squeezed it. She moaned. He moved it downward and massaged her crotch. She kissed him even harder as her body screamed "Fuck me!" She felt him unbuckle her jeans then unsnap her buttons one by one. She almost came when he eased his hand down into her panties and gently explored her cunt. He was only the second man ever to touch her there. He had her now. There was no way that she wanted to stop him.

He slid her jeans and panties down a few inches. She let them fall to her ankles then kicked them off. In the darkness, she heard him unzip his pants and she quivered with anticipation as his swollen knob moved between her thighs. She moaned loudly as he entered her.

"Yes!" she said as they started fucking.

It was a nice, slow and easy fuck, too. His prick filled and unfilled her cunt nicely with each thrust. He was gentle. She wrapped her legs around his hips. He gripped her cheeks and pinned her against the wall then fucked her harder. She moved with him now and stuck her tongue in his mouth again. This kiss was almost explosive.

She was his slut now. His fucking machine and she thrust her hips at him with incredible wantonness. She felt his finger enter her asshole and quivered as she gripped his shoulders. It felt like she was in some sort of porno flick and she let herself go wild.

"Yes! I want it! Fuck me!" she whispered

They fucked for several delicious minutes. As she drew closer and closer to coming, she moved faster. He got her message and fucked her back just as fast, thrilled with his luck at being able to put his prick into her marvelous cunt. She moaned and shook all over as she came. The orgasm was a nice, deep one. The kind she usually got from her husband. He gripped her ass tighter and fucked her faster and faster. Then she felt him stiffen inside her and felt the warm liquid gush into her cunt.

"Oooh yes! I love it," she moaned. "Fill me!"

They kept going until he went limp and popped out of her. She felt his cum ooze down her inner thigh as her heartbeat returned to normal.

"You're fantastic! I thought you said that you didn't cheat," he teased as he felt her stick cunt.

"I don't," she said. "This was business."

He laughed.

"Can I see you again sometime?"

"I don't know. Maybe if we're both here," she said. "We'll see."

"That's fair enough," he replied as they kissed again.

He handed her $200 and ran his hand over her behind. She giggled and squeezed his prick, then got down on her knees and slid it into her mouth. He gasped and moaned as she made him hard again. She stood up, turned around and leaned against the wall with her legs spread apart. Then she sighed as he fucked her. This time, it was a good, soft long fuck. They came simultaneously and she sighed happily as she felt him fire yet another stream of cum up into her cunt.

"Wow!" he said after he caught his breath.

She handed him one of her cards and told him to call her when he wanted to do it again. He promised he would.

They readjusted their clothes just as they heard someone coming down the hallway and hurriedly left the before the guard could find them. Ron grinned happily at her and squeezed her hand. She just nodded and stuffed the bills into her pocket.

He'd given her an extra $100.

She went to the ladies room to clean up and returned to playing the slots. As she did, she took out the bills and counted them. Ron had given her $300.

"I love being a hooker," she thought.

She went back to playing the slots with her extra cash. She played for another hour and finally hit a small jackpot that recouped her earlier losses. She walked over to the cashier to get her money and wondered where Eva was.

At that moment, Eva was in a hotel suite taking on two clients at once. She was on her knees in bed sucking on one man's dick while the other fucked her from behind.

They'd approached her a few minutes earlier. When they asked if she could handle them both at the same time, she said she'd try it for $500. They paid her on the spot and took her up to their suite.

They each took turns eating her pussy and she played with and sucked each of their dicks. When they were good and hard, she got onto the bed. The one fucking her had a long, thin dick that deliciously massaged her g-spot with each deep thrust. The other guy had an average sized dick. After the first guy came in her cunt, they switched. The second guy hammered her hard and fast and made her come twice. The first guy spurted a good load down her throat. They rested for few minutes. Then one guy lay down with an erection. She spread her cheeks and lowered herself onto his prick. When he was inside her ass, the other guy entered her cunt. She moaned and sighed and screamed for more as they fucked her and fucked her and fucked her. She came several times and was covered in sweat by the time they were finished with her. It was the most intense sex she'd ever had.

When she left the suite, she was visibly worn out. She checked her watch and smiled. They'd been at it almost two hours and she had pools of cum in both orifices. They had each tipped her an extra $50, too.

"That's $300 an hour! Not bad," she smiled.

Rinna and Eva left the casino two hours later. They stopped at a small café for a late snack.

"This younger man came up to me while I was playing tonight and asked me what I had under my jeans," Eva said.

Rinna looked at her.

"What did you tell him?" she asked.

"I said that my pussy was under my jeans. Then he asked me if it was a pretty one, so I said yes and offered to show it to him. Before we could get anything going, his damned girlfriend showed up a ruined everything," Eva said. "But the other two guys more than made up for it."

"You mean that you really had sex with both of them?" Rinna asked.

"I sure did—and at the same time. It was great, too," Eva replied as she put her hand on Rinna's thigh. "I'd love to see what under your jeans."

"You can," Rinna said as Eva gently stroked her inner thigh.

"I'm starting to become crazy about you," Eva said softly. "In fact, I've been thinking about you a lot lately. I can't help it."

Rinna just sat and looked into her eyes. Eva slowly undid Rinna's zipper and gently teased her cunt through her panties like she'd done many times before.

"I've been watching a lot of girl on girl porno online and I'd really love to try some of the things I saw with you. You're so sexy and beautiful. I want to make love to you again and again," Eva whispered.

"I feel the same way about you," Rinna asked as Eva's fingers danced along her labia.

"I want to do lots of things to your pussy," Eva said as she massaged Rinna's clit. "Lots of things."

"Maybe I'll let you," Rinna said as she grew more and more aroused.

The waitress walked over with their check and interrupted it. Eva stopped and paid her. They walked back out to the car, got in and headed home.

"I've never been attracted to a woman in my life until I met you. The more time we spend together, the more attracted to you I become.

Lately, I've been thinking about having sex with you. A lot of sex. You make me horny, Rinna," Eva said.

"You make me horny, too," Rinna admitted. "I don't understand it, but I'm crazy about you."

Eva grinned. She looked down and saw that Rinna hadn't zipped her jeans up. She stopped the car in a nearby park and smiled at her. Rinna smiled back and maintained eye contact as Eva unbuckled her belt and slid her hand down into her panties.

"Yes," Rinna sighed as Eva explored her slit.

Eva noticed that her pussy seemed to be unusually moist and a bit sticky. She slid her fingers into her slit and moved them around. Rinna opened her legs wide and quivered as Eva played with her.

"Oh—my—God!" Rinna gasped as she came.

Her cunt convulsed around Eva's fingers as she writhed around. Eva moved her fingers in and out a few times and watched as Rinna came again. When she finally withdrew her fingers, she was surprised to see they were coated with thick, white sticky goo. She knew what it was, too.

"Your pussy is still full of cum!" she said.

Rinna nodded as she slowly fell back to Earth. Eva jokingly smeared some of the cum on Rinna's lips. Rinna wiped it away quickly and looked at her.

"It's very fresh, too," Eva joked. "From the way it looks and feels, I'd say that it was put there less than an hour ago."

"Your pussy is also filled with cum," Rinna said as she slipped her fingers into Eva's slit. "Lots of it."

Eva leaned back and closed her eyes as Rinna moved her fingers in and out of her cunt. After a few thrusts, Eva undid her blouse and played with her nipples. Rinna smiled and ran her tongue over the left one, and then she sucked it.

They got into the back seat and removed their skirts and panties. Then Eva climbed on top of Rinna and began to fuck her. With both of their cunts flooded with cum, their labia made slurping sounds as they caressed. Each back and forth movement sent wild tingling sensations through their bodies. When they came, it was explosive and Rinna felt Eva's juices flood into her cunt and mingled with the cum left behind by the men she'd fucked. Their orgasms merged into one. They kept fucking and fucking to see just how high they could take each other. It was the most exquisite fuck of their lives.

They held each other close as their labias caressed. Both were bathed in sweat now. Orgasm followed orgasm followed orgasm.

"I love you, Eva! I love you!" Rinna moaned. "I'll love you forever!"

They waited a few minutes to come back to Earth, then exchanged kisses. When Rinna got home, it was nearly two a.m. and Al was fast asleep. She smiled at him as she got into the bed. Her pussy ached deliciously now.

"Tomorrow," she said as she kissed his cheek.

The next day, she told Al what happened over breakfast. He grinned at her.

"I can hardly believe what I'm hearing. You're a far cry from the innocent young virgin I met and married years ago. I never imagined you could be this wild or slutty," he said.

"I'm surprised at myself, too. I never thought I'd become a prostitute but once men started paying me for sex, I thought I should take their money and keep going until I get tired of it," she said.

"Just don't try to fuck every man you meet," he said.

"I won't if you promise not to fuck every woman you meet," she returned. "I know you like that Vietnamese woman who works with you, too. So if you want her, that's okay. She seems very nice and quiet so I know she won't cause any trouble."

She was referring to Li.

Al liked Li—a lot. She had shapely, slender legs and a cute behind and she weighed about 105 pounds at most. She was one of those women who never seemed to put on weight no matter how much she ate.

She was very self-deprecating, too. She really didn't think she was attractive enough for any man to want her. Hell, her last "date" was way back in high school and both were so shy that it was a disaster. But she really liked Al. She even cooked special lunches for him once in a while to show she appreciated his friendship.

"I've considered her," Al said.

"I think you should go for her. She is very nice to you and never asks for anything in return. I like her personality, too," Rinna said.

They had met on several occasions. Rinna had invited Li to the house for holiday meals and even asked her to bring her parents. So they knew each other well.

Al looked at her.

"Why are you trying to get me to have sex with other women all of a sudden?" he asked. "You've always been real jealous and possessive and you get upset when I even talk with other women."

Rinna picked at her food and stayed quiet. She didn't dare tell him that she'd had sex with a man at the casino. But she did admit that she was thinking about having sex with Vince again and might fuck other men, too.

"I don't know. I guess I just want to let myself go wild for a while," she said. "Is that okay?"

"I already said it was. I'm just surprised at your change of attitude, that's all. So you want to experiment and I want to know why," he said.

"I'm not really sure. Maybe I want to see if other men find me attractive. Maybe I just want to find out what it's like to have sex with different men. Anyway, it's what I'd like to do for a while. So if I do it, I think it's okay for you to do it, too," she replied.

He laughed.

"You're crazy," he said. "But if this is what you really want to do, I'll go along with it. Don't go too wild. I don't want to lose you."

"You won't. I promise," she assured him. "So when are you going to go after Li?"

"I'm not sure. I have to take things slow with her," he said.

"I bet she has a very nice pussy," Rinna said. "I can tell she has a very nice ass."

He laughed.

"Does that mean that you're going to go after her, too?" he asked.

Rinna smiled and shrugged.

Eva again attempted to get Vince to have sex with her. Much to her dismay, he gave her his usual half-hearted fuck and pulled out after he came inside her cunt. He didn't even try to make her come. He got up, dressed and sat in front of the TV while drinking a beer. She was left in tears on the bed. She had to get herself off by rubbing her clit. As she came, she imagined she was fucking Al again.

When the weekend rolled around, Eva simply went shopping at the mall. Rinna and Al were out of town on another one of their romantic weekend trips and Eva didn't feel like going to the casino by herself. Vince had also done his usual vanishing act. She knew he'd be gone until late Sunday afternoon. Most likely, he was off fucking some other woman. She had no doubt that he was cheating that's why she didn't feel guilty about having sex with Al—or any other man who showed an interest in her.

Frustrated and horny, she drove to the nearest sex shop on Monday to look at some "toys" to help get herself off. What she saw amazed her.

There were literally dozens of dildos of all shapes, sizes and purposes. Some were just long latex pricks that looked and felt almost like the real thing. Others had bumps or ridges or extensions designed to stimulate the clit. Some twisted and wiggled when turned on. Others had thrusting actions and one, according to the package, was a longer, thinner model with a tapered tip that was designed to enter and stimulate the womb. There were also about two dozen models that were designed for anal use. These intrigued her.

After a lot of thought, she bought an eight inch latex prick that felt real and vibrated. She also chose one for anal sex and the one that was designed for the womb. She also bought a bottle of lubricant and some sex DVDs. Since her husband didn't want to fuck her, she was determined to do the job on herself in between visits to the casinos.

That night, she decided to try the one that looked and sort of felt like a real dick. She took it out of the box and studied it with interest. Besides having a set of "balls" where the batteries went, it had an extension at the base that was designed to stimulate the clitoris.

She removed all of her clothes and ran her hand up and down the shaft. It felt warm and almost like a real one. It was about eight inches long and at least an inch and a half in circumference. She opened the tube of lubricant and coated the dildo with it. She slid a pillow under her ass and laid back with her hips raised and her thighs open wide and slowly eased the dildo into her cunt.

"Not bad," she thought as she moved it in and out a few times.

She turned up the power to level one and sighed as the vibrations caressed her cunt walls. The sensations grew even more pronounced as she fucked herself. After a few minutes, she turned it up to level two.

The vibrations doubled.

So did the sensations.

She fucked herself a little faster then slid it in all the way. She gasped and convulsed when the stimulator made contact with her swollen clit and sent intense waves of pleasure surging through her body. She lay quivering and moaning with pleasure for a few moments then turned it up all the way.

And came!

Harder than she'd ever come before.

"Ooohh, yeah! Yeah!" she cried as the orgasm intensified.

She felt her entire body shake and shake as she came and came again. She then fucked herself as fast as she could until she came one more time.

She pulled the dildo from her cunt and turned it off. She smiled. It had worked better than she hoped it would. The orgasms were deep and nearly sensational. Much better than the ones she ever had with her husband.

She walked into the bathroom and cleaned it off then took a long, hot shower.

She used the dildo each morning for the next eight days. By then, she decided she was ready to take it to the next level.

She would fuck herself in her womb.

This dildo was longer and slightly curved to fit the contours of her cunt. It also tapered to a long, thin tip designed to be inserted into the womb itself. It also came with an instruction DVD which she watched twice to be sure she had it right. It showed her in detail how to know when she'd touched the opening to her womb and the best methods for easing the tip inside.

The next day, she decided to put it to use.

It took a little while for her ease it through the opening of her womb. It felt kind of strange, but not uncomfortable. Once she was sure it was in, she turned it on—and screamed!

Her entire body grew suddenly rigid as the vibrator sent pulses of energy racing through her womb. They danced through her entire body and caused her muscles to lock up like the ground does just before a huge quake. She could barely utter a sound. She just lay there with her legs apart and knees bent, clutching the dildo.

Then she came.

It was sudden and very powerful.

Her muscles contracted several times and her arms fell to either side. All she could do was lay there moaning as the vibrations shook her to the core.

It was the most intense sexual experience of her life. The most powerful and deepest orgasm. She felt helpless to stop it. She laid moaning and shaking for what felt forever, physically unable to pull the dildo out her cunt. Her entire body shook uncontrollably as orgasm after orgasm rippled through her. She gripped the bed as the intense vibrations grew stronger.

"Fuck me! Oh, God! FUCK ME!" she screamed.

It ran wild for ten minutes then turned itself off. She lay bathed in sweat as she panted for air. Her heart was racing and her insides throbbed. When calmed down minutes later, she pulled it out of her cunt and looked at it. It was covered with her juices.

"You're a keeper," she said.

When she tried to stand, her knees turned to rubber. Her cunt dripped as she staggered to the shower and turned on the water.

That night, she decided to go to the casino alone. Rinna was out with her husband having fun anyway. She went to a different casino than usual and sat down to play the slots. It was a warm night, so she wore shorts and a t-shirt.

As she played, she noticed that one of the security men had been watching her. About a half hour later, he walked over.

"Hello," he said. "My name's Jack."

"Eva," she said as they shook hands.

"I've seen you here a few times. You look different now. Have you been working out?" he asked.

"Yes I have," she smiled, pleased that he'd noticed.

"You look terrific," he said.

"Thanks," she smiled.

"Are you married?" he asked.

"Yes," she sighed.

He laughed.

"Do you fool around?" he asked.

"Maybe," she teased. "What do you have in mind?"

"I have a private lounge upstairs. We could go there and get better acquainted if you want," he suggested.

She smiled.

"It's gonna cost you," she said.

He took out four large bills and placed them in her hand.

"Is that enough?" he asked.

"Sure," she said. "Let's go."

They entered the suite. It was one of the largest in the hotel and really decked out. Without a word, they walked to the living room.

He took her in his arms and pressed his lips to hers. She sucked his tongue eagerly and held him tight as every cell in her body screamed, "FUCK ME!"

After a long, hot kiss, she sat down on the couch. He knelt before her and removed her shorts and panties. She opened her legs wide and sighed as he explored her cunt with his tongue. He was good, too. So good that she grabbed him by the hair and fucked his tongue. Her wildness surprised and delighted him, too. He inserted a finger up into her asshole and moved it in and out rapidly while he ate her. She screamed and came.

He kept eating her until she came again.

The he stood, unzipped his pants and pulled out the biggest prick she'd ever seen. She reached out and gave him a few jerks. To her surprise, it got longer and thicker. She swirled her tongue over the knob a few times then sucked it while she played with his balls.

"God! You're great!" he gasped. "I can't wait to fuck you."

She stopped, put her feet up on the couch and opened her legs wide. He got between them and slid his prick home. She took every bit of it, too. They fucked like crazy for a long, long time. Eva came again and again. His prick massaged every nook and cranny of her cunt. It was a deep, intense type of fuck that made her feel fantastic.

"Can I come inside of you?" he asked as he fucked her harder and harder.

"Yes! Oh God, yes! Come in my pussy! Fill me!" she gasped.

After a few more thrusts, she felt his cum jet into her and fucked him back with everything she had. She was his slut now. His fuck toy and she loved the way his prick felt as it moved in and out of her hungry cunt.

When it was over, he eased out of her. She smiled at the river of white that ran out of her lips. She reached down and massaged it into her cunt while she sucked his prick. When it was good and hard again, she got onto her hands and knees and let her take her from behind. This fuck lasted a little longer. She came just as he spurted another load into her cunt. They kept fucking and fucking until he went limp and slid out of her.

"Jesus! That was terrific!" he said as he sat down next to her. "Do you cheat often?"

"No. This is only my third time," she said.

"I'd love to do this again soon," he said as they dressed.

"I'm game. Next time I decide to come here, maybe I can give you a call?" she suggested.

He took a card from his wallet and handed it to her.

"Call me the night before to make sure I'll be here," he said. "Does your husband have sex with you often?"

"He used to. He hasn't bothered with me lately," she said.

"What an asshole. Oh, well. That's his loss," Jack said as he escorted back to the casino. "If you were my wife, I'd fuck you every night."

She laughed.

Jack was her newest client and she didn't feel the least bit guilty about it. She loved sex and if her husband didn't want to give her any, she'd find it elsewhere. Jack was good, too.

Real good.

"Yes. I would fuck him again," she decided.

The next day, she called Rinna. She and Al had just returned from their trip and Rinna bragged about how they had worn each other out. The next morning, they got together for breakfast. Rinna told her about the conversation she'd had with Al and how they had given each other the green light to have sex with other people.

"That includes you," Rinna said. "I told Al that he could fuck you whenever he wanted and he said I could fuck other men."

"So you like having strange cum in your pussy?" Eva teased.

"Along with strange dick," Rinna smiled. "Just like you."

Eva laughed.

"Want to go to the casino and try our luck?" she asked.

"At the slot machines or with men?" Rinna asked.

"Both," Eva said.

"Okay. Let's go now. We have nothing better to do anyway," Rinna agreed.

They went to their usual casino. When they reached the slot machines, they split up. Eva settled down at her favorite machine and started playing. Rinna went to her spot on the other side of the room. The place was nearly deserted at that time of day, except for the usual old men and women with their oxygen bottles and walkers. About an hour later, some younger people began to drift in. Most were the usual ghetto and trailer park trash looking for a place to blow their unemployment checks.

Rinna sighed.

The prospects looked pretty slim. She walked over to the coffee urn and poured herself a cup. That's when she caught the eye of a rather good-looking young man. He walked over to get some coffee and smiled.

She smiled back.

He was tall and about 30 years old.

"Hello," he said. "Kind of dead here today, isn't it?"

"Yes. It is," she said.

"I'm Stan. What's your name?" he asked.

"Rinna," she replied.

"Are you as bored as I am?" he asked as they sat down.

"I'm pretty bored," she admitted.

"Well, maybe we can do something about that. If you're interested," he suggested.

"What do you have in mind?" she asked.

"I have a room upstairs in the hotel. Maybe we can go there for a while," he said.

"And what would we do there?" she asked,

"Relieve our mutual boredom," he said with a grin.

"How?" she asked.

He put his hand on her thigh.

"Oh. I don't know about that," she said without asking him to remove his hand. "I don't even know you."

"We can become better acquainted upstairs," he said. "What do you say?"

She sat and looked him in the eyes as he moved his hand up her thigh. When he slid it under her shorts, she parted her legs. He ran his fingers along her labia through her panties. She felt her heart beat faster and faster and parted her legs further.

"What do you say?" he asked as he felt her. "I'll even pay you."

"Let's do it," she said.

Here she was again in a hotel room with a man she just met. They were going to have sex, too. Maybe lots of sex and he was going to pay her for it.

They walked over to the bed and sat down. He pulled her to him and stuck his tongue into her mouth. It felt electrifying, too. Enough to where she sucked it as hard as she could. When he massaged her breast she quivered. Before long, he had undone her blouse and was busy sucking on her left nipple. He soon pushed her down on the bed. She lay there as he slowly undressed her. When he beheld her nude body, he whistled. Her body was flawless. Lean, tan and athletic.

She watched as he undressed and stared at his huge, hard prick. She reached up and started beating him off, amazed at herself for even daring to do this. At the same time, he fingered her cunt. Here legs were wide open now and she was quivering all over.

He put his face between her thighs and licked her cunt. She moaned and gripped his hair as she fucked his tongue. It felt wonderful, too.

Exciting.

When she came, she virtually exploded. She rolled from side-to-side and screamed with pleasure as he held onto her thighs and kept licking. He soon stopped and sat up. He grabbed a pillow and stuck it under her ass to elevate her hips. Then he plunged his prick into her. It went in deep and hard.

"Yes!" she cried as she grabbed his arms. "Yes!"

She lay still as he started to fuck her. He withdrew almost all the way and plunged in deep with each and every stroke. She felt his prick massage he walls each and every time. Each inward thrust made her moan with delight, too.

She soon began to move with him. After a few thrusts, they moved as one. The fuck became faster and harder. Rinna saw stars as she came again and fucked him back with everything she had left. He stopped in mid stroke to let her work his prick, then started fucking her again. Rinna came again.

"Yes! Fuck me! Fuck me good!" she cried.

He fucked her harder and harder. She felt him stop, spasm, and plunge into her as hard as he could. This was followed by what felt like an entire river of cum. She held on and milked his prick of everything he had. It was a strong and very intense fuck, too.

When Stan finally withdrew, Rinna looked down at her cunt and watched a stream of cum ooze from her cunt. Stan smiled. His prick was still half erect, so Rinna grabbed it and jerked him off until he got rigid again.

Then she closed her eyes and smiled as she felt him slide his prick back into her cunt for another round of great, intense sex.

Eva also hit a jackpot.

A good looking man in his 40s spotted her at the slots and ambled over to start a conversation. After a few minutes of flirting and teasing, she agreed to have sex with him in his room. Once they negotiated a price, they hurried upstairs.

They spent several minutes at foreplay while they slowly undressed each other. Then they started with a nice, easy 69. He seemed to have an especially long tongue, too. It hit spots that she didn't even know she had and he also loved to lick her asshole. His prick was about eight inches long and thick, but she did manage to get most of it into her mouth so she could give him a nice, easy blowjob.

They finished their tryst with a long, pleasant fuck. She was surprised at how long he could go, too. Their fuck seemed to last an hour and when it was over, she could barely move. She even lost track at how many orgasms he'd given her. He was good at it. Real good and he really wore her out. He was really delighted that she let him come inside her cunt.

"You know, you're the best woman I've ever had. And your body looks and feels so perfect," he said. "I'd love to do this again sometime."

"We can, if you want. Here's my cell phone number," she said as she wrote it down on the hotel stationery. "Call me when you want me again. This was great!"

She met Rinna in the lobby and they went to lunch. As they ate, they compared notes and giggled a lot.

"Did you wash the cum out of your pussy this time?" Eva joked.

"No. I like the way it feels squishing around in me. What about you?" Rinna said.

"Not yet. I guess we both hit the jackpot today," Eva beamed. "We both came here to get laid and we did. So it was a good day."

"A very good day!" Rinna agreed.

They went to the mall to window shop, and then headed back home. Rinna immediately showered to wash the cum from her cunt. She knew Al would be horny as usual and wanted to be fresh and ready for him.

Eva had no such aspirations. She showered, ate a sandwich for dinner and went to sleep early. Vince never bothered to come home that night and she had stopped caring about that weeks ago.

Three days later, she felt horny again.

Instead of going back to the casino to get laid, she decided to give the anal dildo a try. She'd never had anything up her ass before, but she figured that after the powerful womb orgasms, the anal one couldn't be all that bad.

She went into the bedroom and took the dildo and the tube of lubricant from the boxes. Then she removed all of her clothes and lay down on the bed.

"Here goes," she said.

She massaged the lubricant into her asshole then coated the dildo with more of it. She lay back with her hips elevated on a pillow, spread her legs wide and placed the head of the dildo against her opening. She took a deep breath, exhaled, and slowly eased it up into her ass.

Little by little.

The sensation was odd but not unpleasant. She kept pushing it into herself until she felt the plastic base touch her spread cheeks. She turned it slowly a few times to get accustomed to having something up her ass, the fucked herself with it. The more she did it, the more she liked it. After a few minutes, she turned the vibrator on low. The surge tingled throughout her asshole and rippled through her body.

"This is nice," she said. "Real nice."

She moved it in and out faster as she turned up the power.

"Oh yeah! Yeah!" she moaned as the waves rippled through her.

She fucked herself faster and faster as she writhed on the bed. Just as she neared her first orgasm, she shoved it all the way in and turned the power up to full. When she erupted, she saw stars!

Lots of them.

She let her legs fall to the bed and rocked from side to side as she came and came and came again. She moaned and sighed and cried out as she let the vibrator run and run. She wanted to see how long she could take this. She reached down and started fucking herself again. She did it slowly to savor each and every thrust as it moved in and out of her tingling ass. As she did, she imagined she was with a real lover.

"Fuck me, darling! Fuck me forever!" she cried.

She kept going and coming until the batteries finally died. She took a deep breath and exhaled as she slid the dildo out her ass. She held it up in front of her and smiled. She had no idea how long she'd been lying there. That didn't matter. What mattered was that she really loved doing it.

"Next time, I'll put one in my ass and pussy at the same time to see how that feels," she said as she forced herself to sit up.

At that moment, Rinna was on her hands and knees in a hotel room at the casino getting fucked from behind by a younger man with a long, thick prick. She had met him two hours earlier while at the slots and he had made her an offer she couldn't refuse.

This was their third good, hard fuck that afternoon. The first two times, he did her missionary style. Each time, they came together in a shower of sparks that left Rinna gasping for air. Each time, he came inside her cunt.

God, he was good, too.

His thrusts were deep and strong and she threw her hips up at him each and every time to take his prick as deep into her cunt as possible. He was amazed at her passion, too. Amazed at how she loved to fuck and the way she used her cunt walls to caress his prick. She moaned and sighed with each thrust now as her orgasm built.

"Yes!" she thought. "This is what my pussy is for. This is what I love!"

When she came, she screamed and shook all over. He gripped her cheeks and fucked her harder and harder. She felt his cum jetting into her and fell to her elbows. He leaned over her and kept fucking until she felt his prick go soft and slip out of her.

They lay still for a few moments. He got up and smiled. She rolled over and opened her legs wide as she grabbed his prick and beat him off until he got good and hard again. He draped her legs over his forearms and slid his prick home for yet another, good long fuck.

By the time she left his hotel room, it was past ten p.m. They had fucked several times, too, and Rinna's cunt felt sore. The man had paid her $600 for her time and services. She smiled as she drove home.

They had never even bothered to exchange names.

Chapter Ten

Rinna had an odd sexual adventure later that week. It was very warm day, so she put on her light, silk shorts and went shopping. She walked into the largest department store and got onto an elevator with several other people. When more people got on at the next floor, she found herself pressed against the man in back of her.

"I'm sorry. It's so crowded," she apologized as he turned her head.

"That's okay. I really don't mind," the man replied with a smile.

Her butt was pressed right against his crotch, too. Somewhere between the fifth and sixth floor, the elevator suddenly stopped. At the same time, the lights went out plunging the car into pitch blackness. For some reason, the person directly in front of her stepped back which caused her to step back against the man behind her.

"Excuse me," she said.

"That's okay. I don't mind it at all," he said. "It's nice to be trapped by someone as pretty as you."

After about five minutes, Rinna felt something that was pressing her behind grow harder and harder.

She realized that the man she was leaning against had gotten an erection. A big one! She felt him "hump" her a few times. This caught her totally by surprise and she didn't want to make any sort of embarrassing scene. She just stood there quietly as he humped her a few more times. She had nowhere to move and she wasn't really sure she wanted to move anyway.

Seconds later, she felt his fingers move up the back of her thigh and under her shorts. Intrigued and excited, she stood still to see how far he'd go. His fingers explored her crack for few seconds then moved toward the front and beneath her panties to her cunt. She felt his finger enter her slit and shivered as it moved in and out. She was allowing a total stranger to touch her pussy and he was making her very horny. She leaned into him and opened her stance to see what he'd do and to let him know it was okay.

He fingered her a little while longer. When she was good and wet, he stopped. She thought it was over until she heard him unzip his pants. He pushed aside her shorts and panties and she felt his hard prick move between her legs and along her wet, quivering labia. When it found her opening, it slowly entered her cunt. Horrified and excited, she stood still as she felt his prick move in deeper and deeper. After a short rest, she felt it move in and out nice and easy.

Once.

Then twice.

It went in deep.

Three times.

Instinctively, she leaned against him. She was trapped in a pitch dark elevator with a strange, hard prick moving in and out of her now very wet cunt. She was excited and horny beyond belief. And her actions let him know that she wanted more.

He fucked her faster and faster.

Her heart raced faster and faster as she enjoyed her strange "rape". She knew it was wrong on so many levels but her pussy was screaming "fuck me!" loud and clear. And he was getting the message.

Faster and faster. She could hardly believe how big his prick felt. How wonderfully hard it was and how it deliciously massaged her cunt. My God, it felt so good.

"Yes," she thought. "Yes!"

He fucked her faster for a minute or two, and then rammed his prick up into her as hard as he could. The sudden jolt made her come and she bit her knuckles to keep from moaning out loud. He rammed her hard again. That's when she felt it. A sudden gusher of cum that shot into her cunt and coated her inner walls. He kept at it for few more thrusts and she came again.

She shook all over and nodded to show him she loved this. That she wanted him to keep fucking her, keep making her come and come. It was the most highly erotic moment of her life.

He fucked her harder and harder. She felt him shoot off again in her cunt as she suppressed another urge to moan. She was getting one of the best fucks of her entire life and she had no idea what her "friend" even looked like.

She felt his breath on her neck and heard him whisper that she had the best and tightest pussy he'd ever fucked. She just quivered all over as he moved in and out and wondered when he'd go limp.

Her cunt was flooded with strange cum now and the stranger just kept adding more and more to the pool as he continued to fuck her. She felt his prick start to shrink after a little while and took a deep breath.

The elevator jolted. He quickly withdrew his prick and zipped up just as the lights flickered back on. Most of the people got off at the next floor—including him. She got off on the ninth floor and headed directly to the Ladies Room to clean up.

She had just received a terrific anonymous fuck from a total stranger on a crowded elevator while stuck between floors and she had loved every second of it. It was the single dirtiest episode of her life and she now wished that she could have at least seen his face while they fucked.

She used a tissue, soap and water to wash the cum from her pussy. As she did, she couldn't help but smile.

Eva decided to ramp up her workout routines. After another week of working out at the YMCA, Eva checked herself in the mirror. He belly was nearly flat and her ass now looked tight and perfectly round. Her thighs had also slimmed down. She looked and felt 20 years younger.

Other people she knew also noticed.

Men began to watch her walk by again. Co-workers complimented her and even Rinna's husband whistled at her and stopped by her place for a good, long, leisurely fuck and suck session that left them both satisfied and exhausted.

When they made love, she put everything she had into it. She wanted to show him how much she loved him and wanted him. Al responded in the same way.

So did Rinna.

But Vince remained indifferent.

That Monday, Al and Rinna went out of town for a vacation. By Tuesday, Eva was horny and frustrated again and her attempts to stir up Vince didn't go well.

On Wednesday morning, she decided to go to a casino in the nearby town. She located the slots and sat down to play. Since it was a warm day, she wore a sleeveless blouse, loose tan shorts and no panties.

She was also fishing.

After about an hour of playing, a handsome man walked over and watched over her shoulder. She turned and smiled at him.

"I hope you don't mind my watching you," he said.

"I don't," she said. "Why don't you just sit down next to me so we can talk?" she offered.

He took the seat next to her.

"My name's Harry. What's yours?" he said.

"Eva," she replied.

"Is this your first time here?" he asked.

"Not really. I come up here every once in a while," she said.

"Are you with anyone?" he asked.

"No," she said.

"Would you like to be with someone?" he asked.

"Maybe," she smiled. "You have someone in mind?"

"Yes. Me," he replied.

"Okay. What do you have in mind?" she asked.

He put his hand on her thigh. She parted her knees and smiled more as he slid his hand under her shorts to her bare pussy.

"I have a room in the hotel," he said as he slowly ran his fingertips over her labia.

"Can you pay me?" she asked.

"Definitely. How does $200 sound?" he offered.

"That sounds perfect. Let's go," she replied.

They spent the first few minutes kissing and undressing each other, then fell onto the bed naked. Eva showed off her cocksucking skills while he buried his tongue deep inside her cunt. Eva didn't care that she was cheating. She was horny and needed sex.

Lots of good, hard sex.

And his prick was good, hard and long. And it felt wonderful as it moved in and out of her hungry cunt. They fucked and fucked in as many positions as they could imagine. Eva came more times than she could count and her cunt became filled with lots of hot, thick cum.

They stopped to rest around eleven and went to lunch. He paid for everything, too. After they ate, they returned to the room.

This time, she even let him fuck her in her ass. To make it easy on her, he got the bottle of lotion from the bathroom and coated his prick with it. Then he massaged the rest into her asshole. She put a pillow under her belly to elevate her body. Harry got behind her and eased his prick all the way up into her channel. Then he fucked her with long, easy strokes. Her asshole was so tight, that he came within a few thrusts and flooded her with cum.

She rolled over and sighed as he proceeded to eat her until she came, too. By then, he was rock hard again and he slid his prick into her cunt for yet another good, hard fuck. This time, she fucked him back until they came together.

But Harry wasn't finished. He was very energetic and bounced back very fast. Especially when she sucked his prick. And he was amazed at how much she loved to fuck. So for the entire day, they were a perfect match.

When she left the casino around six that evening, she could barely walk to her car. Harry had literally fucked the daylights out of her and she had loved every second of it. They even exchanged cell phone numbers.

"I'll call when I get back to town," he promised as he gave her $400.

"You'd better!" she responded.

She had no doubt that she'd fuck him again and again. She smiled as she drove home. Her pussy and ass were filled with cum now and she felt really happy and satisfied. She knew that she'd have no trouble picking up any man she wanted, too.

"They think I'm sexy! Everyone thinks I'm sexy but my own husband!" she said. "From now on, I'm going to fuck as many different men as I can and he can go to Hell."

She returned to the casino the next three nights and had lots of sex with lots of different men. She didn't even bother to come home on Thursday. That's when she agreed to spend the entire night with one of her regulars.

If Vince cared, he didn't mention it.

"It's his loss!" she said as she admired her figure in the mirror.

She was still happy when Al and Rinna returned from their trip the next evening. Now, she would have someone to hang out with when she went hunting at the casino.

Al thought about what Rinna had said about Li.

Li was kind of cute and very petite. She never wore makeup and kept her hair short and neat. He began by complimenting her on the way she looked. His compliments weren't unusual to her. He often said nice things. Mostly, they made her blush.

"I'm surprised that you never married," he said at lunch.

"No man wants a woman like me," she said. "I'm almost built like a boy. I have very small breasts. You have to look real close to even know I have them."

"I know one man who thinks you're really sexy and would take you in a second," Al said.

"You're nuts!" she smiled.

"I'm serious," he said.

"Okay. Who is he then? Do I know him?" she asked.

"You know him alright. In fact, you're having lunch with him right now," Al smiled.

She stopped eating and looked at him.

"You think I'm sexy?" she asked.

"I think you're very sexy, especially when you smile. If I weren't married, I'd have asked you out a long time ago," he said.

"I don't wear makeup," she said.

"You don't need it. You're pretty enough without it," he said. "You're comfortable in your own skin. There's nothing fake about you. What I see is who you really are and you're very modest and have a good sense of humor."

"Wow! But I'm built like a stick," she said.

"Then you're a very attractive stick. You have a nice, slender figure with great legs and a cute behind. In fact, I don't see a thing about you that I would change. You're perfect just the way you are," he said.

She sat quietly and looked at him.

"How long have you thought of me this way?" she asked.

"Ever since we met," he said.

"I can tell by the way you say things that you are being honest. Thank you. Those are the nicest things anyone has ever told me," she said. "You've always been real nice to me. You even invite me to your house on special occasions. You even get along very well with my parents. In fact, my mother is crazy about you. She always said that she wished I could marry you. To be honest, so do I. But that's impossible.

You have a very beautiful and nice wife. You would have to be insane to leave her for any woman."

He smiled. Then he took her hand and held it. She blushed but didn't pull it back. She just sat and gazed into his eyes for a few seconds.

"This is totally insane," she thought. "Is he making a play for me? My God. If he is, I'll let him play me. But how far should I let him take this?"

He smiled.

"You look like you're lost in thought," he said.

"I am," she replied. "I think we'd better get back to work before we get carried away."

They got up and tossed their food wrappers into a nearby trash can. As they walked back to the locker room side-by-side, he again held her hand. The physical contact made her feel flushed all over.

When she got home, Li studied her reflection in the mirror and wondered what Al saw in her that other men didn't. To her, she looked plain. Almost boring. She spun around and checked out her body.

"Al said he thought I had a sexy body. Maybe I do have nice legs, but the rest of my body sucks. Why is he attracted to the likes of me?" she asked herself.

"I think he is more attracted to who you are," her mother said. She'd been watching Li from open door. "You are a very honest and good natured woman. He knows this and that is why he likes you."

Li smiled.

"No one's ever said he was attracted to me before. Just my luck, the man I really want is married! Do I discourage him?" she asked.

"You do whatever your heart tells you," her mother advised. "Do you trust him?"

"I always have," Li said.

"Then you two already have a strong foundation. And you know his wife very well. This complicates matters, does it not?" her mother asked.

"Big time!" Li said as she sat down. "I don't want to do anything to disrupt their marriage. They are both good friends of mine. I don't want to hurt anyone."

"I understand. But he has now admitted how he really feels about you. If you believe he is being truthful, then I advise you to allow nature to run its course," her mother said.

Li smiled.

"Why do I feel that my entire world is about to turn inside out?" she asked.

"That is because it is," her mother smiled.

When Al got home, Rinna had dinner waiting for him. They sat down and chatted while they ate. Rinna was an exceptionally good cook and Al had always loved her meals. He told her about his lunch with Li. She listened and smiled.

"So it went well?" she asked.

"I think so. I think I kind of scared her, too. She wasn't sure what to say or how to act. Me neither. I haven't done this since I courted you," he said.

"So you're courting her?" she asked.

"I think that's the best way to approach her. It helps that I've always liked her, too. We're comfortable around each other. You saw that at our last get together," he said.

"I did. That's why I suggested that you go after her. I think she's always been crazy about you but was always afraid to say or do anything about it. She's very sweet and shy. I think she's a virgin," she joked.

"She is. She told me that she's never even been asked out for a date. I can't understand why," he said.

"I can. She's very shy and she has no breasts. American men aren't attracted to flat chested women. That never seems to matter with you. I know you like nice legs and asses instead," she joked.

"You have all three," he smiled. "You're a complete and very sexy package."

"So I've been told," she smiled. "Eva is especially crazy about me now. We have a real hot love affair going."

"I've noticed," he teased. "So, do you think I should continue with Li?"

"Definitely. Don't leave the poor woman hanging. You've already started, so you have to go through with it. She wants to be yours, Al. Make her yours," Rinna said.

He smiled.

"Are you sure about that? What if things work out in ways you don't count on?" he asked.

"I'm not sure. I guess I need to think about this more," she said.

"If I make Li mine, she may not want to let go—ever. Can you live with that?" he asked.

"I'm already sharing you with Eva. One more woman won't matter," she said.

"Li might not want to share," he warned. "Do you still want me to go through with this?"

"Do you?" she asked.

"Yes," he replied. "I want to see how this plays out."

"So do I," she said.

He stood and held out his hand. She smiled and clasped it as they headed up to the bedroom...

The next morning, Eva decided to try the double penetration idea. That afternoon, she stripped naked, lubed up her asshole and laid down on the bed.

She looked at the dildos and smiled.

She slid one up her ass as far as it would go and the second one into her cunt. After moving each one in and out a few times, she turned them both up to full power.

The intensity of the double vibrations made her body contract several times and sent her sailing over the edge within seconds. She rolled and bucked and cried out as the waves of pleasure surged through her entire body.

"Oh God! God! I love it!" she screamed as she came and came and came again.

It felt so extraordinary; she decided to let the vibrators run wild until they ran out of juice. The series of orgasms continued relentlessly and made her quiver and sweat. She came so much that her juices ran out of her cunt and she kept begging for more and more.

After what felt like an eternity, the batteries in her ass vibrator finally quit. She pulled it out and tossed it aside as she enjoyed the one that was still running in her cunt. She lay there moaning for several minutes more until it, too, finally died.

She quivered uncontrollably for several more minutes. It was several more minutes before she could pull the dildo out of her cunt and sit up. She was soaked in sweat and the entire room smelled of sex. So did the bed.

She wobbled to the bathroom and showered. Afterward, she went back to bed and fell into a very exhausted sleep for several hours.

That evening, she could barely walk. Her lower back, ass and pussy ached.

She smiled.

The aches were worth it.

She had spent more than an hour playing with her toys. It had been an hour of nearly non-stop orgasms and intense vibrations.

"Toys are fun and they do the job fine enough, but I want a real dick in my pussy tonight," she said as she the water washed over her tired shoulders.

She had tried without success to reignite the passion between her and her husband. But she realized that he simply wasn't attracted to her anymore. She'd even lost a few pounds thinking that would help.

She got nothing.

Zilch.

Still feeling frustrated and horny, she thought about the card in her purse. She took it out and sat down at the computer and logged onto the site.

It came up immediately.

"GET LAID NOW!!

Discreet sex with men or women. Just fill out the online questionnaire and open the door to a world of unbridled, passionate sex with no strings attached!"

She scrolled through the site and studied the explicit and provocative photos of the women. They covered all ages, colors and sizes and body shapes. They were ordinary woman. Bored housewives looking for discreet sex with lots of different men.

"Hell, I look much better than any of those women," she thought, although some of their pussies looked attractive.

The site also had a section strictly for women. She clicked on the logo and was surprised at the number of women wanting to have sex with other women or both men and women. She found herself drawn to a couple of the Asian women

She decided to fill out the questionnaire.

It asked the usual questions, and then asked whether she'd prefer men or women. She wrote in "men mostly but I am open to having sex with women, too."

She also described what she would never do, sex-wise and a few more personal things. When she was finished, she took a nude selfie with her legs spread apart and uploaded it to the site. She also wrote that she was looking for hot, discreet sex in the early morning or afternoon hours from Mondays to Thursdays and added her phone number.

She got an immediate response from the site administrator which gave her details about how it worked. Basically, men looking for sex pay a set fee to the site to be able to view girls' photos and get contact numbers. Then the men call the women and set up a meeting to have sex for a fee that she negotiates with the clients. In other words, it was an online prostitution service and if she agreed, the contract would be for four months.

Eva smiled and hit AGREE.

She reasoned that since she was already selling her pussy to men at the casinos, a few more clients wouldn't hurt.

Another page came up asking if she knew anyone else who would be interested in joining the service. She immediately typed in Rinna's name and cell phone number.

She turned off the PC and laughed.

Ten minutes later, her cell phone rang,

It was a man named Rod. They chatted for a couple of minutes, and she agreed to have him come over in a half hour. He agreed to pay her $200. When the doorbell rang, she was pleasantly surprised to see a tall, dark haired and handsome man.

She led him to the bedroom.

She was nervous as all Hell as she watched him undress and her eyes immediately want to his prick which was already half erect. When he was finished, she let her loose robe drop to the floor. He ogled her with more than a little interest, too, and she watched as his prick grew to full salute. The idea that another man got an erection just from looking at her excited her.

"You like?" she asked as she spun around slowly.

"Oh, yeah. I like," he assured her. "Are you ready?"

He took a Trojan out of his pocket and was about to open when she shook her head.

"You don't have to use that if you don't want to," she said.

He put it on the side table and smiled.

"This is going to be much better than I hoped," he said.

They spent a few minutes kissing and touching each other. She looked down at his sizeable hard-on and wrapped her fingers around it. He sighed as she gave him several good pumps. He sighed even more when she bent down and slid the knob into her mouth.

While she sucked his prick, he gently licked her cunt. To his delight, she came quickly and let out a happy moan. She rolled onto her back and opened her legs wide. He smiled and slid his prick home.

"Ooh yes!" she cried.

He proceeded to fuck her with long, deep strokes. She wrapped her arms and legs around him and started fucking back. They settled into a good, strong rhythm that lasted for several delicious minutes. It was a truly wonderful fuck.

"Yes! I love it! Fuck me harder! Use my pussy!" she begged as she felt herself about to come.

"Oh yeah! You're fantastic! The best!" he moaned as he fucked her faster and faster.

She sensed he was about to come and held him tighter as she fucked him back with everything she had.

"More! More! Fuck me!" she gasped as she erupted.

He didn't hear her. He was too busy emptying his balls deep inside her cunt. She felt his cum spurt into her and fucked him even harder. She wanted all of it. Every last drop.

When it was over, they kissed for a while. She gave his prick several strokes then slid it into her mouth. This time, she sucked away until he spurted a second load of cum into her mouth. He gasped and moaned as she kept sucking away until he had nothing left. She sat back and wiped the cum from her lips.

"Wow!" he said. "Fucking wow!"

She grinned, pleased that he really enjoyed it.

He got up and dressed. She sat on the bed and watched. She didn't bother to dress. He took out his wallet and handed her $200. She looked at the cash and smiled.

"Was I worth it?" she asked.

"Oh Hell yeah," he said. "After I go online and rate your performance, you'll get a lot of calls," he smiled.

"Oh? You really enjoyed it?" she asked coyly.

"Hell yeah. I especially loved the way you let me come in your pussy. Most other women make men wear rubbers or shoot off outside their cunts. Lots of men love women who let them do that!" he said.

She grinned, almost proudly.

"You have a good, tight pussy and you know how to use it. You can bet I'll be back to see you real soon—and often. Do you do anal?" he said.

She nodded.

"Great! I'll call you again next week," he said as she escorted him to the door.

After he left, she sat on the bed and looked at the cum oozing from her cunt. She now had a pussy filled with strange cum and she loved the way it felt inside of her when she walked. She looked at the mantle clock.

Her next "client" would be there in 15 minutes. She also had two more lined up for the next day and another one for the day after. That would give her $1,000 in cash and all she had to do was open her thighs and let them fuck her.

She smiled.

Most prostitutes ended their careers long before they reached her age. She was just starting out and was surprised at how many men wanted to fuck a middle aged woman. But her 50 year old pussy was in high demand. She was surprised at how many men wanted to fuck her. She knew that she looked better than most of the other woman on the site and being exotic seemed to make her even more attractive. She also knew that if her clients gave her good reviews, she'd really be in demand.

"How many men can I really handle in one week?" she wondered.

Her cell phone rang and snapped her out of her thoughts. She answered it and made another appointment for the day after tomorrow.

"Wow. That's six in three days," she smiled.

The second man was of medium height and build and had an arresting smile. She led him up to the bedroom and quickly dropped her robe to the floor. Then she walked over and stripped him naked. She knelt before him, gave his prick a few tugs, and then stuck it into her mouth. He gasped at her expertise as she swirled her tongue around his knob.

"Let's fuck now," he said.

She nodded and got onto the bed and parted her legs. He climbed on with her and they spent the next few minutes kissing and engaging in foreplay. While he sucked her nipples and stroked her cunt, she wrapped her fingers around his prick and jerked him off. He kissed his way down her belly to her cunt and buried his tongue in it. She stiffened up suddenly, moaned loudly and came seconds later. While she was still in the throes of her orgasm, he slid his prick deep into her cunt and marveled at how tight she was.

"Wow! That's nice! Really nice," he said as they fucked.

They moved together deliciously for several minutes. He gasped and moaned as her inner walls squeezed his prick with each thrust and she loved the way it felt as is moved in and out of her. They kept moving faster and faster and faster.

"I'm gonna come!" he gasped.

"Do it inside me! Come in my pussy!" she shouted as she fucked him harder.

The orgasm that followed was amazing. It was far better than she'd ever gotten from a dildo and he kept fucking and fucking as he emptied what felt like a gallon of cum deep inside her cunt until he became totally spent.

After he dressed, he handed her $200.

"Damn, you're great," he said.

"So you want to do it again soon?" she asked.

"Oh yes! I'll call again next week. You know, you can make a lot of money doing this. You have looks and experience. That's a great combination," he said as he left.

She smiled and plodded upstairs to shower. This had been the most sex she'd had in one day in a long time. It was great sex, too.

Both men had made her come and both had promised to come back for more.

Just as she stepped out of the shower, the phone rang. It was her husband.

"I'll be home later than I expected tonight. I have to work overtime. I'll be home around seven," he said. "Don't bother with dinner. I'll grab something here."

"Okay. I'll see you later," she said.

Her cell phone rang seconds later. It was another man who had seen her picture on the site and wanted to fuck the daylights out of her. She agreed to see him in a half hour. She hung up the phone and looked at herself in the mirror as she ran her fingers through her pubic hair and massaged her still swollen clit.

She laughed.

"Everybody wants my pussy but my own husband," she said. "And they're willing to pay for it. I guess I still have enough to attract men."

The third guy proved to be very good. They ended up fucking like crazy three times in three different positions. One was on her back with her legs draped over his arms while he leaned into her and fucked her as hard as he could. This was very intense and it made her come several times. She then finished the day off by sucking his prick and swallowing whatever cum he had left in him.

When he left, he gave her an extra $50 and said she was the best he'd ever had and he really loved the fact that she let him come in her pussy.

"I'll see you again—soon," he promised as he left.

She smiled.

"Three out of three satisfied customers," she said. "I like being a whore!"

While she was doing that. The site administrator called Rinna.

"Hello?" she asked.

"Hi. Are you Rinna?" the man asked.

"Yes. Who are you?" she asked as she wondered about the strange voice on the other end.

"My name is Frank. I run a website that finds good paying clients for women in the business. A friend of yours gave me your name and number and said you might be interested," he said.

"What business?" Rinna asked.

"Call girl," he replied.

"You mean like a prostitute?" she asked almost in shock.

"Yes. Are you interested in using your body to make a lot of money? Our clients will pay you in cash only and you don't have to report on your income tax return. If you look anything like your friend, you can make thousands of dollars a month doing this," he said.

"I don't think—"she began.

"Look. Hear me out before you decide. The average pay per client is around $200 or more. Even if you only do five per week, that's an extra $1,000 cash in your pocket. Our contract runs for four months, so you can easily make $16,000 during that time," he explained.

That's when Rinna realized that Eva had already registered and she had given Frank her information. She wasn't sure how to react. She's already fucked a total stranger for free and she knew that her pussy was a real asset.

"I'm still not sure about this. It sounds like fun, but I'm married," she said.

"So? Most of our women are married. Their husbands either don't know or they don't care about it. You can also service women if that's your thing," Frank said. "And it doesn't cost you a thing to sign up—ever."

"Um, can I look at your site first?" she asked.

"Sure. Here's my URL. Take all the time you need and get back to me. Your friend joined earlier today and I understand that she's already had two clients. There's no sense letting her make all the money, is there?" Frank said.

"Okay. I'll look it over tonight and get back to you," she said as she hung up.

She laughed.

"That fucking Eva!" she said.

Rinna went online and checked out the site. Although it looked interesting, she decided to talk to Eva about it first. She picked up her cell phone and dialed her number.

"Why'd you give my name and number to that dating site you joined?" Rinna asked.

Eva giggled.

"I thought that since you're already fucking a lot of different men, maybe you'd like to make even more money for doing it," she said.

"Have you made any money yet?" Rinna asked.

"Oh yes! I've already had three clients since yesterday and I have two lined up for today. I get about $200 each time, plus tips. Look, Rinna. We're both fucking men at the casinos for money and we both really enjoy doing it. This will let you make even more money with that pussy of yours than you imagined," Eva said.

"Really?" Rinna asked.

"Really. You have a great pussy and you know how to use it. So go all out with it. Give the site a try. You can have as much strange dick as you can handle and they'll pay you good money for letting them fuck you," Eva said.

"Where do you go with them?" Rinna asked.

"I'm fucking them here at my house when Vince is at work. You have two free days each week, so you can do the same," Eva said.

"I don't think I'd want to have strangers come to my house. I'll just stick to fucking men I meet at the casinos. I think that's safer and I'm already getting all the men I can handle," Rinna said.

"I understand. I'm just going to do this for a month or two. After that, I'll just stick to the casino like you or fuck Al to death," Eva said.

Rinna went online and emailed Frank to tell him she wasn't interested at this time. He didn't reply, so she figured that was that.

She really didn't want to fuck strange men at her own house anyway. Besides, the casino provided her with more clients than she could handle and she could pick and choose as she saw fit based on the way they looked and talked.

That day, she put on her "come and get it" shorts and went to the casino right after breakfast to see how many clients she could attract in one day. She left a note for Al telling him she'd be back around midnight and to have fun with Li.

She arrived at the casino around eight and played the slots for few minutes. By nine, she was up in a hotel room fucking the daylights out of a handsome man that was half her age. She stayed with him for two hours, during which time he fucked her four times.

At 11 she was back at the slots, feeling tired and happy. By 11:30, she was fucking her second client. He didn't last long, either. She finished him off with a good blowjob and returned to the casino for lunch. At one, she was back in a hotel suite fucking like crazy again. This one lasted until three and came in her cunt three times. He was good, too. He made her come each time and the last orgasm almost made her pass out.

At four, she was in another hotel room fucking and fucking until she could barely see. She returned to the casino at five thirty and went to the restaurant for dinner. She met another man while there. He bought her dinner and a couple of drinks and she followed him up to his room where he fucked her in her ass and cunt like a madman. He also made her come twice.

She returned to the casino at seven and hoped for a breather. She playue4d for another half hour when a fifth man approached her. Fifteen minutes later, she was in his suite fucking him.

He lasted about an hour.

She went back to the casino and played the slots for another 45 minutes. She was starting to feel relaxed again, when yet another man approached her. She said she was tired but he made her an offer. She accepted and went up to his suite.

When he was finished some two hours later, she could barely walk straight. She'd fucked six men in one day and sucked each of their dicks. She was about to go home, when she bumped into another man...

When she got back into her car at midnight, she wondered how she managed to survive. She had actually fucked 10 men in one day. She had more orgasms than she could count and her ass and cunt were filled with lots of cum.

"I was the ultimate hooker today," she thought. "I have a tired pussy and $3,500 in cash in purse."

Al was still up when she got home. She smiled weakly at him and sat down on the sofa next to him.

"You look half dead," he commented.

"I'm glad it's only half!" she laughed.

"How many?" he asked.

"Ten. I had sex with 10 different men today," she replied.

"Wow. That's a lot of dick!" he said.

"They just kept coming up to me all day and night. I guess I'm really attractive, huh?" she joked.

"You're too attractive," he said. "You'd better take a break."

"I will. I'm taking the rest of this week off," she said. "Except from you, of course! How did it go with Li?"

"We just went out to dinner and chatted. I'm trying to get her to open up more and more. She's real shy and sweet," he said.

"I know. I've met her. Do you think it will go anywhere?" she asked.

Al shrugged.

"That's up to her," he said.

Li sat looking into her mirror. She still didn't understand why Al was attracted to her or even why he'd asked out to dinner.

It was at a local Italian place and the food was good. They sat and talked for a good three hours then he drove her back home. Her mother watched her get out of the car and smiled. Li looked happy.

"I guess tonight went well?" she asked when Li walked in.

"It was a very nice evening. He kept the conversation light and funny and I was almost sad when it ended. I can hardly wait to see him at work tomorrow. I think I'll bring him one of my special dishes for lunch. He likes my ban xao," she said.

"He likes most of our dishes and he knows what they are," her mother said. "Don't forget, he was in our country many years ago, during the war. He understands our culture and he knows our history."

"I know," Li said. "I think I am still young enough to bear children."

Her mother laughed.

"You and Al would make wonderful parents," she said. "And your children would be beautiful."

Chapter Eleven

Rinna went to the casino like she always did on Saturday night. She wore her shortest skirt and a T-shirt to see how many men she could attract. Whenever she went out by herself, men tried to hit on her. They'd come up and start chatting with her. Sometimes she spoke with them. She sometimes joked with them and teased them back.

Sometimes, she fucked them.

But she had to find them attractive first.

A couple of men did try to talk her into fucking. The first one she turned down flat. The second guy offered her money.

They settled on a price and she went up to his room with him where they undressed each other and got onto the bed. They stared with a nice, long "69" and ended with a slow, easy fuck that left her cunt flooded with cum. She then finished him off with another blowjob.

As she returned to her slot machines, she smiled as she thought about the first time she'd been offered money for sex. The first time was kind of comical and she really didn't understand why it happened.

About four years earlier, she had gone to some local fair. She ended up with a T-shirt from a dentists' booth that had his name on the back and "ORAL EXPERT" printed on the front. She really didn't think anything of it but her husband laughed at it when he saw it and told her not to wear it in public.

The following week, she decided to go for a jog along the riverfront. She had on her jogging shorts and that T-shirt. It was also "Fleet Week" and several small US Navy vessels were docked at the pier and hundreds of sailors were roaming the park grounds. When she passed them, they stopped to watch this hot, sexy Filipina run by. When they saw her shirt, they whistled and shouted. Several men asked her how much she charged and if she swallowed or was any good.

Embarrassed, she stopped running and went back to her car. She had no clue what that was all about. It never registered in her mind that most sailors considered Filipina to be little brown fucking machines or that her T-shirt proclaimed she gave great head.

Then her husband explained why it happened and what the shirt advertised. She put it away in her drawer and said she wouldn't wear it again. His explanation mortified her.

But now, when she thought of it, she smiled. Although she was by no means an "oral expert", she kind of like the idea of being a "little brown fucking machine". She was also pleased that men found her attractive enough to offer her money.

The very next day, she decided to find out if the incident would repeat itself. She put on the T-shirt and again went jogging along the riverfront. About eight a.m., she passed a group of young sailors. When they saw her, they whistled and asked what she charged. She slowed down to them catch up this time.

One of them smiled.

"I like your shirt," he said.

"We all do, said another.

"Thanks," she said.

"You have really sexy legs," the first sailor said. "And a nice ass."

"Are you?" another one asked.

"Am I what?" she asked.

"An oral expert? Do you suck dick?" he asked.

"Better yet, do you fuck?" the first one asked.

"You guys are rude!" she said.

"Well, you're wearing that shirt so we figured you're in the business," the first one said as he pointed to her shirt. "We just want to know how much you'd charge."

"We're willing to pay you," the second said.

"Yeah. This was pay week, so we have the cash," the third one said.

"Even if I was, you guys couldn't afford me," she teased.

"Wanna bet?" the first one challenged.

"Yeah. Name your price," the second added.

"Make me an offer," she said much to her own surprise.

"How about a hundred bucks from each of us?" the first one offered.

"And what would I have to do for that?" she teased.

"Lets us fuck you and you suck our dicks," the second sailor said. "I bet you have a real tight pussy, too."

"I don't know. Like I said, I'm not in the business," she said.

The first sailor called the other three into a huddle while she watched. After a few seconds, they all nodded. She saw them take money from their wallets, count it out and place it in the first one's hand. He smiled and walked over to her.

"There's $640 here. That's $160 from each of us," he said as he showed it to her.

"That's a lot of money," she said.

"So? Do we have a deal?" he asked.

She looked at him.

"If I said yes, where would we go?" she asked.

"That's a good question. We're new here. You have any ideas?" the second sailor asked.

She looked at them and thought it over. The idea of fucking four handsome young men in one day excited her. She'd never fucked anyone else but her husband before and she wondered if she should. She tried to envision the way four good, hard dicks would feel as they moved in and out of her cunt. The more she thought about it, the hornier she became.

"If Al finds out, he'll kill me," she thought. "But how would he ever find out? I'd never tell him and none of these guys even know him, so they sure as Hell wouldn't tell him."

"There's a small, grassy area just behind that building up there," she said, pointing. "It has bushes and trees. No one will see us there."

"Then we have a deal?" the first sailor asked.

She smiled and took the cash from his hand.

"Deal!" she said as they followed her to the hidden area.

One of the sailors took his shirt off and laid it on the grass. Rinna nervously undressed and laid down on it. The first sailor stood over and unzipped his pants. His prick was already good and hard so he knelt between her thighs and slid it into her already wet cunt. She moaned at the alien invader then sighed happily as he proceeded to fuck her. She opened her legs wide and gripped his shoulders as he fucked her faster and faster. She moved with him and tightened her inner muscles.

He groaned and fucked her faster.

"Damn! You're so tight!" he moaned.

The other sailors pulled out their dicks and stroked them while they watched their friend fuck her harder and harder.

"Can I come in your pussy?" he asked.

"Yes!" she moaned as she threw her hips up at him.

After a few more deep, hard thrusts, she felt him tremble. Then he came—a lot. So did she. She held onto him until he emptied his entire load into her cunt. He pulled out and looked at his buddies.

"She's great!" he said.

The next sailor immediately slid his prick into her cum-filled cunt and proceeded to hammer away. She felt his prick squish as it plunged in and out of the cum inside of her and fucked him back as hard as she could.

While they were fucking, the first sailor placed his prick against her lips. She opened her mouth and almost gagged when he slid it in but managed to suck it. She soon heard him groan deeply and felt a gush of salty liquid shoot into her mouth. She sucked it harder and harder until he finally had enough and pulled out.

That's when the second sailor suddenly began thrusting harder as he added his cum to his buddies inside her cunt. He eased out and nodded at the others.

The third guy stroked his dick to make it harder. She reached up and helped him and was amazed at the length of his dick. She got onto her hands and knees and shivered when she slid it into her cunt. Then he gripped her hips and gave her one of hardest, most intense fucks of her life. Each thrust hit places that had never been hit before and sent shivers through her sweaty body. She smiled at the second sailor and opened her mouth.

He laughed and stuck his half-erect dick in it and gasped when she sucked it. By some wild coincidence, both men came at the same time. The third man flooded her cunt with cum as the second shot lines of cum down her throat.

She came, too and it was a beaut!

She shook so hard that she fell on her elbows and emitted a long, deep moan. She was still lost in her orgasm when the fourth man flipped her onto her back and started fucking her. This was a nice, long and easy fuck with long, deep and gentle strokes that made her feel warm all over.

She barely noticed when the third sailor stuck his dick in her mouth or that he came within seconds. She was took lost in the deep, pleasant fuck she was getting. She held onto his hips and moved with him as he body trembled with each thrust of his dick.

"Oh yes! Yes! Fuck me! I love it! Fuck me!" she moaned as her orgasms soared to places she never thought possible.

The sailor moaned.

This was the best pussy he'd ever sunk his dick into by far and he was determined to make this last as long as possible. The other men stood and stroked and stroked their dick as they watched. It was several minutes more before he finally came. When he did, he slid his dick into her as far as he could and unloosed what seemed like a gallon of cum into her cunt.

The gusher of cum made her orgasm even harder. She gripped his arms and fucked him as hard as she could.

That's when she felt warm liquid splatter against her breasts. She looked up and watched as one of the men shot line after line of cum onto her while he jerked himself off. When he was finished, the next guy did the same and so did the third guy.

The guy fucking her finally pulled out. When he did, a river of white good ran out of her pulsing cunt. Since his prick was still half erect, she reached up, grabbed it and slid it into her mouth and sucked away until he begged her to stop.

She looked down at the streaks of cum on her breasts and slowly massaged it into her nipples while she smiled at them. The sailor clapped and cheered.

"You're the best fuck I ever I ever had!" the fourth man said. "Hell, I almost proposed!"

The others laughed.

One handed her clothes to her. They watched her dress. Three of them walked back up to the road. The fourth sailor pulled her to him and stuck his tongue in her mouth.

"Can I see you again? I'll be here for five more days and I'd really love to do this again," he said.

"So would I. What's your name?" she asked.

"David. What's yours?" he replied.

"Rinna," she said as they kissed again. "We can meet again tomorrow. I get free rooms at the casino hotel up the street. Meet me in the lobby around two."

"Uh, how much?" he asked.

"Nothing. I just want to feel what it's like to have you all to myself for a whole day," she said.

"I'll be there!" he promised.

She watched him join the others and waved. They waved back. Everyone seemed more than happy and the sailors all agreed that she lived up to the slogan on her T-shirt.

She now had a pussy flooded with cum from four hot, young men and she had committed her first act of adultery and prostitution. She smiled as she went back to her car and thought how very easy it was to make $640.

"And all I had to do was let them have sex with me!"

She went home, showered for a long time, and never said a word to anyone about what she'd done. She thought that would be a one-time slip. Something that she'd never do again.

She met David at the hotel the next day and they hurried up to the suite. He was more attentive and gentler than he'd been the day before. This time, he went down on her and he was even better with his tongue than he was with his dick. He made her come several times, then slid his dick into her for another nice, long and easy fuck.

No one, she thought, could fuck better than him.

Not even her husband.

She gave everything she had to him that day and then some. They tried several different positions and he made her come more times than she ever did in one day. Several times, she cried out to him to make her his.

"I'm yours now! Yours! Make love to me!" she moaned as she came again and again.

At nine o'clock, David announced that he had to get back to the ship. They dressed and stopped for another good, deep kiss. David walked her to her car and watched her drive away as she waved.

"Wow!" was all she could say as she headed home.

They did exchange cell phone numbers and he did promise to call her before he left. In the back of her mind, she wanted to do this again.

She also knew that there was no way she could disguise that "just fucked" look she always had after great sex. Al would notice that immediately. She hoped like Hell he wouldn't be home when she got there.

He wasn't.

He was still out with his baseball team and probably wouldn't be home for another hour or two. She also knew that he'd be horny, so she got herself ready for a long night of more sex.

Two days later she went for a jog along the riverfront. The sailors were still in town and she caught the eyes of three more handsome young men. When they whistled and waved to her, she stopped and walked over to them. She was also wearing that same T-shirt.

"Are you really an oral expert?" one of them asked.

"It will cost you money to find out," she teased.

"Are you a Filipina?" another asked as he ogled her legs.

"Yes I am," she replied.

"I bet you're a terrific fuck. How much?" he asked.

They negotiated a price of $450. Once the cash was in her hand, she led them to the same secluded area where she did her best to show them that everything they heard about Filipinas was true for the next two hours.

These guys were good, but not as good as the first group. But they were young, handsome and energetic so each of them fucked her twice and she sucked all of their dicks. When they left, they each gave her a long hug and told her she was terrific.

As she watched them leave, she waved and smiled.

"My pussy is like my own personal cash machine! All I have to do is open my legs and men will pay me a lot of money to have sex with me!" she thought as she went to her car.

Much to her disappointment, David didn't call. She sighed and threw away his cell phone number. She figured that she'd never see him again anyway. When Fleet Week came around next year, there would be a different ship and crew. She decided to put her T-shirt away until then.

The week after that, she fucked a guy she met at the casino after he offered her $200. She used one of her complimentary rooms and they spent two hours fucking in three different positions. She finished him off with a long blowjob. An hour later, she was back in the room fucking another guy.

She'd stopped for a while. Now, here she was in the casino, waiting to sell her pussy to any good-looking man who was willing to pay for it.

She smiled.

She had now become a bar girl. She was just like the women in Angeles City that she always looked down upon. She still did because while those girls would sell themselves to any man who offered to pay then, she was very choosy about who she wanted to fuck. If she didn't like a man for any reason (and there were lots of men she really didn't like), she'd simply rebuff his advances. Being a prostitute didn't mean she'd sleep with every man who approached her.

Around ten, a tall, dark haired man approached. He sat down next to her and smiled. Rinna smiled back and kept playing. She noticed that he wasn't gambling.

"Why aren't you gambling?" she asked out of curiosity.

"I'm about to gamble real big but I think the payoff might be worth the risk. At least it looks very interesting," he said.

"And what are you betting on?" she asked.

"I'm betting that you and I will be making love within the next few minutes," he said with a sexy smile.

She blushed.

"You're going to lose that bet," she said. "I'm married."

"Is your husband here now?" he asked.

"No," she said.

"Then what he doesn't know can't hurt him, can it?" he said.

"I guess not," she smiled.

"My name's Mark," he said as he held out his hand.

"Rinna," she said as she shook it.

"I've been watching you all night. You have the sexiest legs I've ever seen and I'd love to get at what's between them," he said.

"You're very bold!" she said.

"I'm a gambler. I have to be bold in order to take risks. You're also a gambler. Are you willing to take a risk?" he asked as he put his hand on her knee.

His touch was making her excited. When she didn't object, he slid it up her thigh. Rinna parted her legs slightly and smiled at him.

"Yes," she said. "I'm willing to take a risk—for a price."

"Wonderful. I have a room upstairs in the hotel," he suggested as he took her hand.

Minutes later, she was on her back naked with her legs wide open and moaning loudly as Mark's tongue explored her cunt. At the same time, he moved his finger in and out of her slit. The dual sensations magnified her pleasure and sent shivers up and down her body. Rinna quickly exploded and let out a deeper moan. While she was still coming, Mark rammed his prick into her cunt hard.

"Ooohhhh!" she cried as she came again.

When he fucked her, he used short, hard thrusts that kept her orgasm going and going. She gripped his shoulders and moved with him, loving each and every thrust of his hard prick. He was different than her other lovers.

His thrusts were stronger and harder.

They felt deeper, too.

His timing was perfect.

"Fuck me, Mark! Fuck the Hell out of me! I love it!" she cried as she came again and again and again.

"Can I come in your pussy?" he asked.

"Oh yeah! Fill my pussy!" she moaned.

He began thrusting faster and faster. She heard him grunt and felt him ram his prick into her harder as he came. He kept fucking and fucking and fucking for what felt like an eternity before he stopped and eased his prick out of her cum filled cunt.

Rinna lay there, bathed in sweat and gasping as her heartbeat slowly returned to normal. She smiled up at Mark.

"Wow!" she managed. "Where did you learn to do that?"

He laughed.

"I'm a male stripper. I work bachelorette parties so I have to stay hard for a long time. It's mostly just practice. I guess you really enjoyed it, huh?" he said as she stroked her breast.

"I sure did. You're great," Rinna said. "I'm glad you showed up tonight. I was getting kind of bored."

That's when she saw that he was rock hard again. His prick had to be at least ten inches long and fairly thick. She wrapped her fingers around it and gave it a few pumps.

"Are you ready for round two?" he asked.

She just smiled and opened her legs...

By the time she got home, it was past nine in the morning. Al was already at work. She and Mark had fucked the entire night and she had no idea about the time or the number of orgasms he managed to give her.

She was sore—but in a good way.

Her cunt tingled and it was filled with so much cum that it now ran down her inner thighs. She staggered upstairs to shower. As soon as she stepped out, her cell phone rang.

It was Eva.

"I've been trying to call you since last night. Where have you been?" she asked.

Rinna told her about her tryst.

"You have all the luck. You get laid almost every time you go to the casino. What did Al say when you got home?" Eva asked.

"Nothing yet because I just got home a few minutes ago. I spent the entire night with Mark," Rinna said. "He paid me $500 so I decided to give him his money's worth."

"Al's gonna kill you!" Eva said.

"Maybe," Rinna laughed. "I just forgot all about the time. That man really knows how to use his dick, too!"

"Slut!" Eva joked.

"You say that as if it's a bad thing," Rinna joked back.

Al was too occupied with Li to even think about Rinna at the moment. He was seated in the break area with Li having coffee and she was gazing into his eyes like she was star struck.

"Do you really mean all those things you said to me?" she asked.

"Every word," he assured her.

"I'm very flattered but I still don't understand why you're attracted to me. I'm so plain," she said modestly.

"What you've just said is one of the reasons I am attracted to you. You're very modest. Most women flaunt themselves then get upset when men go after them. You're quiet and shy and a lot prettier and sexier than you realize," he said.

"I'm not pretty at all—and I sure ain't sexy!" she said.

"But you're both of those and more," he said.

"You make me nervous, Al—but in a nice way. I can tell that you're sincere," she said. "I wish you weren't married so that we can have a real, close relationship and maybe even get married one day. I guess that will never happen."

"Never say never," he said softly as he took her hand.

She really blushed then.

"You have such a beautiful wife. Why would you even notice anyone like me?" she asked.

"To begin with, I noticed you the moment I saw you," Al said. "You're cute and sexy and you have a great personality. Those are terrific qualities and yes, I noticed you."

"Wow. I never thought you felt like that. I'm flattered, Al. I really am. I'm also a little scared," she replied.

"Don't be," he said. "Relax and let things take their course."

"I don't know what that course is," she said.

"You will," he assured her.

When Rinna sufficiently recovered, she decided to return to the casino. This time, she told herself that she'd abstain from having sex with anyone but her husband for a while. She was afraid that she was turning into too much of a slut and sure as Hell didn't want to get that sort of reputation with men at the casinos. She knew that Eva didn't care about that. She was busy fucking as many men as she could and didn't care who knew it.

She sat down at her usual slot and started to play. After an hour, a somewhat inebriated man swaggered up to her. She ignored him.

"How would you like to have a nice fuck?" the man asked.

"Are your parents giving you away or something?" she replied.

He laughed.

"That was good. You think fast on your feet. I like that," he said. "I've seen you around here before. You usually leave with a different guy each time. Are you in the business?"

"What business?" she asked as she grew irritated.

"You know what I mean. Are you a hooker?" he asked.

"I certainly am not! I think you'd better go and bother somebody else before I ask security to throw you out," she threatened.

"I have lots of money," he offered.

"No!" she almost yelled.

"I'll pay you $300," he said.

"I said no," she insisted. "I'm not a prostitute. Leave me alone."

"How about $400?" he asked.

"No way! Now get lost," she said angrily.

"Suit yourself," he mumbled as he staggered away.

Rinna sighed with relief.

She would normally have said yes to his first offer, but she had taken an instant dislike to him from the way he approached her. He was very blunt and boorish, kind of like a gorilla. She just wanted him gone.

While she continued to play her favorite slots, a broad shouldered, casually dressed and rather good looking man walked over. He watched her play for a little while then sat down at the slot next to hers.

"Hello," he said.

"Hi," she replied without bothering to look at him.

"My name's Brad. What's yours?' he said.

"Why do you want to know?" she asked in an irritated voice.

"I'm just trying to make conversation. I saw you here last week but you left before I could speak to you. You come here often?"

"Not really," she said, although she went to the casino nearly every Saturday. It was something to do when she didn't feel like hanging around the house or had nothing else going on.

"You like to gamble?" he asked. Apparently, this stranger wasn't going away anytime soon.

"Sometimes—when I win," she replied.

"Are you winning tonight?" he asked.

"Not really," she said.

"What's your name?" he asked again.

She held back. She figured if she told him, she'd never get rid of him. She glanced at him. He was tall, sandy haired and handsome. He was dressed nicely, too. And young.

"Why won't you tell me your name?" he asked.

"If I do, you'll keep bothering me," she said.

"Yes I will," he laughed.

She giggled.

"Are you married?" he asked.

"What do you think?" she said as she showed him her wedding band. "Go find some single woman to bother."

"Do you know any?" he asked.

"No," she said.

"In that case, I'll just stay here and talk to you," he said. "Can I get you something to drink?"

"No. I'm okay," she said. "I don't drink anyway. If I do, I won't be able to drive home later."

"Oh. You're a lightweight. How about some iced tea or coffee? I'm headed that way anyway."

"Okay. Iced tea," she said hoping to get rid of him.

He nodded.

"Iced tea it is. I'll be back in a few minutes," he said as he walked away.

She was about to leave the slot machine when she started winning. Caught up in the thrill of the moment, she forgot about him and kept playing. A few minutes later, he showed up with her drink in hand.

She smiled and took it.

"Thanks," she said.

"I like your accent. Where are you from?" he asked.

"The Philippines," she said.

"Is your husband an American?" he asked.

She nodded.

"He's one lucky guy," he said.

"He thinks he is," she smiled. "Oh. That's it for me. I'm going to cash this and go home."

He watched her remove the card and winnings slip and walk off. As she did, he studied her behind with interest. It was small and, by the way her jeans hugged her body, he could see it was perfectly shaped. So were her legs.

"Next time," he thought.

Rinna had decided to do her best to avoid having sex with men she met at the casino. At least for a while. But Brad was good looking and she nearly gave in to him. She wondered if she'd see him again. If so, would he still come on to her?

She went to a different casino two days later where she was able to play the slots in peace. She even managed to win a few dollars and went home happy. And when she was happy, she made Al happy.

A lot.

Al kept working on building his relationship with Li. The more time he spent with her, the more he liked her. In fact, he was falling for her big time. Li was also falling for him but held back because she didn't want to be the one who torpedoed his marriage. Her morals and sense of decency kept getting in her way.

But even those lines of defense were starting to falter.

Her mother saw her dilemma but decided to refrain from offering advice. This was something she knew her daughter had to think through on her own. She didn't like to see her in such turmoil but this was one of life's snags.

She smiled.

Li smiled back.

"This is crazy, Mom," she said. "The first and only man ever to pursue me and he is married! And I am good friends with his wife. What is really crazy is that she encouraged it so she could have sex with other men."

"What does he say about it?" her mother asked.

"He said that whatever comes of this will come of it. If we happen to fall in love along the way, he said that would be wonderful. I'm scared, Mom," she said.

"Is that because you have already fallen for him?" her mother asked.

Li nodded.

"I feel like I have entered a dragon's den," she said.

"If his wife encouraged him as you say, that removes all blame from the both of you. It is a very strange marriage but it is what they have decided to make of it. I don't see it lasting much longer," her mother said.

"Me neither," Li agreed. "So I should let Al catch me?"

"Yes. When he does, he may want to keep you," her mother smiled. "You are a rare treasure and he knows it."

Li smiled.

Eva kept busy that entire week. In between her trips to the YWCA, she met four more men from the website. Each man came to her house and fucked the daylights out of her. Three of the four actually gave her multiple orgasms. The fourth guy only gave her one—but it was a beaut! It happened suddenly, too.

He had a prick that was at least 10 inches long and very thick. It was so big; he had to ease it into her cunt a little at a time. After he had most of it buried inside her, he rotated his hips several times. This caused his prick to deliciously massage every nook and cranny of her cunt. It felt so damned, that it triggered an orgasm. While she was in the throes of it, he fucked her for a long, long time.

And she kept coming all through it. Over and over and over again. The orgasm lasted so long and was so deep, that all she saw was white. Her body writhed with each deep, hard thrust and she held him tight and begged him to keep going.

"More! More! I love it! Give it to me harder! More!" she creamed as she fucked him with everything she had.

It was the deepest, most complete and intense fuck of her entire life. When he finally came in her cunt, it felt like gallons of cum. It ran out of her cunt and down between her cheeks and stained the sheets.

"Ooohhh, yeah! Fuck me!" she moaned as he body went limp. "Fuck me forever!"

He kept at it for another minute or so then pulled his still half-hard prick from her pulsing cunt. She looked down at what seemed like a river of cum that followed it out of her cunt. She smiled up at him.

"Wow!" they both said at once.

That was so great that when he tried to pay her, she refused to take his money.

"That was the very best sex of my life!" she said. "I'm not taking your money for that! Wow! You can come over and fuck me anytime you like from now on."

He smiled.

"I'll be sure to call you when I come back," he promised. "My name's Dan."

She shook his hand.

"Eva," she said. "Here's my cell phone number. Don't forget to call me."

"Believe me, I won't!" he said. "You really know how to use your pussy, Eva. You're the best."

She felt proud to hear Dan say that. All of her lovers said the same things. Everyone loved her pussy but Vince.

"I wonder who he's fucking these days?" she thought as she watched Dan drive away.

While she was busy with Dan, Eva's husband made a surprise visit to Rinna. She smiled when she opened the door and let him inside. Without saying a word, he grabbed her and stuck his tongue in her mouth.

"I've been thinking about you lately," she said. "It's been a long time since I felt that great big dick of yours in my pussy and I'm dying to feel it again."

She led him upstairs to the guest bedroom where they quickly undressed each other. Rinna immediately grabbed his prick and beat him off until he was fully erect. Just playing with it made her cunt wet and her heart race. Vince pushed her down on the bed. She parted her legs and sighed happily as he buried his tongue in her cunt.

"Oh yes. I've missed you," she sighed.

Vince ate her until she came twice. Before she recovered, he shoved a pillow under her ass and slid his prick into her cunt. They quickly settled into a nice, rhythmic fuck. They took their time so they could really enjoy it.

Rinna moaned as they fucked. She loved every second of their tryst, every deep, delicious thrust of his prick. And he absolutely loved the way her cunt wrapped itself around his prick as she moved with him.

This time, it was perfect.

This time, they came together.

"Oh yes! I love it! Fuck me, Vince!" Rinna cried as her orgasm rippled through her. "I love your dick! Give it to me!"

He was too busy pumping his cum into her cunt to even hear her. To him, Rinna was his dream girl and the fact that she was willing to fuck him thrilled him to no end. It was one of the benefits of what had become a very open marriage.

He got to fuck Rinna and Al got to fuck Eva whenever they got the chance.

After he filled her cunt with his cum, he went down on her. This caught Ri9nna by surprise and she writhed and moaned as his tongue moved in and out of her cunt. She realized that Eva was right when she said that Vince loved the taste of his own cum.

Vince was hard again. He turned her over onto her stomach. Rinna grabbed a pillow and slid it under her belly elevate her ass. Vince spread her legs wide and slid his prick into her cunt for another long, deep fuck.

They fucked twice more that day. The last time, Rinna was on top and she fucked him like she was possessed. It was as if she just couldn't get enough of his prick. He didn't mind because no woman he ever had in his life could fuck better than Rinna. Not even Eva.

"I'm glad you came by today. It's been much too long since we had sex. Don't be such a stranger, Vince. I'm here whenever you want me and you know how much I love to fuck!" she said.

"I came by today because I had a day off from work and no other obligations," he said.

"Oh? You mean none of your other women were available?" she asked.

"Actually, I've been thinking about you quite a lot lately. I'd love to make this a regular thing between us, too," he said.

"You mean like an affair?" she asked.

"Something like that," he said.

"Let me think about that for a while. An affair sounds so exclusive and I'm having too much fun fucking other men right now. Maybe after I get this out of my system," she said.

"You still fuck other men?" he asked.

"Uh-huh. I meet them at the casinos and we fuck—a lot," she admitted.

"Wow," he said. "So you're doing what Eva does?"

"Yes and it's too much fun to stop right now. But you can have me whenever you like. You know where to find me," she assured him as she stroked his prick.

They dressed and she escorted him to the door. Before he left, they kissed. It was another deep kiss, too. She watched as he got into his car and drove away then shut her front door.

Vince laughed at the situation.

"As long as she's willing to fuck me, I don't care who else she's fucking," he said.

When he got home, he saw a man leave the house, get into a car and drive away. When he walked inside, Eva was stark naked and walking into the bathroom. She smiled at him.

"Yes we did," she said.

"How much?" he asked.

"He was so good, I refused to take his money. I told him to call me whenever he felt like fucking again. Jealous?" she teased.

"A little bit. But I've just finished—" he began.

"—fucking Rinna," she finished. "How does it make you feel to know that I am a prostitute?" she asked. "How does it make you feel that I fuck a lot of other men for money and I let them come in my pussy?"

She reached between her thighs, parted her cuntlips and allowed several dollops of cum to fall to the floor.

"'It makes me incredibly horny and, if Rinna hadn't fucked the Hell out of me, I'd pick you and carry into the bedroom right now," he said.

"How about later?" she asked.

"Definitely!" he said.

She smiled and went into the bathroom to shower.

Chapter Twelve

The next day, Al asked Li to have dinner with him after work.

"Are you asking me out on a date?" she asked.

"Yes I am. Will you go with me?" he replied.

"Of course I will. Where shall we go?" she accepted.

"How about the Mekong?" she suggested.

"Perfect. I love Vietnamese cuisine," he said as he hugged her.

This caught her totally off guard. She wasn't expecting a hug and she reacted by hugging him back.

"Um—won't Rinna wonder where you are?" she asked.

"I doubt it. I'm sure she'll be busy herself tonight," Al said. "Besides, I've already called her. She said to have fun."

Li did a double take.

"Your marriage is very strange," she said.

"Tell me about it!" he said.

The restaurant was modern and dimly lit. They chose a booth in the second dining room and the waiter hurried to take their order. To Li's surprise, Al ordered in Vietnamese. She sat and smiled approvingly as they chatted back and forth. When the waiter left she stared at him.

"Where did you learn to speak my language?" she asked.

"In Vietnam. I was there during the war," he replied with a smile. "Some things just stay with you over the years."

"You mentioned that before. I want to know all about what you saw and did there," Li said.

They sat and talked for a long time while they ate. Even the waiter stopped by to listen as he related his experiences. Li was completely enraptured by him now. The esteem she'd always had for him climbed several notches that night.

They left the Mekong around nine. He called a taxi and took her home. During the ride, he put his arm around her and she snuggled up to him. She thought how perfect the evening had been and wished it would never end.

When the taxi pulled up in front the Li house, he got out and escorted her onto the porch. They held each other tight for a little while.

"Thank you for a wonderful evening," she said softly.

"Thank you," he said.

Li's mother was in the living room watching TV when she walked in. She saw the expression on Li's face and smiled knowingly.

"I know that look," she said.

"What look is that, Mom?" Li asked.

"The look that tells the entire world that you are in love," her mother said.

When Al got home, Rinna was seated on the sofa. He sat next to her and hugged her. She smiled.

"How was your date with Li?" she asked.

"I took her to dinner. I think I have to be slow and gentle with her. I am the only man who ever showed an interest in her and I think that scares her," he said.

"I understand," Rinna said.

"What did you do today?' he asked.

"I stayed home and cleaned the house. I prepared some light snacks for us in case you feel hungry later. It's still early and you don't have work tomorrow," she said.

"I love the way you think," he said.

"You'll really love what I have planned for us tonight," she smiled.

The following afternoon, Vince got home just minutes after Eva's last "lover" left. He was so energetic that he wore her out. After she escorted him out, she fell asleep on the bed. She was still naked and her legs were wide apart. Vince looked down at the line of cum running out of her open cunt and smiled. For some reason, the sight of his wife lying there with another man's cum oozing from her cunt gave him an erection.

A big one.

He quickly removed his clothes, climbed onto the bed and slid his prick into her. The feeling of the cum squishing around as he fucked her felt oddly erotic. Eva woke and smiled at him then moved with him. They fucked nice and easy for a long, long time. Eva came first and shook all over. Vince followed seconds later and added his cum to the pool inside his wife's well-fucked cunt.

He smiled at her.

"So the sight of another man's cum running out of my pussy makes you horny?" she asked as she used her fingers to open her labia. "Horny enough to want to have sex with me?"

"I can't explain it, Eva. When I saw you lying here like that, I got this terrific urge to fuck you," he said.

"How does it feel to put your dick into another man's cum?" she asked.

"Insanely erotic," he admitted. "I like the way it feels when I move in and out. It's squishy and sticky and crazy exciting."

"Maybe I should let you fuck me after Al does. How would it feel to put your dick into your best friend's cum again?" she teased.

He thought about that for a few seconds. As he did, his prick got hard again.

"I see you like the idea. Maybe I'll let you both fuck me at the same time. Rinna, too. We can go somewhere nice and spend an entire weekend fucking each other silly," she said as she stroked his prick.

"I'm game. Let's discuss that with them next time we get together. Maybe we'll just trade spouses for a weekend. That should be easy enough since Rinna likes fucking me and you love to fuck Al," he said.

Eva lay back down and opened her legs wide. Vince shut up and slid his prick back into her cunt for another, good and even longer fuck.

Li was practically dancing in the clouds now. At work, she went out of her way to be close to Al and she even brought him a special lunch that she had cooked the night before. They sat and talked as they ate. Anyone who saw them could plainly see that they were enchanted with each other.

"What are you doing tomorrow night?" Al asked.

"Nothing," she replied.

"I have two tickets to Miss Saigon. You said that you've always wanted to see that play, so I got the tickets last week. We can have dinner near the theater then see the show," he said.

"Of course I'll go with you! I'll go with you wherever and whenever you want me to," she said without thinking.

Then she sort of blushed when she realized what she said. He beamed at her and held her hand. She smiled back.

"He understands," she thought.

The next night, Rinna and Eva went to the casino. As usual, they went to the bar before playing. Eva ordered a light wine and Rinna ordered a sweet ice tea. As they drank, a man walked over and sat down next to Eva.

Rinna watched as they struck up a conversation. During the course of their chat, the man put his hand on Eva's thigh and moved up between her legs. Eva just sat and smiled at him. Then he leaned over and whispered in her ear.

"That all depends on what you want to do," Eva said back.

"We can talk about that in my suite," the man suggested.

Eva nodded. She turned to Rinna.

"I'll meet you in the lobby around eleven," she said.

Rinna watched as the two left together and laughed. She finished her tea and headed for the slots like always. An hour or so later, Brad made an appearance. She noticed him when he came in. He saw her, smiled and walked over.

She kept playing while he sat next to her. At first she tried to ignore him. After a few minutes, she began chatting with him. He was funny and he even made her laugh a few times. And her unique way of mangling the English language made him laugh, too.

She also noticed that he was winning.

Often.

"How do you keep winning like that?" she asked.

"I guess I'm just real lucky. I normally win several thousand dollars a month playing the slots. I usually don't play the penny slots, though."

"Then why are you?" she asked.

"Because you always play them and I like talking to you," he said. "Do you like talking to me?"

She hesitated. Eventually, she admitted that she did.

"So what's your name?" he asked.

"Rinna," she said.

"That's cute. It fits you, too," he said. "You told me you're married. Do you also have a boyfriend?"

"Of course not!" she said, surprised at his question.

"Too bad. Would you like one?" he teased.

She scowled.

"I just asked as a joke," he said.

"What if I had said yes?" she asked.

"I'd offer you myself," he smiled. "Then, if you liked the idea, we could start an affair."

"You're nuts!" she said.

He laughed.

"I've been told that many times before," he said.

"Maybe you should listen. Maybe you should see a doctor or something," she said.

"Maybe I will one day. I'm having too much fun right now," he said. "I see you're wearing shorts tonight. You have great legs."

"Um, thanks," she said, pleased that he'd noticed.

She was a little uncomfortable around him now and regretted wearing the shorts. She looked back at the slot screen and muttered under her breath. She'd lost another round. She pulled her card out and stuck it into her pocket.

"I think I lost enough tonight. I'm going home," she announced. "Bye!"

"See you next week," he said.

"Not if I see you first," she said as she walked away, secretly disappointed that he hadn't made her an offer.

He laughed.

Upstairs, Eva was on a bed bouncing up and down on a huge, hard prick while her lover played with her taut nipples. This was their third good, hard fuck of the evening and his prick never seemed to grow soft.

It was thick, hard and it stretched her inner cunt wonderfully. He'd already come in her twice and his prick made slurping sounds as she bounced up and down on it. She loved every second of it, too. Eva knew that her body was made for sex and the more sex she got, the more sex she wanted.

She felt him shudder inside of her and add yet another load of cum to his previous deposits. This time, it ran out of her cunt and stained the sheets. She kept fucking him harder and harder as she also came. After a few more deep strokes, she fell to the side, exhausted. She looked over at him and smiled. His prick had finally gone limp. He smiled at her.

"You're the best," he said.

She got up, wiped his cum from her pussy with a tissue and dressed. He just took several bills from his wallet and gave them to her. She counted it and grinned happily. He'd given her $300.

"You're worth every cent of it, too," he said. "I hope we see each other here again soon. I come to town about every other month. So I'll look for you again."

She grabbed the notepad from the desk and wrote her cell phone number on it. He laughed when she gave it to him.

"This way, you won't have to waste time looking for me. Just call me the night before and I'll be here," Eva promised.

"Pretty lady, you have got yourself a deal!" he said.

Rinna didn't leave. Instead, she went over to a slot on the far side of the casino. After a few minutes, she saw Jake walking toward her. She smiled and hugged him.

"I guess that means we're on for tonight?" he asked.

"Definitely!" she said as she walked to the hotel with him.

Brad watched from a distance and smiled.

"I thought so," he said. "Now I know how to nail her."

As usual, Jake and Rinna fucked each other silly for as many times as he could get it up. Rinna loved to fuck him and she put all of herself into it. When she left the suite around 11:30, Jake was too worn out to move and she could barely stagger to the elevators.

When she met Rinna in the bar, Eva noticed that she looked tired but happy.

They both giggled and nodded at each other.

"Jake was here tonight," Rinna said. "He really made my pussy purr, too. Tonight, I didn't charge him."

"My guy paid me $300 because he wanted to fuck me in my ass, too," Eva smiled. "It was okay. He had a normal sized dick and it didn't hurt at all."

"With all of the big dicks you've had up there, I didn't think anything would hurt you," Rinna said.

"Oh some dick still hurt!" Eva assured her. "We fucked three times! He was great, too."

"What about your husband?" asked Rinna. "Is he bothered by what you do?"

"No. He knows I fuck other men. Hell, it even excites him," Eva smiled.

She told her what happened the day before. Rinna laughed.

"Vince fucked both of us this week," she said. "Then Al fucked me when he got home. So we both had very good days."

"I'll say. I'd already fucked two other men before Vince came home. He said he really liked fucking when I have a pussy filled with someone else's cum, too. That really turns him on," Eva said.

"What's next?" Rinna asked.

Eva shrugged.

"Want to swap husbands for a weekend? Vince said he'd really love to fuck me or you after Al did so he could feel what that's like. We could go away for the weekend. Somewhere nice," she said.

"Sure," Rinna said. "Can we also have sex with each other? I really loved my last time with you."

Eva laughed.

"That was nice, wasn't it?" she asked as she put her hand on Rinna's thigh.

Rinna nodded.

"I'd kiss you, but I've been sucking on a dick tonight," Eva said as she slid her hand under Rinna's shorts. "I'd really love to eat your pussy."

Rinna sat still and allowed Eva to play with her pussy for a while. She liked the way she touched her and was very willing to give herself to her. Eva smiled and withdrew her hand.

"I'd better not start anything. I'm pretty tired and my pussy is filed with a lot of cum, so it would be too messy for you tonight. Maybe we'll do it next time," Eva said.

Rinna didn't press the matter. When Eva dropped her off at home, Rinna went straight up to the bedroom where she knew her husband would be waiting...

Al took Li to dinner at a steakhouse next to the theater. Li was thrilled with the show and during the intermissions, they went to the bar and had drinks. Li didn't drink much as a rule, so she felt very light-headed when they left.

She was amazed to find a horse and carriage waiting. Al helped her on and they went for a ride through the nearby Victorian park. During the ride, she snuggled up to him and he held her close.

The ride lasted 30 minutes.

Al drove her home.

Just before she got out, he leaned close and kissed her gently on the lips. She kissed him back and blushed.

"That is my very first kiss," she said happily. "It's nice. This was the most beautiful night of my life, Al. It's like a fairy tale or something."

They kissed again.

This time, it was a deep, passionate kiss.

Li smiled and got out of the car. Her parents watched as she practically danced onto the porch, turned and waved to Al as he drove away.

They looked at each other and laughed.

"It looks like our daughter is in love," he father said.

"Very much so," her mother agreed.

"I hope it goes well for everyone. I doubt that Li imagined that her life would go down this crazy road," he said.

"No one did," her mother smiled.

The next morning, the two ladies met at a café for breakfast. Rinna remarked that Eva still looked a little tired.

"I am. That guy fucked the shit out of me last night," Eva said. "And he paid me well, too," Eva almost boasted

Rinna chuckled.

"You really like being a prostitute, don't you?" she asked.

"Yes. I make lots of money and I'm having lots of fun. You should know after all the men you've fucked. I know you like doing it as much as I do," Eva said.

"I've fucked a few different men lately. Most of them paid me. A couple didn't because at that time, I wasn't selling my pussy. My pussy is made to be fucked, Rinna. And the more dicks it gets in it, the happier I am. I know that you love sex as much as I do and you also love getting paid for it," Eva continued.

"Yes I am a prostitute and yes I like doing it. I never thought I'd do anything like this, but it's a lot of fun. I also get enough sex from my husband. We make love nearly every night and he knows I fuck other men. Right now, he's too busy chasing after Li to think much about what I do," Rinna said honestly.

Eva smiled at her.

"Besides, what I really want to do is to fuck Vince more often. The idea of fucking him for an entire weekend sounds great. My pussy gets wet just thinking about it!" Rinna said.

Eva stood and unzipped her shorts to reveal her cunt.

"What about me? Do I make your pussy wet?" she asked.

Rinna replied by pulling her shorts all the way down and running the tip of her tongue up and down Eva's slit.

Li was in a tailspin.

Al actually said he thought she was sexy and that he'd go after her if her weren't married. No man ever told her anything like that before. He said she was perfect the way she was and he wouldn't change a single thing.

She smiled.

"What should I do if he tries to make a play for me? I kind of want him to. But I don't want to cause his wife any grief. I've never been in this position before. I don't know what to do!" she told her mother.

The older woman just smiled and hugged her.

"Let your feelings guide you," she said. "Perhaps something very good will come from this."

"If it ruins his marriage, that won't be good for anyone. I'll feel guilty about it forever. But what he said excited me. I feel so confused about it all," Li said.

"I know. As they say here in America, life has thrown you a curveball," her mother said.

"It's more like a knuckleball, mom," Li said.

Al was also in a spin.

His wife and her friend had set things in motion that he'd never imagined. Not only did Rinna admit to being attracted to Eva, but she had told him that she likes to have sex with her—and other men. She had also given him the green light to pursue Eva and Li. At the same time, he knew that Eva was cheating on Vince and that he was cheating on Eva. These were circumstances he never imagined would happen.

"Just where in Hell is this all leading us to?" he wondered.

Rinna talked over her dilemma with Al. He listened in disbelief as she described her mixed feelings. When she was finished, he just smiled at her.

"So you and Eva want to swap husbands for a weekend?" he asked.

"Yes. Vince and I can spend the entire weekend having sex and you can fuck Eva as much as you like. Since we're already doing it, lets' make it easier for everyone. Vince said he's up for that and so are me and Eva," she said. "This way everyone gets what they want without any guilt attached."

"It sort of makes sense," he said.

She told him what Eva told her about her last time with Vince. He looked at her and laughed. The idea that Vince would fuck Rinna right after him, while she was still filled with cum seemed weird and funny.

"Does Eva expect me to fuck her after she fucks Vince, too?" he asked.

"That's up to you," she said.

"And you really want to spend an entire weekend fucking Vince?" he asked.

She nodded.

"And another man is hitting on you at the casino, but you're not sure if you should let him fuck you?" he asked.

"Right. I mean, part of me wants to do it and another part doesn't. He's kind of handsome and I know he won't give up," she said. "What do you think I should do?"

Al laughed.

"You realize how ridiculous this conversation is? No normal couple would even discuss anything like this," he said.

"I know," she said.

"You want my advice on what to do about having sex with other men? Really?" he asked.

"Um, yes. What do you think I should do?" she asked.

"I really can't answer that one, Rinna. Only you can decide such things. I can't tell you who to fuck or not fuck. Since you decided to travel down this road and take me with you, all I can say is follow your instincts—and be prepared for whatever consequences that may follow," he said.

"Consequences?" she asked.

"Yes. You and Eva are creating an entirely new set of intimate relationships and have dragged me into this neat little web with you. Lives can either be made better or shattered over this. You may have set in motion something that no one expects or can control. Eva's marriage is nearly over with. I saw that coming months ago. Our marriage is still good, but can you really share me with Eva or Li or both? You've always been jealous and possessive. You seem to have undergone a complete personality change," he said.

"Wow. I never thought about that," she said. "But I still want to experiment. That's why I'm okay with it if you want to do it, too. You must think I'm crazy!"

"Definitely," he smiled.

"So now what?" she asked.

"I figure that you're going to fuck a few other men no matter what I say. You already admitted that you liked it, so I know you'll just keep doing it. In that case, I'm going to keep fucking Eva whenever I can and I'll go after Li. We'll do this for as long as you want. If you stop, I'll stop—maybe. Eva and Li may not want to stop," he said. "In fact, I doubt that you will."

She smiled.

"I guess you're right. What about the swap?" she asked.

"Okay. I'm up for that. Any idea when?" he asked.

"Whenever it happens," she said. "Are you gonna have sex with Li?"

"That's up to her, isn't it? I'm not going to pressure her into doing anything she doesn't want to do. But I warn you, she may decide to try and make it a permanent thing. Can you handle that?" he said.

"I'm not sure. It kind of scares me a little," Rinna admitted. "But I said you should do it and I'm going to stick with that decision. Besides, if you stop now, you might crush the poor thing. I don't want to see her hurt in any way."

"Neither do I," Al said. "You're being far too nice and eager about this. Care to tell me why?"

"I really can't answer that one, Al. I don't know myself," she said with a smile."

Three nights later, Rinna returned to the casino. Brad spotted her from across the room and decided to give it another try. He walked over with two drinks and handed her one. She scowled and sniffed the drink.

"What is it?" she asked.

"Rum and coke. I went real light on the rum because you said you don't drink," he said. "Try it."

She took a sip and put the glass down on the console.

"Thanks," she said as she returned to her game.

"I see you're wearing shorts again," he observed. "They're a little shorter than the ones you wore last week. I like them. They really show off your legs nicely."

She said nothing and kept playing. He watched her for a few minutes. She was losing, too, and not real pleased by it.

"Bad night?" he asked.

"Sort of," she said. "How did you do?"

"I won $2,000 at poker, so I decided to shut it down while I'm ahead. I was about to leave when I saw you," he said.

"Why?" she asked.

"I'm attracted to you. You're drop-dead cute and you keep trying to ignore me. That's why I keep talking to you," he replied.

"You need to find some other woman to bother," she said.

"I'm not interested in other women. I'm interested in you," he said.

"Why me? I told you that I'm not interested," she said as she pretended to be annoyed.

"You're a real challenge for me. I normally get what I want," he said.

"Well, you can't have me. I'm married and I'm very happy with that," she said. "So bother someone else."

"No," he smiled.

"Why not?" she asked without looking at him.

"You're the sexiest woman I ever met and I'm going to try everything I can to get into your panties," he said.

She scowled at him.

"What did you say?" she asked uneasily.

"I said that I'd like to fuck you," he repeated. "I want to take you up to my suite and fuck you until neither of us can move."

"I should slap your face off for being so fresh. I'm not that kind of woman," she said as she glared at him. "Get away from me."

"I'm sorry I offended you. I just say what's on mind," he said. "You're really cute and very sexy. And you're Asian on top of that. That makes you even more attractive."

"I don't care. Leave me alone," she said.

He looked at her slot total and smiled. He could tell she was on a losing streak and was already in the hole about $150.

"Still not doing too good, huh?" he asked.

"Not tonight," she said.

"I tell you what—I'll cover all of your losses tonight if you'll agree to have sex with me," he offered.

"No!" she said. "I'm not a prostitute. Leave me alone or I'll call the guard."

"You're not fooling me, Rinna. I've asked around. That's exactly what you are. I don't care about that one way or the other. I still want you and I'm willing to pay," he said.

"Okay. So you know. You're still not getting anything," she said as she actually grew annoyed with him.

"How if I cover your losses and add your usual fee on top of that?" he offered.

"That's a lot of money," she said.

"I'll give you whatever you've lost tonight if you just let me see what you have between your legs," he offered. "Think about it. That's $150 plus your usual $200 fee. What do you say?"

"No," she said adamantly. "I'm not in the mood."

"Suit yourself," he said as he walked away.

Rinna smiled. She knew that sooner or later, they'd end up fucking each other. But for now, she was enjoying her little game. And Brad had upped the ante. That showed he really wanted her. She thought the harder to get she played, the more he'd offer her. When she thought it was enough, she'd accept.

She looked around for Eva, but didn't see her. She knew that she had left the slots area with another man. Most likely, they were upstairs fucking. And he was paying her well for that hot, tight pussy.

Rinna smiled as another man came over to her. She'd fucked him before so there was no pretense between them. He slid his hand up her inner thigh and massaged her cunt. She smiled and nodded. Ten minutes later, they were on his hotel bed, naked and fucking like crazy. After he made her come a few times, she returned to the casino. She had an extra $250 in her pocket and a cunt full of cum.

She sat down at the slots and played again. About 20 minutes later, another man approached her. He was a friend of the man she had just fucked.

"I have $250," he said.

"And I have a nice, tight pussy," she replied with a grin.

She returned to the casino and hour later feeling tired. He'd fucked her in her cunt and ass and she had sucked his dick. It had been an hour of nonstop, energetic sex, too. Before she sat down, she spotted another of her "lovers" walking toward her. She walked up to him and fondled his crotch.

"Oh yeah!" he said as he led her up to his room…

She returned to the casino floor an hour or so later with a pocket full of cash and a well-fucked pussy and ass.

Eva walked up and tapped her on the shoulder. Rinna laughed when she saw how she looked.

"You should at least comb your hair," she said as they walked to the car.

Eva giggled as they got in.

"What a night!" she said. "He fucked me three times and I sucked his dick. Then he gave me $300. I even let him keep my panties as a souvenir. See?"

She opened her shorts to show Rinna her bare cunt.

"I let him come in me each time, too. Men really like that a lot. So do I. I like having a pussy full of cum," she said.

"So do I. I had sex with three men tonight. My pussy feels nice and warm now and I'm really tired," Rinna said.

"Let's go home. It's nearly three a.m.," Eva said.

When Rinna walked in, Al was still up watching TV. He grinned at her.

"Did you get lucky tonight?" he teased.

"Yes—maybe too lucky," she smiled as she sat down next to him.

Li decided to pack a special lunch for Al the next day. She made Vietnamese pancakes and spring rolls and put them in a decorative cardboard box. She handed him the box when they clocked in that morning and blushed when he gave her a "thank you" hug.

At lunch, they sat together in the park.

"Thank you again for this beautiful lunch," he said. "I've always enjoyed your cooking, so I know these will be great."

"It's just a simple thing. It's nothing special," she said shyly.

"Oh but it is special. Just like you," he said.

They ate and chatted. Al made her laugh and he commented on how much he liked her laugh. He had told her these things before, but for some reason, they really registered with her now. She gazed at him and smiled as they talked.

"You know, no one has ever entered my rose garden. That's because no man has ever shown any interest me. I think most feel that I am not voluptuous enough or too plain. But you always say nice things to me and make me feel good. If you were not already married, I would consider giving myself to you," she said.

"And I would be deeply honored to have that privilege," he said as he touched her hand.

She blushed again.

His touches excited her. She looked into his eyes and smiled again. He leaned close and kissed her on the lips. Startled, she just let him do it. That's when they both felt that special, sudden surge of electricity. She sat back and stared at him.

"Wow!" she said.

"Yes, it was," he agreed.

They headed back inside to complete their work day. When Li got home, her mother saw the expression on her face. She sat her down at the dining room table and asked what happened. Li told her.

"It sounds as if you are in love with him," her mother said. "And he is certainly interested in you. You have yourself in quite an interesting place now. What are you going to do?"

Li shrugged.

"I have no idea," she said. "Maybe I'll let nature take its course."

"I see," her mother smiled. "Please be careful, my daughter. He is married and his wife may be very jealous once she sees that you don't plan to give him back."

Li nodded.

"I plan to sleep with him," she admitted. "I plan to give myself to him as many times as he wants me."

Her mother laughed.

"In that case, I think he will decide to keep you, too," she said.

While this was happening, across town, Eva lay on the bed and moaned loudly as her latest "lover" ate her pussy. They had just finished igniting each other with some prolonged foreplay and now his thick, warm tongue was buried inside her cunt and doing things that drive her wild. When she came, she grabbed his hair and fucked his tongue as hard as she could. He responded by sliding a finger up inside her asshole and wriggling it around.

Eva screamed and came a second time.

While she was still writhing in ecstasy, he moved between her thighs and slid his prick into her cunt. She immediately wrapped her arms around him.

"Fuck me! Fuck me hard!" she said.

It was a good, long and hard fuck, too. One of the longest she'd ever experienced. He fucked her hard and slow and she moved with him. She loved the way his prick felt as it moved in and out of her and kept perfect rhythm with him. He was a repeat customer, too. This time, he called her directly and she told him to hurry over. When he arrived, she greeted him at the door naked and led him straight into the bedroom.

He loved fucking Eva.

Her cunt was warm and tight and she really knew how to work his prick. He also loved the fact that she let him cum inside her.

She felt move faster and faster. She matched him and begged him to fuck her harder. He did. The sudden hardness of his thrusts triggered yet another orgasm. Eva screamed and fucked him faster as she came. He grunted, rammed his prick into her as deep as he could and let it fly. The feeling of his cum flooding into her cunt made her moan and they fucked each other faster and faster until both were totally spent.

They rested a while. He got up, dressed and handed her $250.

"You're the best pussy in the world," he said. "The very best."

"Come back soon, Cal," she smiled as she escorted him to the door. "My pussy's yours whenever you want it. Just call and we'll set things up."

"You know I will, Eva," he said as he left.

She laughed as she walked into the bathroom to shower. Cal was her second client of the day and the fifth this week.

"My 50 year old pussy is getting a lot of action these days," she said as she stepped into the shower. "I love being a whore!"

Chapter Thirteen

The next morning, Rinna was jogging in the park by herself. After about 20 minutes, she realized that a young man was jogging beside her. He turned and smiled.

"Hi," he said.

"Hello," she smiled back.

"I've seen you here several times and I've always liked what I saw. So today, I decided to try and speak with you—if that's okay with you?" he said.

"I don't mind," she said as they turned down a more secluded path.

"You have terrific legs," he said.

"Thanks," she smiled.

"What's your name?" he asked.

"Rinna. What's yours?" she replied.

"James," he said. "Like I said, I've watched you several times. You're incredibly sexy. Are you married?"

"Yes I am," she said.

"Rats. I should have guessed. A sexy woman like you sure as Hell wouldn't be single," he said.

"Are you married?" she asked.

"Almost. I might as well be. I've been living with my girlfriend for the last year," he replied.

"You don't sound happy about it," she said.

"I'm not," he said. "She's got a real nasty disposition which I didn't know about until after she moved in. Now I can't rid of her."

"Too bad," she smiled. "Sorry I can't help you."

"I know. Can I be real blunt? Promise me you won't hit me or anything?" he asked.

"I'm sure you won't say anything I haven't already heard," she smiled. "What's on your mind?"

"You, actually," he said.

"Me?" she asked.

"Yes. In fact, you've been on my mind ever since I first saw you. You look so good in your running shorts that you always give me an erection."

"Do you have one now?" she teased.

"Hell yeah. If you don't mind my saying so, I'd love to take your shorts off and fuck the daylights out of you. I bet that you have the tightest pussy on Earth, too. In fact, I'd like to fuck you every day."

She smiled at him.

"Are you insulted?" he asked.

"Not in the least," she replied. "You really want to fuck me?"

Whenever Rinna jogged, her pussy became hot and sweaty and she became horny, Real horny. She was feeling pretty horny right now and the sight of the bulge in his shorts was making her even more so.

"Hell yeah," he replied.

She stopped and looked at him. He stood with his hands on his hips and a very obvious erection in his shorts. She ran her fingers along his bulge and squeezed the tip. She took his hand and led him into a secluded, shady area.

"This is your lucky day," she said.

They walked over to a tree. Rinna leaned over and put her hands on the trunk. James walked up behind her and ran her hands all over her ass. His touches excited her, too. She reached behind her back and grabbed his prick through his shorts. It was rock hard and really big and she knew it was going to feel wonderful inside her cunt.

He pulled her shorts down to her ankles. She stepped free of them and opened her stance. He pulled his shorts down and gently teased her crack and slit with the tip of his prick. She shivered in anticipation. That's when she felt it slip past her labia and penetrate her cunt. It went it nice and deep. He stayed still as she worked it with her inner muscles. When she stopped, he began to move it in and out. He fucked her with long, easy and deep strokes and she sighed with each and every one.

He reached around and played with her nipples as he fucked her faster. She moaned and gripped the tree harder as she thrust back at him. He could hardly believe his luck. Here we was, in the middle of a public park, fucking this red hot Filipina and it was without a doubt, the best fuck he'd ever had.

She felt him move faster and faster. He reached down and swirled his fingertip over her clit. Rinna gasped and came. When she did, her cunt clasped and unclasped his prick several times. The sensations caused him to fire his load deep into her cunt as he fucked her even harder. When it was over, he held onto her as she gripped the tree.

"Holy shit! You're even better than I imagined! Great! Really great!" he said as he caught his breath.

His prick was still hard inside of her. She turned and when it slipped out, she grabbed it and beat him off until he was again at full mast. She then lay down on the grass with her legs wide open. James got between her thighs and rammed his prick home. She gripped his arms and sighed as they fucked as hard as they could. Again, she came before he did. When she did, she fucked him even harder. He leaned over and stuck his tongue into her mouth. She sucked it eagerly as she felt his cum jet into her cunt again.

When it was over, he helped her stand. She picked up her shorts and slipped them on. Then she watched as he dressed. He pulled her to him for another prolonged kiss.

"Can I see you again?" he asked.

"Maybe. When did you have in mind?" she teased.

"The same time tomorrow?" he asked hopefully.

"Alright. I'll meet you back here. This time, bring something for us to lie on," she said. "Oh, by the way, I usually charge for sex."

"Okay. How much?" he asked.

"I get $250. But you're damned good with that thing, so you can pay me what you can afford," she said.

"Deal," he replied as he reached into his sock and took out $100. She smiled and nodded. As good as he had made her feel, she would happily fuck him for free.

They met again the next morning. This time, James spent several wonderful minutes eating her pussy and fingering her asshole while she jerked him off. He made her come several times, and then fucked her after a short rest.

He fucked her missionary style and doggie style. Each time, he made her come hard. Each time, he filled her cunt with cum. She had to admit that he was very good at it, too. Maybe too good. She didn't even bother to ask him for money. She just liked fucking him.

"Can we meet again tomorrow?" he asked.

"Are you trying to start an affair with me?" she teased.

"Yes. Interested?" he asked.

"Maybe. We'll see," she smiled.

Of course they met again the following day and it was pretty much a repeat of the last two days. James's fucking got better and better each time and the last orgasm almost blew the top of her head off it was so intense!

She lay there gasping and smiling as he massaged his cum into her body as if was fine lotion. At the same time, she kept playing with his prick. She really liked his prick, too. It was at least nine inches long and almost two inches around and he was uncut. His cockhead was large, smooth and shiny and she loved the way it felt inside her cunt.

But he was less than half her age, so he'd never really be more than a fuck buddy. That was fine with her. She loved to fuck and he was good at it. And he really loved the way her cunt hugged his entire shaft with each thrust. It felt so damned perfect to him. And she let him cum inside of her. Even his girlfriend didn't let him do that!

"Are we having an affair yet?" he asked.

"Maybe," she said.

"Can I see you again tomorrow?" he asked.

"Yes!" she replied.

They met and fucked for three more days. Each time, it felt more and more exciting. They tried several positions and she even sucked his prick a couple of times. Each time, he came in her mouth and she swallowed his cum.

She was starting to like the taste of cum, too.

And dicks.

James was tireless. They fucked in the woods. They fucked in his car and she even brought him home with her so they could fuck in a bed.

That was really an experience!

It was the first time both were totally naked and she got a good look at his lean, athletic body as she played with his prick. Once she got it at full length, she sucked it. This time, she managed to get more than half into her mouth so that his knob touched the back of her throat as she fucked him with her mouth. He groaned and fired his load straight down her throat. She pumped him a few times, and then stopped.

She grinned.

He was still hard.

She grabbed a pillow and stuck it under her belly so her ass was elevated. He moved behind her and licked her asshole as he fingered her cunt. Rinna shivered and sighed as he played with her until she came. As she lay moaning, he slid his prick into her asshole. Rinna cried out as he pressed into her. It was, by far, the biggest prick she'd ever had up there and it the sensation of it spreading apart her inner walls was sort of painful.

James stopped to allow her to get used to it, then fucked her nice and easy. After a few thrusts, she moved with him and even began to enjoy it. She decided that he could fuck her this way any time he wanted, too. He fucked her for what seemed like a long time. Somehow she even orgasmed. It was good, strange kind of orgasm that touched different places in her body. He kept fucking her as she lay quivering and moaning. After a few more deep thrusts, he grabbed her cheeks and flooded her ass with cum.

They rested and talked for a few minutes while Rinna played with his prick. When it was good and hard again, she pushed him onto his back and impaled herself on his prick. This was the first time they'd fucked like this and she used her inner muscles to squeeze his prick with each up and down movement. She rode him faster and faster and faster until they both came again. This time, she fell on top of him and stuck her tongue into his mouth for a long, passionate kiss.

They fucked three more times that day. Each time, they tried a different position. By the time James left, he could barely walk. She escorted him to the front door and they parted with another long, deep kiss.

Rinna looked at herself and smiled.

James's cum was streaming down her thighs and she felt terrific. He had made her come six times in one day. No one had ever done that before and she figured no one else ever would again. What's more, she agreed to meet him again tomorrow.

"Oh yes. We're having an affair! A damned hot one, too," she said as she went up to shower.

They met each other for six more days and Rinna would have been more than eager to continue. The more she fucked him, the more she wanted to fuck him. And he sure as Hell couldn't get enough of her. She had stopped charging him after the second day, too.

But on the last day, he told her he had to leave town to attend a special training course for his employer and would not be back for at least five weeks. She said that she was really going to miss him and gave him her cell phone number.

"When you come back, call me. I'll meet you anywhere you want and we'll see how far we can take this," she said.

"You know I'll call you, Rinna. That will be the very first thing I do when I get back. Maybe then, we'll get a nice room at a hotel and spend an entire week together," he said.

She smiled.

"I'd like that," she said.

James had caught her at the right moment and things had snowballed from there. She had no regrets, either. The sex was great and the idea of having someone his age enamored of her titillated her even more. While she was fucking him, she totally forgot about the casino and any other men she usually fucked. There was only James and she gave herself to him completely.

She had told Eva about this and Eva ribbed her about being a cougar. She even told Al. He didn't seem too happy that she was fucking him almost every day, but conceded there was nothing he could do about it.

"You have a terrific pussy, Rinna. And I hate sharing you with other men. But we decided to give this a shot, so I'll go along with this for a while," he said.

"How far have you gotten with Li?" she asked.

"Not very. I'm trying to do it a way so she won't fall in love with me," he said.

"Fat chance of that! She's always been crazy about you, so once you start this, I think you'll end up with a second wife," Rinna said. "And yes, I'd be jealous."

They both laughed.

"Of all the lovers you've had, who's the best?" he asked.

"You are," she said.

"Who's your next target?" he asked.

"Vince. I'd really love to fuck him again. Mostly because you're fucking Eva," she said.

"Right now, I'm going to concentrate on Li," he said.

"I knew you would," Rinna laughed. "I bet she has a nice, tight pussy, too."

Eva was also very busy.

While Rinna was fucking James, she was busy entertaining six other men at her house. They all contacted her through the website and she happily arranged to meet and fuck every one of them.

By the time Friday morning rolled around, Eva was too tired to do anything. She had been fucked nearly 20 times that week, both in her ass and in her cunt and had sucked six good, hard pricks and swallowed lots of cum.

And all her "lovers" paid her well for her services.

Vince got home one afternoon just as her lover got into his car and drove off. She greeted him at the door in nothing but her robe. It was open and he could see the line of cum oozing down her inner thigh. She smiled and walked into the bedroom. He laughed and went in after her, eager to once again dip his prick into another pool of sticky cum.

Eva didn't care that her husband enjoyed fucking her when she was filled with cum. If this excited him, so be it. At least they were fucking again. Lately, they'd been fucking a lot. Vince always tried to time it so that he got home right after Eva had fucked her last client so he could slide his prick into a pool of warm cum.

"Ever think about getting gang-banged?" he asked.

"No. Why?" she asked.

"So I could see what it feels like to fuck you right after three or four other guys have cum in your pussy," he said. "If one feels this good, three or more would be great!"

She laughed.

"Maybe I'll arrange it for you one day," she said. The idea of fucking more than one man at a time also turned her on.

That night, while Vince watched over her shoulder, Eva went online to that sex dating site and typed in an ad requesting multiple partners for a gang-bang just so she could see what it was like. Her ad said she wanted at least three men and no more than five. To her delight, five of her regular customers responded within minutes.

Vince watched as she set it up for the day after tomorrow at two p.m. She had said they could fuck her as many times as they wanted and they could pay whatever they wanted. When it was all set, she smiled at Vince.

"Can you handle five?" he asked.

"We'll see," she said as she grabbed his prick and slid it into her mouth.

That day proved to be a very wild one indeed. The men arrived on time and eager to fuck. She led them all into the bedroom, stripped and laid down on the bed with her legs wide apart. Then the fun started. While one man fucked her, she sucked off another and beat off two more. After he came in her pussy, the next man jumped in. This kept going for a good four hours, during which each man came in her cunt at least twice and she had sucked each of them off and swallowed their cum.

The men let themselves out after they each gave her $200 and promised to return real soon. Vince arrived about four minutes later. He saw her lying spread eagled on the bed with what looked like a river of cum oozing from her open cunt. He immediately peeled off his clothes and proceeded to fuck her like mad as he reveled in the squishing sounds his prick made as it moved in and out of the pools of cum in her cunt.

He was so turned on over this, that he fucked her three times before he finally wore out. By then, pools of cum were all over bed and Eva's belly. She reached down and massaged it into her nipples and chest while she sucked his prick. It was like she was sucking six dicks at once now and the idea made her come again.

Vince asked her not to shower just yet. He wanted to fuck her at least one more time...

Eva told Rinna what happened.

"Vince is getting really kinky now. As soon as he sees another man's cum in my pussy, he gets an erection and just has to fuck me. The gang bang thing was his idea, too. I can't believe he wanted me to do that just so he could find out what it feels like to fuck me afterward. It's so crazy!" she said.

"How much did you make last week?" Rinna asked.

"Two thousand," she said. "That's more money than I make in a month at the store and its tax free."

She showed Rinna the cash she had in her purse and bragged about how valuable her pussy had become.

"Yours is just as valuable. You have a beautiful pussy and men love to fuck you and they pay you whatever you ask. Imagine how much money you could make by joining this service! I can get laid three or four times a day and I don't have to leave my house. They email me and set up appointments. So far this week, I fucked 10 men," Eva said.

Rinna looked at her.

"You're already a slut. Why not get paid more for being one?" Eva said. "Just think of your pussy as an ATM that accepts deposit of cum and cash. Men will pay to fuck you and they'll pay a lot," Eva said. "You could have twice as many customers if you want."

"Maybe I'll think about it," she said.

"No maybe, Rinna. Do it," Eva said. "Use your pussy to make money."

"I am making money, Eva. A lot of money, so I don't really need to join that service. I'm already getting as much dick as I can handle," she said. "What I'd like to have is more pussy…"

"Well, you know where to find it…" Eva smiled as Rinna slid her hand up her thigh.

Al and Li were growing closer and closer. Each day, she brought him something she'd cooked and they sat together at breaks and during lunch and any other time they had nothing to do. Anyone who saw them could see there was something very special going on between them and neither of them bothered to hide it.

While he was with Li, Al didn't care what his wife was doing or with whom. This was her idea in the first place. He warned her that he might fall hard for Li—and he had. He wasn't trying to seduce her anymore. He was courting her.

Rinna knew it, too. But she also knew this was something she'd have to live with. Sex between her an Al was still terrific and frequent and she was secretly pleased that he was so busy with her that he wasn't fucking Eva.

But since he was only making love with her and she was fucking other men, Rinna felt more than a little bit guilty. But not guilty enough to stop.

That night, after her chat with Eva, Rinna stood in front of her mirror naked. She studied her cunt carefully and decided it was much prettier than Eva's. She was so sexy that even Eva wanted her.

"I bet I could make lots more money," she said.

Al watched her as his prick grew hard. He walked up and put his hands on her shoulders. She turned and grabbed his prick.

"Are you thinking of selling your pussy to even more men?" he asked.

"Maybe. Do you think I should?" she asked as they climbed onto the bed.

"Since you're a lot sexier than Eva, I'm sure a lot of men would pay you for sex," he said. "Just don't sell yourself to every man you meet and be sure to keep yourself ready for me."

She giggled.

"I'll always be ready for you," she assured him.

The next morning, Rinna got an unexpected call from Li. She told Rinna what was going on with her and Al and said that it wasn't her fault. Rinna assured her that it was okay and that she gave Al the green light to pursue her. When she explained why she did it, Li almost went into shock.

"So you two have an open marriage now?" she asked as she still tried to process it all.

"Yes. I told him that I wanted to experiment with other men and he could fuck other women. I suggested that since he's always felt attracted to you, he should have an affair with you—if you want it. He really likes you. He always has. So I think it's a good idea," Rinna said.

"And you have sex with other men?" Li asked.

"Yes," Rinna said.

"Um, how many other men have you had sex with?" she asked.

"I'm not sure. I lost count. Most of them pay me," Rinna almost boasted.

"You're?" Li asked.

"Yes. I fuck a lot of different men and they pay me lots of money," Rinna said.

"This is crazy. You're crazy! I have to warn you." Li began.

"You've fallen in love with Al, haven't you?" Rinna asked.

"Yes I have. Do you think he feels the same about me?" Li replied.

"Probably," Rinna said.

"Wow," Li remarked. "Now what do I do?"

"I suggest that you let Nature take its course, Li. You might end up as Al's second wife," Rinna said. "That's okay. I don't mind sharing him with you or Eva."

"I don't know how to handle this, Rinna. You're far too nice about it and I'm amazed that you encouraged him," Li said.

"I just told Al to follow his heart and it led him straight to you," Rinna said. "Relax and enjoy the moments you'll have together. You have my permission and my best wishes."

Li thanked her and hung up the phone. She looked at her mother and shook her head.

"It's true. Everything Al told me is true. Rinna just confirmed it," she said. "This is insane, Mom. I'm not sure how to react to any of this. But I do know that I look forward to being with him every day. What should I do?"

"I have already told you," her mother replied. "You have already told me that you love him, so make him yours and let destiny run its course. After all, you did not start this. He pursued you. Let him catch you."

Li smiled.

"I would do the same if I were lucky enough to be in your shoes," her mother added. "And once he caught me, I would never let him go."

"What about Rinna?" Li asked.

"As the Americans say: fuck Rinna. She started this so she must suffer whatever becomes of it, even if it means that she loses her husband. But tell me, Li—do you truly trust Al?"

"Yes, I do. He has told me the truth and he hides nothing from me. If he wanted to, he could have lied about everything. But he has let me know what is happening and why and I know how he feels about me," Li replied.

Her mother nodded.

"If you trust him, then I will trust him," she said.

Eva lay on her back with her legs wide open. Her eyes were half shut and she moaning as she enjoyed the deep and thorough fuck her latest client was giving her. He had arrived at her house an hour earlier and, after some chit-chat, they undressed each other and went straight into a good, long "69".

He proved to be real good at it, too. While she was coming very hard, he even licked her asshole. This caused her to come harder and she had a tough time sucking his prick as she writhed around in ecstasy.

They rested after he shot a good sized load down her throat. His prick was at least nine inches long and very thick. When they started fucking, it filled her as well as she hoped it would. And they had been fucking for what seemed like an amazingly long time.

Eva erupted first. As she came, he fucked her faster and harder and emptied another good sized load deep inside her cunt. They kept fucking for a few more good strokes then he pulled out. Her cunt felt like it was filled to overflowing with his cum, too.

"Wow," he said. "You have the tightest pussy I ever fucked and you're terrific at oral."

He handed her the usual fee plus an extra $50. She smiled and escorted him to the door as drops of cum oozed from her cunt.

About a minute after he left, Vince drove up. Eva smiled as he walked in and led him to the bedroom. She lay down and parted her legs to show him the pool of thick, white cum in her cunt. Vince immediately undressed and plunged his prick into her. Fucking his wife right after she'd fucked another man turned him on like nothing else. He loved the way his prick felt as it moved in and out of the pool inside her cunt and the squishing sounds that came from each and every thrust.

Eva thought this was more than weird. She didn't know why this turned him on and she didn't care as long as it got him to fuck her.

"I can hardly wait to fuck you right after Al comes in you pussy," Vince gasped as he added his load to the pool. "I think that would feel amazing!"

Eva laughed and held on for the ride.

She hadn't seen much of Al since he started his romance with Li. She wonder4ed if she'd ever get a chance to have sex with him again. Rinna was also keeping him very busy. Eva thought it was because Rinna was afraid she might lose Al to Li.

The next afternoon, Li had with Al at their favorite Vietnamese restaurant. As they ate, Li told him about her conversation with Rinna and her mother. Al smiled and laughed.

"I told you it was crazy," he said. "You just can't make stuff like this up. I have no idea what got into Rinna. I think she was influenced a lot by Eva. But whatever it is, it's enabled us to come together."

"I don't understand it either, Al. I'm fine with it as long as we can be together. My parents approve of you and they said that whatever happens is fine. They just don't want me to get hurt," she said.

He reached over and took her hand.

"You won't. I promise you that," he assured her.

Li smiled.

"Do you think Rinna will get over this one day?" she asked.

He shrugged.

"I think she will once she either finds another man she's totally nuts about or decides that our marriage is worth keeping. It's all up to her. She started this and she'll have to finish it. I hope she doesn't get hurt," he said.

"I like her. I don't want her to get hurt, either. That's why this is so confusing," Li said.

Rinna wasn't the least bit confused. Now that she'd started down this road, she wanted to keep going for as long as possible. She was like an escaped nun. She hadn't run as wild as Eva and decided that she probably never would. And, in her own strange way, she was still quite devoted to Al.

But she enjoyed exploring.

That Saturday, Rinna went to the casino by herself. It was early and the place was almost empty. She played the slots for about an hour and noticed it was starting to fill up. That's when she saw Brad.

He walked up and handed her a mixed drink. She looked at him as he put it in her hand.

"Hi. Remember me?" he asked as he sat next to her.

She shook her head.

"Last time, you were really mean to me," he smiled.

"Oh," she said as she sniffed the drink.

"It's just rum and coke," he said. "I went easy on the rum again."

"Thanks, I guess," she said. "You got real fresh with me and you made me mad."

"I'm sorry if my offer upset you," he said as he sat down. "Be truthful: weren't you even a little bit tempted?"

"Not really. I was kind of insulted," she replied with a slight, playful smile.

She noticed he was looking at her legs again. Her shorts had ridden up a few inches and most of her inner thigh was revealed.

"I've been thinking about you all week. So when I saw you tonight, I had to come over and try again. I'm real persistent when I want something," he smiled.

She tried to ignore him as she made her bet. He watched and sipped his drink when it came up nothing. She did this several times without hitting anything.

"Why are you still here?" she asked with pretend irritation.

"I like being close to you," he said.

"Get close to somebody else for a change," she said as she continued playing.

"I prefer to stay with you. When do you normally leave here?" he said as he watched her lose again.

"I usually leave around eleven," she said.

"How long have you been married?" he asked.

"A long time. Why are you being so nosy?" she said.

"I want to get to know more about you. I like you. Is your husband here?" he asked.

"No. He doesn't like casinos. He's really not happy that I come here, either," she said.

"Why do you?" he asked.

"I'm bored and sometimes I win a lot of money," she said.

"And you also make lots of money in other ways," he added.

"Yes," she admitted.

"Do you tell him about it?" he asked.

"He knows all about that," she said. "He doesn't exactly approve but he admits there's nothing he can do about it. He also fucks my best friend."

"I see you're losing again. My offer still stands, in case you're interested," he said.

"What offer?" she asked.

"I'll cover all of your losses if you agree to sell me what you have between those gorgeous legs of yours," he said.

"My answer is still the same," she said.

He noticed her drink was empty and signaled a passing woman for two more. She frowned at him.

"I don't want another drink," she said. "Are you trying to get me drunk?"

"Maybe," he said. "Maybe if you get good and loose, you'll take my offer."

"No way!" she said.

"We'll see," he said.

He watched as she lost three more rounds. He ordered another round of drinks. She took a sip, put it down and continued to play. He watched as she cursed under her breath. She was now $175 in the hole and looked disgusted.

"Think about my offer. You can get all of that back in just five minutes," he whispered as he placed his hand on her knee. That's $375."

She tried to ignore him but the hand on her thigh was making her nervous. She couldn't believe he was touching her or that she was letting him. She knew this game was about to go up another level, too.

"Come upstairs with me," he whispered as he inched his hand upward.

"No," she said softly as she felt his hand move upward along her inner thigh.

"Your legs are so smooth. So very sexy," he said.

She just sat and looked at him as he moved his hand under her shorts and wondered why she was letting him touch her. She took another sip of the drink and looked into his eyes. It was like she was in some sort of trance now.

"You're the sexiest woman I ever met and I want you so much," he said softly as he moved his hand upward to the edge of her panties. She was amazed she had let him get this far but still did nothing to stop him.

"Come upstairs with me," he urged.

She felt his fingers dance lightly over her panties and slowly parted her thighs. He traced her labia with his fingers. She quivered. He saw the look in her eyes and did it several more times. He felt her grow moist.

Her thighs were slightly apart now and the sensations of his finger playing with her labia were sending her through the roof. She sipped her drink as she wondered how she had this go so far and how she could get out of it. He started teasing her harder. She quivered harder and opened her legs a bit more. He accepted her invitation by locating her clit and massaging it through her now damp panties.

"Please stop now," she whispered.

"Are you sure that you really want me to?" he asked as he rubbed faster. "Let me see your pussy. I'll give you $175 for just five minutes. No one will ever know."

"I can't," she said as she trembled.

"Yes you can. All you have to do is come up to my suite and do with me what you usually do with other men," he said as he rubbed faster and faster.

Her legs were wide open now and she was incredibly horny. His touches made her squirm and breathe harder. She looked at him.

"O-okay," she agreed.

He stopped playing with her and smiled.

"Let's go upstairs," he said.

"Pay me first," she said.

He laughed. He took out his wallet, counted out $400 and placed it in her hand. She stared at it for a few seconds as she began to realize what she had just agreed to. She put the cash in her purse and followed him to the elevator.

They got off on the 12th floor and walked to his suite. She gasped when she entered. It was incredibly lavish to say the least. He had brought her to the verge of an orgasm then stopped. She now wished he had finished her.

The suite was incredibly fancy and had a well-furnished living room area and three steps that led up to the master bedroom. The bed was king sized. They walked up to it and she turned around to face him. He smiled.

"Are you ready?" he asked.

"Yes," she said as she wondered why she had agreed to this.

"Can I undress you?" he asked.

She nodded nervously. He knelt in front of her and slowly unbuttoned her shorts and slid them down her legs. He reached up, hooked his fingers in the waistband of her panties and eased them down to her ankles. The he sat back and whistled as he stared at her cunt with a mixture of awe and lust.

"It's gorgeous!" he said softly. "You have the most beautiful pussy I've ever seen."

He leaned closer. She felt his breath on her cunt and quivered slightly. She could hardly believe that she was in a hotel suite letting a perfect stranger ogle her cunt. She felt embarrassed—and a little excited. She was still feeling horny from the way he'd touched her. For some reason, she reached down and used her fingers to pull her labia apart so he could see the pink inner walls of her cunt. He gasped and moved even closer. His warm breath wafted over her cunt and made her even hornier. He leaned forward and inhaled her sexual aroma.

Then he gently ran his tongue along her slit. She quivered and moaned as he ate her. The game was over now. She was going to let him take her as far as he wanted. He gripped her behind and pulled her closer. She felt his tongue dart in and out of her cunt and humped his face. Seconds later, she came.

He picked her up and carried her to the bed. She smiled up at him as he undressed her.

"You are gorgeous!" he whispered.

"Fuck me!" she said as she parted her thighs.

He laughed and moved between her legs and slid his prick into her. It was a slow, deep thrust that made her sigh. She wrapped her arms around his hips and shut her eyes as they fucked and fucked and fucked.

Rinna came again.

It was a good, deep come that made her shake all over. She fucked him faster then. He flipped her over so that she was on top and let her take control. She smiled and fucked him as hard as she could, savoring each and every up and down movement. She came a third time and a fourth.

"I'm gonna come!" Brad moaned as he fucked her back faster and faster.

"Come in me! I want to feel it! Fill my pussy!" she cried as he began firing lines of cum up into her cunt.

They stopped, rested and fucked again.

This time, they went slower, so they could really pleasure each other. Rinna decided that this was the best sex she'd ever had in her life. Brad told her the same thing. After several long minutes, they came again.

Simultaneously.

It was deep and awesome.

She lay next to him as he stroked her breast.

"Did you know I was a prostitute?" she asked.

"Yes. But I figured I'd let you play your little game because I felt you would be worth waiting for. And you were," he replied.

She grabbed his prick and gave it several pulls, then leaned over and sucked it. He moaned as she worked him. At the same time, he fingered her cunt which was still filled with his cum. Seconds later, they were fucking again.

They finally exhausted each other around one a.m. Rinna dressed. Brad handed her several large bills. She looked at the money and at him.

"That's $500. You're fantastic, Rinna. The best. Can we do this again next week?" he asked.

"I'll be here around five," she said.

"I'll see you then," he said as they kissed.

The kiss was electrifying!

She was all smiles as she drove home. Brad had pushed every single one of her sexual buttons. He had made her come harder and more often than anyone else ever did and she didn't want it to stop.

At the same time, Eva was at home fucking two more clients she had met online. One was a tall, handsome Black man with a long, hard dick. The other one was a tall, muscular man with a good, thick one.

Both men had fucked her twice and flooded her cunt with cum. The last mad actually made her come several times and she made sure he was totally spent when her left.

She smiled at hers elf before she stepped into the shower.

"That was an easy $400," she said. "Selling my pussy is a lot more fun than working every day and it pays more."

But it was illegal and she knew she'd be in trouble if she ever got caught. She also reasoned that she had enough cash stashed away to pay bail and any fines she might get.

"Business expenses," she told herself.

She knew that Vince was out fucking the women he met at work. He wouldn't be home until the next afternoon. Al was going after Li, so she decided to ramp up her online trade. She'd fucked seven men that week. Four were repeat customers. She had a lot of repeats. They really loved to have sex with her and she made sure they got their money's worth each time.

She laughed.

"I waited 50 years to cut loose! Now I'm a first class slut!" she said.

Chapter Fourteen

Li decided to wear shorts to work the next day. She usually wore tight fitting jeans or slacks, but she wanted to show Al a different look. She studied herself in the mirror after she dressed. Her legs were thin and shapely and very smooth.

She smiled.

"Al's right. I do have nice legs," she thought.

When she arrived at work, Al whistled at her. Li blushed and thanked him for the compliment.

"I just wanted to feel cooler. It's been real warm lately," she said as the headed for their assignment.

This was the day of the week she usually liked because she and Al always got teamed up. They spent most of the day working side by side and chatting and joking.

"You look stunning," he said when they were alone. "Those shorts show off your legs well."

"I'm glad you like it," she said.

Before she knew it, they were locked in a nice, long kiss that sent shivers down her back. She shivered even more when they locked tongues. When they stopped, she was obviously flushed. She smiled at him and touched his cheek.

"You do things to me, Al. Magical things," she whispered.

"You do the same to me, Li," he said. "The more I see you, the more I want you."

"This is nuts. You are a very married man with a beautiful wife. I'm just a plain woman. Why would you want me?" she asked.

"I can't explain it, Li. I just know that I do," he replied as he held her hand.

"I have never been with a man, but I admit that I am tempted to give myself to you," she said. "I'm excited and frightened by this."

He pulled her close and they kissed again. This time, she felt his hands roam down her back to her behind. She felt him caress her then gently squeeze her cheeks. That's when she realized that he had an erection. The idea that any man would get an erection for her amazed and thrilled her. Without thinking, she began to undulate against his bulge.

He just held her close and moved with her. She began to breathe harder and harder as she moved faster and faster. Her cunt was on fire now. She realized that if they weren't at work, she let him take her right now.

She forced herself to stop. She smiled up at him.

"I am yours now," she said softly. "Use me as you wish."

"Are you sure?" he asked.

"Yes. I'm very sure. You will be the first to enter the rose garden. You will be the only man to enter it—ever. I'm not sure I should even say this, but I love you, Al. I think that I have loved you for a long time. So if you really want me, I am yours," she said.

"Let's make this first time very special for both of us," he said.

"What do you have in mind?" she asked.

"I'll surprise you. Just leave everything to me," he said.

When Li told her mother what happened, the woman smiled and touched her hand. She could see the excitement in her eyes.

"He doesn't know it yet, but he is about to gain a second wife," she said. "How will you deal with his wife when that happens?"

"He told me that he and his wife have an agreement. He has given her permission to have sex with other men and she has given him permission to have sex with other women and she specifically mentioned me. Rinna likes me and she thinks I would be a perfect match for her husband. It's all very strange, but I am willing to take advantage of it," Li explained.

"I always thought Americans were crazy," her mother said. "You are still young enough to bear children. What if you become pregnant?"

"Then I will bear the child and raise it with love as I am sure Al will," Li said. "I will bear him as many children as he desires because I know he will always be there for me and them. I have faith in him."

"Rinna will not like that at all," her mother said.

"That will be too bad for her, then," Li said. "This was her idea anyway and she should be prepared to take whatever comes of it."

Eva stared at Rinna when she told her about Li's call.

"Well you told him to go after Li. I think that's a mistake. He always says that he thinks she's cute and sexy. You may have started something that you can't control later. Li might not give him back. Then we'll both be screwed," she said.

"Both?" Rinna asked.

"Yes. Remember: I like fucking Al, too. Once he starts his affair with Li, she won't leave him with enough energy to handle either one of us," Eva said.

When Al came home, Rinna prepared his favorite meal.

"So how are things going between you and Li?" she asked.

Al told her what happened at work. Rinna smiled at him.

"So, does she have nice legs?" she asked.

"Yes," he said. "But they're not as sexy as yours."

Rinna smiled.

"When are you going to fuck her?" she asked.

"I'm not sure. I have to take this easy. I have to be careful of her feelings," he said.

"You're right. Just remember who you're married to," Rinna said.

"Like you do when you're fucking other men?" he shot back.

That stung like a slap. She sensed more than a little resentment in his remark.

"Do you want me to stop?" she asked.

"Can you? Do you want to?" he asked.

"I'm not sure yet," she admitted.

She really enjoyed getting her pussy plowed by different pricks now. And she was enjoying it too much to stop any time soon.

"Would you stop fucking Eva?" she asked.

"I'm not sure she'd let me stop," he said. "She doesn't take 'no' for an answer. How come you didn't ask about Li?"

"That's simple. You are the only man who has ever shown an interest in her. If you stop now, she'll be emotionally crushed and never trust anyone again. I think you have to follow through with her. I don't want to see her get hurt," Rinna said.

He nodded.

"That makes a certain amount of sense. I don't want to hurt her, either. She's too nice and I like her a lot," he said. "So I guess we'll just keep doing this?"

"That works for me," she smiled. "I wonder what Li's pussy looks like."

He laughed.

"Why? Are you thinking of going after her, too?" he asked.

"Maybe. Thanks to Eva, I kind of like pussy now. I'm thinking about having more than one girlfriend," she said. "I guess that I've always been kind of a slut. I was afraid to let my fantasies run wild until I fucked that first guy in the casino. Then Eva and I purposely went to the casino to get laid. After that, I've just allowed my inner slut to wild."

"You always got kind of slutty when you drank. Now, you don't have to be drunk. With all the men you keep screwing, you might end making a lot of money," he joked.

"I've thought about that. Eva said the same thing. She said my pussy could get me a lot of money," Rinna said.

"She's right," he agreed. "It's tight and hot and you really know how to use it. I think you can make lots of money."

"Does Eva charge you?" she asked.

"She didn't the last time," he replied. "I would much rather make love with you than pay any woman for sex. You're hard to beat in that category."

"You always say the nicest things," she joked.

The next day at work, Al walked up to Li and grabbed her hand. She smiled and leaned into him.

"You and I have a big weekend ahead of us," he said softly.

"What do you mean?" she asked.

"I booked us the honeymoon suite at the Rialto for Friday and Saturday. It comes with room service and champagne. We'll go there right after work. The suite also has a hot tub," he said.

"That costs a lot of money! Why did you do such a thing?" she asked.

"I want our first time together to something very, very special," he said. "Because I feel that you are very, very special."

She fought back a sudden urge to cry.

"So you are treating this as our honeymoon?" she asked.

"Yes," he said as he pulled her close.

"I like how you think," she smiled.

That same morning, Rinna called Eva and asked if she'd like to meet for breakfast.

"I'd love to but I have a client coming over this morning. He's a repeat customer and he has a real long dick. I'll give you a call when we're finished. Maybe we'll meet for lunch but I have another appointment at two. My pussy is going to be well fucked today," Eva said.

"How about tomorrow then?" Rinna asked.

"That's good. I don't have anyone scheduled yet. Should I wear panties?" Eva joked.

"Of course not. I don't want to have anything between me and your pussy," Rinna answered.

"Great. I'll see you then," Eva agreed.

She looked at the clock and went into the bedroom. She took off all of her clothes, splashed some light perfume on her body and slipped on a filmy robe. Ten minutes later, the doorbell rang. Five minutes after that, she was lying on the bed trying to take every bit of a ten inch prick deep inside her hot, wet cunt.

Chaz was her third customer that morning. She had two more scheduled for the afternoon. The first two men fucked her a couple of times and came in her pussy. One guy came so much that it ran out of her pussy and down her ass crack. She massaged it into her asshole then bent her legs back and spread her cheeks.

He plunged into her asshole and fucked her nice and easy until he shot his load deep into her channel. She sighed when he pulled out. She loved getting fucked like this now. Hell, she loved getting fucked every way imaginable.

Then they paid her and left. She didn't come either time.

Chaz was different.

He held her legs wide apart and bent them back toward her breasts. Then he eased his giant prick into her cunt, moved his hips around and started fucking her. His prick felt so good that she quivered with each and every thrust. He knew what he was doing, too.

After about 20 thrusts, she began coming. Her orgasm built up slowly then suddenly erupted. She cried out and shook like a leaf as he fucked her even harder. She came again and again and again. Then she heard him grunt and felt what seemed like a stream of cum fill her cunt.

"Ooh yes! I love it!" she moaned.

When he was sure his prick was slickened by their combined juices, he eased out of her cunt and slid it up into her ass. Eva gasped as he penetrated her. It was, by far, the biggest prick that had ever gone there and it slowly spread her inner walls as he went in balls deep. She closed her eyes and smiled as he fucked her with long, deep, easy strokes.

He came again a few moments later.

When he was totally spent, he withdrew. Then he beamed down at her. She smiled back.

Chaz dressed and handed her $300 and told her it was money very well spent. He said he'd call her again soon as she escorted him to the front door. She had trouble walking now and was glad that she had another hour before her next man arrived.

She looked at the cum dripping onto the floor and smiled as she massaged it into her cunt.

"I have a very happy pussy," she said.

Rinna headed for a different casino. She was feeling a little bored and horny and was hoping to get lucky. But it very early in the day and the casino was mostly deserted. She sat down at the slots and started playing. She sat there for nearly an hour, then stopped and went to the bar to get something cold to drink.

Bar drinks were free to slots players and other gamblers. She sat down and ordered a sweet tea. As she sipped, she noticed a medium built, younger man eying her from across the room. She smiled at him.

He smiled back and walked over.

"Hi," he said. "Excuse me for staring at you like I did, but I couldn't help it. You're the most beautiful woman I've ever seen here."

"I think you say that to every woman you met," she smiled.

"Well, yes I do. But in your case, I really mean it. My name's Troy. Remember me?"

"Of course I do," she said with a smile.

"Have you thought about my offer?" he asked.

"Yes," she replied.

"Good," he said.

They chatted for almost an hour. During the course of their chat, Troy put his hand on her knee. When she didn't seem to mind, he eased it slowly upward. She simply smiled at him and slightly parted her legs to let him know she was willing. When he reached the edge of her shorts, she opened her legs more. He eased his hand under them and smiled when he realized she wasn't wearing panties.

"I have a room on the sixth floor," he said.

"That's all yours if you want it," she said as he played with her cunt.

"I want it," he said.

"Then let's go to your room and fuck," she said. "A lot!"

Eva was lying on her back, moaning and trembling as her "lover" hammered away at her cunt. His prick touched and massaged places in her cunt that no other prick ever had. Each thrust sent delicious shivers all through her body.

This was their second one of the morning. He had already made her come very hard the first time and had practically flooded her cunt with cum. Then she had grabbed his half erect prick and sucked it until he was good and hard again. He didn't miss a beat, either.

He just rammed it home and they started fucking again. At first, she matched him thrust for thrust. But she came again after only a few thrusts. Caught up the throes of an even stronger orgasm, all she could do was lay there with her legs wide apart and let him continue.

And it felt so damned good!

She soon felt him move faster and faster. She wrapped her arms around his sweaty body and fucked him back with everything she had left until she felt him erupt inside her cunt again.

"Oooh yes! I love it!" she cried as she fell back. "I really love it!"

He kept fucking her until he went limp. When he pulled out, a stream of white oozed from Eva's throbbing cunt.

They rested for a few minutes, and then he got up and dressed. She just threw her robe on and walked him to the front door. Before he left, he handed her $200 and smiled.

"Next week again?" he asked.

"I'll be waiting," she said.

She walked into the bathroom and cleaned herself off good to get ready for her next date.

"Not bad for a Monday," she smiled as she washed her cunt to be fresh for her next appointment.

When Vince got home later that afternoon, she was standing at the bedroom door naked. She smiled at him. She ran her fingers over her cunt then held them up to show him she was still full of cum. She turned and walked into the bedroom.

Vince laughed and followed her.

Moments later, he was also naked and on the bed plunging his erection into Eva's hot, tight and cum filled cunt while she fucked him back and moaned happily.

Rinna and Troy hit it off great. They spent a good 15 minutes at foreplay, during which Rinna found out he had one of the longest pricks she'd ever played with. While she took delight in watching his foreskin move up and down while she pumped him, he buried his face between her legs.

That's when she found out he also had a nice, long tongue. After he made her come more than once, she opened her legs wide and smiled at him.

"Fuck me, Troy. My pussy is yours now. Use it!" she said.

He grabbed her legs and draped them over his arms. Then he rammed his prick home and fucked her. It was a hard, fast and deep fuck. Really hard.

She moaned and writhed with each thrust as he leaned into her and fucked away. His prick went where no others had ever gone and his knob knocked on the opening to her womb each and every time.

And he had staying power.

Lots of it.

He fucked her and fucked and fucked her. Each thrust was hard and deep and she quivered with pleasure as she laid there. She came once.

Then twice.

Then again.

"More! More! Give it to me, Troy! I love it!" she screamed as he sent shivers through her body.

Even though he fucked her hard, his strokes felt gentle inside of her, as if his prick was caressing her cunt in order to give her the most pleasure possible.

She held onto him and arched her back as she came yet again. She was giving him all she had now and using her cunt muscles to squeeze his shaft in order to return the pleasure. Troy was amazed at how this felt. At how well she used her pussy. He'd never felt anything like it before and as they fucked, he began to fall madly in love with her.

"I love you!" she heard him whisper as they moved faster. "I love you."

She moaned as she shook all over. The orgasm was so intense that she saw white.

"Can I come inside you?" he gasped.

"You better! I want to feel it!" she screamed.

She felt him stiffen, stop and fuck her a little erratically. Then she heard him grunt and felt the stream of warm cum fill her cunt. He gave her a few more good thrusts then eased out. He fell next to her, panting.

She smiled.

"Man, that was terrific," he said. "The best ever."

"Wow," was all Rinna could say.

"Not only are you the most beautiful woman on Earth, but you are without a doubt the best lover I ever had," he said as he caressed her breasts.

Rinna pulled him to her and stuck her tongue in his mouth for a kiss that sent thrills up and down her spine.

He got up, walked to the fridge and took out a bottle of white wine and two goblets. He filled the goblets and handed her one. She smiled as they clinked glasses.

"To us," Troy said.

They fucked twice more that day. They finished with Rinna on top, riding his prick until both were too exhausted to even move. She was really worn out and her cunt tingled. This had been the most intense sex she'd ever had and she needed a long, warm shower to recover from it.

Troy watched her dress.

"What can I pay you?" he asked.

"Whatever you want," she joked.

He grabbed his wallet, peeled off several bills and handed them to her. She was shocked at the amount when she counted it.

"There's almost $500 here," she said in amazement. "That's a lot of money,"

"Then consider it a gift. Believe me, Rinna; you are worth every bit of that and more. So please accept it as a gift," Troy said.

"Okay. Thanks," she smiled.

"Want to get together again?" he asked.

"Sure. When?" she agreed.

"How about the day after tomorrow?" he asked.

"Same time okay?" she asked.

"Yes," he said.

"Then we have a date, Troy," she said as she kissed him.

When she drove home, she smiled. When she got home, Al laughed at the way she was walking.

"You look like somebody fucked the daylights out of you today," he said.

"He did," she admitted as she plopped down on the sofa. "How are things with you?"

"You won't see me for a couple of days. I've booked the honeymoon suite at the Rialto for the weekend," he said.

"You and Li?" she asked.

"Uh-huh. Jealous?" he teased.

"Very! But I still give you permission to do it. After what I did today, I really can't say anything about that," she replied.

The next afternoon, she met Eva for lunch. They talked about what they'd been doing lately. When Eva found out about Troy, she laughed and gave Rinna a playful shove.

"It sounds like you have yourself a real boyfriend now. And I do mean 'boy'. How's it feel to fuck someone who is young enough to be your son?" she teased.

"Actually, it feels terrific," Rinna admitted. "Troy is very good and he knows how to please me. Would you fuck someone like him if you had a chance?"

"Damn right I would! Hell, I might never let him out of my house," Eva joked. "So when are we gonna swap husbands again?"

"I don't know. Maybe when Li gets tired of Al," Rinna said.

"If you're waiting for that to happen, we might never swap again. We're gonna have to make it happen," Eva said.

But Rinna knew that Al and Li had become nearly inseparable. This was mostly her fault, too. After all, she had told Al to go after Li and she knew what might happen. It did. LI had fallen in love with Al and he with her. She explained it to Eva. She frowned and sat back with her arms crossed.

"You never should have told him to do that," she said. "I love him, too. I was hoping to have to share him only with you. Now Li is in the picture and he's crazy about her."

"What are you bitching about? You fuck dozens of men each month, so it's not like you're not having sex," Rinna said.

"I know. But Al is different," Eva said.

Rinna nodded.

"Yes he is," she agreed.

Li lay on the grass looking up at the sky while Al lay next to her. They had just gone for a stroll in a nearby park and decided to relax and talk. Li told him about her childhood hopes and current wishes, which surprisingly matched his own.

"But my greatest wish is to become the mother of our children. I want to bear you as many children as you desire and I wish to care for you for the rest of my life," she said. "I know this is crazy because you are still very married, but the circumstances will allow us to pursue our dreams."

He smiled.

"I love you, Li," he said as they kissed.

They had been working together for almost 15 years. In fact, he had been the one to train her when she was hired and they became good friends almost immediately. There had always been something special between. Something deep and unspoken. All it needed was the right spark to ignite it. Rinna had provided that very spark.

"I like your wife very much. She has always been very kind and friendly toward me. In fact, she is one of my best friends. I never imagined she would allow this or do what you say she is doing. I will never stray from our bed or bring any sort of shame or dishonor to us. I am yours and yours alone, Al. I am yours now and forever," she said.

Al was in Heaven now.

"This weekend, we will be on our honeymoon. Let's make it a real honeymoon," she said.

"It will be," he promised.

Two days later, Rinna met Troy at the hotel. He took her hand and they hurried up to his room where they spent most of the morning and afternoon trying to figure out how many different positions they could fuck in.

Her favorite was when they lay facing each other so they could kiss and he was able to finger her asshole while they fucked. Just before Troy came, he pulled his prick out of her cunt and eased the knob into her ass. To her surprise, he slid it into her a couple of inches and came. The weird sensation of his cum flooding into her back channel triggered her orgasm and she sucked his tongue even harder. As his cum lubricated her asshole, he slid his prick in further and further and started fucking her again. She dug her fingers into his arms and moaned loudly. No one had ever used her like this and, once she became accustomed to this strange invader moving in and out of her ass, she actually enjoyed it.

Troy fucked her nice and easy as she trembled in his arms. He was the first man ever to use her this way. And it felt unexpected pleasant. She sighed and moaned now with each thrust as he continued to go where no one else had gone before. When she felt him spasm inside of her, she fucked him back, determined to milk him of every drop of cum. He held her tight and let her ride him.

"God you're great! So great! I love you, Rinna!" she heard him say as they kept fucking and fucking.

When they were finally exhausted, Rinna looked at the ceiling and smiled as Troy ran his hand along her body.

"You have the most perfect body I've ever seen," he said. "It's too bad you're married. If you weren't, I'd beg you to move in with me so we could fuck every day."

"I'm not sure I could handle that, Troy. You're a terrific lover but you really wear my pussy out. I like to fuck you—a lot. I'd like to keep fucking you—a lot. But not every day," she said.

"I'll be out of town for a few weeks. I leave tomorrow morning ay six. I'll be back next month. Can I call you?" he asked.

"You'd better. That's why I gave you my cell phone number," she said as they kissed.

Before she realized it, Troy's prick was once more deep inside her cunt and they were fucking nice and easy. This time, it felt nice and gentle. It was the way lovers fuck.

"Use me, Troy. But make it last," she sighed.

He did.

His strokes were slow and deep and he stuck his tongue into her mouth for another long kiss. She sucked his tongue eagerly now and threw herself into their lovemaking. With each thrust, she used her inner muscles to gently squeeze his prick. He suddenly rolled her over so that she was on top. She smiled and slowly moved up and down on his prick while he played with her nipples.

When she felt herself nearing orgasm, she bounced up and down faster and faster. He gripped her behind and thrust harder. She let her head fall back and moaned as she came. He felt her entire body tremble around his prick as her cunt spasmed. Then he came, too. When he did, he slammed his prick as far up into her as he cold and let it fly.

"Yes! Oh God, yes! I love it! Use me, Troy! Make love to me!" she moaned as she came again.

And he was making love to her now.

Passionately.

They kept fucking and fucking until their bodies ached and she collapsed on top of him. When she did, she stuck her tongue in his mouth as he stroked her ass.

"Perfect," she whispered. "Absolutely perfect."

"Yes. You are," Troy said.

To his delight, she leaned over and slid half his prick into her mouth. He moaned and stroked her cunt. When he was fully erect, she straddled his prick and slid it up into her cunt.

"Yes," he said softly. "Like we just had and are having now and what I'd love to do for the rest of my life."

She really went slowly now. She wanted to take her time and really feel his prick and to give him as much pleasure as possible. She realized that this went far beyond just great sex. There was something special between her and Troy now. Something magical.

Troy flipped her onto her back and slow fucked her again. She gripped his arms and moaned happily with each good, deep and gentle thrust. She realized that he wasn't just fucking her anymore. He was making love to her and she was making love to him.

"I'm gonna cum," he sighed.

"In my ass, Troy! Use my ass!" she gasped as her orgasm triggered.

He pulled out and slid it up into her rear channel; again. After a few deep strokes, she felt his cum spurt into her and came again.

"Yes! I love it! I really love it!" she cried.

She rode him until he went limp and rested next to him. He smiled at her.

"Would you like to have an affair? You know—a real love affair. Something special between the two of us," he asked.

"Like we just had?" she asked as she stroked his prick. She smiled when she saw it begin to rise again.

She leaned over and sucked it until, he became rigid, then lay on her back with her legs wide open...

She left the hotel an hour later. It was nearly midnight. She and Troy had literally spent most of the day fucking each other. The last one was special, too. When he came, he buried his prick as deep inside her cunt as he could and just let it go. The orgasm that followed was deep and strong. Like the ones she had when she fucked Al.

When Troy tried to pay her again, she refused. But he kept insisting she take the money. She agreed to take after he stuffed it into her purse.

"It's a gift, not a fee," he said. "I think you're real special. I want you to take this money and buy yourself something nice."

She relented and kissed him again.

"Call me," she said.

"You can count on that," he said as he walked her to her car.

"So—would you like to have an affair?" he asked again.

She laughed.

"Let me think about that, Troy," she said. "I'll see you next month."

She smiled as she drove home. Troy was the second man to ask to have an affair with her. She had to admit, their last time seemed to be something really special. And she had begged him to make love to her, not just fuck her.

"My God," she said to herself. "And we did it. We made love. It was more than just a good fuck. It was much more."

She realized that she had gotten emotionally involved with Troy. That was never her intention but it happened. He had done things to her, made her feel things, that she'd never felt before. They had made love several times. After some thought, Rinna smiled. It was a warm, happy smile. She took out her cell phone and dialed his number. When she heard his voice she smiled more.

"Yes," she said. "I will have an affair with you. I'll be your mistress, your lover or whatever else you want me to be. Just call me when you get back."

Troy promised that he would.

She wondered if that was also Brad's intentions.

Brad was persistent and he did manage to get her panties off. And she was thinking about fucking him again.

Maybe too much.

She also thought often about having more sex with Vince and her own husband. She was still worried that she would lose Al to Li or even Eva.

When she got home, she was really dragging. Al saw the tired but happy expression on her face and knew that she'd been ridden hard and put away wet—again. His pretty little and formerly innocent wife had turned into a real little brown fucking machine. He laughed because she'd always thought of women who did this as real lowlifes.

"He's that good?" he asked as she plopped down next to him.

"Yes," she said. "He's that good."

"Are you gonna see him again?" he asked.

"Definitely," she smiled.

"When?" he asked.

"Whenever her gets back into town. He's asked me to have an affair with him and I said yes," she admitted.

"Wow. He must be good," he smiled.

"He is," she said softly. "But I'm still yours. No matter what happens, I'm yours. You know how it is lately."

He nodded and hugged her close.

"What about the other guys? Are you still going to have sex with them?" he asked.

"Oh yes—and any other men who want to pay me. I'm a prostitute now. I sell my pussy to other men. I'm just like Eva," she said almost enthusiastically.

"My wife the sex toy," he joked.

"Definitely!" she giggled.

She told this to Eva the next day at breakfast. Eva smiled and ran her hand along Rinna's thigh.

"So you're really going to have an affair with Troy?" she asked.

"Yes. He makes me feel incredible. He's a wonderful lover, too," Rinna said.

"I guess that's okay. After all, you cleared the way for Al to have an affair with Li. She may decide to keep him all to herself after this weekend, though," Eva said as Rinna parted her legs.

"That means you and I can have a red hot affair, too," Rinna said.

"I'd love that, Rinna," Eva said as she moved her hand between Rinna's legs. "I really love you, Rinna. I have for a long time now and I want to make love to you—a lot."

"Are you still going after Al?" Rinna asked.

"Maybe. Are you going after Vince?" Eva asked.

"Maybe," Rinna said as Eva slid a finger into her cunt.

Rinna leaned back and smiled as Eva pulled her panties off. Then she opened her legs wide and closed her eyes. She sighed and quivered as Eva ate her. It felt so good.

Rinna soon exploded. As she came, she seized Eva's hair and held her in place as she fucked her tongue. She came a second time and a third before she let her hair go and fall back panting. She watched as Eva unbuttoned her jeans and slid them off.

"Your turn," Eva said as she sat down on the loveseat with her legs wide apart. Rinna beamed. She moved from the sofa to the floor and got between Eva's thighs. Her cunt smelled heavenly.

She ran her tongue from Eva's asshole to her clit and sucked it. Eva moaned loudly. When Rinna slid two fingers into her cunt, Rinna moaned louder.

Rinna smiled up at her.

"I love you," she whispered as she buried her tongue in Eva's snatch.

Al and Li were at work. At break time, they retreated to a secluded area of the building. Li looked into his eyes and smiled as he wrapped his arms around her. Soon, they were locked into a long, passionate kiss.

Al's attentions made Li's heart soar. The more time they spent together, the more she realized that she loved him. If he wanted her, she was more than happy to give herself to him anytime and anyplace he wanted.

To Al, her kisses said everything. They told her that she was his. That she would always be his and no one else's. It was far more than he'd expected, but he was elated nonetheless.

As they kissed, he ran his hands over her behind. His caresses made her quiver a bit. The bulge in his jeans that now pressed against her body made her quiver even more. She was delighted that she had such an effect on him. Delighted that he found her sexually attractive. Delighted that she actually gave him an erection!

When they stopped, she smiled up at him.

"I can hardly wait until Friday," she said.

"I feel the same way," he said.

"I have fallen in love with you, Al," she said. "I have never felt this way about a man before. I am yours now. Forever."

"This is nuts, Li. But I feel the same way about you," he admitted.

Her heart soared into the stratosphere. When she regained control of herself, she smiled.

"What about Rinna? How are things going with her?" she asked.

Al told her everything. Li listened in dumbfounded silence as it sank in. When he was finished, she sat down and looked at him.

"That's totally nuts. And it's wrong on so many levels. Hell, it's even immoral. How could you let her do such things?" she asked.

"Once she and Eva made up their minds to do it, I had no choice but to go along for the ride. What really amazed me is that Rinna suggested that I pursue you because she knew I was attracted to you. She said she even expected us to fall in love and that although she isn't crazy about the idea; she was willing to accept it as long as I allowed her to do what she wanted. So I agreed," he explained.

"And why would you agree to that?" Li asked.

"This is why," he said as he pulled her to him for another long warm kiss.

Rinna and Eva had gone upstairs to the bedroom where they removed all their remaining clothing. Eva immediately lay down on the bed with her legs apart. Rinna climbed on top of her and began rubbing her cunt against Eva's.

Eva held her close and matched her. Fucking Rinna was much better than fucking a man. They always moved together so perfectly and it felt magical when their cunts "kissed" like this. She loved the way Rinna looked, felt and smelled. She loved the look in her eyes when they fucked. She loved the taste of her cunt and the way Rinna ate her or fingered her cunt and ass. Most of all, she loved the way they always came at the same instant.

They were a perfect match in more ways than one.

They were both sluts.

They both cheated on their husbands.

They both sold their pussies to men.

And they were perfect lovers.

"Maybe I should avoid the casino this weekend. I doubt that Brad would give up and go elsewhere but he might stay interested enough to up the ante," she told Eva at lunch. "I've decided to sell myself to him a little at a time to keep this game going."

Eva asked her why. Rinna told her about Brad and what had happened.

Eva laughed.

"If you don't fuck him, I will!" she said.

They laughed.

"Tell me something—do you really love Al?" Rinna asked.

"I'm not sure if it's true love but it's damned close. How do you feel about Vince?' Eva asked.

"I like him but other him being a good fuck buddy, that's as far as it goes," Rinna said. "And he is good to fuck."

"So when are we gonna swap again?' Eva asked.

"Maybe soon. I've been talking with Al but right now he's more interested in Li. It's almost like he's courting her or something. He's being real slow and nice with her because this is all so new for her. She's kind of a wall flower and never had a man show any interest in her before," Rinna said.

"Wow. What if he is courting her? I know that he's always felt attracted to her because he's said so several times," Eva asked.

"I'm not sure how I'll handle that. He might just end up with two wives. What scares me a little bit is that Li is still young enough to bear children and Al's always wanted kids," Rinna said. "That would make things hard to deal with for me."

"Well, it's your fault, right? You told him to do it so you could fuck other men. Now you have to live with it," Eva said.

Rinna nodded and smiled as Eva slid her hand along her inner thigh.

"I'm all yours," she whispered.

Al and Li went to a local park after work. They walked over to the boathouse and sat next to the lake. Al ordered drinks and a light snack. The evening was warm and pleasant and Li was completely enchanted by it all.

"This is such a beautiful place," she said as she gazed at the ducks and swans swimming around. "I've never been here before. I think that's because I didn't want to see all those couples on dates or come here by myself. Thank you for bringing me here."

"I'm pleased that you agreed to come with me," he said as he held her hand. "I can't explain it, Li. But when I'm with you, my heart beats faster. I can hardly believe that you and I are here together like this."

"I feel like this is a dream and I'm afraid to wake up because it might go away," she said. "I asked my mother for advice about us. She said that I should relax and enjoy these moments and that we should follow our hearts no matter where they lead."

"We are," he assured her.

Rinna and Eva had just finished another good, gentle fuck. Rinna lay on her back with her legs apart as she caught her breath while Eva stroked her thighs. Eva's touches drove her crazy. She knew exactly where to touch her to make her feel excited.

"Do you use rubbers when you fuck other men?" Rinna asked.

"I did a few times. Mostly, I don't bother with them. Men prefer not to use them and they really love to come in my pussy. And I love to feel them do it. How about you?" Eva said.

"I never have. Um, do you let them fuck you in your ass?" Rinna asked.

"Sure. I kind of like that," Eva admitted. "How about you?"

"Sometimes if their dicks aren't too big. I let Troy do it. It felt kind of good," Rinna said. "He said he wanted to have an affair with me."

"And?" Eva pushed.

"I said yes," Rinna replied. "It felt different with him. Kind of nice. But he's like half my age so I don't know how long we'll last. I guess that doesn't matter anyway."

"So you're really going through with it?" Rinna asked.

"Sure. He's really nice and he knows how to make me feel very special. I also would like to have an affair with Brad. But I also want to keep making love with you and try other men as well. I guess I've become a real slut lately because all I think about is having sex," Rinna said.

"I think we are both just a couple of walking pussies now," Eva smiled as she kissed her way down Rinna's body to her cunt.

When Friday rolled around, Li showed up at work carrying a small overnight bag. She smiled at Al when they clocked in.

"I'm all set for our honeymoon," she said as she squeezed his hand.

"That's a small bag," he said.

"I just brought a change of clothes and something special and sexy for the occasion," she explained."

"I can hardly wait," Al said.

He phoned Rinna to remind her that he wouldn't be home until Sunday night. She laughed and told him to have fun. When she hung up, she frowned.

She didn't really like the idea that he would be with Li for an entire weekend in a honeymoon suite. She knew that Li would treat it like a honeymoon, too. Al was going to be her first and maybe only lover from now on.

"Well, if they can have an affair, I can, too," she said.

A few seconds later, her doorbell rang. She walked over and opened it to find a grinning Vince standing on the doorstep. She smiled and let him in. As soon as she shut the door, they locked into a long, passionate kiss.

"I told you I'd be here," he said as he felt her cunt through her filmy nightie.

"And I told you I'd be waiting and ready," she said as they went up to the bedroom. "And I am yours for the entire weekend—if you like."

"I like," Vince said as he fondled her ass.

Eva knew Vince would be at Rinna's. She put on her sexiest shorts and headed for the casino around two in the afternoon. She played the slots for an hour before a man finally walked up. They smiled at each other and chit-chatted for a few minutes.

"I'd sure love to have sex with you," the man said as he stroked her bare thigh. "A lot of sex."

"Well, it just so happens that I'm free for the entire weekend," she said seductively.

"I have a suite upstairs," he suggested.

"Let's go," she said. "We can spend the entire weekend doing anything we can think of if you want."

"That sounds great. Um, what's this gonna cost me?" he asked.

"Nothing. Like I said, I am free for the entire weekend," she smiled as she grabbed his prick.

"That sounds even better!" he said.

When they arrived at the hotel, the bellman took their bags up to the suite. Al tipped him. He opened the door and watched as the bellman put the bags inside. When the bellman left, he turned to Li. She was startled when he scooped her up in his arms and carried across the threshold. He placed her onto the bed and sat down next to her.

They gazed into each other's eyes for a moment then kissed. It was a sweet, deep and romantic kiss that fit the moment. She smiled at him as he held her close.

"We're both still sweaty from work. Let's shower together first," she suggested, excited that she was about to allow him to see her naked for the first time.

They walked into the bathroom together. Li blushed noticeable as she slowly undid her shirt. She let it slide off her arms and shoulder to the floor. Al watched as she unclasped her light bra and noticed that her hands trembled. She let it fall and smiled shyly at him as he appreciated the view.

"Are they okay?" she asked.

"They're perfect," he assured her. "Just like you."

She grinned and undid her shorts. She slowly stepped out of them and stopped. She stood up and turned around. Al whistled.

She giggled as he ran his hand over her behind.

"Are you ready?" she asked softly.

He nodded. She smiled as he knelt before her and slowly tugged her panties down. His gaze went straight to her cunt, which was dusted with light, black hair. He could tell by the way her clit was growing that she felt excited. He was the only man ever to see her naked. The only man who would make love with her.

"Your turn," she said.

Al undressed. Li noticed that his prick stood out straight and hard. It was the greatest compliment she ever had.

As they showered, they kissed several times. She quivered all over as he gently washed and explored her body. His touches ignited her passions and she almost came as he gently felt her cunt and ran his hands over her breasts and ass. At the same time, she played with his erection, her heart racing as she rolled the foreskin back and forth over his knob.

After the shower, they dried each other off. As soon as they stepped out of the bathroom, he scooped her up in his arms and carried her over to the bed. She put her arms around his neck and kissed him as he laid her down. She was all his now. All his forever.

He kissed and licked his way down her body. When he stopped to swirls his tongue over each of her nipples, she moaned excitedly. She moaned even louder when he buried his tongue in her cunt. She was so excited that she came within seconds. She lay moaning and rocking as he kept at it until she'd come several more times.

Or was it just one long, sensation orgasm?

She smiled up at him and opened her legs wide. He moved between them and slowly penetrated her. His prick went where nothing else ever had before. The initial pain wasn't as bad as she expected and it vanished completely after a few deep thrusts. She wrapped her arms around his body and moved with him. It was automatic. As if they'd been doing this all their lives. And each movement felt perfect.

"I love you, Al!" she sighed as they both climaxed at the same time.

She was beside herself now. She was making love with the man of her dreams and they were locked together in a good, powerful orgasm. Her eyes were filled with tears of joy as her body moved to accept his love—his seed.

"Oh yes! I am yours now! Fill me with your love!" she whispered as she felt his cum spurt into her. "Make me all yours forever! Give me your seed!"

Al realized that Li wanted him to impregnate her. She wanted to have his baby, knowing that by doing so, it would bind them together forever. He kept fucking her and firing line after line of cum into her cunt.

"I love you, Li!" he said. "I love you."

His words made her come even harder.

Rinna lay with a pillow beneath her belly and her ass slightly up in the air while Vince slow fucked her from behind. He was going especially slow now, moving his prick all the way in and almost all the way out with each stroke.

She sighed happily as he fucked her. He was real good at this. Maybe too damned good. The more they fucked, the more she wanted to fuck him. His prick felt so perfect in her cunt and she let herself run wild each time they got together.

Vince was in Heaven.

Rinna's cunt felt so good as it wrapped itself around his prick. That's why he was fucking her slow this time. He wanted to really savor the way it felt and to make it last longer and longer. He had already made her come by eating her. To Vince, she had the best tasting cunt on Earth and whenever he saw her, he just had to go down on her.

Rinna felt him fuck her a little faster. She realized he was about to come and squeezed his prick as hard as she could with her cunt walls to increase his pleasure.

And hers.

Vince groaned and fucked her even faster. She soon felt his cum spurting into her. The sensation of the warm liquid splashing against her cunt walls sent her over the edge. She screamed and came again. As usual, Vince kept fucking her until he was totally shot. He eased out and lay next to her. She smiled, turned around and grabbed his prick.

"I want more!" she said as she beat him off until he became rigid...

In the honeymoon suite, Al and Li were enjoying a slow, easy "69". She had discovered that she loved the way he ate her pussy and had decided to do everything she could to please him in the same way.

Their timing was perfect, too. As soon as Li's body began to shake with another good orgasm, Al fired a long stream of cum into her mouth. This time, Li expected it and was able to swallow almost every warm drop. Al rolled onto his back. His prick was still straight and hard, too. Li straddled him and lowered her cunt onto his prick. When she had all of it inside her, she ground her hips into his nuts.

Al moaned.

She smiled and started fucking him with nice, easy strokes. She wanted to give him—and herself—as much pleasure as possible. To show him that she was his perfect match and was willing to do whatever it took to make him happy.

As far as she was concerned, they were husband and wife now. She would never let him go. Ever. She understood the bizarre circumstances and didn't care. Al would have two wives from now on. And while Rinna was busy selling herself to other men, she would be exclusively Al's and no one else's.

"Forever!" she said as they fucked.

Rinna moaned loudly. She was on her hands and knees and shuddering as Vince fucked her in the ass for the first time. His prick was kind of large and his first few thrust hurt a little. But she quickly got used to the way it felt inside her and moved with him. He was just the second man to use her this way and she was starting to enjoy it.

Vince had often fucked Eva like this, but Rinna's asshole was tighter than Eva's. That means they both felt it a lot more. And enjoyed it a lot more.

"Yes! Oh yes! Use me, Vince! I'm your fuck slut now. Fuck me!" she cried as she came.

Vince came, too. He filled her asshole with cum and kept fucking her harder and harder until he finally went soft. Rinna stuck her tongue in his mouth for a long, fiery kiss.

"Yes," she thought. "I really am his fuck slut now."

Al woke early. He propped himself up on his elbow and gazed down at the sleeping Li. She looked so serene. So happy. He leaned over and kissed her. She opened her eyes and wrapped her arms around him. As their kiss grew more passionate, she opened her legs and quivered as he entered her again.

"You are mine now and I am yours," she thought as they made love. "And I will never let you go."

They made love twice that morning. Afterward, they showered, dressed and decided to have lunch in a nearby restaurant. All through the meal, they gazed at each other and smiled. Anyone who saw them could see how they felt about each other.

"I love you," they both said together.

Li blushed and giggled. It was spontaneous and from their hearts. They had made love at least eight times since they checked in. Each time, he'd made her come. Each time she felt him empty his seed deep inside her cunt. Each time, she eagerly accepted it.

"I love you so much that I want to bear you a son," she told him. "I want him to be the product of our love for each other and I want us to raise him together. Will you stay with me if I become pregnant?"

"Definitely. I will stay with you even if you don't," he vowed.

She beamed at him and squeezed his hand. It was the very declaration she had been hoping for.

"What about Rinna?" she asked.

"We'll worry about that when we have to. Right now, I'm sure she's at home having sex with Vince or someone else. She's probably not even thinking about us," he said. "Right now, I feel that I have two wives and I'm really crazy about you."

"We have put ourselves into a most interesting and improbably situation," she said. "I don't want to be your "second" wife. I want to be your "only" wife. I want us to live together and have children. I want us to be a family. But I know how you feel about Rinna and I understand that I must accept this situation for now."

"You're very pragmatic," he said with a smile.

"That is the Buddhist in me," she said. "I accept what I cannot change. But I will always hope and love you with all of my heart and soul."

"I feel the same about you, Li," he assured her.

Rinna was growing a bit concerned.

She had not heard from Al since he and Li checked into the hotel the night before. She envisioned them fucking. No—making love. They were both doing what they'd always wanted now and he was treating her like his new bride.

"Right now, he's fucking the Hell out of her tight little pussy and she's doing everything she can think of to please him. Al probably won't bother to call me at all this weekend. I guess he'll tell me all about it later," she thought as she bounced up and down on Vince's prick with wild abandon.

She loved the way his prick felt inside her cunt and was doing her best to show him exactly how much. He held her hips and fucked her back with equal vigor, delighted that he was getting another chance to have sex with Rinna. The more they fucked, the more drawn to her he felt.

Rinna knew this.

For the time they would be together, she was all his and only his. His personal fuck slut and she was determined to wear them both out.

As she felt herself about to come, she rode him faster and faster. He drove his prick up into her as hard as he could with each and every thrust. Each thrust caused her to moan appreciatively and shake all over.

"Oh yes! I love it! Fuck me, Vince! I'm yours now. All yours!" she ranted as she came.

He came, too.

Rinna felt his cum jet into her and used her muscles to squeeze his prick tighter. He moaned and kept fucking her until he was drained. Rinna dismounted and lay next to him. She reached over and grabbed his prick. It was slick and sticky with their combined juices. He lay there and smiled as she proceeded to beat him off nice and slowly.

"I'm going to fuck you and fuck you all weekend," she said. "When I'm finished, we'll both be too worn out to move."

"I love the way you think," he said as they kissed.

Eva's new lover proved to be gentle, caring and very good at oral. He spent several minutes eating her. At the same time, he either played with her nipples or fingered her cunt. And he made her come.

Several times.

Each time, she gripped his hair and fucked his tongue like there was no tomorrow.

While she was still quivering through her last orgasm, he slid his prick into her cunt and gave her one of the deepest, gentlest most pleasant fucks she'd ever had. She loved the way he moved his hips so that his prick swirled around inside her cunt and massaged every part of her. After a few moments, she moved with him and their fuck grew steady and strong.

"Can I come inside you?" he asked.

"You damned well better!" she said as she felt herself coming.

He came a moment after and virtually filled her cunt with his cum. He came a lot, too. Much more than she had expected. They kept going for a long time, during which he made her come yet again.

Damn, he was good.

In fact, he was the best.

"I love it! I love it! I love it!" she cried as she clung to him.

"God!" he gasped as she teased him with her cunt muscles. "That's incredible!"

They stopped to rest awhile. He smiled at her.

"What's your name?" she asked.

"Joe. What's yours?" he replied.

"Eva," she said. "Nice to meet you, Joe."

They laughed.

"Are you married?" he asked.

"Sometimes. How about you?" she asked.

"Divorced," he said. "Want to make this a steady thing?"

"Maybe. Let's see how the rest of this weekend goes first," she said as she opened her legs for round two.

He eased into her and leaned forward. She draped her legs over his arms and sighed as he gave her another good, steady fuck. She lay there and moaned and gasped with each long, deep thrust.

"Yes," she thought. "Yes he's great!"

This fuck lasted a long, long time. A few thrusts before Joe came, Eva's body quivered out of control. This orgasm was stronger and deeper than the others and she cried out in pleasure. Joe rammed it into her as hard as he could and added another load to his earlier one. Never had he fucked anyone like her. Her cunt felt so perfect around his prick and it tasted as heavenly as it looked.

They kept going for a few more thrusts. When Joe finally pulled out, a river of white cream ran out of Eva's open slit.

"Want to have dinner? I can call for room service," he suggested.

"That sounds perfect," she smiled.

Chapter Fifteen

Vince left Rinna's house on Sunday afternoon. Just like she said, they had fucked and fucked until neither of them could hardly walk. They sure as Hell didn't sleep much and they only stopped to eat and shower together a couple of times.

He wobbled out to his car and drove off. Rinna watched him from the living room window and waved. She smiled.

Her cunt and ass had been well-used more times than she could count. Both orifices were flooded with Vince's cum and her cunt felt sore in a happy sort of way. It had been one Hell of weekend.

She wondered if Al and Li were still going at each other.

"I hope she gives him back!" she said.

Eva and Joe parted right after breakfast at 11 a.m. Joe had a plane to catch and Eva desperately needed to get some sleep. Joe had proven to be a terrific and tireless lover. He had made her come in several positions and he really knew how to hit all of her buttons.

He also wanted to go steady.

The way he made love, Eva was seriously considering it. He was so good; he had made her forget about all of her other lovers.

"I might as well do it," she told herself. "After this weekend, I'm sure Li and Al will become inseparable. She will never let him go."

When Al got home Sunday night, Rinna greeted him with a long kiss and a nice dinner. They sat and talked for a long time about where their lives were going. Rinna told him that she had spent nearly two full days and nights having lots of sex with Vince and that she'd like to do it again soon.

"He wants us to become a steady item," she said. "But I know he's seeing two other women, so I doubt it would be exclusive. I'm not sure I want that anyway. I want to keep trying other men and charge them for sex like I've been doing."

"You might as well. A hot piece like you would make serious money doing it," Al replied. "When we started this swapping, I never thought it would go this far. So you really like fucking different men?"

"Oh yes," she smiled.

"Do you have a favorite?" he asked.

"You," she said. "It will always be you."

"Besides me," he said.

"Right now, that's Vince. That might change, though," she said. "And I also like pussy now, thanks to Eva. So I might try other women, too. How did it go with Li?"

"Better than we both expected. She didn't hold anything back. Neither did I. We plan to keep doing this whenever we can. Li said she's my "second wife" now and she plans to keep me. She also wants to have my baby. This is a development I didn't expect, but I admit I like it," he said.

She looked down and nodded.

"I expected this," she said. "You swept her off her feet—like you did me. Li loves you now. I guess I'll have to learn to share you. That shouldn't be so hard because I'm going to keep having sex with other men. That should give you and Li a lot of time to be with each other."

"You know this is nuts, right?" he asked.

She nodded.

"But this is fun and exciting," she said. "By the way, Eva found herself a man she's crazy about. She said the sex between them is perfect and they are going to get together a lot. I also have another lover who wants to become steady, so I'm thinking about seeing him often. You know that I really love sex. And I really love having sex with several different men—and women—now."

"So I see," Al said with a smile. "Just be careful. There are a lot of creeps out there and I don't want you to get hurt."

"I'm careful," she said. "Do you still have anything left for me tonight?"

"What do you think?" he smiled.

Li was still up on Cloud Nine when she got home. Her mother watched as she virtually danced into the house. She smiled.

"You look happier than I have ever seen," she said.

"I am happy, Mom. I am the happiest woman on Earth right now. I have given myself to the man I love and he has given himself to me. As far as I am concerned, Al is my husband and I am his wife," Li replied happily.

"I'm glad things went as you expected," her mother said. "Now what?"

"We spend as much time together as we can and I told him I want to bear his child," Li said.

Her mother raised an eyebrow at this.

"And he said?" she urged.

"He said that was the most wonderful thing he ever heard," Li beamed. "He promised that if it happens, he will be by my side forever to raise and care for it. I know he means it, Mom. Just like I do when he tells me that he loves me."

Her mother smiled and touched her hand. Her only child had finally found someone to love and who loves her back. His being married complicated things but neither Li nor Al seemed to feel that was an obstacle.

"If you are as sure of him as you say you are, then I am happy for you both," she said.

"We're sure, Mom," Li asserted.

Eva got back home about an hour after Vince did. They looked at each other and laughed.

"What a couple of cheating sluts we are!" Eva said. "We each spent the entire weekend fucking other people. So, have you gotten enough of Rinna?"

"I'll never get enough of her," Vince said as he got them each a beer. "Who were you with?"

"A new guy I met at the casino. His name is Joe and he wants to see me often," she replied.

"How do you feel about that?" he asked.

"I'm thinking about it. But I don't want to limit myself to just a couple of guys," she said.

"Is he good?" he asked.

"Oh, Hell yeah!" she smiled. "He's really good."

"As good as me?" he asked.

"He's better than you," she smiled.

"Then maybe you should see him more often," Vince suggested as he feigned being offended. He was secretly glad she found someone she really liked and hoped she make it a steady affair so he could run wild.

"Okay," she said.

"Wow. You sound real anxious!" he joked.

"I am. He makes my pussy purr," she said. "A lot!"

"How do you suppose Al and Li did?" he asked, changing the subject.

"I think they did great. I also think that they really love each other," she said. "Do you still want to set up another swap?"

"Sure. Maybe we can go away for a long weekend or something—provided, of course, Li allows Al to go," he said.

She laughed.

But the rest of that week was fairly normal.

Eva spent Tuesday morning and afternoon fucking two new clients at home. Al and Li became more inseparable at work and Rinna made sure she had dinner waiting for Al each night and fucked the daylights out of him afterward. She was making sure he understood that no matter what happened between him and Li that she was still his wife and she had no intentions of letting him go.

Li understood it. She even called Rinna about it. Rinna assured Li that she would not try to put an end to her newfound love affair with Al, but she also let her know that she couldn't have him all to herself.

"But you're free to have him on any night or day that I'm with someone else. On those days, you're his wife," she said.

"You're very nice about this, considering the circumstances," Li said.

"I have to be, Li. First of all, it was my idea for the two of you to have an affair. I mostly did it because I really like you a lot and I think that you and Al are a perfect match in many ways. When he is with you, I'm free to have sex with other men—or women—and I don't have to feel guilty about it. Neither should you or Al. Now that you both love each other, this kind of makes it interesting. Now Al has two wives," Rinna reasoned.

Li was silent for a few seconds.

"You said that you'd be free to have sex with women?" she asked.

"That's right. Eva got me started on that," Rinna said.

"Really? You really have sex with her? Like the women in those movies?" Li asked.

"Yes I do. Why are you asking? Are you curious?" Rinna asked.

"Kind of," Li admitted.

"Well, if you ever want to satisfy your curiosity, give me a call," Rinna offered.

Li giggled. Rinna could almost see her blush and smiled.

"Maybe I will," Li said.

Eva met Joe at his hotel on Wednesday. She made it obvious that she was more than a little happy to see him again. They went out for lunch, during which he told her how crazy about her he was and how he'd love to make her his steady.

She remained non-committal.

After lunch, they went up to his room where they spent several minutes kissing and undressing each other. They did it slowly. Deliberately. When they were both naked, she laid back and smiled. Joe kissed her lips then moved down and sucked each nipple while he stroked her cunt. She wrapped her fingers around his prick and slowly beat him off as she squeezed it tight. Before much longer, she was moaning with pleasure as his prick plunged in and out of her eager, hot cunt.

Joe changed the tempo of his thrust several times as they fucked. Each time, he either sped up or slowed down or combined it. Each time, she tried to change with him. Eventually her body went on auto pilot and moved with him.

She came first and let out a deep, happy "YES!"

He fucked her faster and emptied his first load deep inside her cunt. Eva sighed happily. She knew that this was just the first one. At least two more would follow and each would be better than the last.

That Saturday, Rinna returned to the casino. She sat down at her usual slot machine and inserted her card. When it lit up, she started playing.

About 20 minutes later, Brad walked up holding two drinks. She smiled as he handed one to her and sat down next to her. He watched her play and made small talk for a while. She chatted idly as she played and played. Since he was a gambler, she decided to try and increase the odds to see if he'd take the challenge.

Then he heard her curse under her breath. He looked at her score. She was $200 down.

"I'll cover your losses again," he offered as he placed his hand on her thigh.

"I don't know—" she hesitated.

He moved his hand upward. When he reached the edge of her shorts, she parted her legs. He smiled and raked his fingers over her panties. She quivered slightly but kept playing. He watched as she lost again and again, while he kept playing with her cunt. Her legs were wide apart now. He moved his fingers past her panties and into her hot, most slit. She looked at him but said nothing. She just sat there and allowed him to finger her.

"Damn!" she said as she lost again.

"You're down $240. You can make that up real easy if you want to," he said as he teased her clit. "Is our date still on?"

"Yes," she said as she looked at him.

"Maybe you'll let me do other things," he said.

"Like what?" she asked as she grew hornier.

"Let's talk about it upstairs," he said.

She stared at him.

She was on the verge of coming. Her legs were wide apart and he was playing with her g-spot and sending waves of excitement racing through her body.

"I want you, Rinna," he whispered. "I couldn't stop thinking about you all week."

He "fucked" her faster and faster. She squirmed and held onto the edge of the seat as his fingers went in deep.

"Let's go, Rinna," he said again as he teased her g-spot.

She looked at him and nodded as she came. It was a nice, easy come that made her shake all over. He withdrew his fingers from her cunt, took out his wallet and counted out $240. He placed the money in her hand. She smiled and slipped the bills into her pocket then followed him to the elevator.

They headed straight for the king sized bed. Her head was up in the clouds. She let him remove her shorts and panties like he did last time while she eyed the huge bulge in his pants and wondered what his prick looked like. Her cunt was still swollen from her orgasm and she was very edgy as he stared at her.

"Lay down," he said.

Nervously, she got onto the bed. He got in next to her and spent a few minutes running his hand over her inner thighs and cunt. She was now breathing hard and her legs were wide apart. He got between her thighs and slowly kissed his way upward.

"You smell like heaven," he said.

He ran his tongue slowly along her slit. She quivered and widened her legs. He licked hers several more times as he fingered her slit. She gasped and trembled as his tongue discovered her clit. He was good, she thought. Real good.

She moaned as he inserted his tongue into her cunt. She moaned even louder as her proceeded to go down on her and licked and sucked her clit. At the same time, she felt his finger moving in and out of her cunt faster and faster. Her entire body felt like it was on fire as she gripped the sheets and rocked from side-to-side. Brad's tongue felt exquisite, too. She closed her eyes and arched her back as the first wave rippled through her.

"Oh God damn!" she cried as she came.

Brad lapped up every drop of her juices as he continued to eat her. She came a second time.

Then a third.

She gripped his hair and fucked his tongue like mad now.

"Oooh yes! Yes!" she cried as she came again.

He stopped and smiled down at her. She smiled weakly back at him. Her head was still reeling from the orgasms. She lay on the bed and sighed as he gently ran his fingertips through her cunt hairs.

"That was nice," she said after a few seconds. "Very nice."

She sat up and unzipped his pants. She reached inside and pulled out his erect prick. She sat and studied it for a few moments. It felt warm and stiff in her hand as she watched it grow longer and longer until the knob peered out from its fleshy hood.

It was huge—at least nine inches long and real thick. To his delight, she wrapped her fingers around it and slowly beat him off. As she did, she watched his foreskin roll back and forth across his red knob. The way it looked and felt made her heart beat faster. She soon realized that she liked to play with his prick.

A lot!

After a few beats, precum oozed from his slit and ran down the knob. She spread it over his prick and continued jerking him off. This caused him to moan with pleasure. She tightened her grip and did him slower. Brad quivered and begged her to keep going.

She tightened her grip on his even more prick and beat him faster and faster. Seconds later, he erupted and fired a long line of cum straight up in the air. She kept at and watched as line after line of thick white cum shot upward and landed on him and the bed. She kept going and going and going until he begged her to stop. She took a tissue from the box on the table and wiped her hand.

She jerked him faster and faster and gasped as he moved his middle finger in and out of her cunt. A minute later, she came. She shook all, over and emitted a long moan but held onto his prick. To her surprise, he grabbed her and stuck his tongue in her mouth. She hungrily kissed him back and kept jerking his prick and pulling it closer and closer to her cunt until the knob actually touched her swollen clit.

Brad moaned as she rubbed his knob across her clit a few times to tease him. The more she did this, the hornier she became.

"Fuck me now!" she screamed as she drove her hips upward.

His prick slid all the way in and out with each delicious thrust. It was a good, hard and deep fuck this time.

"I'm yours, now! All yours!" she moaned.

They moved faster and faster. When they came, it was together. A perfectly times explosion of intense pleasure that rocked both their bodies to their cores. He got her to get into an all-fours position. Rinna squealed with delight as he licked her anus and fingered her cum filled cunt.

"Ready?" he asked.

She nodded and gritted her teeth as he slowly entered her rear channel. His was the largest prick she'd ever had up there and it was at that moment he truly made her his.

It was a nice, slow and easy fuck. Each stroke felt better and better. More exciting. He reveled in her exquisite tightness and the way her rear channel fit his prick like a velvety glove. He fucked her a long time, too.

Rinna came first.

She moaned and shook all over. Her quivering triggered his eruption and he emptied his nuts into her ass as he fucked her faster and faster. When he pulled out, a river of white cream flowed from her opening and she laid there sighing with pleasure.

They rested a while, and then Brad called for room service. She smiled when he ordered two medium well steaks, salads and a bottle of wine.

"I hope you don't mind eating in," he said.

"I don't mind it at all," she replied.

Eva was in a casino hotel across town. She was on her back naked and getting the daylights fucked out of her by a tall man with a huge prick. A second man knelt on the bed and moaned as she sucked his dick and played with his balls. Two other men stood nearby, stroking their hard-ons and waiting their turn.

They had picked her up in the casino and, after negotiating a price, she agreed to take them all on in a good, long gangbang. When the first man finished, he shot his load into her cunt and pulled out. A second man immediately replaced him. When she made the guy she was sucking come, he shot off into her mouth and stepped back so another guy could get a blowjob.

This marathon continued for a good five hours. By the time they were finished, she had sucked each of their pricks and each man had fucked her in her ass and her cunt. Eva herself had totally lost track of how many orgasms she'd had.

The men left her sleeping face-down on the bed and returned to casino. Eva woke the next morning. She was sore and ached all over, so she decided to take a shower. As she passed the side table next to the bed, she saw eight $100 bills.

Al had been with Li the entire evening.

She had invited him to her house so she could cook him a traditional Vietnamese meal and so he could get to know her parents better.

It was a long, pleasant evening for everyone and it further strengthened the bone between Al and Li. Now, she had made him part of her family. To her it was very important that her parents liked Al and she was very nervous at first. But everything went better than she'd expected. Her parents had many questions for Al, which he answered honestly. Her father liked his open attitude and the two of them had fun.

Al and Li went for a walk around the neighborhood afterward, hand-in-hand.

"My parents really like you," she said. "I am pleased."

"I like them, too. I think they'll be wonderful grandparents," he said as he squeezed her hand.

"My dad was pleased that you understood our culture and are willing to learn more about it. He said that you seem to feel very much at home with us. I guess your time in Vietnam was very special to you."

"It was," he said. "It was a growing experience."

She smiled.

"So is my time with you," she teased.

Rinna and Brad fucked twice more that night. For their last one, Rinna got on top and slow fucked the Hell out of him. As she moved up and down, she also used her inner muscles to caress his entire shaft. The sensations just about drove Brad wild. They finished with a good, long "69" during which Rinna tried to suck Brad dry until he begged her to stop.

"Holy shit, Rinna! Each time with you is better than the last! Nobody can make love to a guy like you do!" he said after he caught his breath.

"So you like having sex with me?" she asked.

"I love having sex with you! If you weren't already married, I'd beg you to marry me," he said.

"Well, I love having sex with you, too," she said as they kissed.

She looked at her watch.

It was already six a.m. They'd been together for 13 hours. She smiled at him.

"I have to get home now," she said.

He grabbed his wallet, took out a wad of cash, and put the bills in her hand. She beamed at him. At this point, she really didn't want to charge him. She got dressed, put the cash into her pocket and Brad escorted her to her car. They parted with another long kiss and agreed to do it again the following week.

Inside the car, Rinna counted out the cash and was shocked to see that he had paid her $650.

"He must really love my pussy!" she smiled as she drove home.

Al had already gone to work by the time she got home. She sat down and thought about what was happening with her life.

She now had three steady lovers. Vince, who dropped by once in a while for a good fuck. Troy who had asked her to have an affair—which she agreed to. And Brad who had jumped to the top of her list as her favorite.

Brad was good, caring, adventurous and handsome. He had taken the time to pursue her and said she was special. He knew what she was and that didn't matter to him at all. It didn't matter to Troy, either.

But she was married and she loved her husband more than any of them. She had woven a very tangled web for herself and Al.

"Oh well. I asked for it. It'll work itself out one day," she told herself.

Eva had no misgivings.

She threw herself into her profession with a vengeance. Even though she had been gang fucked the night before, she went online and agreed to see clients the next day.

She fucked two men that day. The first one was a repeat customer with a 10 inch dick and a great tongue. After a good, hot 69, he fucked her missionary style. It lasted a long, long time, too. In fact, he made her come twice more before he finally emptied his load deep inside her cunt while she begged him to fuck her harder.

She barely had time to clean herself before when the next man arrived. He had great staying power and was able to get it back up in a hurry—especially after she sucked on it. They fucked three times that afternoon and he finished off by coming in her ass.

Tired and happy, she stumbled into the bathroom to shower. Before she stepped into the tub, she stopped in front of the mirror to admire the stream of cum oozing from her cunt. She loved being a hired slut. She knew what her pussy was for and loved to use it. She was also beginning to love getting fucked in her ass.

She smiled.

Rinna was also busy that day with Vince.

He had dropped by right after work. He'd called earlier, so Rinna expected him. She greeted him at the door in a very sheer robe and stuck her tongue in his mouth. After a few minutes, she unzipped his pants, grabbed his erect prick and led him up to guest bedroom. Before much longer, they were both naked and fucking.

Nice and steady and hard.

Vince's prick felt so perfect as it moved in and out of her cunt and she met his thrusts with thrusts of her own. He knew how to read her, too. When he knew she was coming, he fucked her faster and faster.

She dug her nails into his back and fucked him back as hard as she could.

"Fuck me, Vince! I'm yours now. All yours!" she moaned.

They moved faster and faster.

Rinna came and began shaking all over as she emitted a deep, happy moan. He rammed his prick into her hard and coated her cunt with cum. A lot of cum, too.

They kept going and going for several more thrusts then Vince pulled out and fell next to her. They kissed again, and then he moved down and sucked her nipple while she beat him off. When he was good and hard again, she mounted him and began to bounce up and down on his prick. He gripped her thighs and held on for the incredible ride, amazed that this beautiful woman even let him put his prick inside her cunt.

"I love it! I love it! I love it!" she cried as she fucked him as hard as she could.

"I love it, too!" he gasped as he felt himself starting to come again.

He gripped her ass and drove his prick harder and harder. With each hard thrust, he fired more and more cum into Rinna's cunt. He felt it running down his shaft and onto his balls as they fucked.

Rinna's head was back and she was moaning loudly as she orgasmed. When she reached her peak, she fell on top of him and stuck her tongue into his mouth again. He gave her several more shorts thrusts and finally went limp.

"Holy shit," he said after he caught his breath. "You're fantastic!"

"So are you. We seem to be perfect together, don't we?" she asked. "Maybe too perfect."

"You know, I've been having sex with two other women at work on a regular basis, but I'd give them both up if you agree to have an affair with me," he said. "And I mean a very long affair, too."

She smiled, pleased that he even said that.

"While I love to do this with you as a regular thing, I still love to fuck other men. I'm not ready for a long affair yet. Let's just keep doing what we're doing and see where it goes. Okay?" she said.

"That works for me. I hope Al is okay with it," he said.

"As long as he's fucking Eva and Li, I'm sure he won't mind a bit," she said.

Rinna stayed home for the next two days. She busied herself with cooking and cleaning the house and making sure Al had nice meals waiting for him when he got home. Over dinner, they talked about their weird situations and laughed at how they came about.

"Strange—but I really did expect Li to fall in love with you. I think she's been in love with you for a long time but was always too shy or polite to do anything about it. I think she knew that you liked her, too. So I accidentally pushed you into her arms and now you have two wives. Maybe even three, if you count Eva," Rinna said.

"I think Eva is too busy with her clients to bother with me anymore," Al said. "That's fine because I'd rather be with you or Li. How are things going with you and Vince?"

"Very well," she said. "He keeps pushing for me to become his steady or something, but I'm not ready for that."

He laughed.

"I can't believe that you're the same shy and innocent woman I married 20 years ago. You're an entirely different person now," he said. "I like what I see but this kind of scares me, too. I'm afraid that you're going to get too wild."

"Well, they pay me a lot," she admitted. "Do you think I should keep charging them?"

"Definitely. You might as well make some good money while you're doing this. Just don't get caught. It is illegal you know," he cautioned.

"I know," she said. "I'll be careful."

Eva was very busy that day. She had serviced two clients early that morning and had nearly been fucked into the mattress by her third.

When Vince got home from work, he saw another man get into a car and drive away. He smiled. That meant Eva and him just finished fucking. He walked in just before she was about to enter the bathroom. She smiled at him and nodded.

He pulled off his clothes and followed her into the bedroom. Eva lay down and opened her legs wide. Then she pulled open her cuntlips to show him that she still had a pussy full of cum. Vince grinned, got onto the bed and rammed his prick into her. As he fucked, he actually savored the way the pool of cum felt as he pumped his prick in and out of her. And Eva loved the weird, squishy sensations that surged through her body. She didn't understand why Vince loved to fuck her while she was filled with another man's cum and she didn't care.

It was weird.

It was really kinky.

And it was crazy sexy fun!

They fucked and fucked for a long time. Eva soon came again and began to writhe and moan beneath him. Vince fucked her even faster as he added his own load of cum to what was already in her cunt.

Even he couldn't explain why the sight of another man's cum inside his wife's cunt turned him on. It just did. Even the idea of seeing her like this gave him a massive erection and he just had to fuck her then and there.

Naturally, Eva didn't complain a bit!

The next morning, Eva drove to Rinna's place. To her delight, Rinna greeted her at the door stark naked and immediately stuck her tongue into her mouth.

"No more games," Rinna whispered.

They raced upstairs to the bedroom where Rinna just about tore off Eva's clothes and dragged her onto the bed. This was the first time they had seen each other naked and they spent several long, delicious minutes exploring each other with their fingertips and tongues. As they did so, all inhibitions quickly melted away and both resolved to make to the other.

They started out by using their fingers to make each other come while kissing or sucking each other's nipples. They kept at this until they'd come several times. Each orgasm seemed to be more powerful than the last.

After a short rest and more foreplay, Eva rolled over and buried her tongue in Rinna's cunt. Rinna gasped and cried out as her friend ate her. Then Eva straddled her face so Rinna could do the same to her.

She did.

As they made love, they both realized that they loved the way their pussies tasted. They even tongued each other's assholes and rammed their fingers up them while they did this. Rinna moaned and exploded. As she did, she fucked Eva's tongue. She also managed to keep licking away at Eva's cunt until she came, too. They kept doing this until they came again.

And again.

They ended up with a long French kiss.

"I never realized how beautiful your body is. It's so smooth and sexy," Rinna said as she ran her fingers over Eva's body. "Now that we've finally done this, I'm going to want you more and more. I love you, Eva. I truly love you."

Eva pulled her down so she could suck on her nipple again. Rinna was very good at this, she thought. Very good. Rinna kissed her way down Eva's belly to her cunt. Eva sighed and opened her legs wide. Then Rinna swung her body around so Eva could get at her cunt, too.

"Ohhh, God! I love you, too, Rinna!" Eva sighed.

They kept at this until both were exhausted. Rinna watched as Eva got up and put her clothes back on. She left off her panties and didn't bother to button her shorts. Rinna threw on a light robe and walked her to the front door. Just before Eva left, Rinna kissed her again and slid her hand down into her shorts. Eva responded by gently feeling her cunt.

"I'll see you again—soon," Eva said.

"I love you," Rinna said softly.

She sighed.

She had crossed a boundary she never imagined she would. She had just made love with her best friend again. Now that it happened, she didn't feel weird or anything else. She felt happy, satisfied and excited.

"I'm in love with a woman!" she said with a smile.

The next day was Saturday. Rinna went to the casino alone because Eva was busy with another client. She went to her usual slot and started playing. After a few minutes, Brad appeared next to her holding two drinks.

He handed her one.

She smiled at him as she sipped.

"I was hoping you'd be here," he said. "We had a lot of fun last time."

"Yes we did," she smiled.

"I'm glad you enjoyed it. Want to do it again?" he asked.

"Yes," she replied.

"Great. Let's go upstairs," he said.

She took his hand and went to the elevator with him. She followed him up to his suite and into the bedroom again. He had a bottle of champagne on ice and two glasses on the nightstand. She watched as he popped the cork and filled the glasses. He handed her one and sat next to her on the bed. She smiled and sipped as he felt her cunt again. When the glass was empty, he refilled it. She drank this faster and got a case of the giggles as he undressed her. When she was completely nude, he pushed her onto her back and started sucking her nipples while he fingered her slit. She writhed and moaned with pleasure as he kissed his way down to her cunt. As soon as she felt his tongue touch her clit, she threw her legs wide apart. Like before, he fingered her slit as he ate her. She gasped and moaned and came. He kept eating her and eating her. This triggered more orgasms and she began humping his tongue and screaming for more.

When he stopped, she watched from her drunken-orgasmic fog as he undressed. He was lean, tanned and muscular. And his prick was big hard and straight. God how she wanted to fuck him! He got back onto the bed.

She sat up and wrapped her fingers around his prick. He gasped as she started jerking him off. As she did, she stared at his knob. She was drunk, still on Cloud 9 from her orgasms and her inhibitions were gone. She leaned over and ran her tongue over the knob a few times. After she decided it didn't taste so bad, she slid the tip into her mouth and proceeded to suck. As she sucked, she pumped him with her hand. His prick tasted kind of pleasant and it was just the right size for her mouth. She squeezed his balls and moved her mouth back and forth.

Brad moaned.

For some reason, she tried to get more of it into her mouth. As soon as his knob touched the back of her tongue, Brad came. The sudden gush of cum down into her throat surprised her. She almost gagged, but somehow managed to swallow every last drop. She kept beating him off and sucking away until he was totally spent.

His cum was a little bit sweet, too.

"Not bad," she smiled as she looked at him.

She let him go and fell back onto the bed. He rolled over and buried his tongue in her cunt once again until she came and came. When he was finished, she saw he had another erection. She grabbed it and aimed it right at her open slit and started pumping it nice and easy. With each pump, she moved it closer and closer to her opening until she felt his knob moving against her labia.

Brad gasped as she moved it slowly along her slit. She moved it back down then slowly up again. This time, she slid the tip into her cunt. Brad groaned and closed his eyes as she repeated it twice more. Each time, she eased a little bit more of his prick into her cunt.

"Let's do it, Rinna," he whispered.

By now, half his prick was inside her and she was so excited and oh-so tempted to let him fuck her. She held his prick in place and squeezed the tip with her inner muscles, Brad moaned louder.

She moved his prick up and down her lips again. It felt so damned good, too. She relaxed her grip and quivered as he slid his prick all the way inside her. Brad smiled and started fucking her. She wrapped her arms around him and bent her knees, then fucked him back. His thrusts were long and powerful. His prick felt wickedly good as it moved in and out of her cunt and she threw herself into this with a wild abandon.

Fucking him felt as good as she expected it to be. He knew how to fuck as well as he ate pussy and she happily showed him that she was just as good at it. They fucked at a nice, strong, steady pace for a long, long time. Rinna soon came again. It was the kind of come that sent waves of pleasure rippling through her. She held him tighter and fucked harder. He matched her pace and stuck his tongue into her mouth which she eagerly sucked.

She felt his prick stiffen suddenly and knew he was about to come. She held him tight and fucked even harder. He moaned, rammed his prick all the way into her and came.

A lot!

And she kept milking his prick for as long as she could.

"Fuck me, Brad! I love it! Make my pussy scream!" she cried as she came again.

He just buried his prick inside of her and held on for the ride. When they finally returned to Earth, he pulled out and fell next to her.

"Jesus! That was terrific!" he gasped.

"It sure was," she agreed. "Wow! You sure know how to fuck!"

"How much do I owe you for this one?" he asked.

"I don't know. Surprise me," she laughed, as she realized that he was so good, she would have been willing to pay him.

They lay still for few minutes. When Brad rolled over to kiss her again, she grabbed his prick and jerked him off. He was soon rock hard again and she smiled at his recuperative abilities. This time, instead of letting him enter her, she jerked him off until he came all over her cunt. He gasped and moaned as she pumped and pumped until he had nothing left. By then, his cum was all over her belly, cunt and thighs. Some had even found its way inside her cunt and was running down between her cheeks. She finished him off by licking the cum from his shaft and knob as she played with his balls.

"Jesus! You're fantastic!" he said. "The best!"

She giggled and fondled his half hard prick. When it didn't respond, she let him go. He watched her clean herself off and dress. When she was finished, he grabbed his wallet and gave her $850. She stared at the cash.

"Is it enough?" he asked.

She smiled and nodded.

"It's enough. Was I worth it?" she asked.

"Hell yeah, Rinna. You're the best," he said happily.

She looked at his naked body. She was still drunk and horny. She reached down and gave his prick several easy jerks. When it grew hard again, she knelt down and slid it into her mouth. Brad gasped as she sucked away and played with his balls. She kept sucking and sucking for several minutes until he finally came in her mouth again. As he came, she jerked him off until he was totally drained. He watched her swallow it all, then stand up and wipe her lips with a tissue.

"That was a bonus," she said.

"It sure as hell was!" he agreed. "Damn! You're great. I can't wait to fuck you again."

She laughed. It was a nervous kind of laugh, too.

As she drove home and the alcohol cleared from her mind a little, she realized that she was becoming Brad's personal prostitute. She had done everything, including fuck him, and he had paid her very well for those favors. And he was damned good. And he seemed to have more money than he knew what to do with and he was more than willing to spend it on what he wanted.

And what he wanted was her.

Her life would never be normal again now that she and Eva had become lovers. In fact, it had been spiraling out of control ever since the first wife swap. Now, she was sucking Brad's prick for money and fucking him.

And Vince.

And anyone else who caught her interest.

When she got home, the house was empty. She walked into the kitchen and saw the note Al had left on the fridge. She smiled when she read it.

"I'm at the Rialto with Li. Don't wait up."

She picked up her cell phone and called Eva. To her delight, she answered.

"I'm free all weekend," she said.

"Me too. Want to get together?' Eva asked.

"Of course I do," Rinna said.

"I'll be there tomorrow morning. We can go out to breakfast then spend the rest of the day making love until we're too tired to move," Eva said.

"I'm all yours," Rinna said with a smile.

Chapter Sixteen

Al and Li didn't just fuck the entire weekend. In between long bouts of lovemaking, they had meals in fine restaurants, walked through the city park hand-in-hand, and even visited the art museum. And Li had decided to do anything and everything she could to please Al and make him happy.

To make him hers.

Each time he came, she held him tight and fucked him harder to make sure he shot every bit of his cum into her cunt. Each time, she begged him to make her pregnant. She wanted his child and she knew if she gave him one, their relationship would be unbreakable.

And each time they made love, it felt better and better. They were perfect together. They knew exactly how to please each other in many different ways and Li was more than eager to learn more.

And he loved her body.

She was lean and perfectly shaped. Flawless.

And her cunt was marvelously tight and she knew how to use it.

Rinna had accidentally created a rival. And Li wasn't about to let Al go.

"You are mine now and I am yours. I will be with you forever and ever," she said as they made love.

Rinna spent most of the next morning and afternoon making love with Eva again. They tried everything they could think of, too. They ate each other through several good comes and fucked each other with dildos. They even figured out how to pussy fuck each other, which sent both of them soaring into places they'd never been.

The sensations surging through their sweaty bodies as their cunts massaged each other were deep and exquisite. It was something Rinna had seen in a porno movie and this was the day they decided to try it.

She was on beneath Eva and she shivered uncontrollably each and every time her cuntlips caressed Eva's. She had never felt so excited or wet. They were now fucking. Actually fucking just like the women in the movies. She could feel Eva trembling with each pass, too. This was intense lovemaking.

Deep.

That's when Eva found out that she actually ejaculated. They were frantically rubbing their pussies together while French Kissing when they both came. To Rinna's delight, she felt Eva's warm cunt juices gush into hers and literally flood her cunt. Rinna kept fucking her back as hard as she could as she begged Eva to keep coming inside of her.

"Fill my pussy, Eva! Fill me with your cum!" she cried.

By the time Eva was finished, Rinna's cunt was covered with cum. Eva's cum!

"Oh God! I love you," she moaned. "I'm yours, Eva. I'm yours forever!"

They rested a little while then did it again. Again they erupted together. Again Eva squirted into Rinna's willing cunt. They fucked until they couldn't fuck anymore.

Vince was busy, too.

He'd met a very cute, dark-skinned woman at work and the two hit it off right away. Her name was Tina. She was five feet four inches, about 120 pounds and had a near perfect figure and a very pretty smile. She also had a wacky sense of humor which he appreciated.

She was also very direct.

While they were having lunch that afternoon, she looked directly at him and said: "I want to fuck you."

Right after work they went to her apartment. They wasted no time undressing each other and Tina laid down and spread her legs wide. The second he saw her pretty, neatly trimmed cunt, he dove between her legs and started eating her.

Tine was surprised and delighted. She'd never been eaten before and she almost pulled his face into her cunt as she humped his tongue. He made her come at least four times and she was spread out on the bed, trembling and bathed in sweat by the time he finished. While she was still gasping for air, he rammed his prick into her wonderfully tight cunt and they fucked like crazy. Tina was so horny and excited; she'd forgotten to ask him to use a rubber. She just fucked him like mad and savored the feel of his prick as it moved in and out of her cunt.

She was on the pill anyway.

Also to her delight, they climaxed together. And it was a long, body pleasing one. After a short rest, Tina sucked his prick until it was full and hard again, then got on her hands and knees and begged him to fuck her in her ass.

This proved to be a longer, more intense fuck. By the time Vince flooded her rear channel with cum, she was lying face-down on the bed and quivering through another series of powerful orgasms.

"Holy shit! That was amazing!" she said after a while. "I could really get to love this."

"Me, too," he said as he stroked her behind.

"Let's make this a regular thing. Okay?" she suggested. "I don't want to let you get away."

"That's fine with me," he agreed as they kissed.

The next day, Eva met two more men who fucked her silly. Both were early morning appointments so there wouldn't be any pools of gooey cum left in her cunt for Vince to put his dick into.

It didn't matter.

The first guy started out by eating her pussy until she literally screamed for him to fuck her. And he had a 10 inch prick which he knew how to use to make her scream even louder. He lasted long, too.

In fact, he fucked her for more than 20 minutes before he finally loosed a good load of cum into her throbbing cunt. He paid her $200 and said he'd call her again soon.

The second guy was normal sized and energetic. In fact, he fucked her twice and she finished him off with a blow job.

Right after he left, Eva received calls from two other clients. They were her regulars now. She fucked one right after lunch and the other at four, and then decided to shut down for the rest of the day. She already had three more lined up for the next day, anyway and she needed some rest.

Vince didn't get home until nearly 11 that night anyway and he looked worn and happy. That's when he told her about Tina.

"She just started working there a few days ago. She's some sort of temp, so I guess she'll be gone in a few weeks. Of course, they could offer her a permanent position. In that case, I'll be seeing a lot more of her and less of you," he explained.

She frowned.

"Whatever," she said.

She wasn't real happy with the way the situation was playing itself out. She really wanted to have a lot more time with Al, but now he was crazy-mad about Li and nearly out of the picture. Now Vince was banging a woman half his age and might not have anything left when she finished with him.

Vince was thrilled because Tina filled the void left by Rinna's pursuits of other men. To him, this was a win-win for everyone involved. Everybody was fucking everybody.

Rinna stayed home to rest and cook dinner for Al, who came home after four p.m. looking tired and happy. Rinna saw the look on his face and frowned but said nothing.

What could she say? After all, she was fucking other men. Plus she suggested that Al go after Li. She had known the risks in that, but as long as Al was fucking her, she could feel free to fuck other men—like Brad.

The next three days were fairly lame. Rinna busied herself with housework and cooking and making sure Al was too tired to have sex with Li. Al didn't mind a bit, either. On Thursday he told her that he'd be with Li at a hotel several miles away, so she was free to do what she normally did.

"So I am your wife from Monday to Thursday and Li is your weekend wife now," she joked.

"And you can fuck as many men as you like while I'm with her. That way, we're all happy and satisfied," he said.

But Rinna wasn't sure that she was satisfied.

Or very happy.

She decided to return to the casino that Saturday.

She walked in and smiled when she saw Brad. He smiled back and followed her to her favorite machine and sat down next to her.

"Hello", he said as he handed her a drink.

"Hello," she smiled as she took a sip.

"Long time, no see," he said.

"I've been too busy to come here for a while," she said.

He looked at her slot total and saw she was up by $120. He smiled.

"Remember our last night?" he asked as he placed his hand on her knee. "It was one great night. You have no idea how glad I am to see you tonight."

"Oh? Why is that?" she asked coyly.

He slid his hand upward. She watched as his fingers crept under her shorts. It made her tingle all over and she parted her thighs. He moved it up and started teasing her labia. She smiled and kept playing. As his fingers moved into her already wet cunt, she watched as she hit another small jackpot. Her total went up by another $22. By now, his finger was moving in and out of her cunt and she was fidgeting.

"I want you again," he said. "Come upstairs with me."

"Good because I want you, too," she said as she parted her legs more.

"Let's go to my suite," he said as he rubbed faster.

Her legs were wide apart now and her cunt was sopping wet. She looked at the bulge in his pants and ran her fingers over it as she realized that she wanted him as much as he wanted her. She really wanted to fuck him.

She suddenly came. It was a good, hard orgasm that nearly knocked her off the chair. She pushed his hand away and took a deep breath to calm down.

He put his hand on her thigh again. Her cunt was still throbbing from her orgasms. She watched as he eased his hand up and under her shorts again and parted her thighs. This time, he slid two fingers into her cunt and proceeded to "fuck" her with them. She opened her legs wide and closed her eyes. His fingers sent waves of pleasure surging through her body. She was glad this part of the casino floor was pretty dark so no one could really see what was happening.

Brad was hitting all the right buttons. She quivered hard and came again. Then he eased his fingers all the way in and found her g-spot again.

"Oh my God!" she gasped as he massaged it.

She came again, only harder.

Her cunt was on fire now and her thighs were wide open. She felt his fingers moving around inside of her as she breathed harder and harder. She wanted to stop but something held her back. She was too horny now and a huge part of her wanted to scream "yes!"

"You like what I'm doing?" he asked.

She nodded as she felt another explosion coming on.

"Then imagine how you'll feel when we fuck. Imagine my prick moving in and out of your hot, tight pussy over and over again," he said as he fingered her. "Let me fuck you."

She did imagine it. That's why she didn't stop him. That's why she let him bring her to yet another hard come that nearly blinded her. As she came, she seized his wrist and pushed his fingers deeper into her cunt, then fucked them.

"God! Oh my God!" she gasped as she came again.

Since they were in a very dimly lit area, she unzipped his pants and pulled his prick out. She smiled, looked at him, then leaned over and slid his prick into her mouth. Brad sighed as she sucked away. While she did, she thought about how good his cock tasted and how much she enjoyed sucking it.

She slid as much of his cock as she could into her mouth and squeezed his balls several times. Brad gasped at the intense sensations and pushed her head downward so that the knob of his prick touched her tonsils. She responded by sucking harder and pumping his shaft as fast as she could. He came moments later. Rinna again swallowed his cum as she beat him off. When he was drained, she sat up and wiped her lips.

"Let's fuck, Rinna," he urged.

Her cunt throbbed deliciously now, but she said nothing. She was afraid of the words that might come from her mouth.

"Let's do it, Rinna," he pressed.

"Okay," she said softly.

It proved to be even better than their last time.

They spent several minutes with foreplay and Brad sucked each of her nipples before they went into a nice, easy 69. This time, she teased him by bringing him almost to a climax three times and stopping before her came. She finally let him come on the fourth one and he emptied a large amount of cum into her mouth which she happily swallowed. In the meantime, he had made her come twice and she was so out of breath, she fell back with her arms and legs wide apart. Brad was very hard again and he mounted her and slid his prick deep into her cunt. She bent her knees and gripped his waist and they moved together.

Brad fucked her like a man possessed and she fucked him with unbridled lust. She loved the way he used her. Loved the way his prick felt as it moved in and out of her cunt. There were no games no. No holding back. She was his well-paid slut and he was her fuck toy and nothing else on Earth mattered.

And how many times he made her come.

Brad was enchanted with her. She was, by far, the very best sex partner he'd ever had. He didn't care how much money she asked for as long as he could put his prick inside her wonderfully tight cunt and eat her, it was money well spent.

They spent nearly four hours in his suite having sex in as many ways as they could think of. Rinna finished him off with another blowjob that left Brad totally spent and he left her with a tired, tingling feeling in her cunt.

"God, we're so good together," he said.

"Perfect," she agreed.

"You want to keep doing this?" he asked.

She grinned at him and ran her fingertips along his prick.

"What do you think?" she replied. "I am your personal slut now, Brad. I will meet you here whenever you like for as long as you keep paying me. I am your personal prostitute."

"I prefer lover to prostitute," he said.

"Call me what you like. Just keep feeding my pussy," she joked.

On the way home, she grinned like the Cheshire Cat. Brad, she decided, was a terrific sex partner. He was good at locating and hitting all of her buttons and the orgasms he gave her sent her into space. He was so good; she was almost willing to fuck him for free. But since she wasn't forcing him to pay her, she thought she might as well make some good money for her services

Fucking different men was a lot of fun. Getting paid to fuck was even more fun. Even so, she would never charge her husband for sex. After all, she knew that Li wasn't charging him. Neither did Eva. He wasn't her customer. He was her lover and the three of them were deeply involved in a bizarre affair.

She laughed.

"I never thought I'd be getting paid for sex at this stage of my life!" she thought.

But in the back of her mind, she realized that she would open her legs for almost any man who had enough money. Especially Brad. She liked playing with his dick and sucking it. She loved the way he ate her and the way he fucked her. And she really loved the money.

When she got home, Al was sound asleep. She showered and got into bed next to him and fell into a deep slumber. When she woke, Al was already at work. She called Eva and they met at a nearby café for breakfast.

"Al usually waits up for me. Last night, he didn't bother to. Hell, he didn't seem to notice when I got into bed next to him. This morning, he left without waking me. That's not like him," Rinna complained.

"I know what you mean. I haven't had a chance to fuck him since Li became part of his life. Does he still fuck you?" Eva asked.

"Yes. But not as much as he used to. That's okay for now. It lets me do my whore thing as much as I want. But I think I created a monster when I told him to go after her," Rinna said.

"You started fucking him a long time ago and never stopped. But you'll have to pry him away from Li. I doubt you can do that, though. They're crazy about each other and she wants to have his baby."

"And I'd like to keep having sex with you," Eva continued as she put her hand on Rinna's thigh.

Rinna giggled.

"Well that's yours whenever you want it, too," she said. "We're lovers now and I want us to stay lovers."

"Well? Are you gonna fuck Brad again?" Eva asked.

"We'll see. I'm sure that I'll keep fucking Brad for a while," Rinna replied. "And I'd like to fuck other men like I've been doing. Let's see how this works itself out."

Rinna noticed that Eva's hand was on her thigh again. This time, she decided to see how far she intended to go. She looked at her and smiled.

"I've always thought you were very pretty," she said. "In fact, I was always worried that you might try to steal my husband from me."

Eva giggled.

"I sort of tried," she said. "I am crazy about him. I always have been."

"He's always felt attracted to you, too," Rinna said. "It was only a matter of time for you and him to have sex. When we started swapping, it opened an entire new world for us."

"In more ways than I ever imagined! I can't even count how many different men I've fucked. Hell, Rinna. I don't even know how much money I've made. All I know is that it's a lot. How about you?" Eva said as she caressed Rinna's cunt through her panties.

"The same," Rinna said. "Let's finish eating and go to my place."

"Let's!" Eva agreed.

When they got there. Rinna took Eva's hand and led her upstairs to the bedroom. They began by kissing and feeling each other all over then undressed each other. They spent several minutes exploring each other. Rinna became fascinated with Eva's cunt. It looked so perfect. So sexy.

That's when she felt Eva's tongue move across her labia and realized that her friend was licking her pussy. Caught up in the moment, she did the same to Eva and ignited what would prove to be a very torrid love affair.

When Al came home, they were still at it. He heard the sounds coming from the bedroom and investigated. He watched in awe as they 69ed and quickly got a hard on. Eva was on top and she winked at him as she finished making Rinna come again. While she was coming, Eva rolled off and sat up. Before Rinna could react, Eva unzipped Al's jeans, pulled out his dick and proceeded to suck away. After a few seconds, she looked at Rinna and nodded. That's when Al got the surprise of his life as his wife grabbed his prick and slid it into her mouth.

He came fast.

And Rinna swallowed every drop.

Eva stood and helped him undress. Rinna watched for a second and joined in. By then, Al had another good erection. Eva gave it several licks, then lay down and parted her legs.

"Fuck me!" she cried.

He looked at Rinna. She nodded that it was okay, then sat back and watched as AL and Eva fucked like there was no tomorrow. After a few seconds, she straddled Eva's face and sat down. Eva grabbed her thighs and started sucking her clit

The sight was so erotic that Al began spurting lines of cum into Eva's cunt. She pushed Rinna off and wrapped her arms around Al's body as she fucked him back as hard as she could. Rinna watched as she came.

"Yes! Yes! Yes! I love it! Fuck me!" Eva shouted.

When Al pulled out, Rinna shoved him aside and buried her tongue in Eva's cunt. He got another erection watching them go at it. He got behind Rinna and slid his prick into her cunt for another good, hard fuck. When he pulled out this time, Eva ate Rinna.

Eva dressed and smiled at them.

"That was the best sex I ever had. We need to do this again soon," she said.

Rinna laughed.

"I'm okay with that if Al is," she said.

"Are you, Al?" Eva asked.

"Definitely!" he said.

"This was our time," Rinna said. "I guess it got out of hand. We didn't expect you to be home so early."

"So when I saw you, I thought it was time to live out one of my fantasies and have a three way," Eva said. "This was fun!"

"Yes it was," Rinna said. "Wild, too."

"I don't know what got into the two of you, but keep it up. I like this," Al said.

They all laughed.

At that very moment, Vince was in Tina's apartment pumping another load of cum into her hot, tight ass. She loved getting fucked there and she knew how to work her muscles in ways that drove Vince nuts.

Tina also shaved her cunt. Vince loved the perfectly smooth mound and flower petal lips and the way her dark pink inside stood out against her dark skin. They had both left work early so they could spend the entire afternoon and evening fucking in as many ways possible.

In fact, their affair had ignited big time.

They managed to find time each and every day to have sex, either at work or at Tina's place. And she was so good that he barely thought about fucking Rinna or Eva.

Tina also loved to suck his prick. In fact, she could hardly keep her hands off it. They weren't in love. They were in lust. They had become daily fuck buddies now and she intended to keep this going for as long as she could.

The next morning, Rinna got together with Eva for breakfast at the IHOP.

"That was terrific yesterday. If your husband were available to fuck me every day, I'd give up selling my pussy to strangers. He really knows how to hit all my buttons in a big way. No wonder you don't want to fuck anyone else!" Eva said.

"I have to admit that watching him fuck you like that was a real turn-on. I almost came while you were doing it. And I loved the way your pussy tasted with his cum in it! Wow, that was exciting!" Rinna said.

"So are you going to fuck Brad again?" Eva teased. "You've already had sex with him a few times, so why not keep doing it? I bet he'd pay a lot, too," Eva said. "I'd fuck him into the mattress for the money he's paid you. You have a beautiful pussy, Rinna. You could make lots of money with it, too. Just like me."

"Well, I am a prostitute," Rinna said.

"You sure are!" Eva smiled. "There are lots of good, hard dicks out there looking for nice, tight pussy to play in."

"Yes there are," Rinna said. "You going to the casino with me tomorrow?"

"No. I'm meeting Harry at his hotel," Eva said with a wink. "You're on your own."

Rinna nodded.

She went to a different casino the following night. In the back of her mind, she hoped to avoid Brad to make him that much more anxious to have sex with her and to up the ante. Tonight, she wanted to bag other game.

While she was playing the slots, a younger man walked up and started a conversation. He was very handsome and funny, so she talked with him. His name was Jessie and he was over six feet tall with shaggy brown hair and green eyes.

While they talked, he kept ordering them drinks.

"You're real cute," he said as he placed his hand on her thigh.

She smiled and pushed it away. He smiled back.

"Are you married?" he asked.

"Very," she said.

"Happily?" he asked.

"Very," she assured him.

"In that case, I'm sorry if I bothered you," he said.

"That's okay. You're not bothering me. I kind of like talking with you," she said.

"So it's okay if I hang around a bit longer?" he asked.

"I guess so," she replied.

"Do I have any chance at all with you?" he asked as he touched her leg again.

"Chance at what?" she asked as he slid his hand up her thigh.

She was kind of drunk now and a little bit horny. She smiled as he eased his hand under her shorts. Instead of pushing him away, this time, she parted her legs and allowed him to feel her pussy.

"You already know," he whispered as he fingered her clit.

She opened her legs further. He responded by sliding his finger deep into her cunt. She sighed as he moved it in and out gently. He could hardly believe she was letting him do it. He smiled and did it faster. She twitched around in her seat and wondered why she had let him do this to her and why she didn't stop him.

"Maybe I don't want to stop him," she thought.

"Let's go up to my room," he urged.

"No. I shouldn't," she replied. "I'm married."

"Forget you are for a little while," he said as he slid a second finger into her cunt.

"No," she said half-heartedly.

"What if I offered to pay you?" he said as he fingered her.

"How much?" she heard herself ask much to her own surprise.

"What would I get for $100?" he asked.

"Nothing," she said.

"What about $200?" he asked.

"I'll suck your dick and let you eat me," she said. "But nothing else."

"How much to fuck you?" he asked.

"Three hundred," she said.

"Okay," he said.

"Pay me first," she said.

He smiled, took six $50 bills from his wallet and gave them to her. She stuffed the bills into her purse and followed him to the elevators.

Once inside, they went directly to the large bed. Rinna sat down on the bed and unzipped his pants. He undid his belt and let everything fall to the floor. She watched him finish undressing. His prick was already very straight and hard. She reached out and gave it several slow pulls then slid the end into her mouth. He gasped as she explored it with her tongue. He gasped louder when she sucked it and played with his balls. She bobbed her head back and forth as she sucked away. A few seconds later, she felt his cum splatter against the back of her throat. She swallowed it and kept sucking and pumping his prick until he went limp. She wiped his cum from her lips and smiled up at him.

"Your turn," she said.

She lay back on the bed and allowed him to undress her. When she was totally naked, he leaned over and sucked each of her nipples while he rubbed her cunt. She opened her legs as wide as she could as he licked his way down her body and sucked her clit. She moaned and moved against his face. He licked her from clit to asshole and back again several times, and then concentrated on her clit. He ate her for a long time, too, before she finally came.

It was a long, explosive orgasm that rippled through her entire body.

He kept eating her until she came several more times, and then smiled down at her.

"You have the sexiest body I've ever seen. It's so smooth and perfect," he said as he stroked her cunt.

She was still on fire from the way he ate her and her cunt throbbed. As he played with her, it throbbed more and more. He leaned over and sucked her clit again. She moaned and writhed as he licked away. She came again within seconds. She looked at the huge prick in her hand and ran her fingers over the knob. She let him go and opened her legs wide. He got between them. She trembled as he teased her labia with his cockhead a few times, and then sighed as she felt it push past her lips and plunge deep into her cunt. He went in all the way, too. Every bit of his massive prick was now inside her cunt and she quivered as it filled every part of it.

It felt strange and exciting. She looked up at him and smiled the used her inner muscles to squeeze his prick.

"My God! You're so tight! You feel so fucking tight!" he whispered.

"You like it?" she asked.

"Oh yeah! I love it!" he said as he pushed in deeper. "What about you?"

"It feels nice," she admitted. "Now fuck me!"

He pulled back a few inches. To his delight, she thrust her hips up at him so that his entire prick was once again inside her cunt. Then she pulled back and did it again and again. He responded by moving with her. She was on auto pilot now. She had a huge dick inside her cunt and she wanted to feel it moving in and out of her. Given the circumstances, it was impossible not to fuck him. No woman could lay there with a massive prick in her pussy and not fuck. Especially not her.

"Yes!" she whispered as he thrust into her.

Caught up in the moment, they moved together faster and faster. She dug her fingers into his shoulders and fucked him back as hard as she could as his prick deliciously massaged her inner walls.

Since he had already come a few minutes earlier, their fuck lasted for several minutes. She loved the way his prick felt now and he became amazed at her sexual prowess. Her cunt was tight. Perfect. And she was an amazing fuck.

"Yeah! Yeah! I love it!" he gasped as he drove into her as hard as he could.

She moaned and gasped with each deep, hard thrust and fucked him back. Seconds later, she came. It was a good, deep hard come, too. She held on tight as she trembled uncontrollably. The sensations were intense.

She drove her hips upward to take him all the way in time and again. At the same time, she used her inner muscles to squeeze his prick. He remained still and let her work him, amazed at damned good she really was. She was amazed with herself. They weren't supposed to fuck, but once she felt his prick enter her cunt, there was no holding back

"I'm gonna come!" he moaned.

"In me!" she cried.

She felt his cum spurt into her with each inward thrust. She moaned and thrust back with everything she had. She wanted to keep going. To take him deeper because his prick felt so damned good.

After a few more strokes, he withdrew.

"Wow!" he said. "I didn't expect that. That's great."

She sat up, grabbed his prick and sucked it until he came again. He caught his breath, then took another $200 from his wallet and gave it to her. She cleaned herself off and dressed. He then escorted her to her car.

"When can I see you again?" he asked.

"I don't know. I don't come here often. Maybe we'll meet again later," she said as she drove away.

At that very moment, Eva was on her hands and knees on top of bed in a hotel room getting fucked slowly from behind by a Harry. He had become her favorite client and she was more than eager to fuck him again.

He was good at it, too.

They had started out with a long, easy "69" and she had swallowed what felt like a gallon of cum. After a few minutes of rest, she rolled onto her back and fucked him missionary style until he made her come and he shot his load deep into her cunt.

She lay moaned and sighing as he continued to fuck her with log, deep and slow thrusts. She had brought rubbers with her, but once she saw his massive prick, she wanted to feel every bare inch of it inside her cunt. As soon as he slid it home, she let her "wild hooker" side take over and fucked him back with every bit of energy she could muster.

And even as she came, she gripped his prick with her inner muscles and milked him of every drop of cum she could while begging him to fuck her harder.

Right after that, she sucked his prick until get good and hard again and let him take her from behind. She really liked this position because it enabled him to play with her nipples or clit while he fucked her. The entire time, he kept telling her how gorgeous she was and how he loved how tight her cunt felt. And she told him how much she loved the way his dick felt as he fucked her.

And she really did love it.

He was giving her the best sex of her entire life and he seemed to be almost tireless. She felt him grip her hips and dive his prick all the way into her. Then he came again. So did her. This time, it was almost mind-numbing.

"More! More! More! Fuck me more!" she cried as her entire body shook.

After a few more thrusts, he slipped out of her cunt and rolled onto his back. She fell next to him.

"God! What a fuck!" they both said in unison.

Then they laughed and laughed.

When they were finished, he handed her $250. It was the most she'd ever made from one client. He also handed her his business card. She gave him her cell phone number and told him to call her when he wanted another good, hard fuck.

On the way to the car, she laughed.

Not only did other men want to fuck her, they were even willing to pay for the privilege. And the sex had been damned good. Much better than any she'd ever had with her husband.

Chapter Seventeen

Rinna and Eva hatched a scheme to draw Li into their circle. Since they were all friends, Li thought nothing of accepting an invitation to come to Rinna's house for a wine and cheese party. Li was already aware of the fact that Eva and Rinna were lovers and that they both fucked several different men.

"I'm glad you decided to have an open marriage," Li told Rinna. "It gave me the chance to be with Al. But aren't you afraid that I'll steal him from you?"

"You've already stolen him," Rinna said. "I kind of expected that because he's always found you to be very attractive. But that's okay because it gives me the chance to fuck whoever I want to fuck. So we're all getting what we wanted."

"You ever think about selling your pussy?" Eva asked as she touched Li's thigh.

"No! Never!" Li said.

"Too bad. A sexy woman like you would make a lot of money. American men love Asian pussy and they're willing to pay a lot for it," Eva said. "And I bet you have a beautiful pussy."

"I think I'll just stick to Al," Li said as she watched Eva stroke her thigh. Since it felt exciting, she didn't object.

"Ever want to try having sex with a woman?" Eva asked.

"Not until Rinna told me about the two of you. I'm kind of curious," Li admitted.

"Maybe tonight we'll satisfy that curiosity," Rinna said with a smile.

As the evening grew later, the wine flowed more freely. By eight, all three women were tipsy and Rinna swung the conversation around to girl-on-girl sex. Li sat and listened as both Rinna and Eva described their lovemaking and how Eva usually ejaculated into Rinna's cunt. As Li listened, she barely noticed that both women were running their hands up and down her thighs.

"Have you ever thought about making it with a woman?" Eva asked. "Have you ever wondered what it would be like to have another woman eat your pussy or what another woman's pussy tasted like?"

As Li opened her mouth to reply, Eva pulled her toward her and stuck her tongue in her mouth. Startled—and more than a little turned on—Li kissed her back. At the same time, Rinna unbuttoned Li's blouse and started licking and sucking her left nipple while she continued to feel her thigh.

Li was drunk and confused and incredibly horny now. Before she realized it, Rinna had pulled her shorts and panties off while Eva finished undressing her altogether. She was now naked and her legs were wide open on the sofa. Soon, both women were sucking her nipples and playing with her cunt. Li was in a tizzy now. Rinna moved between her open thighs and gently licked her cunt.

Li gasped.

She watched as Eva undressed and stared at her beautiful naked body. Eva sat next to her and placed her nipple on Li's lips. Without thinking, she sucked it, causing Eva to moan happily, Rinna moved her tongue up and down Li's slit then settled down to suck her clit. Li gasped, convulsed and came.

Hard.

Rinna kept sucking until Li came again. She then moved aside so Eva could eat her pussy. Li moaned louder as Eva buried her tongue in her cunt and fingered her at the same time. Before she realized it, she had come twice more.

When Eva stopped, Li was panting hard and her cheeks were flushed. She watched as Rinna stripped. They took her hands and led her upstairs to the bedroom. As soon as Li was on the bed with her legs apart, Rinna mounted her and pussy fucked her nice and easy. Li cried out in pleasure as she got the idea and moved with Rinna. As she lay there fucking, Eva straddled her face and Li got her very first taste of another woman's cunt.

And she loved it!

Rinna fucked her faster and faster. Moments later, they both erupted. Li bounced around but kept eating Eva's cunt. Rinna moved aside and Eva mounted Li and fucked her. This time, Rinna straddled Li's face.

Five minutes later, all three women came at the same time. That's also when Li felt a gush of warm liquid spurt into her cunt and realized that Eva had come inside of her. The idea was so erotic that Li erupted again and lay quivering for several minutes afterward.

When she returned from Cloud Nine, she grinned at the others.

"Oh my God! That was fantastic!" she said.

"We told you it would be. Happy we did it?" Eva asked.

"I'm very happy! How often do you do this?" Li asked.

"About once a week," Rinna said. "Why? Do you want to join us?"

"Yes. I do," Li said much to her own surprise. "Hey! Did you guys just rape me?"

Rinna and Eva laughed.

"Kind of," Rinna said. "It's more like we seduced you."

"Or initiated you," Eva added.

"Whatever it was, it was wonderful!" Li smiled.

"Are you really going to bear a child for Al?" Rinna asked.

"If he wants I'll bear him a lot of children," Li said. "As far as I'm concerned, Al and I are married. So the two of you will just have to share him."

"We can do that!" Eva smiled.

"Yes we can—especially now that we'll get to have sex with you, too. You know, I've always wanted to get into your panties. You taste as good as I expected. Doesn't she?" Rinna said.

"Mm mm-mmm," Eva agreed as she stroked Li's cunt.

When Li left around midnight, her cunt tingled deliciously. Both women had eaten her several times and both had actually fucked her. When Rinna rubbed her cunt against hers, it was the most amazing and erotic thing that Li had ever experienced. She didn't know women could do that and once Rinna started, Li didn't want her to stop. Eva had proved to be even better at it, especially when she actually came in Li's cunt.

She smiled as she drove home.

Now that she'd been initiated, she knew that she'd do this again and again. She also hoped that Al wouldn't object once he found out.

Both women had also urged her to try being a prostitute for a few weeks and they said she had the most erotic and sexy body they'd ever touched. But Li wasn't going to do anything like that. Her mother would be disgraced if she sold herself like a common whore. It went against all of her beliefs and morals.

"No," she told herself. "The only man who will ever see me naked or make love with me is Al. No one else will ever have me. Ever!"

And she meant it.

When Al got home, Rinna and Eva told him about their liaison with Li and how she had steadfastly refused to ever sleep with another man.

He laughed.

"You both underestimated Li. In spite of what's going on between us, she has a strict moral code that she lives by. That code is unshakable. The only reason she gave herself to me is because she actually and truly loves me and she knows I love her. She went into this with both eyes open and she's willing to live with the situation for as long as it takes. She's also determined to bear me a child because she knows how much I've always wanted one. So like it or not, you've created some very fierce competition for yourself," he explained.

They stared at him.

Al was right, too. Li was younger and prettier than either of them. If she really pressed, she could steal Al away.

"Would you leave me for her?" Rinna asked.

"That depends on whether or not you'd leave me for another man," he replied. "I'm leaving that up to you. After all, you started this and you'll just have to live with the outcome."

Rinna thought about Troy and how terrific sex with him was. She was also really fond of Brad now and she wondered what she'd do if Brad wanted to push for something more than just a weekly fuck or two.

"You're right," Rinna said.

He looked at her.

"You've already told me that you're having an actual affair with this Troy and you're thinking about having one with Brad. I know how much you like to fuck and you've really gone crazy lately," he said.

"So have I," Eva said. "Hell, I don't even know how many different men I've had sex with since I went into business. It's like it all spiraled out of control for me. All I really wanted to do was to have sex with you. I wanted just us to have an open affair. That's why I pushed Rinna into swapping. Now, all think about is fucking and I don't care who I fuck as long as he's willing to pay me."

"Well, you're both terrific at it, so you should get paid," Al said.

Eva smiled and slowly unzipped her shorts. Before Al realized it, Rinna had his prick out and she was happily sucking on it. Seconds later, they were all naked and Al found himself lying on his back on the floor while Eva bounced up and down on his prick and he ate Rinna's pussy. They kept at it until everyone came. Al emptied his entire load into Eva's tight, hot cunt while Rinna cried out and gyrated on his face.

After a few minutes rest, they switch positions. This time, Rinna rode Al's prick while he ate Eva. It didn't matter that her cunt was still filled with his cum, either. After all, he'd eaten her, Rinna and Li several times right after they'd fucked.

When it was over, they dressed and went into the kitchen for some cold drinks. Eva smiled at him and ran her tongue over her lips. He laughed as Rinna elbowed her.

"How come you're not in love with me?" asked Eva. "We've been fucking for a long time now."

"It's hard to explain. I love you, Eva. But I'm not in love with you," he said.

"Kind of like I am with one of my lovers?" she asked.

"Yes—and the way Rinna is with a couple of hers. Like Vince or Troy," he said. "It's a weird situation and the more lovers you add to the equation, the weirder it becomes."

"And with Li?" Rinna asked.

"It's totally different because she has given herself only to me. She's vowed that I will be the only man in her life ever. It's kind of like it was with us when we got married. You know, the way it used to be before we went down this crazy road. I think that's why I actually love her," he said.

"It's okay with me if you want to have two wives. Just remember that I am your only legal one," Rinna smiled.

"And you remember who you're married to, too," he said. "At the end of the trysts, we both come home to each other."

"Do you think our marriage can survive this?" Rinna asked.

"Only time will tell," he said.

The next morning, Li greeted Al at work with a warm hug and kiss. At break, she told him what happened with her Rinna and Eva.

"It was quite an experience, too. It was one I never imagined I'd ever have," she said.

"Did you enjoy it?" he asked.

"Yes. It was fun and very exciting. They did things to me I didn't think were possible. Rinna was especially good. In fact, I can't seem to stop thinking about now," Li said.

He chuckled.

"Did you eat them?" he teased.

"Oh yes! I ate both of them," she said.

"And?" he asked.

"I learned why you love to eat me so much. I liked the way they tasted," she admitted.

"So you've been initiated into their circle now?" he asked.

"Yes. Is it okay with you if I have sex with them again?" she asked.

"Go for it. What did you like most about it?" he asked.

"The way Rinna fucked me," she replied. "They both did, but I enjoyed it with Rinna more. She was more gentle and caring."

"You two have always liked each other, so that makes sense," he said, surprised at her use of the word "fucked". He'd never heard her say it before. Apparently, Rinna and Eva were rubbing off on Li in more ways than one.

At ten the next morning, Rinna got an unexpected call from Troy. He was back in town and was staying in his usual room at the casino. Of course, Rinna agreed to meet him. Just hearing his voice made her wet between her legs.

She immediately phoned Al and told him where she'd be and raced off to meet Troy.

As soon as he opened the door his room, Rinna threw her arms around him and stuck her tongue in his mouth. Troy swept her up in his arms and carried her over to the bed where they spent the next few minutes undressing each other and engaging in foreplay. Rinna felt eager to have his prick inside her cunt again and she moaned happily as he slid it home. She wrapped her arms and legs around his body and gasped as they fucked. She loved every good, deep thrust and the way its thickness massaged every part of her cunt each time.

"Oh yes! Fuck me, Troy! I need it! My God I need it," she gasped as they moved together. "I'm all yours, Troy! Use me! Make me scream!"

They fucked faster and faster. Rinna felt herself tremble as her orgasm triggered. She dug her nails into his arms and fucked him back with everything she had as she came and came and came. Troy groaned and fired his seed deep inside her cunt. While she was still rocking and moaning, he withdrew, grabbed her ankles and bent her legs upward and eased his sticky prick into her asshole. Rinna moaned as he fucked her nice and easy. He was the only man who ever fucked her like this and she loved the way he did it.

"I'm yours, Troy! My ass is yours! My pussy is yours! I'm all yours!" she moaned as she came again.

Troy kept going until he was completely spent. Rinna had the best ass and cunt he'd ever fucked and he loved every inch of her smooth, sexy body.

He smiled and kissed her.

"I'm yours," she whispered as she beat his prick until he was hard again.

To make sure he stayed that way, she slipped it halfway into her mouth and sucked and licked the knob while she massaged his balls. She then laid back and opened her legs wide. Troy slid his prick into her cunt as deep as he could. She closed her eyes and moaned.

"Yes!" she said. "Oh, God! Yes!"

They fucked again and went to dinner. Rinna grinned the entire time, too. Troy bounced back very fast and he seemed tireless. As they dined, she played with his prick under the table to let him know she wanted more.

"Can you spend the night?" he asked.

"I thought you'd never ask," she smiled.

She had already called Al to tell him that the house was all his and Li's tonight. She would be back on Saturday night or maybe Sunday afternoon. Or even Monday morning. It depended on how many times she could get Troy up.

"It's been a while since I've seen him so I'm going fuck him until his dick falls off. Why don't you do the same with Li?" she said.

Al laughed as he hung up. Then he located Li and gave her the good news. She smiled and hugged him.

"I am all yours this weekend," she said happily. "I am all yours forever if you like."

"I like," Al said.

Across town, Eva was in a luxury suite of a casino hotel happily sucking the long, hard prick of a man she'd met only minutes before. They'd met at the bar and he struck up a conversation. One thing led to another and he soon had his hand between her legs and his middle finger working her slit.

"Are you available for the entire weekend?" he asked.

"Maybe," she said. "That depends on how much you're willing to pay."

"I'll pay you $500 and even buy all of your meals," he offered.

"Deal!" Eva smiled.

Now here they were in his suite, naked on the bed. And she was going to give him the best sex of his entire life.

Or kill him in the process.

When he undressed she gasped at the size of his prick. It was, by far, the longest she'd ever seen and she wondered just how much of it would fit inside her cunt. After he ate her until she'd come twice, he got between her thighs and slid his entire prick into her hot, wet cunt with one move. She gripped his sides and moaned loudly as he fucked her with long, deep, easy thrusts.

"All of it!" she thought as she fucked him back.

His prick deliciously massaged her cunt with each in and out thrust. At first, she laid still and savored the way it felt. After a few strokes, she moved with him. She was amazed that she was able to tale every bit of it inside her cunt. She clung to his shoulders and sighed and moaned as the fucked and fucked and fucked.

"I'm in sexual Heaven!" she thought.

Vince wasn't exactly idle himself. When he realized that Eva would be spending the weekend at the hotel fucking a client, he called Tina and invited her to his house for the weekend. Naturally, she jumped at the chance.

She now had Vince and his hard, thick cock all to herself the entire weekend and she was going to show him how well she knew how to use her pussy and her mouth to keep him satisfied. She was a bit younger than Vince, but she loved the way her fucked and ate her. He was so good at it, that she decided to ditch her other boyfriends and become exclusively Vince's lover.

Tina's cunt was sweet, velvety and tight. Just the way he loved it. She also had, what Vince considered to be, the most perfectly shaped ass on Earth. The fact that she liked to get fucked in it made it even more attractive to him.

Li put a pillow under her behind and lay down with her legs wide apart. Al spent several minutes eating her pussy while she moaned and cooed happily. After he made her come, she watched him move between her legs. She sighed as he slid his prick into her cunt. After a few thrusts, she moved with him in that slow, easy rhythm she loved so much.

"Tonight we make a baby," she said.

"We sure as Hell can give it a good try," he said as they moved together faster and faster.

Rinna quivered with each good, hard thrust of Troy's prick as he fucked her from behind. Each time they fucked, it felt more and more exciting. Troy had found several different ways to fuck her, several different ways to make her come. Each time he came, he spurted large amounts of cum deep inside her cunt.

Or ass.

Or mouth.

Rinna felt him move faster and faster. The sudden change caused her to quiver harder. Seconds later, she came. And as she did, she screamed out.

"I love you, Troy!"

When she left the hotel on Sunday afternoon, she was bone tired and sexually happy. Troy had fucked her at least a dozen times and she had lost track of how many times he ate her pussy and she sucked his dick. The sex had been great and nearly non-stop.

And she had screamed out "I love you!" more than once.

"I love you," she thought. "I've never said that to any other man but Al. Did I yell out in the heat of passion or did I really mean it?"

She'd fucked several men. Troy was different. She felt connected to him and not just sexually. She had agreed to start an affair with him, mostly because the sex with him was so damned good. It was like his prick was made for her pussy and vice versa. And she just couldn't seem to get him out her mind.

"Yes, we are having an affair. And it looks like it will be a long and hot one," she thought.

When she got home, Al and Li greeted her at the door. She smiled weakly at them and plopped herself down on the sofa. Li brought her some iced tea. Rinna smiled at her and thanked her.

"I guess there's no need to ask how it went," Al joked. "You can barely walk straight. You haven't looked like this since our honeymoon."

Rinna giggled.

"He's that good," she lied.

"So you two are really having an affair?" Li asked.

"Oh yes," Rinna said. "I'm going to see him whenever he comes to town for as long as this lasts. He said he's crazy about me."

"Are you crazy about him?" Al asked.

"Sorta," she said. "Jealous?"

"Yes and no," he replied as he held Li's hand.

Rinna smiled at them and nodded. She understood perfectly. Al and Li were becoming inseparable. She had expected it. Even though she knew that Li was more than eager to bear Al children, she didn't hate her in the least.

"You pregnant yet?" she half-joked.

"I don't know," Li replied. "I hope so."

Rinna giggled.

Vince escorted Tina out to his car early Sunday afternoon. Both were grinning from ear-to ear. They'd had almost nonstop sex since Friday night. Vince's ability to bounce back after a good orgasm amazed Tina. Even after he filled her cunt with cum, he was ready to go again within minutes. He had just about word her out, too.

None of her former lovers had been able to keep up with her. Vince outdid all of them by far.

Vince loved Tina's tight, compact and perfect body. She was flawless and he especially loved the fact that she shaved her cunt. It made going down on her far more enjoyable and she tasted better.

"We're damned great together," she said as they got into the car. "Shit. We're better than great. We're perfect!"

"We sure are, Tina. You're the sexiest woman I've ever known and you certainly know what that terrific body of yours is meant for."

"Want to do this again real soon?" she asked.

"Hell yeah! You name a time and place and I'll make sure it happens," he replied.

Eva got home just in time to see them drive away. She watched until the car vanished around the corner and shook her head.

"I can't really bitch about it. After all, I've spent the entire weekend fucking the shit out of some guy I just met on Friday!" she said to herself as she entered the house.

For the next few days, everything was kind of normal. Everyone needed a few days to rest to recuperate from their sexual marathons.

But when the next Monday rolled around, Eva began taking calls and arranging to meet with clients. In fact, she had three lined up for Monday alone and she threw herself into it with her usual energy and enthusiasm.

Vince walked into the house just as another one of Eva's clients was driving away. He watched until the car was out of sight, then smiled and walked in.

"I'm in the bedroom," Eva called out.

He walked in and saw her lying on her back with her legs apart. She smiled at him and used her fingers to pull her cuntlips apart to show him the fresh pool of cum that was still inside of her. He stripped and got onto the bed. His prick was already rock hard as he rammed it into her cunt. The sensation of the cum squishing around his prick as he fucked her turned him on even more and made him fuck her faster and faster.

Eva moaned and held on for the ride; secretly amused that he loved plunging his prick into someone else's cum. When Vince was like this, he fucked her harder and better than he ever did before and she wasn't about to complain a bit.

She soon moved with him. As she reached her orgasmic peak, she screamed out a name. The fact that it wasn't his turned Vince on even more and he fucked her harder.

"Fuck me, Al! Fuck me good!" she screamed.

That's when Vince added his cum to the pool inside her cunt. But he wasn't finished. He slid his prick out of her cunt and rammed it up her ass. To his delight, he encountered yet another pool of cum and he stayed hard the entire time he fucked her. When he finally came a second time, he was totally shot.

He lay next to her panting. She laughed.

"What's so funny?" he asked.

"You are. When I screamed out Al's name, you seemed to get more excited," she said.

"I did. For some reason, that got me hard all over again. Weird, huh?" he said.

"Yes. But I don't mind as long as it gets you to fuck me like that. Wow! That was great," she smiled. "I don't get to fuck Al now that he's with Li. She takes up most of his time and attention."

"That's because they're crazy about each other," Vince said. "How many men do you fuck each week?"

"Five or six," she said. "That includes the men I meet at the casinos."

"Do they all pay you?" he asked as he felt his prick getting hard again.

"Of course they do. Why? You like the idea of me being a prostitute?" she teased as she watched his prick grow.

"For some reason, the thought of you fucking other men turns me on," he said as he mounted her again.

"So you want me to keep doing it?" she asked as they fucked.

"Yes!" he replied.

Two days later, Rinna lay on the bed and sighed deeply as Eva's tongue danced all over her cunt. Eva didn't just east her pussy. She made love to her. She was gentle and oh-so exciting. At the same time, Eva as slowly moving her finger around in Rinna's asshole and making her squirm as she enjoyed the sensations.

Eva loved the way Rinna's pussy tasted, too. She loved the salty-honey flavor and the way Rinna quivered when she came. She also loved the way Rinna ate her and the explosive orgasms that always resulted.

Rinna soon came again. As she did, she fucked Eva's tongue with everything she had. Eva kept licking her clit and fucking her ass with her finger until Rinna came again and again. Rinna fell back and just moaned as stars erupted around her.

Eva stopped and got on top.

"Fuck me!" Rinna gasped.

Eva began rubbing her cunt against Rinna's. This sent delicious waves of intense pleasure surging through both their bodies. Rinna gripped Eva's ass and fucked her back like she always did. Fucking Eva was better than fucking a man.

"I love you! I love you!" Rinna moaned. "Oh, God! How I love you!"

That's when they both came. As they did, Rinna felt Eva's juices spurt into her cunt. She was actually coming inside of her. Filling her pussy with her love juices. And Rinna eagerly accepted as much as she could.

Eva lay on top of her until she stopped coming. They exchanged several deep kisses, and then sat up. Rinna looked down at the liquid dripping from her cunt and rubbed it into her vulva. She smiled.

"I love it when you come inside me," she said.

"It's strange because I don't ejaculate when I fuck a man. I only do that with you," Eva said. "I guess that's because I love you."

Rinna smiled and nodded.

"So, have you fucked anyone besides Troy lately?" Eva asked.

"Just Al," Rinna said. "I went back to the casino to look for Brad but he wasn't around last night. I was going to fuck him silly, too."

"Did Troy pay you again?" Eva asked.

"He insisted on giving me money even when I told him not to. It was a lot, too. I'm really feeling things for him I didn't expect to. It kind of scares me because he's so young. But the sex is too good to stop and he's fun to be with on top of that," Rinna said.

"So both Troy and Brad pay you for sex and you always take the money?" Eva asked.

"Yes," Rinna replied.

Eva laughed.

"Now it's official. Now you really are a prostitute," she said. "Just like me."

"That's right. I fuck men for money," Rinna admitted. "My pussy has become very valuable."

"So how much are you gonna charge Brad next time?" Eva asked.

"A lot!" Rinna laughed. "But right now, I want to fuck you!"

Eva lay down and opened her thighs...

Chapter Eighteen

A few nights later, Rinna decided to see if she could attract other men. She put on her skimpiest shorts, omitted her panties, and headed for the nearest casino. When she walked in, the sight of her beautiful and sexy legs turned heads. A couple of men even whistled at her. She noticed one rather handsome young man standing at the bar. He eyeballed her and winked as she walked by. She sat down in the stool next to him and ordered a rum and coke.

He sat back and admired her, like a dog admired a slab of meat in a butcher's window.

"Hi," he said.

"Hi," she replied as she sipped her drink.

"If you don't mind my saying so, you are the most beautiful woman I have ever seen. Where are you from?" he asked.

"The Philippines," Rinna replied.

"I've heard a lot about the women there," he said.

"And just what have you heard?" she asked innocently.

"I've heard that Philippine women are the best in the world," he said as he touched her knee. "And that you have the tightest pussies. Do you?"

"Maybe," she said as she let him caress her thigh.

"Are you married?" he asked as he eyed her ring.

"Very," she said as his hand crept higher and higher.

"I see," he said as he slid a finger past the edge of her shorts to her warm, bare muff. Since she didn't stop him, he fingered her slit. She parted her knees and looked him in the eyes. He saw that she was okay with the situation and she liked what he was doing.

"I think that maybe you're not as married as you say," he said.

"Maybe you're right," she teased.

"Do you fool around?" he asked.

She grinned at him.

"Sometimes. What do you have in mind?" she asked.

"I'd like to take you up to my room and fuck the daylights out of you," he said.

She laughed.

"That will cost you," she said.

"Oh. It's like that, huh?" he said with a smile as he moved his hand upward.

"Yes. It's like that," she said.

He took out his wallet, took out a few bills and handed them to her. He watched her count the money.

"Is that enough?" he asked.

"Yes," she replied.

He smiled.

"Let's go," he said.

They stripped as soon as they reached his bed. She knelt before him and gave his prick several slow pulls to make it hard. Then she slid it into her mouth and worked it with her tongue. He gasped at her expertise. As she sucked, she played with his balls. She enjoyed sucking dicks now. She liked the way each one had a slightly different flavor and the way they moved inside her mouth.

"Oh God, you're good," he said.

When he was real hard, she let him go and smiled.

"Let's fuck now," she said.

He took a rubber from his wallet. She snatched it out of his hand before he opened it and tossed it on the nightstand. He smiled. He was going to get to fuck this Asian cutie bareback. Rinna lay down and opened her thighs. He took one look at her cunt and buried his tongue in it. She gripped his hair and sighed and moaned as he ate her.

"Oooh yes! YES!" she moaned.

She came moments later and screamed. As she came, she fucked his tongue with everything she had. He sat up, gave his prick a few strokes, and then entered her. As soon as she felt his prick touch bottom, she wrapped her legs around him and smiled.

"Fuck me!" she said.

He was different in that he withdrew almost all the way on each upstroke and plunged in deep on the down strokes. He fucked her slowly and easy as if he wanted to savor every thrust. After a few strokes, she began to match him.

"Damn! You're good!" he gasped.

They fucked faster and faster.

Harder and harder.

"That's it! Fuck me!" she cried. "Make my pussy yours!"

They moved faster and faster. She felt herself coming and fucked him harder. He responded in kind and she felt his entire body quiver with each thrust.

"I'm gonna come!" he gasped.

She held onto him and fucked him with everything she had left. He grunted and fired several lines of cum deep into her cunt. He was amazed that she let him to that, too. Or that he had made her come—again!

"Yeah! Yeah! Yeah!" he groaned as she continued to milk his prick.

She kept at it until she felt him slip out of her cunt. He fell next to her, panting.

"Jesus Christ! That's the best fuck of my life!" he gasped.

Rinna looked down and watched as his cum leaked out of her half open cunt and smiled. She had crossed yet another line by purposely finding a man who'd pay her for sex. As he lay there, she sat up and started jerking him off. When he was half hard again, she leaned over and slid his prick into her mouth. This time, she kept sucking away until he fired one last load of cum into her mouth. She sat up and wiped her lips off.

"Holy shit! That was amazing! You are amazing!" he said after a few minutes. "No wonder they call you little brown fucking machines!"

She laughed. She'd heard the phrase before.

She cleaned herself off in the bathroom and dressed. She picked up the unused rubber and put it in her purse. He looked at her.

"Souvenir," she said.

He laughed.

He dressed and escorted back to her car in the parking garage. After she got inside, she looked at her watch.

"It's one a.m.! Al's gonna kill me!" she said.

Then she thought about the $375.00 she had in her pocket and smiled.

"What a great fuck!" she thought as she headed home.

But he was sound asleep and hardly stirred when she climbed into bed next to him. He'd been out playing baseball most of the day, so she figured he was too tired for anything else. She snuggled up to him and fell fast asleep.

Two days later, she put on those same shorts and headed for a different casino. She did this while Al was at work and the casino's slots were nearly empty. When she entered, she passed by a handsome younger man. She noticed he was ogling her legs, so she smiled at him and walked over to a slot and started playing. He approached 10 minutes later and sat down next to her.

"Hi," he said. "I'm Bill."

"I'm Rinna," she smiled as she saw that his eyes seemed to be riveted to her thighs.

"You like my legs?" she asked.

"I love your legs. Are you here alone?" he asked.

"Not anymore," she smiled.

"Are you married?" he asked.

"Yes I am," she said as she noticed the bulge in his jeans.

"Do you fool around?" Bill asked.

"Maybe," she said. "What do you have in mind?"

"I have a suite upstairs," he suggested as he put his hand on her thigh.

"I see," she said as she watched his hand move upward.

When it reached the edge of her shorts, she parted her knees to let him know she might be interested. He smiled and eased his fingers past the denim and almost came when he realized she wasn't wearing panties.

"We could go up there and fuck our brains out," he said as he ran his fingertips through her cunt hairs.

"That will cost you, Bill," she said.

"I thought it would. How much?" he asked.

"Make me an offer and I'll tell you if it's enough," she said as she felt his finger ease into her cunt.

He took out his wallet, pulled out several bills and handed them to her. She counted them and smiled.

"I'm all yours," she said.

Eva was also busy.

She was lying on her back on her bed enjoying the feel of the good, hard prick moving in and out of her cunt as she serviced yet another client. This was one of her repeat customers and they had arranged to fuck each time he came to town on business. She had also given him her cell phone number so they could bypass the dating site. This way, he paid her direct and she made double what she normally did.

He was great, too.

His prick was a good nine inches long and thick so it massaged every bit of her cunt with each in and out movement. She was also fucking him back as hard as possible.

Len was her first client of the day.

After him, she had two more lined up. So her pussy would get one great workout today. Ever since she joined the website, she didn't lack for sex partners. So many men, most of them handsome, wanted to fuck her.

Some of them wore rubbers. They didn't have to. After all, she loved the feel of a good, hard warm prick in her cunt. This client never used rubbers and she always let him come inside of her. After they fucked, she usually finished him off with a blowjob to make sure he was totally satisfied.

That's when she heard him grunt.

She wrapped her legs around him and fucked him as fast and as hard as she could while he spurted line after line of thick cum into her cunt. After a few hard thrusts, she also came and she let out a deep, happy moan as her entire body shook.

Her lover slid his half-hard prick out her cunt. To her surprise, he then eased it up into her asshole. She bent her legs back toward her chest to take all of him inside and quivered as he fucked her and fucked her. She felt him grow harder as he expanded inside her ass. To her shock, she came again.

"Oohhh yeah!" she cried as she fucked him harder.

Seconds later, he fired off another load in her asshole and kept fucking her until he grew soft and slipped out. She grinned up at him.

"That was different—and very nice," she said.

"I've wanted to do that ever since I first saw you. Thanks for letting me," he said.

"You can do that anytime you want from now on," she assured him as she watched his cum drip from both of her openings.

He got up, dressed, paid her and left. She looked at the clock. Her next client would be there in 30 minutes.

"I love this life," she smiled as she went to the bathroom to clean up.

Bill fucked Rinna twice and she finished him off with a blow job that left him moaning. It was only seven p.m., so she decided to return to the casino and play the slots. As she played, a tall, dark haired man walked over and struck up a conversation. As they chatted, she let him stroke her thigh.

"You're so sexy. I'd really love to have sex with you," he said.

"Maybe you can," she smiled.

"Oh? Will it cost me?" he asked as he slid his fingers past her shorts.

"Definitely," she said as she parted her knees.

"How much?" he asked.

"Make me an offer," she said.

He leaned closer and whispered in her ear. She smiled and nodded then followed him to the elevator and up to his room.

Al and Li had gone out to dinner and a movie. Afterward, they returned to his house and made love. Their connection was growing stronger by the day now and Li was showing Al that she was only his and was willing to do everything she could to please him in every way possible.

When he was with Li, he didn't even think about Rinna. And that's exactly the way Li wanted it to be.

Rinna grinned tiredly as she drove home.

She had been with him for nearly four hours. They'd 69ed twice and fucked three times. He did her three different ways and she let him come in her pussy each time. When she was finished, he could hardly move.

She thought about the $700 she had in her purse and chuckled. Both men were about half her age and both had found her attractive enough to pay her a lot of money for sex. What's more, the said he wanted to do it again soon. So she gave them her cell phone number and told him to call her the day before they wanted her so they could arrange things.

The only difference between them and her husband was that she had only come once with Bill and twice with the second man. Al made her come every time. He was so perfect at hitting all of her buttons.

"So why on Earth am I doing this?" she asked herself.

Then she thought about the cash in her purse again and smiled as she realized she liked being a pussy for hire.

Eva had just finished fucking her last client when she heard her husband's car pull up outside the house. She hurried the man out through the back door and shut it. Then she grabbed her robe. She was still tying the belt when he walked in. She looked at him and smiled.

He smiled back.

She let her robe fall open and stood with her feet apart. He watched as several drops of cum leaked out of her pussy and hit the floor. Then he laughed and took off his clothes.

That's when he realized that she had transformed herself. Her body was lean. Her stomach was flat again and she had redyed her hair a deep, dark brown. That's also when he realized why other men wanted her now.

And he did, too.

"How many men did you fuck today?" he asked as they got into bed.

"I was very busy today. I fucked four different men," she said. "And they all left something in here for you."

Li looked at the home pregnancy strip and frowned. The strip was negative. Despite their efforts, she was not pregnant.

Yet.

She showed the strip to Al.

"Well, we can keep trying if you like," he said.

She threw the strip in the trash can and put her arms around him. "I like," she smiled.

Vince and Eva lay next to each other as they caught their breath. Their lovemaking had been especially intense this evening and small pools of cum lay scattered all over the bed sheet. Vince leaned on his elbow and smiled at Eva.

She smiled back.

"Does Rinna go around selling herself to different men like you," he said.

She looked straight at him and smiled.

"You'd be surprised," she said.

"No! Not Rinna!" he said in disbelief.

"Yes, Rinna!" Eva said smugly. "She fucks men she meets at the casinos and they pay her."

"Wow. Does Al know?" Vince asked.

"He does," she said as she reached down and stroked his ever-hardening prick. "But she only fucks you at her house. So if you want to fuck her while she has a pussy filled with cum, you'll have to catch her right after she fucks Al."

"Or we could all go away together for a weekend like we did before," he suggested.

"I'm willing but I don't think Li will let Al do it," Eva joked.

The following morning, Al grinned when he saw how tired Rinna looked. She smiled at him.

"I took your advice," she said. "I put on my smallest shorts and went to the casino to see what would happen."

"I guess your fishing e3xpedition worked," Al joked.

"It sure did," she replied.

"So how many men did you have sex with?" he asked.

"Two," she answered. "I made a lot of money, too."

"Are you going to keep doing it?" he asked.

"At least for a little while. Maybe I'll try again tonight. Only this time, I'll go to the casino a little earlier," she said.

"I told you that men would be happy to pay you for sex," he said. "I'm not sure if I should be happy for you or disgusted or both."

"Me neither," she admitted. "Eva told me that she sometimes has sex with four men in a day. That's a lot of fucking!"

"Yes it is. But I read somewhere that a really good prostitute averages that on a good night. So I guess she's really good," Al said.

"Maybe I can be better," Rinna joked.

"You're nuts. But if that's what you want, go for it. Get it out of your system," he said. "That just gives me and Li more time together."

"Oh," she said as she realized what he meant.

"So think about what you're doing for a change," he advised.

Rinna thought about it and decided to give it another try. She went out to the casino at noon. This time, she headed for the bar to get something to drink. A few minutes after she sat down, a well-dressed man walked over and sat next to her. She smiled at him as she sipped her drink. The man started a conversation to see what she was about while she looked him over. Within a half hour, she was in his hotel room on his bed and getting fucked from behind. After she let him come in her cunt, she finished him off with an easy blowjob. After he paid her, she went down to the casino and started playing the slots.

Some 20 minutes later, another man walked up and gave her a drink. She accepted and smiled at him.

"I saw you leave the bar earlier with that guy," he said. "Now you're here flirting with me. Are you in the business?"

"Maybe—for the right price," she said as she let him touch her thighs.

"How much?" he asked.

"Make me an offer and I'll tell you if it's enough," she said.

He did.

"It's enough," she said as she followed him to the elevators.

This man was more energetic. He fucked her missionary style then took her from behind. His prick was good sized and he knew how to use it well enough to make her come twice. Again, she capped off their tryst with a good, long blowjob. When it was over, she gave him her cell phone number and told him to call her if he wanted to do it again.

It was only four p.m.

She decided to keep fishing for a while. She returned to the casino and played the slots. This time, an hour passed before another man approached her. He was young and handsome and well dressed, too. As they talked, she let him feel her cunt to let him know she was available. He said he was there for a meeting and had a suite on the 11th floor.

"I'd love to take you up there and fuck your brains out," he said as he slid a finger into her cunt.

"Maybe that can be arranged," she suggested. "I do love to fuck and I'm real; good at it."

"Now you've got me. What would I have to do to get you into bed?" he asked.

"Well, you can pay me," she said with a smile.

They settled on a price and she went up with him. When he took off his clothes, she stared at his prick in amazement. It was at least 10 inches long and really thick. She gave it a few pumps with her hand then somehow managed to get most of his knob into her mouth. He let her suck for a while, then scooped her up and carried her to the bed. That's when she discovered that he also had a really long tongue!

When she staggered out of the room two hours later, she felt extremely well fucked. He had fucked her four times. Each time, he emptied a huge amount of cum into her pussy. Each time, he also made her come.

Hard.

Their last fuck lasted over 20 minutes, during which she came more times than she could remember. Or maybe it was just one very long orgasm. She couldn't decide which. But wow! He was great.

He was so damned good that she didn't want to take his money. But he insisted and that was that. Her cunt had been stretched to the limits and she tingled all over. It had been very intense, very satisfying sex.

She counted the cash in her purse and smiled. Between the three men, she had made $750. She was being well paid to have great sex with strangers and they were happy because she gave them their money's worth.

It was now 8:35.

Time enough for one or two more.

She finally got back home around nine the next morning. She had never felt so worn out in her life. Her hair was still a mess and she could barely walk upstairs. She had been fucked in her cunt and ass several times and sucked several pricks. Her ass, cunt and belly were flooded with cum and her purse was filled with money.

Lots of money.

She sat down on the bed and sighed deeply. As she managed to drag herself into the shower, she vowed never to do anything this crazy again.

When Al got home, she told him all about it over dinner. He stared at her.

"You fucked eight different men in one night?" he asked.

"Oh yes. I'm really tired, too. Now that I know I can do it, I don't really want to do this again. I'm staying with one man at a time. Two tops," she said.

"Does that mean you're giving up hooking?" he asked.

She shrugged.

"I'll take money if it's offered but I'm not going out looking for it again," she said. "I love sex but this was too much."

He laughed.

"There's a price to pay for being a slut," he said.

She nodded.

For the rest of the week, Rinna stayed home and played housewife. Al was happy to see her doing her normal routine again and wondered how long it would last.

That weekend, Rinna returned to her favorite casino. She settled down to play the slots. After a few minutes, a waitress walked over with a rum and coke.

"I didn't order this," she said.

"Someone sent it over to you, so here it is, hon," the waitress said as she handed it to her.

She knew who'd sent it. She looked around but didn't see him. After a while, she sipped the drink as she played. As soon as she'd finished, the waitress returned with another and took her empty glass. This one was a bit stronger, too.

She looked around but Brad was nowhere in sight. She shrugged and kept playing, wondering when he'd sneak up behind her. Just as she finished the drink, he walked over with two more. He sat down next to her and handed one to her.

"Hello again," he said. "I was hoping you'd show up tonight."

"Hello," she said. "Thanks for the drinks."

"You know what I want, "he smiled.

He looked down and saw she was wearing shorts that left little to the imagination.

"You have great legs," he said.

"Thanks," she said. The drinks were getting to her now.

"The last time was really special," he said as he put his hand on her knee. He slid his hand up her inner thigh and made eye contact. For a second or two, she almost got lost in them. He was almost hypnotic. She felt his hand move a little higher but did nothing. She listened as he whispered to her and told her how much he wanted her and what he'd like to do to her. Before she knew it, his fingers moved past the edge of her shorts and up toward her pussy. She felt nervous now. A little excited, too.

She parted her legs and quivered as he played with her clit. He ran his fingertip up and down her slit slowly and gently. She began breathing heavier but maintained eye contact with him.

She felt his finger move past her panties and slowly enter her cunt. She opened her legs wider and quivered as he moved it back and forth. She was in a sex and alcohol fog now and liked the way his touches felt.

"Name your price," he urged as he fingered her a bit faster.

"I'm very expensive tonight," she said jokingly as she opened her thighs wider.

She felt his fingers burrow deeper and quivered. He moved them in and out slowly. She parted her thighs as far as she could and looked into his eyes as she sipped the drink.

"Name your price," he said again.

"One thousand," she said nervously, thinking that it would be too much for him and he'd leave her alone. "Cash."

"Deal!" he agreed.

She looked at him. His finger was buried deep in her cunt now and moving deliciously around inside of her. Her legs were wide apart now and her head was reeling. She was really wet now. And incredibly horny.

"Are you kidding me? That's a lot of money," she said.

"I have lots of money and I like to use it to get what I want. Tonight, I want you," he said as he eased his finger out her cunt.

He took out his wallet, counted out 10 one hundred dollar bills and handed them to her. She stared at the cash in disbelief.

"Okay," she said.

"How many times can I fuck you?" he asked.

"As many times as you like until I have to go home," she replied. "I told my husband I'd be back by tomorrow afternoon."

"Fantastic! Let's go. My suite is on the 6th floor," he said.

They got onto the bed and spent several delicious minutes exploring each other with their fingers and kissing. She shivered as he sucked each of her nipples then licked his way down to her hot open cunt. As he did, he shifted so he straddled her face and his cockhead touched Rinna's lips. She swirled her tongue all over his knob then grabbed the shaft and slid it halfway into her mouth while he ran his tongue all over her cunt. When she felt his tongue slide into her, she started to suck away.

"Since I'm already a prostitute, I might as well go all out!" she thought as she sucked and licked his long prick. "I might as well make this the best fuck I can."

They 69ed for few more minutes, and then shifted again. He got between her thighs and she opened them wide and bent her knees.

"Fuck me!" she said as she willingly accepted it into her hungry cunt.

He began fucking her with long, easy strokes. Taking his time to enjoy the way her cunt felt. She held his arms and moved with him. His prick felt good inside her. And the longer they fucked, the more Rinna enjoyed it. She sighed and moaned with each thrust as her body raced towards what promised to be an incredible climax.

Rinna came first. As she did, she fucked him faster and trembled all over. He kept going as hard as he could. Then, just before he came, he pulled out and fired several lines of cum on her writhing body. While she was still up in the air, he eased his prick back into her. This time, he fucked her hard and fast. The change thrilled her. She wrapped her arms and legs around him and fucked him back as hard as she could. Each deep, hard thrust caused her to shiver as one mini-orgasm after another rippled through her. She arched her back and screamed as she came. She fell with her arms akimbo and moaned happily as he continued to hammer away at her in what seemed to be the longest, most intense fuck of her entire life.

His thrusting began to grow erratic. Rinna realized he was about come. She gripped his waist and fucked him with everything she had left. He groaned loudly and buried his prick as deep into her cunt as he could. Rinna felt his cum gush into her and came again. They kept at it for a few more unsteady thrusts. He rolled off and smiled.

She grabbed his prick, gave it several jerks then slid it into her mouth. She worked him until he became hard again them slid around and mounted his prick for another good, long ride. She loved the way his prick felt inside of her and she wanted to enjoy every moment she had with Brad.

When he was about ready to come, Brad rolled her over. He draped her legs over his arms and fucked her as fast and as deeply as he could. The intensity caused Rinna to orgasm again. She gripped his shoulders and moaned loudly as he kept fucking and fucking. When he came, he rammed his prick all the way in and coated her inner walls with cum

After a short rest inside of her, he began to fuck her again.

"Oh yeah! Oh, yeah! Fuck me!" she moaned.

He grunted and came again a few thrusts later. She came, too. As she did, she fucked him as hard as she could until they were both exhausted.

They fucked several times that night, stopping only to order dinner from room service. Rinna discovered that Brad was an exceptionally good lover and nearly tireless. He discovered that she also loved to fuck.

A lot.

More than any woman he'd ever known. She was daring and willing to try just about any position and she loved to suck his prick.

"That wasn't so bad, was it?" he said the next afternoon.

She laughed.

"Actually, it was great," she replied. "Really great. Was it worth what you paid?"

"Definitely," he replied. "It was the best thousand bucks I've ever spent."

"Good. I'm glad you enjoyed it," she said as they dressed.

"I think I've fallen in love with you," he said. "In fact, I can't stop thinking about you and when I see you, I want you more and more. If you weren't already married, I'd propose to you. I'm serious, Rinna."

"Wow," she said as she realized her feelings for him went way beyond just great sex. They had eaten meals together and talked and made each other laugh. They'd showered together, gambled together and did just about everything a honeymooning couple would do.

And now he told her that he loved her.

"Don't worry, Rinna. I'm not asking you leave your husband or anything like that. What we have going now is special and fine. I just thought I had to tell you how I feel," he said.

She nodded.

"I'm starting to feel the same about you, too," she said. "This is exciting and confusing and totally crazy, Brad. I don't know what to say or how to act."

He walked her to the car.

"Will you be here again next week?" he asked.

"Yes," she replied.

"Let's get together again. I'll pay you the same price. You're so damned good that I must have you again," he offered.

She smiled at him.

"I'll be here," she said. "But you don't have to pay anything. Ever again."

They kissed.

She got into her car and waved as she drove off. He watched until she was out of sight and smiled as he went back to his suite.

"I've finally found the woman of my dreams—and just my luck—she's married. Her husband is one lucky bastard!" he thought.

Rinna did think about on the way home. She really enjoyed having sex with him a lot more than she expected. And she loved to be with him far more than she expected. They were lovers now. Like her and Troy, only stronger.

But will she be able to juggle two affairs and have other men on the side?

"Of course I will!" she decided.

Chapter Nineteen

While Rinna was fucking Brad, Li was also busy fucking Al. She had shown up at his house wearing nothing but a bath robe, which she dropped to the floor the second he let her inside. This sexual adventure began in the living room with Al eating Li's pussy while she sat with her legs draped over an armchair and ended with him fucking her up her ass. In between they also fucked in two other positions and she had sucked his prick.

This wasn't just sex. They were making love and Li was determined to have his baby. Since Rinna knew they were fucking, Al saw no reason not to have an affair with Li. She had a wonderful tight body and a cunt to match and she really knew how to use both.

As long as he had Li, he didn't care what Rinna was doing or how many different men she fucked. His relationship with Li had blossomed into a strong, deep love and that's all that mattered anymore.

He also knew that Rinna had become just like Eva and was fucking men for cash.

"Several other men," Eva had told him. "She is just like me now. Our pussies are money machines."

When Rinna got home, Li was standing in the living room wearing an open robe. She could see that she had a well fucked look on her face, too. Li smiled at her as if to say "he's mine now. You can't have him back."

Rinna looked at her cunt then walked up and felt it. Li shivered and nodded. She knew what Rinna wanted and was willing to give it to her.

"Tomorrow," she whispered.

Rinna nodded. She was also very tired now. Very satisfied.

Li dressed and left.

"Is she pregnant yet?" Rinna asked.

"We'll know in a few weeks," he replied. "You're okay with this?"

"Not really. But it's what you both want and if that makes you happy, then I'm happy for you," she said with a smile. "I need to talk with you later. I seem to have a problem and I need someone to talk to."

"I'm here. What sort of problem?" he asked.

"I have two men who say they love me and I'm not sure how to handle it," she said.

Al laughed as she went up to shower. It was mostly in the open now. They were all guilty of something. Later over dinner, Al listened as Rinna told him about Brad and Troy. He shook his head and laughed.

"Of course they're crazy about you. Any man who spends time with you will fall in love with you. You're every man's dream girl. But I see where you're confused. On the one hand, you have Troy who is half your age, energetic and totally nuts about you. Then there's Brad who you said is very handsome, fun to be with and has tons of cash. Brad lives in the area, so he's readily available. Troy comes here about once a month and you usually spend the entire weekend with him. What it comes down to is—who do you like more?" he said. "Who are you most attracted to and want to be with more?"

She sighed.

"Vince also wants to make it a regular thing. I like to fuck him but I'm not actually emotionally attracted to him other than as a friend. Then there's you, the man I love more than anything else on Earth. I still want to be available for you whenever you need me. Despite your relationship with Li, I have no intentions of letting you get away," she said.

"When we started down this road, I warned you that things might get complicated. You could carry on your affair with Brad and only see Troy when he comes to town. I'm sure you could juggle the two of them with no problem. But you're also having love affairs with Eva and Li. Then there's Vince and the other men you might decide to fuck for money. What I'm afraid of is that you'll ruin your health at this pace. You really need to slow this down somehow."

She nodded.

"Maybe I'll stop letting men pick me up at the casinos. That might help," she said.

"It's a start," he agreed. "I've limited my extra marital activities to just Li and Eva. They're more than enough for me because I still have you. So maybe you should limit yourself to two or three lovers," he suggested.

"I'll try. But you know how I am," she said.

He laughed.

"Do I ever!" he said.

The following Saturday, Rinna went back to the casino to meet Brad. They met at the bar, had a couple of drinks and went up to his suite. They were naked and locked in a torrid 69 within seconds after hitting the bedroom. Rinna sucked his prick until she felt it was perfectly hard. Then she stopped and looked up at him.

"Fuck me, Brad," she said.

Brad got between her thighs. She bent her knees and smiled, then trembled as he slid his prick deep into her cunt. She closed her eyes and relaxed as he began fucking her nice and easy. It felt nice, she decided.

Very nice.

After a few good thrusts, she wrapped her legs around him and began to fuck him back. Brad increased the tempo. Rinna moaned, dug her fingers into his shoulders and moved with him as he fucked her harder and harder. They immediately began moving together. This time, the rhythm was faster and a little bit harder.

"Oooh, yes! Yes! Fuck me, Brad! Fuck me good!" she moaned

They fucked faster and faster. Rinna gasped, arched her back and cried out as she came. It was a good, deep orgasm, too. One that shook her entire body.

"Yes! I love it! Fuck me!" she cried

He leaned into her and fucked her as fast as he could. Rinna moaned and gripped his arms as she matched him stroke for stroke. Then she came again.

Brad did, too.

He filled her cunt with every drop of cum he had. Then they kissed and caressed each other for a while before fucking again. This time, Brad picked up the pace.

"Oooh yes! Yes! Fuck me, Brad! Fuck me!" she cried.

Brad slid his prick all the way in. Rinna quivered and used her inner muscles to squeeze him several times. Brad moaned. It felt exquisite. Then he began to move. Rinna moaned on each thrust then began to fuck him back. They soon fell into a good, easy rhythm. Rinna wrapped her knees around his hips and smiled up at him.

"That's it, Brad! Fuck me!" she said. "That feels so nice. So nice!" she moaned. "Fuck me harder now!"

Brad did as she asked. He thrust into her faster and faster. Rinna quickly matched him thrust for thrust.

"Oooh yes! Yes! That's the way I like it! Fuck me!" she cried. "Use my pussy! Make it yours!"

They kept at it for a few more good thrusts. Then Rinna came. While she moaned and trembled, she felt Brad's cum jet into her. He always came a lot, too. So much that she wondered where he was getting it from. Just before he finished, he withdrew from her cunt and slid his prick up into her asshole. The sudden switch caused her to come again and she fucked him with everything she still had.

She loved the way his prick felt as it worked her ass. It was the perfect size for her. He was still coming, too. With each deep thrust, he shot another wad into her ass and her cries of pleasure encouraged him to keep going. When he finally pulled out, he was totally limp. They lay next to each other for a little while.

That's when he made another proposal.

"How would you like to go away to a resort with me for a weekend? I'll pay for everything," he asked.

"Like where?" she asked as he stroked her cunt.

"Pick whatever place you like. We can even go for an entire week if you want," he said.

"I think that sounds great," she said as she sucked the tip.

By now, his prick was rock hard again. He got between her thighs and rammed it home. She wrapped her legs around his hips and moaned as he fucked her. He was good at this, too.

Real good.

They moved faster and faster. She matched him thrust for thrust, loving the way his prick felt as it moved in and out of her cunt. His thrusts grew longer and faster. She realized he was about to come again and fucked him back with everything she had. It was a hard, intense kind of fuck that took her breath away. She felt his body stiffen as he thrust harder.

He was coming again.

So was she. She gripped his back and thrust her hips upward and let out a deep moan. They kept fucking and fucking until he finally collapsed on top of her with his prick buried in her cunt. She used her inner muscles to milk him until he finally softened and eased out.

"Wow!" he said after a while.

She smiled.

"Sex with you is really terrific," he said as he sat up.

"I really love doing this with you, too," she said. "My pussy gets wet whenever I think about you, too."

"So you'll go away with me?" he asked.

"I need to think about that for a couple of days. It's very tempting to even imagine being somewhere with you for an entire week and just fucking our brains out," she said.

"Be daring, Rinna. Let's do it," he pushed. "We can treat it like a honeymoon. I just want to be with you."

She smiled, then leaned over and sucked his prick...

Once again, Eva and Joe were heating up their love affair. This time, he went over to her house because her husband was out of town for the night.

Eva greeted him at the door dressed in her very sheer robe. As soon as he walked in and shut the door behind him, Eva let the robe slide to the floor and stood before him completely naked. He gawked at her smooth, lovely body as his prick hardened. She walked up to him and groped him. Within seconds, he too was naked and Eva was kneeling before him stroking his cock. She had a hungry look in her eyes. Sort of like a cat ogling a canary.

Joe led her to the dining room and had her lean forward on the table with her legs apart. Then he knelt behind her and lovingly licked her puckered anus for a few seconds before sliding his tongue up into her cunt. Eva gasped as he explored her soft, flowery lips and nibbled at her clit. It was a very pleasant and exciting sensation that made her fidget. At the same time, Joe reached up and massaged her nipples. That really made Eva squirm.

Now that she was good and wet, he stood up and eased his prick into her channel. She sighed as his knob pushed past her labia and sunk deep into her pussy. She felt him moving in and out. He did her slowly at first, trying to find his balance. When he did, he began fucking her faster and faster. Eva sighed and trembled all over. He grabbed her behind and humped her even faster. This caused her to shriek with delight as his knob raked across her g-spot several times.

He loved the way her cunt convulsed around his prick each time he thrust into her. She felt so good, too. So tight. So silky smooth. In fact, this was one of the best fucks he'd had in weeks.

And Eva had one of the best cunts.

Each time his prick moved inside her pussy, Eva sighed happily and trembled with lust. She felt herself growing wetter and hotter as they fucked and she began thrusting her hips back at him to match his rhythm.

Each time, he pushed into her all the way to his balls. Each time, he thrust harder. And each thrust caused Eva to moan.

Eva felt herself coming. It was a good one, too. From deep inside her cunt. Joe realized what she was going through and picked up the pace of his thrusting. Eva moaned and threw her head back.

"Oohh! That's it! Fuck me, Joe! That feels so good! So fucking good!" she moaned.

He fucked her even faster. He soon felt his balls spasm a few times and held onto her even tighter as he hammered away at her sopping cunt. Eva shook wildly and sighed. Then she fell across the table and lay trembling while he continued to fuck her like a madman. After several more deep thrusts, he pushed his prick as deep into Eva's cunt as he could and released a flood of cum. The sensations caused by the hot cum slamming into her cunt walls triggered another orgasm in Eva and she began groaning loudly. Spurt after spurt jetted into her. She felt each and every one of them, too.

And they felt delicious.

So wonderfully delicious.

He kept humping away until his prick slid out of Eva's cunt. As it did, a shower of cum dripped from her open slit and splattered onto the carpet. He fingered her slit while she slowly fell back to Earth. Eva turned and wrapped her fingers around his half-hard shaft. To her delight, it began to get hard again.

"Let's finish this upstairs," she said.

Al got home from his date with Li a few minutes after Rinna did. She smiled as he sat down on the sofa next to her.

"Brad wants me to go away with him. He said I could pick any place I liked and we could stay as long as I wanted," she said.

"I see. What did you tell him?" Al asked.

"I said I needed time to think about it. Brad excites me and I'm developing strong feelings for him, but that sounds like he wants me to make some sort of commitment with him. I'm not sure I want that. Not yet," she said.

"What's your gut feeling about this?" he asked.

"I want to do it but I'm scared to," she said. "I'm scared where it might lead me."

"You definitely have a problem," he said. "So do we. I'm not crazy about having you going on a week-long trip with anyone. You're still my wife and I don't want to lose you."

"What if I told you it's okay if you want to go on a long trip with Li? Would that make it easier?" she asked.

"Now that's something I need to think about!" he said.

Rinna decided that as much as she cared for Brad, she still wanted to play the field. She enjoyed fucking many different men and was reluctant to settle down with just one or two. Al had told her to do what she felt she really wanted to do. She decided that he was right.

Two nights later, Rinna went to another casino. As usual, she wore her tiny "fuck me" shorts just to see if anyone would try to pick her up. A few minutes after she sat down at a slot and started to play, a handsome young man walked over and sat beside her.

"You look terrific in those shorts. What would it take for me to see what's in them?" he teased.

"Money," she replied with a smile.

"I have money. How much?" he asked.

"That depends. How much are you willing to pay?" she teased. "What I have can be expensive."

"I'll bet it is," he said as he stroked her thigh. "How about if I offered to pay you $250?"

"That's a start," he said.

"I have lots of cash on me. I just won big at poker," he said as he opened his wallet. "Take what you think is fair."

She smiled.

"Are you sure?" she asked as he stroked her thigh more and more.

"Go for it," he assured her.

She reached down and took out several bills. It was at least half of what he had in the wallet. He smiled.

"My room is upstairs," he said.

Li was on her back with her legs wide apart and her arms wrapped around Al as they fucked. It was a nice, long, steady and deep fuck. The kind she loved. The kind that made her feel warm all over. She matched him thrust for thrust and sighed happily each time he plunged into her.

Al was in Heaven, too.

Li's cunt felt exquisite.

Perfect.

When they made love, neither held anything back. It was like magic.

Across town, Eva had just finished fucking her third client of the day. He was tall, muscular and energetic. He'd stopped by at two and they spent the next two hours fucking and sucking almost nonstop. Evan lost track of how many times she came. He was damned good with his prick, too.

And he'd virtually flooded her cunt with thick, warm cum when he came. And came. She lay there panting while she watched him dress. He helped her back to her feet and paid her. She smiled and escorted him to the door. She was still naked and lines of cum were running down her inner thighs.

"It's fun being a hired slut," she said as she walked to the shower.

Rinna left the casino three hours later. Her new friend had fucked her three times and she had sucked him dry afterward. She really loved to suck pricks now and she loved the way cum tasted and felt as it slid down her throat.

She even enjoyed getting fucked in her ass because the orgasms she experienced during anal sex were incredibly intense and her lovers went nuts over the way her ass muscles convulsed around their pricks.

This man was no exception. She was sort of amazed that she was able to take his good sized prick all the way up her ass like she did. It hurt at first, but once they got into it, it felt better and better.

She now had two loads of cum in her pussy, one in her ass and another went down her throat. She was amazed at how quick he was able to get it up each time and she really enjoyed it when he ate her pussy and made her come several times.

She was tired, too.

He was so good that he'd worn her out. When she was finished, she gave him her cell phone number and told him to call her when he came back to town. He promised that he would and said she was worth every bit of what he paid.

They dressed and he escorted her to her car. She waved when she drove off and smiled at the $400 she made. That was very good money for doing something that she loved to do.

"How much longer will I be able to keep this up?" she wondered. "What will Al say when he sees me?"

Al arrived the same time she did. They smiled at each other and hugged. They stumbled upstairs and showered together as they talked and laughed. Rinna knelt down in the shower and sucked Al's prick. This was one side benefit of her fucking several other men. She never wanted to suck his prick before. Now she actually loved it. And she was damned good at it.

When he was good and hard, she stood, placed her hands on the wall and presented her ass to him. This was yet another benefit. She now enjoyed getting fucked in her ass. He moved behind her and eased his prick into her. He was surprised at how easily she took it. Then he realized that her last client probably used her this way, too.

In his mind, he pictured another man using her this way and his prick got even harder. Rinna noticed it and drove her ass into him harder. He reached around and massaged her clit as they fucked. She felt herself quivering all over as waves of pleasure surged through her wet body.

"Fuck me, Al! Fuck me like you always do!" she gasped.

The more her slutty side emerged, the harder they fucked. Her ass felt good and tight as she used her muscles to grip his prick. She fucked him like he was one of her clients now. There was no need to hold back.

It proved to be a long, vigorous fuck, too. To Rinna's delight, Al made her orgasm. It was a long, deep come that shook her entire body. She let out along moan and squeezed his prick with her ass muscles several times as she begged him for more.

Al came seconds later and flooded her ass with his cum. They kept at it until they were both spent and their skin felt wrinkly from being under the falling water for so long. They got out and laughed as they dried each other off.

And after she wore him out in bed that morning, he didn't seem to have a care in the world—which was just the way she wanted him to feel.

And to take his mind off Li for a little while.

Vince got home just as Eve stepped out of the bathroom. When he saw that she'd been showering, he scowled in disappointment.

"Sorry," she said. "I didn't think you'd be home so early, so there's nothing for you."

"How many today?' he asked.

"Three," she replied. "That's enough to keep me satisfied at least until tomorrow. I'll have three more and they'll be here during the late afternoon. So I'll have a pussy full of cum waiting for you."

"Good," he said as he walked up and kissed her.

"You like being a slut?" he asked.

"I love it," Eva said. "I get to fuck a lot of different men and they pay me for the privilege. It seems that everyone wants my pussy. You said I was too fat. Funny how other men don't think I am fat. They love my pussy. They all tell me that it's nice and tight and that I'm very good at what I do."

"You've always been very good at that," he said.

"Then why did you become involved with those other women?" she asked. "I was always right here in front of you. I was always ready and willing. But you decided you don't want me anymore. You threw me under the bus. The trouble is, I refused to stay there and feel sorry for myself. How do you like me now?"

"I'm not real sure how I feel about you to be honest," he said. "You're really different. You're sexier, too."

"But you only like to fuck me if my pussy is full of cum! And when it isn't, you don't want to touch me? That's sick but I'll get used to it. I kind of like it in a way, even if I can't understand it," she said. "I often wonder what you have in mind for us. Do we still have a future?"

"I'm not sure. Do you want a divorce?" he finally asked.

"I don't know. Let me think about that for a while," she said. "Do you?"

"Maybe," he said.

She nodded.

"Then you shall have it," she said with a big smile. She saw the expression on his face and laughed.

"That wasn't the answer you expected, was it?" she asked.

"No," he admitted.

"That's too fucking bad," she said. "We'll make it easy. I'll keep the car you bought me and take half your savings account. You keep everything else. I don't want alimony and I won't touch your pension. Okay?"

He nodded.

"Then we have a deal. I'm going to the casino. Don't bother to wait up for me," she said as she left.

When she got to the casino, she went straight to her favorite slot machine. She played for about an hour, and then noticed a man standing behind her. She smiled at him. He walked over and sat down at the machine next to hers.

"I'm Fred," he said.

"Eva," she returned.

"Are you here alone?" he asked.

"Not anymore," she said.

"I like you. You're direct," he said. "Wanna have some real action?"

"Maybe. What do you have in mind?" she said as she batted her eyes.

"Well, we could go up to my suite and fuck all night," he suggested.

"All night? Can you last that long?" she joked.

"I'd like to give it a try," he said.

"Okay. I'm game if you are," she agreed. "But this will cost you."

"I figured that. How much?" he asked as he slid his hand between her legs.

"How about $350?" she asked.

"For an all-nighter? You have yourself a deal," he agreed.

They headed for the elevator and took it up to his suite. Once in the bedroom, Fred removed his pants. Eva slid onto the bed and smiled as he climbed in next to her. They kissed for a little while, and then he pulled up her shirt and licked and sucked her nipples. Eva moaned and writhed but kept pumping his prick nice and slow. Then Fred slowly peeled off her panties and kissed his way down her belly to her cunt. When he ran his tongue along her labia, Eva opened her legs wide and pressed his face into her cunt.

"Yes! Eat me, Fred! Eat my pussy!" she cried.

Fred licked and sucked her cunt until she exploded and began fucking his tongue wildly. He stopped, let her come down a little, and then licked her again. Eva cried out and came harder. In her orgasmic fog, she barely noticed that Fred had gotten between her thighs.

She opened her legs wide and pulled him into her. Fred's prick went in slow and deep. Deeper than anything that had ever been inside of her before. He went in all the way to his balls and stopped to saver the way her cunt closed around his shaft like a fine, soft glove.

"Yes!" she sighed.

Then she closed her eyes and gasped and moaned while Fred fucked her. He used nice, long, deep and easy strokes that seemed to massage every nook and cranny of her trembling cunt. After a few strokes, she began moving with him as her cock-hungry cunt overrode her brain.

"Oooh, yes! That feels good! So good!" she moaned as she fucked him faster and faster. Fred's prick felt delicious. It made her tingle all over. As her excitement boiled over, she tried to match him thrust for thrust.

They fucked a little faster.

"Oooh, God! That's wonderful!" Eva cried as she trembled all over and fucked him back wildly. "Yes! That's what I want!"

That's when she came.

It was a good, strong orgasm that shook her entire body. As she came, Fred fucked her a little faster. Eva quivered and arched her back as she fucked him back with everything she had until she began coming again. Fred drove in and out faster and faster. Eva moaned and trembled with each good, hard thrust and clawed at his arms. Fred felt his balls start to churn. He leaned over, stuck his tongue into Eva's mouth and fucked her as hard as he could. Eva matched his every thrust. She knew that Fred was about to come and she wanted to feel him come inside of her. When Fred came he rammed his prick as deeply into her as he could and fucked her with short, quick strokes as he emptied every drop of cum he had into her hot, eager cunt. They kept fucking and fucking until Fred's prick became soft and slid out of her. He sat back and watched as a stream of thick, white cum oozed out of her twitching lips and ran down between her cheeks to the sheet. Eva emitted a deep, satisfied sigh as she smiled up at him.

"What do you think?" she asked.

"I think this was the best sex I ever had and that you have the tightest pussy on Earth," he said as he ran his fingers over her sticky labia. "That was so good, I didn't want to stop."

"You were great. You really know how to use that dick of yours. I really love the way it feels inside my pussy," she said.

"That was an incredible fuck," Fred said. "I'm glad I met you today."

"Me, too," Eva said as she pumped his prick faster.

She ran her tongue over the knob and shaft. When he was at full salute, she lay down and spread her legs.

"Fuck me!" she said.

"Your wish is my command!" he replied as he slid his prick deep into her eager cunt.

"Oooh, yes!" Eva sighed as his knob struck bottom.

He began moving in and out of Eva's cunt. Eva quivered with each delicious down stroke, then moved with him.

"Oooh yes! Yes! I love it! It's wonderful! Fuck me harder! Give it to me good!" she moaned.

They fucked harder and harder.

"Fuck me! Fuck me! Fuck me! More! More! Make me come!" she screamed as she fucked him with everything she had.

Then she came.

It was a strong, deep orgasm that sent her mind reeling. She moaned and cried and continued to drive her hips upward. Fred fucked her faster and faster. Eva groaned loudly, quivered all over and came second time.

"Oh God! That feels so good!" she moaned as he bent her legs back a little ways and fucked her deeper.

This time, she wrapped her legs around his waist and gripped his arms as he fucked her. She matched him stroke for stroke right from the start and sighed and moaned as they moved faster and faster. Fred fucked her harder and harder. Eva moved with him eagerly and squeezed his prick with her cunt muscles.

"Ooooh, yeah! I love it! This is the best fuck! A great fuck! A wonderful fuck! Give it to me!" she cried as she fucked him faster and faster.

Then she came again. This time, she came harder than she ever came before. As she did, she fucked him wildly and begged for more and more. As she came, she fucked him faster. Fred groaned, drove his prick as deeply into her cunt as he could, and emptied his balls inside of her. Eva shuddered as she felt his cum splash into her cunt walls. And she came again.

Fred gave her a few more deep thrusts, and then slid his prick out of her cunt. A river of cum followed and ran down between Eva's cheeks. He stuck his tongue into her mouth for another, long, deep kiss. Eva held him tight until her sexual fog parted. Then she smiled up at him.

"You're spectacular. The best. What if I want you every day?" Fred asked.

"In that case, we'll have to work something out. After all, I have other people I like to fuck," she said.

She gave him her business card with her cell phone number. He slid it into his wallet and smiled. She reached down and started pulling on his prick again. When it was nice and hard, she mounted him and they fucked like it was their last night on Earth...

Eva got home sometime after nine the next morning. The house was empty. She was tired and well fucked. Fred had managed to keep her up all night and they'd fucked in several different ways. Her pussy was sore in a nice way. She'd never had so much sex in one night before and she had agreed to see him the following week.

She laughed to herself as she walked into the bathroom to shower. Men were easy. They all wanted to get laid by a beautiful woman and they were more than willing to pay for it. She examined her pussy in the full length mirror and smiled.

"Yes," she thought. "I have a terrific pussy!"

She looked at the clock and smiled. She had four hours to get some sleep and get ready for her first client. He was another repeat. They'd fucked three times before. Each time, he tried something different.

Li was waiting at the clock when Al staggered into work that morning. She gave him a good hug and kiss. He smiled at her.

"I love you," he whispered.

"I love you," she said softly. "I am looking forward to our future together. I think we will have a good life and several children. It's funny, but Rinna knows how we feel about each other. I think it bothers her deep inside, but she won't let it show. Maybe it's because of all the strange turns your lives have taken lately. Mine, too."

"You're probably right," Al said as they headed to their assignment. "We're all being pulled in different directions. But I've been led directly to you and this is where I want to be."

"I feel that, somehow or other, we can make this work. My parents have their doubts but we'll show them they have nothing to worry about," Li said. "The only one who worries me a little is Eva. She's crazy about you and she doesn't try to hide it."

"She's also crazy about you," Al smiled. "So is Rinna. How does it feel to be part of their little circle?"

"A little weird but a lot of fun. I like having sex with them," Li said. "But we haven't bothered with it for a while, so I guess the experiment is over with. You have turned my world inside out, Al. I'm doing things I have never imagined I'd do and I really enjoy doing them. But when our baby is born, I will be yours and yours only. Forever."

"And I will be yours only forever," he vowed.

"Rinna will not like hearing that! But I do," she smiled.

Chapter Twenty

Rinna stayed home to rest for a couple of days and talked out her problems with Al. He was supportive but remained non-committal when it came to advising her as to what to do about her lovers.

She admitted that she had trouble keeping herself from thinking about Brad. He had said that he loved her and he was going all-out to make her his. That scared the Hell out of her, too. She started out fucking him for money. Now, she refused to make him pay at all. When she saw him, she just wanted to leap into his arms and let him whisk her away.

Al just listened.

His wife was obviously enamored with Brad. Just how far she planned to take this relationship worried him, too. Was their long, happy marriage about to disintegrate? Were they too far along the path to turn back?

Li was the biggest factor for him.

There was no doubt that they loved each other now and he had no intentions to turn her away ever. But how could he make it work with both Li and Rinna?

"We're a royal mess now," he said. "I warned you this might happen and it has. Now what?"

"I wish I knew, Al," she said. "I wish I knew."

"All we can do is keep at this and let it lead us to wherever it will," he said. "If I end up with the both of you and the two of you can live with that, then we'll be able to make this work."

"I'd like that," she smiled.

When Al went to work the next day, she put on her "fuck me" shorts and headed for the nearest casino. Instead of going to the slots, she sat down at the bar and ordered a rum and coke. After a few minutes, a tall, dark haired man walked over and sat beside her.

She smiled at him as he studied her legs.

"Hello. My name's Pete. What's yours?"

"Rinna," she replied.

"Nice to meet you, Rinna. You are without a doubt the sexiest woman I've ever met," he said. "And you have the greatest set of legs on Earth."

She giggled at the compliments.

"Thanks," she said.

"I've seen you here a couple of times. I wanted to talk to you but you left with someone before I could. When I saw you today, I decided to act fast before you got away again," Pete said.

"Oh? And what do you have in mind?" she asked.

He put his hand on her knee. When she didn't move away, he slid it up her inner thigh. She parted her legs and smiled as he slipped his fingers under her shorts.

"You're not wearing panties," he said as he explored her soft lips.

"I didn't think I'd need them," she said. "Is this what you had in mind?"

"It sure is," he said as slid a finger into her cunt.

"You can have me—for a price," she said. "I'm not cheap."

"I don't care. I've got to have you," he said as he kept playing with her. "How much?"

"I charge $350," she said. "And you can fuck me as much as you like."

He withdrew his hand, took several bills from his wallet and gave them to her. She smiled and put the bills in her purse. Then she squeezed the now obvious bulge in his pants.

She followed him up to his room. As soon as they undressed, her eyes went straight to his prick. It was the longest and thickest prick she had ever seen. She grabbed it, gave it several pulls then led him over to the bed. She pushed him onto his back and slid the knob into her mouth.

Pete moaned as she swirled her tongue over it. He moaned louder when she started to suck it. At the same time, she played with his balls.

"Turn around so I can eat your pussy," he said.

She moved and straddled his face. Pete's tongue was also long and she quivered as it explored places that no other tongue ever had. He also began to finger her asshole. They kept at this until they both came. For Rinna, it was a long, body shaking kind of orgasm. At the same time, Pete fired what felt like quart of cum into her mouth. It coated her tongue as she lapped it up. It tasted salty and sweet and thick.

They rested for a few minutes. Then she helped Pete get it up again. She lay down and opened her legs wide and shuddered as he slid it home. He went in deep. So deep that she felt it knocking on the entrance to her womb and its thickness wonderfully massaged every part of her cunt.

After a few deep thrusts, she moved with him. Each thrust was long and slow and deep. Each thrust sent delicious sensations racing through entire body. She'd never felt anything like this before. It was so good that she didn't want it to end.

Pete was also in Heaven.

Rinna's cunt was wonderfully tight and he loved the way it hugged his entire shaft with each thrust. In fact, it was the best pussy he had ever sunk his meat into and he fucked her slow so he could savor every second.

"Yes! Yes! I'm yours! All yours!" she moaned.

He moved a little faster. She matched him. It was the most perfect fuck she'd ever had. She felt herself nearing another orgasm and fucked him faster. He caught her message and fucked her back.

"More! More! I love it! Fuck me, Pete!" she cried as she began to come.

Her convulsions worked his prick better than he ever imagined. Before he could stop, he began shooting lines of cum deep inside her cunt. She felt it splattering her walls and fucked him harder as her orgasm took off.

"God yes! Yes! I love it! I love it!" she screamed as she came.

It was one of the most intense orgasms of her life. She saw stars as waves of pleasure surged through her. Pete was still rock hard, so he just kept fucking her. She came again and again and tried hard to fuck him back.

She loved the way his prick felt as he fucked her.

"More! Keep fucking me! Fuck me forever!" she cried.

She felt him come inside of her again. This time, he slowed his strokes until he finally eased his half hard prick out of her. She looked down at the river of cum running from her still convulsing labia and smiled happily.

"My God. That was the best fuck of my life!" they both said at once.

They rested for a while. Then she grabbed his prick, jerked him off and sucked it until he was fully erect again. Pete grabbed a pillow and instructed her to slide it under her ass to elevate her hips. In this position, sex would be more intense for both of them.

And it was.

Since Pete had already come three times, she knew it would be a long time before he'd come again. She was right. This fuck lasted almost 20 minutes and each hard thrust just about made her teeth chatter. She felt it twice as much as before and she began coming and coming and coming.

"More! I love it! Use me, Pete! I'm all yours!" she moaned.

When he finally came inside of her again, he lay on top of her until she finished milking every last drop of cum he had left from him. This time when he pulled out, he was totally soft. He smiled down at her.

"Wow! You're the best I've ever had, Rinna," he said. "I really mean that."

She grinned up at him.

"You're the best I've ever had. I've never felt anything like I did with you," she said. "I really love the way can use that dick of yours."

"Can we do this again soon?" he asked.

She nodded.

"How soon?" she asked.

"Tomorrow?" he asked.

"Oh yes. I'll be here. And you don't have to pay me, either," she replied. "In fact, you don't have to pay me ever again because you make me feel terrific when we fuck."

Pete smiled and kissed her.

"You're one very special lady," he said.

She did meet him again the next day. And the day after. Each time, they fucked each other silly and Pete nearly blinded her with orgasms. Rinna had never fucked so many times in three days and she had never swallowed so much cum. Each time, Pete had come in her pussy. Each time, she begged him for more and more.

"Are we having an affair?" he asked.

"I think so. We can't seem to get enough of each other now," she said.

"Want to keep doing this?" he asked.

"Sure," she smiled.

"Fantastic. I have to leave tomorrow. I'd like to call you when I return," he said.

She wrote down her cell phone number on some hotel stationary and gave it to him. He slid it into his wallet. They kissed again. It was another long, deep kiss.

She dressed.

Pete escorted her back to her car and waved as she drove away. She smiled to herself. She didn't intend to get involved in anything like this, but Pete did things to her that she simply couldn't get enough of. He had gone from client to lover.

She thought about what was happening and got a pang of guilt. This was a total lapse of common sense for her. She was selling her pussy to men for cash and now was caught up in what might become a full blown affair with Pete.

As well as affairs with Troy, Brad and Vince!

"I made a fucking mess!" she thought.

She knew she shouldn't feel too guilty about it. After all, her husband was having a hot affair with Li and made it clear that he wasn't going to stop it any time soon. In that case, Rinna decided that she'd keep fucking other men for cash and carry on her affair with Pete. It was a win-win for everyone.

But she still felt a little guilty.

"I'll get over it," she told herself.

It was five o'clock when Eva's last client left the house. She lay down on the bed with her legs apart and waited. A few seconds later, she heard Vince come in. He walked to the bedroom, saw the cum oozing out of her cunt and immediately disrobed.

She smiled.

"I have cum in my ass and pussy," she said.

"Then I'll fuck you in both places tonight," he replied as he plunged his prick into the pool of sticky goo inside her cunt.

"God! I love the way this feels! It's amazing," he said as they fucked. "Looks like your last lover came a lot today."

"He did—and I saved it for you," she said as she thrust back.

"I really want to fuck you right after Al does. The thought of sticking my dick in his cum really turns me on," he said. "Would that turn you on?"

"I think that will hard to arrange now that Al's involved with Li," she said. "He doesn't even have time for me now. Damn, how I hate that!"

She reached over and beat him off. In a few moments, he was rock hard again. She got onto her stomach and slid a pillow under her.

"You know where to put it," she said.

The next afternoon, Rinna got a surprise visit from Hal, her neighbor up the block. She smiled at him when she opened the door.

"Hi, Hal. What do you want?" she asked.

"Can I come in for a second?" he asked.

She shrugged and admitted him. She noticed that he was ogling her as she had just put on her jogging shorts. He'd never looked at her that way before.

"Is it true that you're in the business?" he asked as they sat down on the sofa.

"What business?" she asked nervously.

"You know," he said as he placed a hand on her thigh.

"Oh," she said as she looked into his eyes.

"Are you?" he asked as he moved his hand upward. "You know, I've always thought you were one of the sexiest women around. I've often wondered what you'd be like in bed but never imagined I'd have a chance to find out. I guy I know at the casino kind of hinted that you were in the business, so I thought I stop by and ask."

She looked at him but said nothing. He moved his hand higher. When he reached her crotch, she parted her thighs and smiled as he gently felt her cunt through her panties. She knew that Al was fucking Eva, so why shouldn't she fuck Hal?

"Are you in the business?" he asked as she opened her legs wider.

"Yes," she replied.

"I have $200. Is that enough?" he asked.

"It's enough," she smiled.

She led him up to the spare bedroom. She let him undress her. As he did, he sucked each of her nipples and licked his way down her belly to her cunt. She laid back and threw her legs open as he buried his tongue in her cunt.

She had to admit he was good at it.

Real good.

In fact, he made her come after only a few seconds. When he was finished, she grabbed his already erect prick and slid it into her mouth. Now it was his turn to be amazed. Rinna was giving him the best blowjob of his life. She was so good, that he soon spurted lines of cum down her throat. Rinna sucked up every drop, too. She kept sucking his prick and playing with balls until he begged her to stop.

She smiled.

"That was great," he said.

"Ready for the big one?" she asked as she lay back opened her legs.

Hal got hard again quickly. He got between her thighs and eased his prick into Rinna's soft, willing cunt. She wrapped her arms and legs around him and they began what was a nice, easy and very pleasant fuck. He had a perfect thrusting rhythm, which she happily matched. They moved together perfectly, faster and faster and faster.

"Can I come in your pussy?" he asked.

"Ohh yes!" she moaned. "Come in me like you own me."

He fucked harder. She matched him and used her inner muscles to squeeze his prick. The change in sensations was so terrific that he came on the spot. He began thrusting faster and faster as he shot streams of cum deep into her cunt. Rinna was coming, too.

"Fuck me. Fuck me harder! I love it! Fuck me!" she screamed.

"I love it! I've always wanted you, Rinna! Always!" he moaned as he came and came.

They kept going until Vince finally pulled his limp member out of her. Rinna beamed up at him as she massaged his cum into her pussy.

Hal reached over and massaged some of his cum into Rinna's asshole. She knew what he was up to and happily responded by stroking his prick until he was hard again. Then she slid a pillow under her hips and pulled her lags back toward her chest. He smiled and pressed his knob against her rear entrance.

Rinna grit her teeth as he slowly penetrated her. His prick was the largest thing she'd ever had up her ass and she wasn't sure if she could handle it. He realized her discomfort and went slower. She nodded at him to tell him it was alright and he kept going until his balls touched her cheeks.

Then he fucked her.

He did it slowly and easy at first until she became comfortable. Then she wrapped her legs around his hips and moved with him. It felt weird at first but each thrust felt better and better. After a few thrusts, she began to enjoy it and fucked him back. To her amazement, she actually came. It was a weird, deep kind of orgasm that shook her entire body to its core. She began to moan and sigh as she came. Hal fucked her faster and faster and finally erupted inside her ass. She felt his cum shoot into her and quivered as she came again. They kept fucking until he shrank and popped out of her ass—along with a river of cum. It ran down between her cheeks and covered the pillow.

She lay there panting and smiled up at him.

"Damn! You're good with that thing!" she said.

"You're fantastic, Rinna. Want to keep doing this?" he asked as he stroked her cunt.

"If you have the money, I have the pussy," she said.

"How does once a month sound?" he asked.

"Pefect" she said.

They got up and dressed. Rinna walked him to the front door and smiled as he walked out to his car. She headed upstairs to shower. When she got to the bathroom, she stripped and studied herself in the full length mirror. As she did, she stroked her cunt.

"Everyone wants to fuck my tight little pussy. I can't blame them, either. I'd fuck me, too, if I could," she joked.

The day before, she and Eva had tried to convince Li to try picking men up at the casinos like they did. They told her that as sexy and pretty as she is, she'd have no trouble at all getting man to pay her a lot of money for sex.

Li adamantly refused.

Such things went completely against her moral code. As far as she was concerned, she was Al's wife and she would only give herself to him and no other man would even see her naked, much less fuck her. But she did agree to keep having sex with them both once in a while.

Rinna laughed.

"It's a start," she said.

Li told Al about it of course. He looked at her.

"The idea disgusts me. I would never do anything like that even if I were not your wife. Such a thing would bring disgrace to my family and myself. I like your wife and Eva but, I hate to say this, they have very questionable morals. I do not understand how you can allow such a thing," she said.

"I told you how it happened," he said. "And if it hadn't happened, you and I would not be together like we are now. So there is an upside to this mess and you're it."

She laughed and hugged him.

"I will never do such a thing to you. Ever! I promise," she vowed.

"I know," he said.

He knew that Li's morals were unshakable. He'd be able to totally trust her at all times.

"You can keep making love with Rinna. After all, she is your true wife. But I am not pleased that you might have sex with Eva. I prefer that you limit yourself to just Rinna and myself. I'm sure between us we will keep you very, very busy!" Li said.

He laughed.

"I know you will. I've already thought about doing that very thing. Eva has more than enough lovers to keep her occupied anyway and I don't have a real emotional attachment to her," he said.

"Then you agree?" she teased.

"Sure," he said.

"That is wonderful. Now let's make a baby together," she said...

That Saturday, Rinna drove to the casino on the other side of town where she met a man named Steve. He was tall, thin, dark haired and handsome. She met him in the bar. After they chatted over a couple of drinks, she went up to his suite with him.

"How much do you want?" he asked.

"I usually charge $350 for an entire night or $1,000 for a weekend," she replied.

Steve took out his wallet. He counted out 10 $100 notes and gave them to her. She smiled and placed the money in her purse.

"I'm all yours until Sunday night," she said.

They spent a few minutes engaging in foreplay while they undressed each other, and then Rinna grabbed his prick and slid it into her mouth. He groaned as she sucked on it and played with his balls.

"Wow," he said. "You give great head."

About two minutes later, he began firing lines of cum down her throat, which she hungrily swallowed it. She wiped her lips with the back of her hand and lay down on the bed. Steve got in with her and started licking her cunt. She moaned and sighed as he ate her while she pumped his prick. Steve kept eating her until she came. When she did, she rocked from side to side and screamed out in pleasure.

They rested for a couple of minutes while he stroked her pussy. She looked at him and smiled.

"Let's fuck," she said.

Steve got between her thighs and pressed the head of his prick against her opening. She opened her legs wider in anticipation. His prick was the longest she'd ever seen, too, and she was eager to feel it inside her.

Steve looked down at her. She was, by far, the most beautiful women he'd ever had sex with and he decided that he wanted this one to last a long time.

"Now," he whispered as he pressed forward.

Rinna quivered with excitement as she felt his prick enter her pussy. When he was all the way in, she bent her knees and moaned. Her pussy felt so damned good, too, as he moved his prick in and out. Rinna gasped on the first thrust. And moaned on the second.

And the third.

Steve fucked her a little faster. Rinna opened her legs wider and moved with him. His prick, she decided, felt so good inside her cunt. She dug her fingers into his arms and fucked him back a little faster. Steve matched her, then did it harder. Rinna moaned and shook with each hard thrust. And she drove her hips upward to take him in even deeper.

"Ooooh! That's it, Steve! Give it to me good now. Use my pussy!" she moaned.

She wanted it now and she fucked him as hard as she could to prove it. Steve stuck his tongue into her mouth and fucked her harder. Rinna quivered, arched her back, and came. As she did, she fucked him faster.

"Fuck me, Steve! I love it! Make me yours now!" she cried as she wrapped her legs around him.

They fucked for what seemed like a long, long time. Then Rinna erupted again. This time, her orgasms was so strong, she rocked from side-to-side. Somehow, Steve stayed in her. When she settled down, he began fucking her again.

Rinna moaned and gasped as he used her. His strokes were slow and very deep now. She could feel his knob massage the entrance to her womb each time he plunged in and felt a delicious tingle when his prick raked across her g-spot she arched her back, wrapped her thighs around him and moved with him. Steve was delighted with her responses. When Rinna fucked, she held nothing back and her warm, tight cunt massaged his prick perfectly with each thrust. He steadily picked up the pace. Rinna moaned and matched him.

Again and again and again.

Faster and faster.

Rinna began thrusting harder and dug her fingers into his arms. Steve let her go for a little while then fucked her back just as hard. He leaned over and sucked her nipple. Rinna cried out, trembled all over and erupted. As she did, she fucked him as fast and as hard as she could. Seconds later, he slammed his prick into her all the way and flooded her cunt with cum. They kept fucking until both were spent.

He rolled off and caught his breath.

"Wow! That was the longest fuck I ever had in my life!" he finally said. "You're good, Rinna! Hell, you're the best!"

She laughed as she leaned over and sucked his prick again and didn't stop until he came in her mouth.

The rest of the weekend was pretty much the same. Steve loved to try various positions and she was more than willing to do the same. They only stopped to have dinners and breakfast or shower together. The weekend proved to be a sexual marathon that finally ended around six on Sunday evening.

Both her ass and her cunt felt tired. She had trouble getting out of bed and standing straight. He watched as she got ready to leave and kept telling her how fantastic she was. She smiled at the compliments as she dressed.

"You're really great, Rinna. I can hardly wait to do this again. Can I call you when I come back to town next month?" he asked.

"Sure. You have my cell phone number. Don't lose it," she said.

She went out to her car and smiled as she thought about how easy it was to use her pussy to make money.

A lot of money!

Li laid back and opened her legs. Al smiled and mounted her again for another nice, long, easy fuck. As long as he got to make love with Li, he wasn't too concerned what Rinna was doing. And, as much as he loved Rinna, he knew that she'd be fucking other men any time they weren't together.

"Does it bother you that Rinna is a prostitute?" Li asked.

"No," he said.

"How come?" she asked.

"Because you're not," he said as he moved faster and faster.

"Yes!" Li moaned as she moved with him.

They kept going for a long time. Then, as if by magic, they both climaxed at once. They held each other tight as they continued to make love and Li sighed happily as she felt his cum jet into her eager cunt.

"I love you!" she screamed.

"I love you, too," he assured as they kissed.

Rinna got home about eight p.m. She wasn't the least bit surprised to see Li's car parked at the curb or the lights still on in the living room. When she walked in, they were seated on the sofa sipping wine while watching a movie on TV. Rinna smiled and sat down on the loveseat.

"Did you have fun tonight?" she asked.

"Oh yes. We had lots of fun tonight," Li smiled. "My pussy is still tingling. How about you?"

Rinna blushed and nodded.

Al waited for her to volunteer some information but she stayed quiet. They chatted a few minutes, and then Li got up to leave. She gave Al a long, passionate kiss and said she'd see him at work.

Rinna walked her to the car.

"Does she know?" she asked when she came back inside.

"Yes," Al replied. "I have no secrets from her or you."

"How is she compared to me? She asked.

"That, my love, is much too close to call. She reminds me of you when we first married," he said. "You remember those days?"

"Always. Are they over now?" she asked.

"Only if you want them to be," he said.

"I'm never letting you go," she said. "I love you too much, even though our lives have taken on some strange turns. I know this is mostly my fault and whatever comes of this will come. I just want you to know how I feel."

"The only way you'll ever lose me is to walk out on me on your own accord," he said. "Our vows were til death do us part and I meant every word."

"Does Li understand that?" she asked.

"She does. She said she can live with it if we all stay together and work at it. What about those other lovers? Do they understand how you feel?" he asked.

"I think so. If they can't, who cares? Nothing with them is permanent anyway. They'll move on when they tire of me," she smiled. "Although one might stay around longer."

"Brad?" he asked.

"Yes. Um, he's invited me to go away on a vacation with him. He wants to take me to any resort on Earth I name for at least a week. I said I'd think about it," she said.

"And have you?" he asked.

"Well, yes. I thought that if I went away with him it would allow you and Li to spend that time together and make that baby you both want. And I'd get to spend the week at a luxury resort with a charming, slightly younger man and do whatever we want as often as we want. It would be a win-win for everyone," she said.

"So? You're going to do it?" he asked.

"I don't know. We've never been apart that long since we got married and you might worry about me. That would ruin your time with Li and I don't want to do that to you. Besides, I'd miss you too much and I'd be thinking about you the entire time," she said.

"You're absolutely right in both cases. What if you called me every night to let me know that you're safe?" he suggested. "Would Brad let you do that?"

"Maybe," she said. "I can ask him."

Al just smiled at her.

"One more question. How is Eva compared to me?" she asked.

"Eva really knows how to fuck," he said. "But you're much better. I guess I feel that way because we've been married for a long time. That's what makes it special."

She nodded.

"I feel the same way about those other men I fuck. They're good and exciting. But what we have is special. That can't be replaced by any man," she said.

"Are you still going to keep fucking other men?" he asked.

"Yes," she said softly.

"Why?" he asked.

"For the money," she said.

"For the money?" he asked almost in shock.

"Yes," she said. "And it's a lot of money."

"A lot?" he asked. "How much is a lot?"

"Hundreds of dollars. So I make $2,000 a month in cash for doing something I really like to do," she said. "I know it's wrong, but the money is too good to say no to."

"They must be rich," Al said.

"Very," she said. "I've also had sex with a few other men I met at other places. I never used to charge any of them but you suggested that I start doing that. You were right. Most men are willing to pay a lot to fuck my pussy."

"Anything else I should know?" he asked.

"You already know everything," she replied.

"Have you made up your mind about Brad?" he asked.

"What would you do if you were me?" she asked.

"I can't answer that. Only you can. Do what you feel is right for you," he said.

She looked at him and smiled. She decided that she needed another woman's opinion. She would ask Eva and Li how they felt about it at breakfast the next morning.

"Are you going to the casino on Saturday?" he asked.

"No. I think I'll stay home with you instead," she replied.

"Great. We can go to a show and dinner," he said. "And after that—"

She put her arms around his shoulders and smiled at him.

"I'm going to fuck your brains out!" she said.

The next morning, she met Li and Eva at the local café for brunch. Rinna explained her problems and they both laughed.

"I'd go," Eva said. "I'd pack my bags and go with him without a second thought. Then I'd make sure it would be a week he'd never forget."

Li shook her head.

"I cannot understand why you even decided to have sex with other men when you are married to Al. But if you go away for a week, that means I'll have him all to myself. Even though it feels wrong on so many levels, I'd get over it," she said.

"So you both think I should do it?" Rinna asked.

"Yes!" they both said at once.

Rinna smiled. She took out her cell phone and called Brad.

"Yes, I'll go with you," she said.

"Fantastic! Where would you like to go?" he asked.

"What's your favorite place?" she asked.

"How about St. Thomas?" he suggested.

"Really? That's so expensive!" she said.

"The sky's the limit as far as I'm concerned. Is that okay with you?" he asked.

"Definitely! When will we do this?" she asked.

"How about next Tuesday? We can be back the following Wednesday," he said.

"That's perfect! See you tonight?" she agreed.

"You know it, babe!" he said happily. "Love you!"

She hung up the phone and looked at the others. They both had big grins on their faces.

"Wow! St. Thomas! I'd fuck him to death if he took me there! You lucky bitch!" Eva said.

"That's crazy" Li said. "That's where Al said he wanted to take me."

"No! When?" Rinna asked.

"Next week," she said. "He said we'd go there for two weeks if I liked. I said I'd think about it as I think it costs too much. I offered to pay half, too. Al said I didn't have to but it was up to me."

"So we're both going to the same place?" Rinna asked.

"I guess so," Li smiled. "Crazy, huh?"

"Yes. But I sort of like it. That's where Al and I went on our honeymoon. Of course, every trip with him is a honeymoon," Rinna said.

"He's very romantic," Li smiled.

"Yes he is!" both Eva and Rinna replied.

They all laughed.

Eva checked her watch.

"I've got to run," she said. "I have a client coming over in a half hour. In fact, I have three lined up today. My pussy is very busy these days."

They watched her leave. Li smiled and leaned back in her chair as she sipped her coffee.

"She seems to be real happy with her chosen profession," she said.

"We both are, although I don't fuck as many men as she does. She sees men almost every day. I kind of limit myself to one or two on weekends," Rinna said.

"I'll just stay with Al," Li said. "We're happy together and I want us to stay that way. I don't like it when he has sex with Eva, though. With you it's okay because you are his wife."

"Eva's been complaining that since you came along, she hardly ever sees Al anymore. She says you take up all of his time. I don't mind because it lets me fuck other men. So his relationship with you is good for both of us," Rinna said.

"I still say you're crazy," Li said with a smile. "But I like you anyway."

Rinna met Brad in the lobby of the hotel an hour later. He immediately pulled her to him for a nice, long kiss that made her feel warm between her legs. She smiled at him and held his hand as they went up to his suite.

"How long can you stay?" he asked as they undressed.

"I can stay until we wear each other out," she smiled. "I've been craving your dick all week and you know what that means!"

They started with a nice, long 69. Each time Rinna felt that Brad was about to come, she stopped sucking and pinched his prick until it subsided. Then she started sucking again. He really liked it when she did this because she wasn't just giving him a blowjob. She was orally making love to him and going out of her way to prolong the pleasure.

He was doing the same to her. He licked or sucked her clit until she started to quiver, then stopped. When she didn't come, he ate her again. They did this to each other several times, and then Brad made her come.

Rinna bounced around and moaned loudly as she sucked his prick harder. When she tasted his first line of cum on her tongue, she beat him off until he begged her to stop. They rested in each other's arms for a few minutes while Rinna kept playing with his prick. When he was good and hard again, she straddled him and impaled herself on his prick. It was a nice and very long fuck, too.

Ten minutes later, Brad gripped her hips and rammed his prick up inside her. She moaned and came with him. They kept fucking for a little while longer, and then Rinna fell on top of him and stuck her tongue in his mouth.

Eva was on her hands and knees. She gasped and moaned as her client rammed his big prick in and out her cunt. It was big, too. When she made him hard by sucking him, she was amazed at how long and thick it became.

They'd already fucked in the missionary position. He was thrilled that she was so sexy and more thrilled that she allowed him to come inside of her. She was thrilled with the way his huge prick worked every part of her cunt, too. When he was finished, she sucked his prick until it was hard again, and then begged him to fuck again.

This position felt far more intense, too. Since he'd already come, he lasted even longer. She came long before he did and was still coming when he final shot his last load into her. He got up and dressed. Just before he left, he handed her $200. She gave him her card with her cell phone number and told him to call her when was in the mood for more great sex.

She looked at the clock and hurried into the bathroom to clean up. Her next lover would be there in 30 minutes...

Al and Li lay next to each other. They had just finished making love for the second time that evening and her cunt was filled with his cum. She felt warm and happy all over. Just like she always did when they were together.

Al smiled and kissed her.

All thoughts of Rinna were a million miles from him now. When he was with Li, there was only him and her. No one and nothing else mattered.

"Are you sure they're going to the Virgin Islands?" he asked.

"That's what Rinna told me. Is that too close for you?" she replied.

"Maybe. How do you feel about it?" he asked.

"It's okay with me if you don't mind. Would we run into them?" she asked.

"That's a possibility. It might prove to be very awkward for all of us," he said.

She laughed as she stroked his prick. When he was good and hard again, she straddled it and lowered herself onto it. He gasped as she ground her cunt against him. He moaned even louder when she started fucking him.

It was nine the next morning when Brad escorted Rinna to her car and kissed her again.

"I love you," he said.

She smiled and nodded as she touched his cheek. She had deep feelings for Brad, but she wasn't sure if they went that deep. They had spent the entire night and most of the morning having sex in as many ways as they could imagine and her cunt was oozing a stream of cum.

"I'll call you when I book the trip," he said.

"I can hardly wait! Bye!" she smiled as she got into her car and drove away.

"Damn it! He said he loves me! Now what do I do?" she asked herself. "The trip will only make him love me more and I might really fall for him, too. It wasn't supposed to be like this!"

Eva had saved her last client for four o'clock. She knew he'd leave just about the same time that Vince got home from work. He'd come a lot, too, In fact, he fucked her three times and each time, he filled her cunt with lots of thick, white cum.

Her cunt was now just the way Vince liked it. She lay down on the bed with her legs apart and smiled as she heard the front door open.

"I'm waiting for you!" she called out.

As soon as Vince saw the obviously deep pool of cum in her open cunt, he pulled off his clothes and plunged his prick into her. As the cum squished around his prick, he sighed.

"Damn! That feels so good!" he said.

He fucked her nice and slow, too, so he could savor the good swirling around his prick with each thrust. He didn't know why this excited him so much and he didn't care. He lust loved fucking Eva when she had a full load in her pussy.

As he fucked, the cum ran out of her cunt and went between her ass cheeks. Vince saw this and it excited him even more. He soon added his first load to the other guy's cum. Instead of finishing in her cunt, he pulled out and slid his prick up into Eva's ass. She moaned loudly as he fucked her and fucked her. A few seconds later, he emptied his remaining load deep inside her ass.

"Damn, that was terrific!" he said. "I love the way that feels."

"Since you like to fuck me when I'm filled with someone else's cum, why don't you eat me, too?" she teased. "Maybe you'll like the way it tastes. I always do. It's kind of sweet and salty. You already know how it tastes. I used to watch when you were so flexible that you were able to suck your own dick. You always did it when you thought I wasn't looking."

Vince blushed.

He thought back to those early days and laughed. He'd started trying that on a whim when he was doing yoga years ago. He was practicing his asanas as he did every morning. He went into the plow position which was lying on his back with his feet stretched back over his head. The idea was to become flexible enough to eventually put his toes on the floor then to bend his knees so they were also on the floor at his shoulders.

At first, he did it just to see if he was that flexible. As the days passed, he was able to stretch more and more. He realized that his crotch was only inches from his face and he could even smell his prick after a while.

The next time, he did it naked to see if he could suck his own prick. As he lay there staring up at his flaccid member, he thought about erotic things. His prick began to get longer and harder. He had never seen his prick this close and watched as it grew. It was very close to his face now and he tried to stretch out his tongue to taste it. It was mostly out of curiosity because Eva always liked to suck it.

But it just didn't happen that day.

The next time around, he actually managed to get his prick close enough to his mouth so he could swirl his tongue around the knob. He did this several times, too. That's when he realized that he liked the way it tasted. And the way his tongue felt as it moved around his knob.

The next time, he actually managed to get the tip into his mouth and suck it for a while. The sensations he sent through his body were exciting. He also realized that he enjoyed the way it felt in his mouth and the taste.

The next time, he actually got half of it into his mouth and sucked away. Turned on beyond belief, he sucked it and sucked it until he came. The feeling of coming in his own mouth made his orgasm that much more intense. It erupted from his prick and splattered over his tongue and the more he came, the harder he sucked. The taste of his own cum surprised and excited him. So he kept sucking and licking until he'd shot his entire load into his mouth and eagerly swallowed every bit of it.

When he finally stopped, he lay stretched out on the floor. He ran his tongue all over the inside of his mouth to lick off every drop of cum. Then he smiled. He knew then that he actually liked the taste of his cum. He liked it enough to keep doing this.

So he did it again the following night. In fact, he just couldn't do the plow position anymore without sucking himself off until he came. He did that several more time afterward and each time, he swallowed his cum.

Until now, he didn't know that Eva had watched him do it. And had masturbated while she watched. The sight of Vince sucking his own prick turned her on, too.

"So you already have sucked a dick. It was your own but it's still a dick and you swallowed your own cum. So why not eat my pussy after another man fills it?" she teased as she held her cunt open. "Look at all that good, sweet cum going to waste. Don't you want to taste it?"

By then, he was rock hard again. He moved between her thighs and rammed his prick into her as hard as he could. Eva shuddered.

"Yes! Oh God! Yes!" she moaned as they fucked.

Just before he came, she grabbed his prick and slid it into her mouth. Vince gasped as she brought him to a climax then jerked him off to catch every drop of his cum in her mouth. When she was finished, she grabbed him and stuck her tongue into his mouth. Caught off guard, he ended up with a mouth full of his own cum and some of the earlier deposit. She held him and kept merging her tongue with his to let him taste it. To her delight, he began sucking her tongue while he moved his fingers in and out her cunt. The taste of the cum in his mouth triggered another good erection which Eva stroked until he was fully erect.

She came and fell down on the bed. She watched as Vince licked the cum from his lips and swallowed.

"Yes. I like the taste of cum!" he said as he mounted her chest and tit fucked her.

When he came, he shot his load all over her chest and nipples. To Eva's shock, he leaned over and started licking it off. The sensation of his tongue moving over body made her come several times. It was the wildest sex they'd ever had.

"Damn! If you keep doing things like that, I'll never fuck another man again!" she said as she recovered. "That was crazy and exciting and wild. I loved it! I can't believe you licked up all that cum!"

"Most of it was mine so no big deal," he said. "It's not like I ate your pussy."

"Why don't you?" she asked.

He laughed, thought about it and buried his tongue in her cunt. As he licked, his prick grew harder and harder as he imagined he was lapping up Al's cum.

But both Vince and Eva knew that now that Li had entered the picture, Al would have little or no time for them. Li was determined to be the only woman in Al's life. But she knew that Rinna was in the way and that she'd have to live with that.

Now, she monopolized almost all of Al's free time and he was thrilled to death about that. Eva was starting to hate Li because of this.

Rinna got home about 20 minutes after Li left. She smiled at Al and gave him a warm hug. He hugged her back.

"You look really tired," she commented. "Like you've been having sex all day."

"I have," he said.

"Li or Eva?" she asked.

"Li," he answered.

"What did you do?" she asked.

"Everything," he smiled. "What did you and Brad do?"

"Everything!" she said.

"What's bothering you?" he asked. "You look like you need to tell me something."

She told him about what happened with her and Brad and how she had agreed to go with him. He sighed and nodded.

"I think this is where we lose each other," he said.

"No," she said. "I won't let that happen. I don't feel the same toward Brad as I do you. I don't feel the same about anyone else as I do about you. Think of this as a vacation from each other. Besides, you'll have Li for the whole time I'm gone. I will call you like I promised. I won't forget," she said.

"If we survive this, it will only make our marriage stronger," he said. "Go on the trip. Have fun and be careful."

"You're so understanding. I'm sorry I started all of this," she said.

"Actually, Eva started all of this. We just got caught up in the avalanche," he smiled. "The one who benefits most from this is Li. I've never seen anyone as happy as she is right now. So let's not do anything to spoil it for her because she didn't ask for this. Besides, I really love her. I love you, too. It's selfish, but I want to keep you both all to myself."

"I think that can be arranged," she smiled. "I like Li a lot, too. She's very sweet natured and honest and she's crazy about you—like I am. I'll even help raise that baby you've been trying for if she lets me."

The next day, Eva conducted business as usual. She spent the entire morning fucking the daylights out of a new client and the afternoon fucking a repeat customer like there was no tomorrow. Then she waited with her cunt full of cum for Vince to get home.

"My pussy is all ready for you again. It's just as you love it—filled with lots of good, sweet cum," she said as she held her labia apart.

Vince smiled, undressed quickly and jumped into bed for another good, hard and messy fuck.

"Oooh yeah!" he said as the cum squished around his prick.

Eva wrapped her arms around him and fucked him back as hard as she could. She was starting to love this now and was thinking about arranging a three man gang bang so they could all come in her. That way, Vince would really be in Heaven when they fucked.

And Vince loved the fact that his wife had become a cum slut so he could fulfill his kinky fantasies. After several good thrusts, he rammed his prick all the way into her cunt and added his cum to the pool. He came a lot, too.

To Eva's delight, as soon as he pulled out, he buried his tongue in her open slit and hungrily lapped at the cum in her cunt. This caused her to orgasm big time and she fucked his face as she screamed out for more.

When he was finished, he lay next to her.

"You're right," he said.

"About what?" she asked.

"I like the taste of cum," he said.

"I guess that means you'll be sucking dicks huh?" she teased as she stroked his prick.

As soon as he was hard again, he slid it into her cunt.

"Don't even think about that!" he said as they fucked.

When Tuesday rolled around, Al watched as Rinna packed for her trip with Brad. A very large part of him wanted to tell her not to go, but he knew she had to. She had to see if there really was anything magical between her and Brad or if he was just another guy she liked to fuck.

Rinna smiled at him.

"Don't worry. I'll be back," she said. "It's just for a week or two."

"I don't like you going away for a day, much less two weeks. I hope you know what you're doing. Can you trust this Brad?" Al asked.

"I can trust him. He's a real nice guy and we like each other a lot," she said as she closed the suitcase. "Besides, you'll have Li while I'm gone. So there's no need to be jealous of me and Brad. I'm sure you and Li will find a lot of ways to keep occupied."

He laughed.

"How do you really feel about this guy?" he asked.

"I'm not really sure. I like being with him and we're real good together," she said. "I guess I'll find out for sure on our trip. How do you feel about Li?"

"You already know how I feel," he said.

She nodded.

"Let's promise each other that we won't forget who we're married to and what we have between us. I don't want to throw all of that away," she said.

"Me neither. But life is funny at times. Things happen. People change. We're not the same as we were before this started. But I still love you. That will never change," he assured her.

"And I still love you—forever," she smiled.

She left for the airport at six that evening and met Brad at the gate. He showed her the two first class tickets.

"That's the only way I ever travel," he said. "Now you will, too."

Al went to work and saw Li at the time clock.

"I've got my bag packed. When do we leave?" she asked.

"Tomorrow morning. We'll be in St. Croix by noon. I've booked the honeymoon suite," he said.

"I can hardly wait. Is there a chance we'll run into Rinna?" she asked.

"No. They'll be on St. Thomas," he said.

"Good. I don't want us to have any awkward moments," she said as they kissed.

Rinna's trip to St. Thomas proved to be as wonderful as she expected. In between the sightseeing, boating and dining, she and Brad found several different ways to fuck. And they did so all over the islands.

Whenever they found a secluded spot, they had sex. Rinna was amazed at his stamina, too. Each time he fucked her, it felt better and better. Their oral sex was great, too. Brad knew how to use that long tongue of his to send her over the edge each and every time and he loved the way she sucked his prick and swallowed his cum.

For seven days and nights, she was all his. He used her cunt and ass more times than she could count and each climax was spectacular. For the entire week, Brad kept professing his love for her and how he'd give anything to make this last forever.

Although she grew fonder of him with each passing day, she always stopped short of saying that she loved him, too. She did love having sex with him. In fact, that was better each time. She didn't even bother to wear panties after their first night so Brad could fuck her whenever he wanted and wherever he wanted.

After a particularly good fuck on their last morning, Brad asked her why she doesn't say she loves him.

She stared up at the ceiling fan and smiled.

"I want to, Brad. You're a wonderful and romantic man and I'm really crazy about you in many ways. In fact, my pussy gets wet whenever we're together," she said.

"But?" he asked.

"The only man I really love is my husband. I know we have an unusual relationship, but I can't change the way I feel about him. I feel almost the same way about you and I'd like to scream out how I feel, but something is holding me back," she said.

Brad moved between her thighs and slid his prick back into her cum-filled cunt. She dug her fingers into his back and moaned softly as they moved together. This time, he went slow and easy. His strokes here deep and her cunt walls caressed his shaft with each and every thrust.

"Yes," she sighed. "That's perfect!"

Brad leaned over and kissed her. She returned it passionately as they moved faster.

"I'm all yours," she whispered. "All yours!"

He felt her body tremble and realized she was about to come. He fucked her faster and faster. Rinna responded in kind. It felt wonderful.

Magical.

Incredible.

They fucked faster and faster. Brad felt himself ready to blow and fucked her harder. The sudden change in tempo triggered Rinna's orgasm and he followed a second later. As his cum merged with her body juices, she fucked him faster.

"I'm yours, Brad! All yours forever! I love you!" she cried.

Her words made Brad hard again and he fucked her even harder. Rinna held on for the wild ride as she came and came and came again.

"I love you," she whispered as they each other tight.

The next morning, they took a bus to the beach and walked hand-in-hand in the snow white sand. Rinna was up in the clouds now. Way up.

She had actually admitted to Brad that she loved him. And she really meant it. She was in the same spot that Al now was. She was loved two men at the same time.

"Don't worry, Rinna," Brad said. "This will work itself out sooner or later. Right now, let's just enjoy this time we have together."

They did.

For the next four days and nights, they explored every way they could think of to give each other pleasure. As they did, their love continued to grow and grow.

"My God. What am I going to tell Al?" she wondered as she and Brad fucked.

On St. Croix, Al was about to experience his own magical moment. Li had purchased another pregnancy test kit as her period was a few days late. She took it out of the box and retreated into the bathroom. She emerged a minute later and placed the strip on the coffee table.

Al watched as Li checked the pregnancy test strip. When it turned blue, they both jumped for joy. Li was pregnant!

"We did it, Al! We did it!" Li shouted as they hugged.

"Yes we did!" he said happily.

He picked her up and kissed her passionately. It was what they both wanted more than anything else on Earth.

"Now you are mine forever," she said as he held her tight.

"And I wouldn't have it any other way," he assured her.

He picked up his cell phone and called Rinna. She reached over and answered it but quickly dropped it as Brad mounted again and hammered away at her cunt. As she moaned and screamed for him to fuck her harder, Al and Li heard everything on their end. They listened and smiled as their fucking grew more intense. That's when they both heard Rinna scream out as she came. As she came, she moaned loudly and said, "I love you, Brad! I love you!"

Al and Li smiled at each other.

"It looks like our dilemma might have solved itself," she said.

"Looks like!" he laughed.

They kept listening as Rinna sighed and moaned while Brad's prick pounded away at her cunt.

"Yes! Yes! Fuck me, Brad! Fuck me forever!" she screamed as she obviously came again.

Li blushed as a male groaned and the fucking noises became faster. Then came a long, oooohhh! This ended with the sounds of heavy breathing and kissing. Li and Al laughed. Rinna and Brad forgot that the phone was still on.

Li smiled and lay back with her legs wide apart. Al laughed and moved between them. Now it was Brad and Rinna's turn to listen while he and Li made love—if they'd stop fucking long enough to hear it.

When Rinna calmed down she glanced over at her phone and gasped when she heard the sounds of Al and Li making love. That's also when she realized that they had heard everything she screamed out as Brad fucked her senseless.

"They heard us! They heard everything!" she said as she turned off the phone.

"I know. I saw you put it down without turning it off, so I figured that you wanted them to hear us," Brad said.

"That means they heard me say that I love you! They heard me begging you to fuck me!" Rinna said as she stared up at the ceiling.

"So?" Brad asked. "We heard them fucking, too. That means we're even."

Rinna laughed.

"Maybe I really wanted them to hear us, Brad," she said.

"Even if you didn't, it's too late to take it back now. I wonder why they called you anyway," Brad said.

"I can guess. They called to tell me that Li's pregnant," she said.

"Shit! Now what?" Brad asked.

"We wait and see what happens," she replied. "This is crazy, Brad. I'm sorry I got you mixed up in this mess. While I love you, I still madly love my husband. He loves me and is also crazy about Li. I'm not sure how to untangle this."

Brad shrugged.

"None of that matters as long as we get to make love," he said. "I knew that I wouldn't have you all to myself when I went after you. This is what it is, Rinna. We'll figure out how to make this work in a way where everyone's happy."

"You're so understanding," she smiled as they kissed.

Vince and Eva were lying in bed after another good, long lovemaking session. This time, he added another wrinkle to his kinky side. He spent several long minutes fucking her and emptied all of his cum into her cunt. While she was still writhing in the throes of her orgasm, he plunged his tongue into her cunt and lapped up as much of his own cum as he could reach. This made her scream and quiver all over as she fucked his tongue.

He soon grew hard again and rammed his prick back into her for a longer, harder fuck that left them both gasping for air.

"Wow! That's the best sex we ever had together! I love it!" Eva said.

Vince propped himself up on his elbow and smiled at her. She smiled back as she realized that all was now right with their world. Lately, Vince couldn't seem to keep his hands off her and she was perfectly fine with that.

"You know that divorce we talked about..." he began.

"Forget it," she smiled. "This is the first time you made love with me without my having my pussy filled with cum. It was just as wonderful as ever. I think our magic has returned."

"Yes it has. Let's take a trip together. We'll go somewhere romantic. Somewhere that has no casinos. We'll have a second honeymoon. Maybe we'll find a nice chapel and renew our vows. We can start all over again. I love you, Eva. I don't ever want to lose you."

"If I give up all the other men, will you give up your other women?" she asked.

"Even Rinna?" he teased.

"Well, maybe not her. But you might not have a chance to be with her much. She's crazy about that guy Brad. Then there's Troy and Al you'll have to compete with. And me, too," Eva said.

"Will you give up Al?" he asked.

"Since Al hooked up with Li, he's pretty much given me up," she replied. "At least for now anyway. So do you want to do this?"

"Definitely," he assured her. "So we have a deal?"

"What do you think?" she asked as she pulled him onto her.